Death in Tallinn

ALLAN MARTIN

First published in 2020 by Sharpe Books.

Dedication

For Vivien

CONTENTS

DEATH IN TALLINN

Prologue

Tallinn, Estonia, March 1933

It was a bad place for a view.

Not because of the view itself. From this vantage point up on the edge of Toompea Hill, the tourist or visitor from out of town, could enjoy a great panorama. Below were the roofs and spires of the Old Town, a miraculous fossil surviving from the Middle Ages: narrow cobbled lanes, the tall houses of the German merchants, and the churches their profits built, the Town Hall with its slender gothic minaret sitting at the edge of the Square. And everything squeezed snugly inside the city walls with their covered walkways and round towers. Beyond the Old Town could be glimpsed the ships tied up at the quays. And if you looked further, and the smoke drifting over from the plywood factory wasn't too thick, there was the deep blue of the Gulf of Finland.

And another view by night. The array of lights measured the extent of the growing city. The lights of the Old Town, irregular and unpredictable, sunk in the narrow alleys, even the cafes on Town Hall Square blotted out by the invisible silhouette of the Town Hall itself. Beyond, to the north and east the regular streetlights of the New Town, and over to the west the dim and random twinkling of the crowded slums and expanding suburbs. And at the water's edge, blackness. But if you stood at the railing, the darkness permitted the living sounds of the city to rise up like a miasma; fragments and slivers of noise, hints of unseen living. A single word called out, a laugh, a trumpet's blue note, a car horn, the whinny of a horse. And the odour of night: wisps of cooking, cigar smoke, malt of the brewery, rendered hoof from the glue plant.

No, the viewpoint was a bad place because of those forty metres of rock between the railing and the footpath below that led to the Old Town. If you leaned out and looked straight down, you could see the hexagonal wooden roof of the kiosk by the path. But that was in daylight.

The man watched the pinpoints of light shimmering below. They seemed to rotate, and the railing reappeared. And then he floated out, and felt himself drifting over the nightbound city. Only the wind in his ears told him he was moving. The darkness thickened. And with a stab in his chest and a flash of light in his head, it was over.

Day 1. Wednesday 22nd March 1933

1

Kaarel Rebane saw the man when he arrived at six to open up his kiosk. The sun wasn't up yet, but there was light enough in the grey sky for him to be visible. He stared at Kaarel with an expression of puzzlement, and at first that was all Kaarel saw, the face, with the short dark hair and neatly trimmed moustache. Then, as he stared up, more of the body became visible, shoulders, and outstretched arms draped either side of the kiosk's roof. Kaarel walked round the back of the six-sided wooden building, looked up again. The man's legs were spreadeagled on the rear of the roof. He was wearing a dark overcoat, grey trousers and black leather shoes, well polished. And, protruding through the dark bulk of the torso, the sharpened stake which pointed skywards from the kiosk's apex. The Estonian flag, which normally fluttered from the makeshift flagpole, was, despite the light breeze, clinging stickily to the pole, the blue, black and white tricolor now a glistening black in the pale pre-dawn chill.

Kaarel knew he must inform someone. The kiosk sat by the path running round the foot of the cliff, near the lane leading into the Old Town. It was only two hundred metres to the Baltic Railway Station, where there might be a policeman on duty. But Kaarel ran in the other direction, towards the Old Town. Only forty metres took him to the nearest buildings, on the right hand side of the narrow street where once the Nuns' Gate had stood. The beauty salon of Marju Simm was not yet open, so Kaarel entered, by a wooden door, the entrance passage next to the shop, ran up the stone staircase to the first floor landing, and rapped on the door. He knew that the Simms had a telephone.

The Simms possessed a telephone because Artur Simm was a newspaper reporter. Even though it was expensive, Artur knew that every tool which speeds communication is a must-have for the modern journalist. There are limits, of course – he couldn't afford a biplane, though he knew that for a big story, his paper, *Pealinna Uudised,* Capital News, would hire one. Artur was ambitious, and he knew that to get to the top you had to think big, seize every opportunity.

So when Kaarel Rebane arrived at his door, gasping that a dead man was impaled on the flagpole of his kiosk, Artur replied without hesitation, "Leave it with me, Kaarel, I'll contact the authorities. You go back and wait for the police, I'll make sure they'll be along in no time. Don't you worry." As soon as Kaarel had gone, Artur phoned his paper and asked them to send a photographer. Then he told Marju to wait five minutes before calling the police, and rushed out himself.

As he came round the curve of the path, and his eyes adjusted to the weak pre-dawn light, he saw him. The man was draped face-down over the roof of the kiosk, the post protruding through his back. He seemed, apart from the flagpole, to be undamaged. But when Artur looked closer he realised that his head was at an odd angle, and a dark train of dried blood crept down towards the roof's edge.

Artur looked the man in the eye. He hoped the man would see him there, blink at him, then, with terrible effort, gasp out a few quotable words before giving up the ghost. But there was nothing in the eye that suggested life. The only thing was, the dead man was vaguely familiar. He looked a bit like Clark Gable. But Artur couldn't place him. And how the hell did he manage to land right on the flagpole, Artur wondered. He'd seen flying squirrels in a short at the cinema, and imagined the man in his dark overcoat swooping effortlessly down from the clifftop, before sinking right onto the sharp post, arms and legs stretched wide, as if to seize the whole roof of the little building.

"Artur, where are the police?" Kaarel interrupted his thoughts. He looked shaken.

"Don't worry, Kaarel, they'll be here any minute. In fact, I thought they'd be here by now."

"Should I open the kiosk? What do you think?"

"Probably not a good idea. I expect the police will want to examine the body and then remove it. You don't happen to know who it is?"

"No, no idea." Kaarel preferred not to look again at the man who stared from his roof.

Artur jotted down a few ideas in his notebook, glancing round to capture the scene in his mind. He would find the right prose as soon as he got to the office. In a few minutes he heard the sound of footsteps, running towards the kiosk.

"Thank goodness," gasped Kaarel, "That'll be the police."

But it wasn't the police. It was a young man in a greenish tweed jacket, with his shirt tails flapping as if he hadn't had time to tuck them into his trousers. Round his neck was a leather case from which he extracted a 35mm Leica camera, before looking up at the dead man.

"Wow!" he exclaimed. "*Tere*, Artur! This is something. Do you ..."

"Shut up, Tõnu, just snap it. The cops will be along in a minute, then you won't get close to him."

"But he is a cop, Artur! It's Vaher. From the CID. He's high up."

"Not any more," said Artur, "Get shooting, Tõnu, we haven't much time."

As Tõnu fiddled with a flash bulb, Kaarel asked Artur, "Where did he come from? I thought you called the police."

"Don't worry, Kaarel, I called them too. I'm surprised Tõnu got here first. I really am. He's only taking a few shots for the paper. Once the police get here we'll all have to stand back. Nobody else will get pictures like this."

Tõnu took several shots, from various angles, starting close to the body, then moving further back. But changing the flash bulb after every shot slowed him down, and soon they heard the rasp of a two-stroke engine, and saw among the trees a motorcycle and sidecar, heading towards them from the direction of the railway station.

Dammit, said Artur to himself. He hadn't expected that. He'd thought a couple of plods would walk over from police headquarters down on Pikk Street. "Tõnu," he hissed, "Get out of here now, and over to the paper. Tell them what you saw. I'll see what happens here, then come over and work up a report. We'll have it ready for the lunchtime edition. If not before. Quick!"

Tõnu dashed off, still clutching his camera, the case swinging wildly from the strap around his neck. He was gone by the time the bike emerged from the trees, roared across the empty ground in front of the path, and slithered to a halt by the kiosk. The patrolmen came over to stare at the dead man.

"Holy Spirit help us!" one of them gasped. "It's Vaher!"

"Is he dead?" said the other.

"Looks that way, but we better check. Come on, Mati, give me a hand up." With some help from his colleague, the patrolman managed to get a foot on the lip of the counter, which protruded beyond the closed shutters at the front of the kiosk and grabbed the edge of the roof. With his own face inches from the dead man's, it was obvious that he was dead. Nevertheless he checked for a pulse in the neck. Nothing.

Now they turned to the two men watching them, the older one middle-aged, short, balding, worried, the other slim with sandy hair and a toothbrush moustache beneath his pointed nose, smirking.

"You!" said the patrolman on the ground to the younger man, "Did you find the body?"

"No," replied Artur, it was him, indicating Kaarel, "I just came by later."

"OK," said the patrolman, "We don't need to talk to you. You get back over there by the trees." He laid a hand on Kaarel's arm. "You,

Sir, just wait with us here. CID'll be along in just a minute."

No sooner had Artur positioned himself discreetly among the trees than a square black Fiat 522C saloon swung off the road and parked on the waste ground by the path. A large man in a black suit clambered out of the passenger seat and walked heavily over to the kiosk. His black hair and his drooping moustache were both in need of a good trim. He looked at the dead man, for several seconds. "Shit!" he said, "What the hell was he doing?"

"It's Chief Inspector Vaher, isn't it, Sir?" said the first patrolman.

"Who the hell are you two?" snarled the big man.

"Liiv and Kask, Sir, motorcycle patrol. Number 17."

"Then don't just hang around. Establish a cordon round the scene. Keep the people back, as far as the trees. We'll have to get the doctor, and the technicians." He went over to the car and spoke into the driver's window. Then the car reversed sharply, swerved onto the road again and rushed off.

By this time it was properly light, though the sun was masked by a blanket of cloud, and the man on the roof was attracting a certain amount of attention from passers-by. Liiv and Kask found it difficult to keep them at a distance.

The big man looked closely at the body, without touching it. "Killed by the fall, there's no doubt about that," he muttered, "Must have come from the viewpoint up there. Jumped, or fell."

"Could he have been pushed?" said Patrolman Liiv.

"Don't be stupid! It's Vaher. No-one would dare. Surely. Must have been suicide. Police work is stressful, all right. But him?" He looked up at the dark bulk of Toompea Hill, looming over them. Was he aiming for the flagpole, he asked himself. He leaned against the kiosk, put his forehead to the cold wood, shut his eyes. He sensed a gnawing emptiness inside. Surely not Vaher. Vaher was the best.

"Are you all right, Sir?" asked Liiv.

He pulled himself together. "Yes, of course. Who found the Chief Inspector – was it him?" He nodded at Kaarel, who was standing awkwardly by the motor bike.

Kask responded: "Yes. Kiosk-owner, Kaarel Rebane. Came at six to open up, saw the body right away."

The big man beckoned Kaarel over. He looked apprehensive.

"Kaarel Rebane?" he said.

"Yes."

"Inspector Sõnn, CID. You found the body?"

"Yes."

Sõnn scowled. "You came to open up your kiosk?"

"Yes."

"What time was this?"

"About six."

"Do you open at that time every day?"

"Yes, more or less."

"You didn't see the man land on the kiosk?"

"No, he was ..."

"And he hasn't moved since?"

"No. He's dead, I think."

"You can let us decide that. Did you touch or move him?"

"No. Not at all. I ran and told Artur. He lives just round the corner. In Nunne Street."

"Why did you contact him, rather than the police?"

"He has a phone. He said he'd call the police. Then he came round here."

"To gawp at the corpse? Did he recognise him?"

"No, it was the photographer who did that."

"What! What was a bloody photographer doing here? Did you call him?"

"No, no, it was Artur. He's a reporter."

Inspector Sõnn groaned. "So a reporter and a photographer were here before the police?"

"Yes."

"Where are they now?"

"The photographer ran off just before the patrolmen arrived. I don't know where Artur's gone. He was here a minute ago."

Inspector Sõnn waved Kaarel away. "Wait over by the trees. We'll need a statement." He looked up again at Vaher. What the hell was going on? He felt for the hip flask in his pocket.

2

Artur Simm arrived at the office of *Pealinna Uudised,* on Narva Street, tingling with excitement. Ever since he'd been promoted from junior reporter to reporter four years ago, he'd been covering agriculture and folklore. Now here was the opening he needed. The death of a top policeman! Policemen don't kill themselves every day; there must be a reason. A scandal? Corruption in the force? Or a personal matter, an affair of the heart. He did look like Clark Gable.

Who could forget that steamy love scene in *Red Dust*? He'd begun to write the report in his head as he hurried across town. This could be a breakthrough, maybe even get him a move to the crime desk.

As soon as he arrived, Kristiina at the reception desk said, "The boss wants to see you, Artur. Right away."

This sounded positive. Artur took the steps two at a time, up to the second floor, and knocked on the door marked '*Toimetaja*.' The editor's lair.

"Come in," called a deep voice. Eirik Hunt, veteran editor, fearless critic of the government, and anyone else who crossed his path. "Sit down. How did you get this, Simm?"

"Er, tip-off from an informant, Sir."

"Hmm, good work. This is going to be big. Smart thinking to call us right away. Tõnu got some good shots. We can get a picture on the front page for the mid-morning. Kallas will write it up as soon as he gets in." Jaan Kallas was the paper's crime reporter.

"But ..."

Artur's protest dried up in the face of Hunt's fearsome stare. "Don't push your luck, laddie! You used your brain here. I won't forget that. Talk to Jaan as soon as he's here, give him anything you've got. See how he deals with it. Learn from him. This informant, can you get more out of him? Did he see Vaher jump?"

Artur forced himself to hold back his response, and rewrote it before speaking: "Hmm," he said thoughtfully, "I'm not sure about that, Sir, I'll need to talk to him again. He may know more than he's told me."

"OK. Get onto that as soon as you've seen Jaan. And I still want your folklore piece for tomorrow."

Dammit, thought Artur. He hadn't done it yet. Still, if he could knock out something quickly, by the time he'd finished, Jaan would have arrived, and he could spend the rest of the day on the policeman's death. Do a bit of digging on his own, show what he was capable of.

He went down the stairs to the floor below, and along the corridor to the reporters' room – that was the room for reporters who weren't yet thought worthy of an office to themselves – and sat down at the battered desk facing into the corner. He sighed, and reached up for his copy of *The Encyclopaedia of Estonian Folklore*.

3

A little later, a hundred miles to the south, on Herne Street in Tartu, *Ülemkomissar* Jüri Hallmets, his wife Kirsti, and children Liisa and

Juhan, were sitting around the kitchen table, having breakfast. On the table were cheese, smoked ham and herring, boiled eggs, black rye bread and butter. Chief Inspector Hallmets, a tall man in his mid-forties, had lost the two outer fingers of his left hand to a Red Army sabre in the Independence War, as well as acquiring a groove across the top of his head from the same source.

"This herring is remarkably good," said the Chief Inspector, to no-one in particular, "So, Liisa, what's the University got for you today?"

"Seminar in Mediaeval History, lecture on the Early Development of the Estonian Language, and German conversation. We're going to discuss cooking."

"You won't have much to say then!" smirked her brother.

"When did we ever see you cook?" snapped his sister, "You schoolboys are all the same – hot air."

"What have you got today, Juhan?" said Kirsti, hoping to avoid another squabble.

"Physics, maths, English. The usual."

"Phone!" shouted Liisa, jumped off her stool and ran from the kitchen into the hall. A moment later she came back, disappointed. "It's just for you, Dad. Some Colonel from Tallinn."

"Ah, Chief Inspector, Colonel Reinart, Interior Ministry. We've a bit of a situation here, and we'd like your help."

Hallmets recognised the name. He'd met Reinart first in 1919 during the Independence War. At that time he was a staff officer. Now he was a civil servant. He wasn't sure what exactly the colonel did. But he was important.

"Yes, Colonel, what can I do for you?"

"You know Chief Inspector Vaher?"

Hallmets hesitated. He knew Vaher, didn't like him. At all. "Yes, Sir. How is he?"

"He's dead. Impaled on a kiosk below Toompea."

Hallmets' mind went blank. Something he'd seen in the war flashed through his head – prisoners impaled alive by the Reds. He shook the thought away. "How did it happen?"

"We don't know yet. The thing is, we need someone from out of town to investigate."

"Why's that? There are plenty of good detectives in Tallinn."

"I'd rather not speak on the phone. Let me come straight to the point. I've spoken to the Minister and the Prefect of Police, and they agree that you're the person we need. So I'd be very grateful if you'd get on the next train up. I'll send a car to meet you. You could be here for a few days."

Hallmets told the family he'd have to go to Tallinn right away.

"Must be a big case," said Juhan, "If they can't handle it on their own. Is it gangsters or Reds?"

"Not clear yet, son, won't know till I get there. Look after your mother and sister." He left the kitchen to loud complaints from Liisa, and packed a suitcase, not forgetting his pistol, a neat black Browning FN1910 automatic. He put on a woollen overcoat over his dark suit, then took it off again and decided to carry it. He promised Kirsti he would phone that evening. A car arrived from police headquarters to take him to the station, and he caught the eight thirty train to Tallinn.

There was only one other person in his compartment, an elderly woman. She must have got on further down the line, perhaps even at Valga, on the border with Latvia, where the train started. She scrutinised him carefully, and finally pointed to his hand.

"You got that in the war?"

"Yes." He didn't want to say any more. Most men he knew who'd been in the Independence War preferred not to talk about it.

"We lost our son. He was only eighteen."

"You have other children?"

"Two daughters. And Tõnis. He wasn't old enough, though he wanted to. I suppose we're lucky, really. Others lost more." She lapsed into silence, staring out the window.

As the train made its way north, through wooded swamp and straggling forest, with occasional stretches of farmland, Hallmets thought about the dead man. Vaher had, like Hallmets, been in the Independence War. He'd come through it whole, unlike Hallmets, and joined the new police force after the war. He'd worked in Tallinn, then moved to Narva, at the eastern edge of Estonia, before returning to the capital as second-in-command of the *kriminaalpolitsei*, the CID. Hallmets had met him a few times, and found him patronising and arrogant, although he could be respectful, charming, even obsequious, when dealing with the top brass.

And he despised Vaher's gung-ho approach to police work. Vaher believed that once arrested, an individual was guilty, and the job then was simply to make the evidence strong enough to get a conviction, or to persuade the suspect to confess. And he seemed to be good at doing that. Hallmets knew many of his own colleagues admired Vaher, and thought, like him, that everybody knew who the bad guys were; you just had to pin something on them. Whether it was something they'd done or not, that didn't matter too much.

As to why he was dead, Hallmets had no ideas about that. Vaher was hardly the type to kill himself – he was too self-important and ambitious. Could somebody have killed him? He'd certainly made plenty of enemies – that came with the job. But killing a police officer was a very rare occurrence in Estonia. However, no point in speculating now, plenty time for that later.

Hallmets had bought the daily newspaper *Postimees* at the station in Tartu, and now flicked through, glancing at the headlines. International news was on page 3. The main article, headed, 'The New Germany Rises,' gave an account of Adolf Hitler's swearing-in as Chancellor the previous day, at Potsdam, near Berlin. Hallmets had been to Germany several times, on police training courses as well as holidays, and liked the country and its people. But the Nazis he viewed with horror: race hatred and violence were not his idea of politics. People had told him not to worry, the extremist rhetoric and the parades were just clever techniques to raise Hitler's profile, and as soon as he was in power, everything would be toned down, he'd become a regular politician. Hallmets wasn't so sure.

4

It was half past eleven when the train pulled in to the Baltic Station in Tallinn. Hallmets exited the grey stone building through the main archway, and waited just outside. The weather was cold, and the sky a grey sheet of cloud; he'd put on his overcoat after leaving the train. He could see before him the silhouetted bulk of Toompea Hill. Amidst its crowded jumble of government buildings, rose the spire of the cathedral that gave the hill its name. He let his eyes run from Tall Hermann, the tower at the far right, along the face of the cliff to the viewing platform near the left hand edge.

"Chief Inspector Hallmets?" A young man in a smart army uniform, clean-shaven with blonde hair, approached him, and saluted. "I'm Lieutenant Kadakas, Sir. I'm to take you to the Ministry." He took Hallmets' suitcase and led the way to a black Volvo Pv652 sedan, a cut above the usual police vehicle. The driver opened the rear door for him while Kadakas stowed the case and got into the other side.

As the driver got in, Hallmets said to Kadakas, "Before we go to the Ministry, I'd like to see the spot where Chief Inspector Vaher was found."

"Colonel Reinart's orders were to go straight to the Ministry, Sir."

"I'm adjusting them slightly."

Kadakas opened his mouth to repeat his orders, then, as he glanced into Hallmets' grey eyes, closed it again. "Yes, Sir, of course."

"So it's the kiosk, then?" said the driver, without turning his head.

"Thank you," said Hallmets.

They were there in four minutes. The body had been removed and the kiosk was now open again for business. And plenty of it. Word had got around.

Hallmets got out of the car and looked closely at the little building, then up at the cliff brooding over them, and the railings of the viewpoint at the top. He walked around the kiosk, then peered at the ground between it and the base of the cliff. Twice he knelt down and poked at something. Then he came back to the car.

As they moved off again, Kadakas asked him, "Find anything, Sir?"

"Maybe," he answered, "We'll see. How come everyone knows what's happened here?"

Kadakas seemed unsure what to say.

"In the paper," said the driver, and, with his left hand on the wheel, passed back with his right a copy of *Pealinna Uudised.* "Special edition. Came out just after eleven. Quick work, eh?"

It was on the front page: '*Ghastly Discovery: Senior Police Officer impaled.*' It described how kiosk owner Kaarel Rebane had been shocked to find a dead man on top of his workplace. The scene was described in graphic detail, and there was a grainy photograph of the dead man's face, staring sightless down from the kiosk roof. Next came a description of Vaher and his methods: he was described as '*crude, perhaps inelegant, but successful and popular*'. '*Vaher always got his man,*' said the writer, '*and was rightly feared by the criminal community. Did one of its members gain his sadistic revenge?*'

Hallmets put the paper back onto the front seat, next to the driver. "Thanks," he said.

They passed along Nunne Street, turned left into Pikk Street, and left again near the bottom to pull up outside the grey stone frontage of the Interior Ministry. Beyond it rose the whitewashed wall of St. Olav's Church, its spire once the tallest in Europe. But that was in a different world.

Colonel Reinart's office was on the third floor, overlooking the lane between the ministry and Police Headquarters next door. The colonel, a tall man with brown hair that matched his eyes, a well-tended moustache, and an immaculate uniform, shook hands with Hallmets. "I remember you from the war," he began, "You distinguished yourself at Võnnu, when we chased the Germans out of Latvia. I was on General Põdder's staff. Sad that the old boy died last year. Didn't the Latvians give you a medal? More to the point, why didn't you stay with the army after the war."

"I've never really been a fan of uniforms. Or of doing what other people tell me."

"But you do that now. Give orders to others."

"It's not like the army. My people can argue with me. It's called teamwork."

The colonel smiled thinly, and ordered the lieutenant to bring coffee. He waved Hallmets to an upright armchair, upholstered in leather, and sat himself behind his large desk. He pointed to an ornately-carved wooden cigarette box on the desk. "Cigarette?"

"No thanks. Spoils the taste of good coffee."

"Hmm." The colonel was about to take one, but checked himself. "How much do you know about this Vaher business?"

"Only what I read in the *Pealinna Uudised.*"

"That's as much as we know at the moment."

"I doubt that," said Hallmets, "Otherwise you wouldn't have called me so quickly. I'm sure there are plenty of good detectives still alive next door."

The colonel glanced out of the window at the building across the lane. Hallmets followed his gaze. At a window opposite, a uniformed police officer was grimly punching the keys of a typewriter, a cigarette in the corner of his mouth.

"The papers got to the body before the police had even arrived," replied the colonel, "This investigation will be very public. I'm sure you're aware of Vaher's reputation for, how can I put it, effectiveness."

"I'm glad you didn't say justice."

Reinart frowned. "We were quite aware of his methods. But the people he put into the frame usually seemed to be those who deserved it. And he was very popular within the force here. There are lots of officers who'd happily round up all the usual suspects and shoot the lot of them in revenge. That's why we want a proper investigation, so that the police are seen to be professional."

"That's very noble, but I'm not convinced," said Hallmets, "There's more."

"That's all you need to know, Chief Inspector."

Hallmets stood up slowly. "What I need to know, Colonel," he said quietly, "is whatever will help me solve the case, which is what I assume you want me to do. If I don't have access to everything, I don't do it. I can find my own way back to the railway station, thank you."

"Please, *Härra* Hallmets, do sit down. I can see that you're indeed as others have described you. Awkward, insubordinate, but also courageous and determined. As you were at Võnnu in '19. If you'd just followed orders, that breakthrough would never have happened. All right, I'll tell you what I know."

Hallmets sat down again. "Let's be clear about this, Colonel. I'm willing to lead this investigation, because I too think that justice needs to be seen to be done. But if I suspect that any information is being withheld from me, I will walk away. You have my word on that. And it's obvious there's something more, otherwise I'd be talking to Captain Lind next door at Police HQ, and not you here at the Ministry."

The colonel smiled. "Yes, I suppose so." He studied his immaculately-groomed finger nails for a moment. "Well, then, I should explain that there may be a political dimension to this."

"You don't say."

"As you know, our democracy is at the moment somewhat fragile. The parties in parliament are constantly falling out, and there's a new government every few months."

"That's a bit of an exaggeration."

"You know what I mean. People are losing faith in the politicians. They think they're too interested in their own careers, and aren't dealing with the problems. Especially the economic ones. I fear more and more people are looking for, shall we say, an extreme solution."

"As in Germany."

"Many other countries too. And there's a movement of that sort here too."

"Are you talking about the Vaps Movement? The veterans' organisation? They're hardly Nazis. I'll admit I don't share some of their views, but it's perfectly reasonable to press the government to make more farms available for veterans."

Reinart picked up an expensive-looking fountain pen, scrutinised it carefully, put it down again. "In the last year or so they've changed. They've become explicitly political, and they're admitting anyone who agrees with their politics, even if they're not veterans. And they've started following some of the habits of other right-wing groups in Europe. Uniforms, armbands, lately even the so-called Roman salute.

This could be a gift for them. Proof that democracy leads to chaos. They want a referendum to change the constitution, create a powerful president who can do without parliament."

"A bit like Hitler?"

"And that's another complication. Our German community. Disgruntled landowners who lost out with the Land Reform. Businessmen who admire Hitler. Plenty of nostalgia for the good old days when they ruled the roost. They could cause trouble too. That's why we need to tie this up quickly, and the investigation has to be absolutely above board. And led by a top investigator with an exemplary war record and a strong belief in democracy."

"You've studied my file."

The colonel smiled. "There's nothing secret there. You don't keep your views quiet."

"Then we'd better get started. Is Captain Lind aware of my involvement?"

"This has been approved at the highest level. The Interior Minister spoke to the Tallinn Police Prefect personally, and he, Prefect Rotenbork that is, has spoken to Lind. But take this, just in case there are any problems – it's a letter from me authorising you to be given whatever resources you need whilst investigating this case." He handed over an envelope. "I'll let you go and see Lind now. I'll send you over our file on Vaher as soon as I've had it copied. We've arranged your accommodation at the Imperial Hotel, on Nunne Street, by the way. It's actually quite close to where the body was found. I've had your suitcase sent there already. And the Ministry will put a car and driver at your disposal – the one that brought you here this morning. The driver's name is Lembit, he's a good man, very resourceful, and discreet. One other thing, which I hope you won't mind. I've allocated Lieutenant Kadakas as liaison between your team and the ministry. Not to spy on you of course. But we need to be aware of what's happening with the investigation on a regular basis. And he might be useful, too. Strictly speaking, he's army, not police, but I've told him to defer to you. If you don't feel he's pulling his weight, let me know and I'll have him shot." He smiled. "Just a joke. Here's my card. Any problems, phone me."

5

As soon as Hallmets crossed the lane and entered Police Headquarters, he was shown to Captain Lind's office on the first floor.

More coffee arrived. The captain, thin, grey-haired and stooping, looked tired. But he shook Hallmets' hand warmly. "Jüri, good to see you. Messy business, this. I'm sorry they've dragged you into it, but I suppose they're right, bringing someone in from outside to run the investigation. I'm just glad it's you."

Lind and Hallmets were old comrades from the war, and both had joined the new police force of the Estonian Republic. Five years previously, when the Tallinn force was expanded, and they were seeking a deputy commander of CID, Lind tried to persuade Hallmets to take the job. Hallmets had refused. He was happy in Tartu. He liked the atmosphere and the culture, his wife had a job at the university, and his children were happy in school. He never regretted the refusal, though he was sorry for Lind when he saw that Vaher had been appointed.

"Good to see you again, too, Peeter, let's hope we can get it tidied up without a lot of fuss."

"Not much chance of that, I'm afraid. The papers are going to have a field day. If *Pealinna Uudised* hadn't put out that Special this morning, we might have been able to persuade them to sit on it for a few days. But of course Hunt – he's the editor – realised we'd try that, and rushed out his scoop before we could do anything. The politicians are furious, as you can imagine. Poor Viktor got a roasting from the Minister. Hardly his fault, but he's the Prefect, so that's where the buck stops."

"What's his view on the case?" Hallmets had met Viktor Rotenbork, Prefect of the Tallinn-Harjumaa Police Division, a couple of times and formed a positive impression of him as a straightforward policeman with a sound legal background.

"He knows this has to be sorted out as soon as possible, and that we need somebody above suspicion to do it."

"What am I above suspicion of? Is there something going on in the police here that I should know about?"

Lind looked uneasy. "Chief Inspector Vaher was, shall I say, a divisive influence here. I was reluctant to appoint him. I'd heard enough about his methods when he was in Narva. But the committee was impressed by his results, and that was that. I'm afraid I never got on with him. But he was popular with many of his colleagues. His approach certainly made the job simpler: first decide who's guilty, then find some evidence that fits, invented if necessary, then beat a confession out of the suspect. Saves a long trial too."

"Weren't the examining magistrates unhappy about that?"

"He tended to work with just a couple of them, people who valued law and order above justice, and were willing to let him get on with it. And you can't argue with a signed confession, can you? Anyway, enough of that, let's be positive. Let's drink to my retirement, eh? Only six months to go, and I'm free." Lind opened a drawer in his desk and produced a bottle of vodka and a couple of shot glasses. He opened the bottle and filled the glasses. "*Terviseks!*" They downed the clear liquid.

"That's good stuff," said Hallmets. He glanced at the bottle. "*Leikari?* Sounds Finnish." But can't be, he thought. Alcohol production was banned under Finland's Prohibition Law.

"A present at Christmas, from Vaher, as it happens. I was waiting for a good moment to open it. Maybe we should drink to him, too." They swallowed another shot.

"And so to business," said Lind, now rather more relaxed than when Hallmets had arrived. "I've got you an office with an investigators' room next to it. And you'll need some people to assist you. Can I suggest you take a couple of people from outwith the city force – that'll underline that your team is above board?"

"I suspect you're going to tell me you've already summoned them."

The captain blushed. "You know me too well, Jüri. So that's saved me beating about the bush. They'll be here quite soon. I've worked with them both in the past. Eva Larsson and Oleg Maslov."

"The names are vaguely familiar. Tell me more. And why I should take them."

"Larsson's Swedish-Estonian, from Saaremaa, currently stationed in Pärnu. Great sportswoman, would have qualified for the Olympic shooting team, er, if women had been admitted, that is. And she's not found it easy in the police; many officers don't think it's a job for a woman. There are very few of them in the force, as you'll know. As for Maslov, he comes from one of those villages down by Lake Peipsi. He's based down at Petseri now, near the Russian border. Great judge of vodka, I hear. But those aren't the reasons you should have them. They're good detectives. Persistent, thoughtful, trustworthy. But of course, if you need other people to do some of the legwork, let me know, and you can have whoever you want. I've also assigned one of the secretaries to you – her name's Marta Kukk. She's reliable and doesn't gossip. What about a car?"

"The ministry have supplied one, plus a driver and a liaison officer."

"Ah. One of those. You're dealing with Reinart at the Ministry?"

"Yes."

Lind nodded. "I came across him during the war. Wherever the fighting's thickest, you can be sure he won't be there. Oh, you should have these – the keys to Vaher's office. I've had it sealed till you decide to look at it. I'll take you up to your office now. But first let's drink a toast to the success of your investigation. *Terviseks!*"

Hallmets' office was on the fourth floor, the windows looking down into the lane between Police Headquarters and the Interior Ministry. One of the windows across and slightly below him must be Colonel Reinart's. His office was spacious and bright, and next door was a large work room featuring an oak table which seemed to have come from the dining room of a manor house.

By the door leading from the work room to the corridor was a small desk behind which stood Marta Kukk, a woman in her early sixties, her grey hair tied in a bun and *pince-nez* hanging from a thin gold chain. She apologised to Hallmets that he must forgive her spelling, she couldn't keep up with the changes in the written Estonian language that the experts kept introducing. "Up to 1918, you see, Sir, I was only typing in German. I worked for Herr Scheelmann then, he imported wine, sent it all over the empire. So after the war I came here, and had to switch to Estonian. Poor Herr Scheelmann went bankrupt. All his stock had been stolen in the war and after it, he couldn't rebuild the business without the Russian market. He eventually went to Romania, I think it was, he had a cousin there."

Having familiarised himself with his space, Hallmets decided to get some lunch. No point in trying to do everything at once.

He suspected the cafes in Pikk Street would be full of policemen, so he walked down to the city wall at the Great Coastal Gate, next to the squat bulk of the 'Fat Margaret' tower. From here it was only a short walk to the harbour area, where he found a reasonably comfortable cafe, and enjoyed a mushroom pie with a bottle of *kvass*, the slightly alcoholic drink made from fermented rye bread.

He knew this wasn't going to be an easy case. He hadn't seen any of the paperwork yet, but he had the feeling that it wouldn't tell him much more than he already knew. Yes, the post-mortem would tell him the exact cause of death, with hopefully an approximate time, and it would be important to confirm that Vaher fell onto the kiosk from the direction of the viewing platform. He wondered if anything had been found up at the platform itself.

He wondered also about Vaher himself. Once he'd settled in and read the paperwork, he must begin the dissection of Vaher's life, for there he would find the reason for his death.

6

At another cafe, a little to the south, on Narva Street, two men were eating sauerkraut with sausage and drinking beer. One was a thin young man with a tuft of moustache below his nose and sandy hair which flopped over his forehead. The other was older, with sparse dark brown hair, greying in parts, a red nose, a paunch and a complexion to which time and alcohol had done their worst. This was Jaan Kallas, crime reporter of the *Pealinna Uudised*. His companion was Artur Simm.

Kallas was talking whilst he ate. "Listen to me, Artur. I appreciate that you're keen to develop your career, and that you want to get away from the tedious stuff that you're having to do at the moment. But let me tell you, there are no short cuts in journalism. You've got to learn from experience, and from those who know what they're doing. And that's especially true when it comes to crime reporting, because the only advantage we've got over the police is that we can talk to the criminals without threatening to arrest them. But that needs trust. I get exclusive stuff because I've got informants who trust me. That took a lot of time and effort, and alcohol. But it's not just the informants, Artur. You have to build up a picture of the whole crime scene in the city. Who the syndicates are and what they control, who the hitmen are, who the various enforcers work for, and where they operate. There's a geography and an economy of crime, and if you don't know it, you can run into some real trouble.

"See this Vaher business. Take my word for it, this means real trouble. Senior cops don't get killed without there being some very heavy stuff out there. If they killed Vaher, they'll kill you without a second thought. Why? Because you're nobody. And the reason I'm saying this is that I can see what's going on in your little head. You're thinking you're going to dash out there when I'm not looking and with a few phone calls uncover a giant criminal conspiracy that caused Vaher's death. Well, forget it. First, because nobody will tell you anything, and that's because they don't know you. And second, once you start snooping, they'll simply bump you off. One morning you'll float into the harbour on the tide, dead as you'll ever be. No indication of who did it, or why. Just another corpse of a bit player who thought he could be a star.

"Yeah, go on, smirk at me. But I'm telling you, your life depends on your listening to me. I won't be doing this forever. I'm happy for you to take over when I've gone. But if you want to do that, you need to learn the job. I'm offering you a good deal here, as well as a free meal.

Work with me and learn the trade. Sure, at the moment it's my name that's on each piece. But one day it'll be yours, if you do it right. Just don't try running before you can even crawl. There's the deal, take it or leave it, buddy boy."

There was a touch of irritation in Artur's frown. "OK, OK, Jaan, I take your point, no need to overdo it. I'm glad to work with you, learn a few tricks. But I'm not just your errand boy, I want a bit of the real action too. If it weren't for me, you wouldn't have this morning's exclusive."

"Sure, kid, that was quick thinking. You happened to be in the right place at the right time, and you made the most of it. You've got an eye for an opportunity, and that's one of the talents any good journalist needs. But you were lucky, the opportunity just fell into your lap. Do you think that's going to happen, week in week out, for the next thirty years. No way. To be successful you've got to make those opportunities happen, pick them off the tree before they fall. Stick with me, and you'll learn how to do that. And as a bonus, you get to stay alive. Now, if you want to work with me, let's get down to business. If you don't, then piss off now." Kallas shovelled a pile of sauerkraut into his mouth, so that loose strands hung out the edges, like skinless worms struggling to free themselves. He shoved them in with the edge of his hand, and took another swig of beer.

Artur nodded. "OK, Jaan, let's get to it. Where do we start?"

Kallas scratched his stomach and burped. "We need to dig up some shit on Vaher. It seems to me this was a revenge killing. That's why it was so public. You don't throw somebody off Toompea Hill unless you want to make a point."

"So what is the point?"

"If I knew that I'd already be writing it up. My guess is that he'd seriously pissed off somebody in the criminal world. Somebody big, somebody who doesn't mind throwing people off Toompea Hill. So we'll need to look at all the people he put away, see if there was anyone well-connected enough to stir up a response. Why don't you do that? I'll contact a few of my ears in the underworld, see if they've got anything to report. A twenty-crown bill buys plenty of talk, but it's working out how much of it was worth twenty crowns that's the tricky bit."

"Maybe I could come along to meet them."

"Is that a joke? Listen, sunshine, to a good reporter, his contacts are part of his body, that's why I call them my ears. If you want some ears, you'll need to grow them yourself. Now, clear off and do some work!"

Artur hadn't finished his beer. But he took the hint. Even though he considered Kallas to be a pompous and self-satisfied asshole, working with him was an opportunity. And despite what Kallas had said, he would do a little digging on his own too. He knew the other man was simply trying to keep him out of his patch. But, he thought, talent will out. He got up, nodded to Kallas, left the cafe, and walked off, trying to effect a relaxed swagger.

A thought occurred to him. What if he were to follow Kallas, then he could find out who his 'ears' were. But that wouldn't happen during the day. Kallas would probably sneak into some dive down by the harbour; maybe he even disguised himself as a sailor. Well, two could play at that game. He needed to write that folklore piece for Hunt, too. Who the hell wanted to read that some old farmer thought it would rain when he saw a mole in his field? There was a weather forecast at the bottom of page four, why didn't they just read that?

Jaan Kallas finished his beer and ordered a coffee. He needed to think. And he had no intention of sharing his thoughts with Artur Simm. He realised that Artur's deference was a sham, that the ambitious little turd simply wanted his job. Nevertheless, Hunt had ordered him to work with Simm. Perhaps Hunt was lining Simm up as his next crime reporter, and wanted Kallas to train him. He couldn't refuse. But he would have to use Simm carefully, give him plenty of legwork, but keep him away from any real insights.

The case worried him, because it was out of the ordinary. Its sensational nature was a gift to the press, of course, but it was also highly unusual. Killing a policeman was in itself a very rare occurrence. The underworld was well aware that the police reaction would be heavy and dangerous, that an attack on their own was the worst crime in the book. The response would be unrelenting: raids on all the usual criminal haunts, sudden arrests and interrogations, random beatings of petty thieves, pimps, and other shady characters, bright lights shone into shadowy places. It was no good for the criminal business. Bribing policemen was a much more successful strategy than killing them.

The public nature of the event added another dimension. Yes, now and again someone jumped off Toompea Hill. It was a convenient spot for a suicide. But Vaher wasn't the suicidal type – he was too fond of himself. So why was he killed? And by whom?

He had no answer to these questions yet. He doubted that Artur would come up with much from his trawl through the court records.

The big players always managed to avoid being put away, and remained in their comfortable houses in Kadriorg or Nõmme. They tended to be discreet, and if a killing was required, it happened quietly, with a knife or a ligature. If it was a warning to rivals, that happened discreetly too. Perhaps a finger sent through the post. But nothing sensational. That wasn't the Estonian style.

Unless it was the Russians. A lot of Russian refugees had ended up in Estonia after the Revolution. There had even been a white Russian army based in Estonia for a while. Until they'd tried to capture St. Petersburg, and been thrashed by the Reds. Most of them had drifted off by now – America was the destination of choice – but there were still plenty of them around, and, unlike the Estonians, they were more attracted to outward displays. But anything too outrageous, and they knew they'd be kicked out of the country.

It was certainly a puzzle. The first thing was to collect some information. And no time like the present. He finished his coffee, paid for his and Artur's meals, put on his coat, and left. As he strode down Narva Street, he failed to notice a slim figure in a raincoat, hat pulled low, lurking in a doorway.

7

Returning to Police Headquarters, Hallmets noticed that no-one spoke to him. He guessed that his appointment to the Vaher case was not popular locally. The Tallinn police would be itching to react to the killing, and no doubt resented not being set off. He would have to deal with this soon, before somebody started doing things without waiting for orders.

As soon as he got to his office, he noticed there was now a phone on his desk. He asked to be put through to Captain Lind.

"*Tere*, Peeter! Jüri here. I'm wondering if you'd mind me having a meeting with all the detectives here later this afternoon. I think I need to let them know what's going on, forestall anyone who's thinking of taking his own private revenge for Vaher. Bring them on board a bit."

"Good idea, Jüri. Leave it with me, I'll organise it and open it. What time – five suit you?"

On his desk sat a brown cardboard folder. On a white label stuck on the front was written, in a flowing hand, in black ink, 'Nikolai Vaher'. This was the case file. But there was not much inside. The first item was a form completed by Patrolman Liiv. It was written in pencil in a simple but clear script. The report indicated that they had been despatched from Pikk Street to investigate a report of a body. They had located the body, on the roof of a kiosk near Nunne Street, and confirmed that it was dead. They identified the finder of the corpse, one Kaarel Rebane, and another witness, Artur Simm, who claimed to have summoned the police using the telephone in his flat in Nunne Street. This information was passed on to Inspector Sõnn on his arrival at the scene. The patrolmen then ensured the security of the site until the medical examiner, photographer and forensic technician had completed their work, and the body had been removed and taken to the transit morgue in the Pikk Street basement. At that point, they allowed *Härra* Rebane, the kiosk-owner, to open up, and returned to Police Headquarters.

The next sheet was Inspector Sõnn's report on the discovery of the body. It was disappointing: brief and written in an almost illegible scrawl that should have gained the writer immediate entry to medical school. Sõnn identified the dead man as 'probably Chief Inspector Vaher' and opined that he had probably jumped from the viewpoint on Toompea Hill. Sõnn had taken a cursory look around the kiosk, and noticed nothing remarkable apart, of course, from the corpse on the roof. He had left the scene as soon as the medical examiner had arrived, and returned to Pikk Street. There was no indication that Sõnn had thought of examining the scene at the viewpoint.

A form completed by the medical examiner indicated that he had arrived at the scene at 6.55 am, and had pronounced the man dead. With some difficulty he and the patrolmen had removed the body from the roof and he had given it a brief examination on the ground. Cause of death appeared to be injuries consistent with falling from a height onto the flagstaff on top of the kiosk. However, this opinion was only provisional, and a post-mortem would be required to ascertain the exact cause of death, and to identify any further aspects which would be of interest to the police. Several large black-and-white photographs showed the corpse in situ and then laid out on the path in front of the kiosk, on a sheet which the doctor had brought.

A report by Einar Sepp, the forensic technician, indicated that there were large numbers of footprints around the kiosk, but that owing to the cold dry weather over the last few days, there were none which could be identified as belonging to the night of Vaher's death. The eroded nature of the prints suggested they were all several days old. The roof of the kiosk had been dusted for fingerprints, but none found apart from those of Patrolmen Liiv and Kask. Large numbers of cardboard cigarette-ends were observed, which was usual for this type of location. Apart from other objects usually found in the vicinity of kiosks – small coins, scraps of paper, sweet wrappers, cracked cigarette holders, etc. – nothing which could be linked to the dead man or his arrival onto the kiosk had been found. It was presumed from this that the man had fallen from somewhere on Toompea Hill directly onto the roof of the kiosk.

That reminded Hallmets of something. He took from his pocket what he had found several metres behind the kiosk that morning, and laid it carefully on the desk. A cigarette holder, about eight centimetres long. Made of ivory, which was unusual, and almost new, which was also unusual. Most cigarette holders discarded around kiosks were cheap and broken. They were usually made of artificial horn, produced from casein, a by-product of butter-making, and were often broken due to firm gripping between the teeth rather than the lips. Replacements were obtainable at any kiosk, hence the likelihood of finding discarded ones nearby, as Sepp the technician had done. But this one was expensive, and it had hardly been used. Why should it have been discarded? He turned it over, and saw that there was something carved into the underside: a coat-of-arms maybe, or set of initials. He opened the desk drawer and was pleased to see that Marta had supplied him with writing materials and stationery. He took out a sheet of thin notepaper and placed it carefully across the incised work, then rubbed with a pencil to reveal, in gothic script, the letters **NV**. Perhaps Nikolai Vaher. Could it be too much of a coincidence for it to be lying there. It had not been there long, he was sure of that. Had it been there much longer it would have been either crushed into the dust by thoughtless heels, or spotted and picked up by a sharp-eyed individual who would either use it or sell it. Had it fallen out of Vaher's pocket as he fell, or been thrown out when he landed? It was a luxury item, hand-carved, it must have cost a good few crowns. He took a small envelope from the drawer and put the cigarette holder inside, then slipped it into the top pocket of his jacket.

Beneath the other papers was a cutting from today's *Pealinna Uudised* describing the discovery of the body. It was the one he had read in the car, but it was useful to have a copy to study at greater length. He noticed that the article was written by Jaan Kallas, head crime reporter at the paper.

There was a polite knock at the door connecting his office to the workroom, and Marta told him the post-mortem would be that evening at six. He asked her to go the Personnel Department and borrow

Vaher's file.

As they spoke, there was a pounding at the door leading to the corridor, and without waiting for an invitation, a man burst into the room and strode towards Hallmets. A large man in a dark suit with a fleshy face, a protruding lower lip, black hair and a drooping moustache. The man lurched towards Hallmets, breathing heavily, and leaned over his desk. Hallmets was engulfed by a smell of sweat and cheap fruit brandy.

"Listen, big shot," growled the man, "We don't need you here to sort out Vaher's death. We can take out all the crime bosses in the city right now. One of them must have done it and no-one'll miss the rest. So just bugger off back to the countryside. Someone's probably stolen a pig by now, so you'd better ..."

He did not get the chance to finish his sentence. In a swift movement, Hallmets grabbed the hair on the left side of his head and banged it down onto the desktop. Then he lifted it up and did it again. The man slumped onto the desktop, dazed. Hallmets got up, walked behind him, twisted the man's arm behind him, and heaved him up. He marched him through the open door into the workroom, and pushed him onto a chair that stood by the window. Then he opened the window, grabbed the man's ear, and thrust his face into the chill breeze that swept into the room. The man gasped.

"Now, my friend, who might you be?" Hallmets asked, as he pulled him back inside.

"Sõnn. Inspector Sõnn. Who do you think you are, let me go," he wailed.

"I'd like to talk to you, *Härra* Sõnn, but not just yet. First, I don't believe it's a good idea to be rude. People will just think you're a thug, and treat you like one. Second, I don't believe it's a good idea to drink lots of cheap alcohol when you're supposed to be working. People will just think you're a drunkard, and treat you like one. Now I'd like you to leave my office and sober up. Get some fresh air, have a wash and drink some coffee. Then come back and see me at half past four, so that we can discuss your report." Hallmets moved him towards the door, which Marta swiftly opened for him, and shoved Sõnn into the corridor. He staggered a few steps before one foot tripped over the other and he fell onto the lino with an audible thump, hitting his head on the floor. Groaning, he crawled off, and Hallmets shut the door.

"You should have thrown him out the window," said Marta, "I can tell you, there are too many of his type in this building. I shouldn't speak ill of the dead, but Vaher encouraged them. You did well to put him in his place, Sir."

"Thank you, Marta," said Hallmets, trying to calm himself down, "Can you note in the diary that I have an appointment with Inspector Sõnn at four thirty. I'm going to go out now to have another look at the site."

There was another knock at the door.

"Don't say he's back again!" muttered Hallmets, and flung open the door. "Yes!" he snarled.

Kadakas stood there at attention. "I'm really sorry to disturb you, Sir," he gasped. "Colonel Reinart asked me to report to you."

"All right, Lieutenant," said Hallmets, "You'd better come with me then."

8

Hallmets led Kadakas at a brisk pace; he needed to get the adrenalin out of his system. They headed up Pikk Street and into Nunne Street then back to the kiosk where Vaher's body had been found. There was still a big crowd there – the death was doing wonders for Kaarel Rebane's business. Beyond the kiosk they came to the Patkuli Staircase, a narrow stone stairway that zigzagged up the cliffside to the viewpoint at the top, and Hallmets led the way up. When they reached the top, they found about a dozen people staring out over the Old Town, and taking photos of the view and each other. Hallmets found a spot at the railing, and looked out for a couple of minutes over the Old Town towards the harbour and the bay, and then down towards the hexagonal roof of the kiosk below, in the centre of which a dark smudge was still visible.

"Well, Kadakas, what do you think happened? How did Vaher get down there?"

Kadakas looked puzzled. "I don't know, Sir."

"Good start. Best not to jump to any conclusions to begin with. That's ruined too many investigations. The first thing to do is to consider the possibilities. What do you think they are?"

Kadakas thought hard. "Maybe he jumped. Climbed over the railing then threw himself off."

"Good. That's number one. Next one?"

"If he didn't jump he must have been pushed."

"OK. That's number two. What exactly do you mean, though?"

"Well, he was up here, like we are, and someone crept up on him and pushed him."

25

"Stand still, Kadakas!"

Kadakas froze, standing about an arm's length from the railing. Hallmets turned rapidly behind him and pushed him towards the edge, but Kadakas instinctively grabbed the railing. "Hey, what's going on?" he gasped.

"If you were Vaher and somebody pushed you, you did what he'd have done."

The light dawned on Kadakas' face. "Ah, I get it, Sir. It needs more than a casual shove to get someone over the edge here. But what if he were drunk?"

"Yes, you'd think it would be easier, but a drunk would still grasp hold of the rail. It's an instinctive reaction."

"So he can't have been simply pushed. He must have been manhandled over."

"Yes. That's option two, he was bundled over. Alright, what else is possible?"

"Hmm. Talking of drunk, maybe he was drunk and climbed over for some reason, then lost his footing and fell. So then it would be an accident."

"That's scenario number three. But not an accident. There is no such thing as an accident. Talking of accidents diverts us from an important truth: everything has a cause. If he had drunk a bottle of vodka, he had a reason. If he clambered over the railing, there will be a reason. If he let go of the rail, there will be a reason."

"What can we call this, then, if we can't say it's an accident?"

"We'll call this option 'death by misadventure', in other words, doing something that wasn't sensible. Is that it, then? Is there another possibility?"

"If he didn't jump, wasn't bundled over, and didn't just fall off, no, I can't think of anything else." Kadakas looked satisfied with his concise summing up.

"What if he wasn't here at all?"

"But he was. He must have been. Otherwise how did he get onto the kiosk roof?"

"I would do it this way. I would shoot you in the chest with a large bore shotgun. Then I would take a ladder and lift you onto the kiosk roof, then lower you onto the flagstaff, so that it poked through the entry wound and out the exit wound in your back. Then I would remove my ladder and go away."

"Clever. So that's how it was done?"

"No, probably not. I suspect he did come off here. But we mustn't assume that he did."

"So option four is that he was killed first, then put on the roof?"

"Exactly. But there is a simple way of testing option four. This evening at six there will be a post-mortem. That will tell us whether he fell onto the kiosk or was placed on it. But, for the moment, we must assume both are possible. So, we have four options, but each could have occurred in different ways. For instance, option two, that he was bundled off. The simplest scenario is that he was up here looking out when some men come from behind, grab him, and manhandle him over the rail."

"Or they could have knocked him over the head, then thrown him off."

"Yes, that's good, Kadakas, because that leads to another possibility. That he didn't come here himself, but was taken somewhere else, knocked out or even killed there, then brought up here and tossed over the rail. So, plenty of possibilities. But the good news is, once we know what they are, we can start eliminating them. Until there's just one left."

"Yes, Sir. Very logical."

"Quite. Now, while we're here, let's see what we can find. Unfortunately, no-one thought to check this spot earlier this morning, and since then it's been walked over by maybe a hundred people, every one of whom has clutched this railing in his or her sweaty hands. So we're unlikely to find any finger- or footprints that we can tie to Vaher. The best we can do is have a good look round and see if there's anything here that might be relevant."

"Were you thinking of anything in particular, Sir?"

"No. Just see if there's anything lying around that looks unusual. Look at the surfaces, and into any corners where things could have got caught."

"Should I get down and crawl?"

"No, I don't think that's necessary. And these people will wonder what we're up to. Half of them are probably up here because they read about Vaher in the paper. So we don't want to attract attention. We're more likely to find something around the edges of this area. The central part will have been well-trampled. We'll start here, go in opposite directions, and meet at the other side. If you find anything, just put it in your pocket."

Twenty minutes later they met by the archway at the rear of the viewing area, that led to the government and diplomatic buildings that crowded Toompea Hill. Hallmets motioned Kadakas through the arch into the narrow lane beyond. "Come on, let's find a cafe where we can look at this stuff in comfort."

He led Kadakas through the lanes towards the onion domes of the Alexander Nevski cathedral, then they turned a sharp left to walk down a sloping cobbled lane that led through an arched stone gateway into the Old Town, to the head of Pikk Street. But instead of heading on to Police Headquarters, they turned right down a lane to emerge into Raekoja Plats, Town Hall Square, dominated by the mediaeval town hall with its arcaded lower level and slim minaret-like tower. There were several cafes facing the square, and Hallmets pointed Kadakas to the *Alt-Revaler-Cafe*. They were soon ensconced at a window table giving them plenty of light to look at their finds. A waitress came over to take their order, giving Kadakas a lingering smile as she went off.

"Well, what did you find?" Hallmets asked the lieutenant.

Kadakas rummaged in his capacious uniform pockets and fetched out two empty cigarette packets, and the top part of somebody's false teeth. "Amazing what you can find, isn't it?" he said, "What about yourself, Sir?"

Hallmets put a torn cigar label on the table. "And there's this." He took from his pocket a dull black-and-gold cylinder. A fountain pen, with the black cap screwed on. Round the barrel was still visible despite a coating of dust, a complicated design in gold and silver, the gold still gleaming

"That looks like something valuable," said Kadakas.

"It is. It's a Pelikan Toledo. Lying on the ground, right up against the wall. Looks new, too. German, only came out a couple of years ago. As you correctly observed, very expensive. I've got a Pelikan pen myself, the 100 model. It's a good pen, but the Toledo is a luxury item. The sort of pen men sign treaties with. Not something a policeman can afford. And certainly, something you'd want to look after very carefully."

"Wealthy tourist with a hole in his pocket?"

"That's possible. But it might also have been dropped by Vaher or one of his assailants. We'll need to check with Vaher's widow, see whether he had one like this. OK, the other stuff. What do you make of the cigarette packets?"

"One's Latvian, *Karmen* brand, the other's Estonian, *Linda*. Both empty."

"Any writing on the inside?"

The lieutenant peered inside each packet. "Let's see. No, nothing."

"The false teeth could be useful. We'll have to check that with the widow too. And his dentist."

"Surely someone would notice losing their false teeth."

"You'd be surprised. Right, now the cigar label; *Laferme*, they're made here, quite popular. We might find a suspect who smokes them, otherwise it's not going to help us. We should see Einar Sepp – he's the forensic technician. If he'd been up here this morning, he'd have got all this and maybe more."

They sipped their coffee in thoughtful silence. Hallmets could see that Kadakas was wanting to speak but not sure how to put his thoughts into words. "Come lieutenant, you've got something to say. Out with it then!"

"Yes, Sir, it's about my position in all this. I'm not really sure what I'm supposed to be doing, apart from reporting back to Colonel Reinart."

"What exactly were the colonel's orders?"

"To make myself useful to you, and report back to him daily on how the investigation is progressing."

"OK. Here's what we'll do. I've no time for people who don't pull their weight, so if you're really going to make yourself useful, I'll use you just like any other member of my team. That means doing police work. I also don't like being spied on, so I want your reports to be strictly factual, and as short as possible. If you're not happy with working on that basis, you can go back to Reinart now. What do you say?"

Kadakas hesitated only for a moment. "Yes, Sir, I'm happy with that. Colonel Reinart didn't specifically say I should report on your handling of the case."

"Good. One more thing. Your military uniform suits you, as our waitress noticed. However, as detectives, the last thing we want is to stand out. You often see more by blending in with the crowd. So when you come in tomorrow, be in civvies."

"But Colonel Reinart ..."

"Is not your senior officer at the moment. I am. As far as I'm concerned, you've been seconded to me for the duration of this investigation. So tomorrow, no uniform."

"Er, yes, Sir."

"Good man. Let's get back to HQ now. We've plenty to do."

9

Artur Simm watched as Jaan Kallas came out of the cafe and shambled along the road. Perhaps he was going to meet an informant now. Artur slipped out of the doorway and followed. But Jaan only led him to the post office, and disappeared inside. Artur hesitated. If he went in, he could be spotted. But then, he could simply be buying a stamp. He pulled his hat down and went in. Luckily, there were a lot of people in there, queueing at the counters or at the shelves by the windows, filling in forms or writing postcards. He joined a queue and looked around for Jaan. Soon he spotted him, in one of the phone cubicles, talking into the handset. After a minute he hung up and left the booth, making for the phone counter to pay for his call. Artur took the opportunity to slip out again into the street, cross the road and wait behind a cart loaded with milk churns, parked behind a sad horse.

When Jaan emerged from the post office and set off, Artur followed, only to be led back to the offices of *Pealinna Uudised.* Whatever meeting Kallas had arranged would surely happen that evening. He could work on his folklore piece for the next couple of hours.

In his small and cluttered office, Jaan Kallas began to write his copy for the following morning. In the absence of any other information, he was going to write something about Vaher's methods, and mention some of the criminals he had put away. He picked up his notebook and a file bound in well-worn cardboard, and headed for the archives in the basement. He'd started as a cub reporter with *Postimees* before the war, and practised his craft with despatches from the front. Then he'd become the crime reporter for *Pealinna Uudised,* ever since the paper had been born amid the excitement and chaos of independence.

He thought he might find Artur down there, but the place was empty. He pulled one of the bound sets of newspapers from the shelves. Each volume contained all the editions for a month. 156 volumes. Approximately. This was going to be a long afternoon.

An hour later Artur arrived. "Sorry I'm late," he said, "I had to get my folklore piece in. About weather predictions. Do you know there's a man in Ruhnu who ..."

"Yeah, yeah. Checks his seaweed every morning. Or something like that. You know what that stuff's called, Artur? A novelty filler. Light-hearted bit of junk that takes people's minds off the real news for a few moments, lets their brains idle for a bit. Do you know what sells papers, Artur?"

"Well, news, I suppose."

"Wrong. Number one, excitement. Number two, entertainment.

Without them, we can print as much news as we like and nobody would buy a single copy. That's why we have to make sure the news is either exciting or entertaining. That doesn't mean making it up, it has to be real news. But it means finding an angle that makes people want to read it. That must be quite a challenge with agriculture and folklore. But doesn't mean you shouldn't try. Did the man in Ruhnu ever save a life?"

"He did stop a ferry sailing when he predicted a storm. Twenty people could have died if it had sailed. The storm came just when he said it would, and the meteorologists hadn't spotted it at all."

"That's your angle, Artur. 'Twenty lives saved by seaweed!' That'll get people reading."

"But that was in 1906."

"That doesn't matter. Once folk are hooked on the story they won't care that it happened a while back. Anyway, my angle for tomorrow is 'Vaher, the man who put away villains.' Retrospective on his past successes, and controversy over his methods. Not too much, mind. People don't want to have to think too hard. But first we need to check out the details."

Artur groaned. "Do we have to go through every single page of all these volumes? It'll take a week."

"People think journalists are disorganised, and drunk most of the time. But the first bit of that's wrong. The best journalists are the best organised, because they can put their finger on information, when others can't." He tapped a file that lay on the table in front of him. "See this file, in here is a list of all the pieces I've ever written for this paper, indexed for names and types of crime. So we don't need to look at every page, we just need to find the serious crimes handled by Vaher, and extract those details. Then I can put something together. So, I started by making a list of dates and victims. We'll take half each, find the articles, and extract the information. Then you can leave it with me, and I'll write the article."

10

Back at Police HQ, Hallmets found that Eva Larsson and Oleg Maslov were waiting to meet him in the work-room next to his office. Larsson was of medium height, with blond hair tied in a braid at the back of her head, and a serious expression. She wore a blouse and skirt of a pale green colour. Maslov was bear-like, his dark beard badly-shaved, and a broad smile on his face. He wore an ill-fitting brown suit, perhaps borrowed. Hallmets, after the introductions, asked them, together with Kadakas, to come into his office. He asked Marta to bring coffee.

Hallmets began. "Thank you for coming here so promptly. You know why you're here?"

"I was told officers from outwith the capital were required to investigate the death of a policeman," said Larsson, "I didn't realise till I saw the newspaper that it was Vaher." She spoke slowly with the accent of the Baltic islands.

"You met him?" asked Hallmets.

"Only briefly, Sir. At a police shooting competition. He didn't speak to me, but made his opinions of women in the police force clear to one of my colleagues. Rolling pins were the proper weapons for women, he said. I don't suppose he was very pleased when I won."

Maslov laughed loudly. "Me, I never met him, boss. But I heard of his methods. More Russian than Estonian, eh?" He spoke with only a slight Russian accent.

"We're going to have to work hard on this," said Hallmets, "Our biggest disadvantage is that we've no feel for the crime scene here in Tallinn. At some point we'll have to bring in one or two of the local CID people, but I'd rather leave that until we know who's worth having. So for the moment it's just us. The post-mortem is at six and that'll certainly move us on, even if it only confirms he fell from the viewpoint. Assuming that's the case, however, we still don't know whether he jumped, was pushed, or tripped."

"So we can't be sure that it was murder, and not suicide?" said Larsson.

"That's correct. It's tempting to see this as a revenge thing by somebody he put away for a good stretch, but we have to remember that the largest number of murders are family affairs. We mustn't exclude the possibility that he was killed by a relative or even a colleague."

"A colleague! Surely that's impossible! Sir!" said Kadakas.

"It may be unlikely, lieutenant, but that doesn't make it impossible. That's why you'll find that a lot of CID work is negative, ruling things out rather than ruling them in. But if you know what it's not, that helps point you towards what it is."

"He could have been involved in something else," said Larsson, " Other than family or police stuff."

"Good point. We need to form a picture of Vaher's day-to-day existence. Somewhere in his life is the cause of his death. It's a big job for just four of us. So, I suggest that the three of you familiarise yourself with the paperwork that we've got so far. Then we'll all go to the meeting at five with the local CID people. After the meeting, Larsson and Maslov, you go and eat in the canteen, get chatting to people, see how they felt about Vaher. Kadakas, the uniform won't help you blend in there, so you come with me to the post-mortem. Let's meet again here at seven."

After the others left, Marta brought in Vaher's personnel file and a sealed envelope just delivered by a messenger from the Ministry.

He began with the personnel file. Nikolai Vaher was born in 1895 on a farm near the village of Sonda, in Ida-Viru county, to the East of Tallinn. He was educated at the village school in Sonda and at the secondary school in Narva. He left school at fifteen and returned to the farm. He was nineteen when the World War began, and managed to avoid conscription into the Russian army until May 1916. But the army seemed to suit him, for within a year he had risen to the rank of sergeant. He returned home, as many Estonians did, when the Bolsheviks seized power, and soon found himself in the new Estonian army, ending the War of Independence as a captain. After the war, in 1920, he joined the fledgling police force, and became a CID officer in Tallinn. He was there during the attempted coup by the communists in 1924. In 1925 he moved to Narva as a detective inspector, and in 1930 returned to Tallinn as Chief Inspector and second-in-command of the CID.

Hallmets hoped that the file from Reinart would add some meat to these bones. He broke the seal and extracted a thin folder from the envelope. Stamped on the front in red were the words "Restricted file – only to be read by ..." – and his own name written in. But inside were only three sheets of thick paper with a smooth, almost shiny, surface. The Ministry had invested in one of the new photostatic copying machines, and this cumbersome apparatus had been used to copy excerpts from various documents. Unfortunately, the header information had been covered up on each document, so its origin or author was not shown.

The first was apparently from a report on Vaher's activities during the 1924 coup attempt, and reported that Vaher showed great energy in tracking down communists who had taken little or no part in the insurrection, but no doubt intended to emerge at a later stage. The writer noted that some of his senior officers regarded his zeal as excessive, adding that, 'It is possible that persons who were neither communists nor even sympathisers were persuaded by V's forceful interrogation to confess to activities which they had not in fact undertaken.'

The second sheet seemed to be part of a report prepared in connection with Vaher's proposed promotion and move back to Tallinn in 1930. It referred to Vaher's approach to policing as 'direct' and his success rate as 'exemplary'. It called him an inspiring leader who would do well in a more challenging post. Apart from the 'incident of Dr K' his record was spotless. Unfortunately the writer did not elaborate.

The third sheet seemed to be more recent, reported Vaher had expressed admiration for the achievements of Mussolini's Fascist Party in Italy, and hopes for a more authoritarian government in Estonia. He was reported – it didn't name the source – as saying that 'it was time to end the chaos that is democracy.'

Hallmets leaned back in his chair and rubbed his eyes. These supposedly secret reports had added little to what he knew of Vaher. He was generally suspicious of reports from people in the Political Department, who would listen to any gossip or hearsay, then add 2 and 2 to make 17. But 'the incident of Dr K' was puzzling. That needed following up.

There was a knock at the door. Marta put her head round. "Inspector Sõnn to see you, Sir."

Sõnn shuffled in and stood just inside the doorway, studying his feet. He muttered something.

"Inspector, please take a seat," said Hallmets, "I'm sorry I didn't catch what you were saying."

Sõnn lowered himself gingerly onto the chair. "I'm sorry, Sir, for this morning. I'm afraid I had too much to drink. I behaved very badly."

"Thank you," said Hallmets, "I agree that you behaved badly – you were, after all, drunk. The question I'd like you to answer for me is this: Are you drunk regularly, or was this a one-off? Please be honest with me."

"It's not a regular occurrence, but it has happened before. Only a couple of times. When there was trouble of some sort."

"What was the trouble this time?"

"The Chief Inspector. We couldn't believe what had happened. Had a few drinks to his memory. I guess I had more than most. I found him, you see. Stuck on that kiosk. I couldn't believe it at first. I still don't understand it. Why would he do such a thing?"

"Can you tell me?"

"No, Sir, I wish I could."

"Tell me something about him, Inspector. You knew him, I didn't. What was he like as a policeman?"

Sõnn paused to think. "Hmm. I'd say he was single-minded. Once he got onto a case, he didn't stop till he'd got the perpetrator. And got him to confess too, usually. He was very methodical, kept his own records too, in addition to what's in our files. The villains respected him. They knew that he knew all about them, that he could pick them up just whenever he wanted. Quite often he'd get a tip-off telling him who the guilty party was, sometimes where to find the blighter as well. Of course, then he had to find the evidence to back it up, or get a confession. And he was good at that too – he could be very threatening without being violent. He was a fine figure of a man – they often compared him to Clark Gable – and could be very persuasive. He could utter the most terrible threats with a really charming manner. None of us could do that. He was the right man to have in charge, Sir, no doubt about that."

"That's very helpful, Inspector. So what would you say Vaher was like as a man?"

"Well, that's a trickier one." Sõnn was warming to his role of expert. "As I said, he could be very charming, very persuasive, threatening too if he wanted. He could be the life and soul of the party, did you know he could sing and dance too? People used to say to him that he should be in films."

"He was a good actor?"

"I suppose so. When one of our lads was killed – there was a shoot-out behind the railway station with some black marketeers – he gave a beautiful speech at the funeral; he had most of us in tears. And he wasn't just talk. It was his trap that caught those guys. And they paid the price when Aleks was hit. Vaher made sure none of the bastards would live to go to jail; he personally finished off two who'd only been wounded. That's leadership, isn't it?"

Hallmets wasn't so sure about that. "What about his private life? Did he have a wife, family?"

"He kept his private life private. He was married all right. His wife was quite a looker. She used to be in films. I've no idea if he had any kids."

"Where did he live?" Hallmets could easily find this out from the file, but wondered whether Sõnn knew.

Sõnn creased his brow. As he had relaxed while speaking, his whole body had become more crumpled. He looked as if he needed a hot bath and a night's sleep. Hallmets could see he was beginning to run out of steam. "Hmm. Out in the suburbs somewhere, I think."

"Thank you, Inspector, you've been very helpful there. There's just one other thing I want to ask you about. You were the first CID man on the scene. Did it seem clear to you that Chief Inspector Vaher had fallen from the platform?"

"Yes, I suppose it did."

"So why not send your forensics technician up there? There may have been footprints or other evidence."

"I don't know. I guess I wasn't thinking. I couldn't believe it was Vaher. How could he be dead? I assumed it was suicide, that no-one could have killed him."

"But the forensics technician, Sepp, wouldn't it have occurred to him to go up there?"

Sõnn looked thoughtful. "Now that I think about it, we already had the body on the ground by the time he arrived. The doctor ordered it, in case he was still alive. So Einar never saw the body in place on the kiosk roof. Though he knew it had been found there."

"Well, let's leave it there for now. But let me assure you, Inspector, I am going to do everything necessary to find whoever did this. It will be done legally, and they will answer for it in court."

Hallmets stood up and offered Sõnn his hand. Sõnn took it hesitantly, and without looking Hallmets in the eye, shook it weakly and shuffled off towards the door.

11

The room was full when Captain Lind led Hallmets and his team in. It wasn't a big room, and it was already half full of cigarette smoke. But at least that covered the smell of sweat and resentment that pulsed from the twenty-odd men who sat on the chairs and on tables and leant against the walls. The captain coughed more than once as they made their way to the desk with the blackboard behind it. Someone had written in white chalk on the board, "We don't need outsiders to fix this." Captain Lind avoided looking at the words. Hallmets made a point of stopping to read. Maslov picked up the blackboard rubber but Hallmets motioned him to put it down.

The Captain opened the meeting. "Detectives! I know you are, as I am, devastated by the sudden death of Chief Inspector Vaher. If it was murder" – a ripple of muttering ran through the crowd, they knew it was murder all right – "if it was murder, we will find the culprit. But it must not be seen as an excuse for the police to take revenge on their enemies." What's wrong with that, the muttering suggested. "That is why the Ministry has appointed Chief Inspector Hallmets to lead the investigation." Hostile glances were directed now towards Hallmets. "Before I ask him to speak to you, I'm going to tell you something about him. Most of you fought in the Liberation War." There was a general murmur of agreement – that was something you never forgot. "Perhaps some of you remember the breakthrough at Võnnu, which finally beat the German barons and their mercenaries?" There were louder mutters of agreement. "This man, Jüri Hallmets, made that breakthrough possible. He was wounded in the process, and was awarded the highest Latvian medal for bravery. I knew him then. He was an exceptional soldier. Now he is the best policeman in our country. It is only fair that we use his skill to solve this case."

There was silence in the room. The sense now was of puzzlement. Hallmets was clearly not just a bumpkin pushed in by the Ministry. Until he entered the room, he had just been an out-of-towner brought in from Tartu – where everybody knew there was no crime anyway. But now he wasn't an unknown. The man from Tartu had a war record – that made him to some degree a comrade – and a good one, which commanded some respect. But it still wasn't clear, despite what the captain said, whether he could cut it as a cop. "What's wrong with using us to solve the case?" called an angry voice from the smoke cloud which now filled the back of the room.

Lind was unsure how to react, but Hallmets laid a hand on his arm, and moved beside him. He allowed his eyes to sweep the faces of the detectives as he waited for silence. Their eyes dropped before his, or looked away, or blinked, as one by one they fell silent. When the room had become quiet, Hallmets spoke, clearly, and audibly, but without shouting or straining his voice. In his few years as a teacher, before the war, he had learned that skill. As with many other skills, it had not come naturally.

"Colleagues," he began, "Many of us here fought for Estonia's independence. Since then we've proved that an independent Estonia is richer and happier and freer than one that was ruled by the Russian Empire and the German barons. Our country needs to be seen to be open and to be just. A senior policeman's dead, probably murdered. What'll it look like to the world if our response is to round up a bunch of petty criminals and beat them till they confess? Then shoot them 'while they tried to escape.' That's how the Soviets do it. We're better than that, aren't we?" He paused, looked round the room. "Aren't we?" he repeated. Reluctant mutters of agreement rippled round the room. "This must be about justice, not revenge. Every move we make will be reported in the press, so they'll have to be the right ones."

"How do you know we'll get them?" came another voice.

"Because we won't stop till we do. Is that clear enough? We won't drag people off the streets and beat them up. We won't try to stitch up some half-wit who doesn't know whether he's coming or going. But we won't leave it either. We'll keep at it, like a dog that's never going to drop that bone."

"I like it," said the voice again.

"Wait a minute," called Hallmets, "I know you. It's Henno Lesser, isn't it? You worked with me on the Teral case, in Viljandi, back in '25."

"Yes, chief, you're right." A tall, thin man in shirt sleeves came forward out of the fug. His receding brown hair accentuated his long nose. Hallmets offered his hand, and the man shook it firmly. Then he turned: "Open the bloody window somebody, it's like the London smog in here! And I'll say it now, this man's good. The Teral case was tough, real tough, everybody thought the two sisters had planned it together. Nobody suspected the uncle. But Hallmets nailed him, fair and square."

A man sitting near the front suddenly stood up. Short and plump, balding, with a fringe of fair hair. Hallmets hadn't noticed him before. A man who could render himself unseen. He nodded briefly to Hallmets. "You won't remember me, Chief Inspector, nobody does. But I worked on the Stachenberg case in Põltsamaa, that was in '27 or '28. Ilmar Hekk. I was the guy who watched the Count for six days until he thought it was safe to collect the stolen painting from the woodshed. As soon as I reported that, you went in. He fired first, but you got him." He turned to the others. "He's OK. We should go with him."

Things had calmed down, and the smoke was clearing. Hallmets noticed Sõnn standing at the back. The inspector raised a finger slightly, gave a hint of a nod. Hallmets decided to bring things to a close. "I've only just arrived," he said, "And I'm right at the beginning of this. We haven't even had the post-mortem yet, that's this evening. But I'll keep you informed on what's going on, and I'll ask for your help if I need it. And one other thing. Please don't try to do your own investigating of this. You might want to, and think it'll help. But you know what it's like when somebody else buggers up your case.

However, if you do hear or find something that might be relevant, let me know right away. Thank you for giving me your time and attention."

As he sat down behind the desk, applause broke out, not wild, but appreciative, acknowledging. Hekk came up and shook his hand. "If you need me, just give me the word." Then he was gone. Lesser hung back as the others left. "Good to see you again, Chief. I knew you could give them a good talking. It's like you used to say, words are more effective than fists. I've got some contacts. Let me see what the word is on the street about this. I'll get back to you."

12

Jaan Kallas read over what he'd just typed out. He wasn't impressed. It lacked bite. There was plenty of detail, identifying most of the petty criminals Vaher had put away since he'd come to Tallinn. But that was the trouble: most of them were petty criminals. None of them were the indispensable sidekick of a Mr Big who'd want public vengeance for their jailing. They were all eminently dispensable, little men who took the rap because that suited both Vaher and the Mr Bigs of the capital. Vaher got his man (again) and Mr Big lived happily ever after. No, as he'd suspected, there was more to this, a lot more. The first job was to eliminate the Mr Bigs from his enquiries. Then he could start looking further.

He found a table near the back of the *Alt-Revaler-Cafe* on Raekoja Plats. The high-backed armchairs gave the table the feeling of a private booth, somewhere you could sit without being noticed and talk without being heard. He glanced at his watch. Almost 5.30. He knew his contact would be on time, and sure enough, as the minute hand slunk onto the half-hour, he sensed a shadow over the table. He looked up and nodded to the man who stood by the other chair. Short and thin, his hair and moustache immaculately trimmed and greased, his pin-striped suit as fresh as new, the creases sharp, the turn-ups clean, the watch-chain gleaming. The image was of a spiv made good. A man who didn't need to sell brushes any more because he employed an army of brush-sellers. This was the man who called himself simply Mr P.

"*Tere, Härra P*," said Kallas, "Please, take a seat."

Mr P was already sliding into the seat, the fedora laid carefully near the edge of the table. An odour of Cologne wafted across to Kallas, and a bored waitress drifted up to the table, regarding the two men as if they were waxworks. Kallas hurriedly ordered coffee, and took from his inside pocket his notebook and a brown envelope. He slid the envelope across the table to Mr P, who weighed it in his hand, nodded to himself, and slipped it into his own inside pocket, nodding.

"All right," said Kallas quietly, "What have you got? I need to know who's behind this Vaher business."

The man leaned forward, smiling with teeth so white they couldn't be real. "I put all my people onto this, *Härra Kallas,* top priority, just like you asked for, devoted a whole afternoon to it. That's a lot of time for a lot of people. Here's what we came up with. He leaned further forward, so that Kallas was immersed in a perfumed cloud he knew would cling to him for the rest of the day. And, as Mr P whispered, Kallas jotted down, in shorthand, the list of Mr Bigs who, it seemed, were not involved in Vaher's death. Mostly names familiar in the capital, and a few from further afield too, Narva, Paldiski, Haapsalu. It was obvious to Kallas what was going on. The gangsters feared a police crackdown in the wake of Vaher's death. They knew the police would assume it was one of them, and that there would therefore be lots of arrests, threats, beatings and general mayhem until somebody confessed. So they were letting it be known that it wasn't them. Hints were dropped in the hearing of men known to belong to Mr P's ring of informers. The same hints would also be reaching the ears of known police informers. This news wouldn't put Kallas ahead of the police, but he wouldn't be behind them. And he could be more outspoken, more speculative, more entertaining.

Mr P took his hat, his brown envelope and his perfume cloud and left. Kallas leaned back in his chair, relieved. He found Mr P repellent, and at the same time pathetic. The pretension at mysterious anonymity was just laughable. As soon as he had begun to deal with him, several years previously, Kallas had done some digging, and soon found him to be Boris Popov, a con-man who'd fled Russia soon after the Bolsheviks took power. Since settling in Tallinn, he had established a network of informers, and sold information to anyone who'd pay. The reason he was still alive was that everyone found his service useful. Even police officers had been known to use him.

Kallas ordered more coffee and a slice of *Kohupiimatort*; cheesecake encouraged a sense of wellbeing in him, and allowed his thoughts to flow. The conclusion was clear. All the local bosses denied killing Vaher. *Ergo*, it wasn't a crime-related revenge killing. It was still possible that it was the work of a new gang out to make a serious mark and earn a reputation. But Mr P had no suggestion that was the case either.

He now had enough to get his article for the morrow finished off. That would give him a bit of time to get some other inquiries moving.

In another corner of the *Alt-Revaler-Cafe*, Artur Simm lowered his newspaper slightly, to watch the man who'd been meeting Kallas take his overcoat from the stand, slide himself into it, and ooze out into Raekoja Plats. Artur put his hat on and pulled it down over his face, turned up his coat collar, and moved out, careful to avoid being spotted by Kallas. The man kept to the edge of the square and turned into Harju Street. Artur followed, keeping a good distance behind. There were plenty people about, so he didn't think he was too visible. The man walked on into Vabadus Plats and made for St John's Church. He opened the main door and went in. Artur hurried after. He found the door unlocked, and, opening it as quietly as he could, went in. The whitewashed walls and plain glass windows made the interior bright, and he felt very visible. The silence in the church was tangible, and nothing moved. There was no-one else there that he could see.

The man must have realised he was being followed, and slipped out of the church through another exit. Artur cursed quietly, then crossed himself – wasn't that what you were supposed to do in a church. He was about to go back out when he thought he caught a movement in the corner of his eye. He tiptoed over to the rearmost pew, and sat down close to the central aisle. He wasn't sure what to do next. He heard footsteps in the side-aisle, up near the altar, but could see nothing because of the heavy stone pillars separating the side-aisles from the nave. Then a door squeaked open and shut. He got up and crept into the side-aisle; it was empty.

At its head however, set into the stone wall, was a small wooden door. He tip-toed up to it, turned the handle gingerly, and opened the door. He found himself in a narrow passage, which soon turned sharply right, leading to another door. In the passage there was a smell of Cologne. The door was unlocked, and when he swung it open he saw a small room containing a table, two chairs, a cupboard and a large wardrobe. In the room the smell was stronger, but there was no-one there. The window was of frosted glass which gave the room a claustrophobic feel. More like a cell. And cold. He shivered. He opened the wardrobe: clerical robes. This seemed to be a vestry or robing-room. The cupboard was below the window, and had two doors with polished wooden handles. He bent down to try one of the doors, and then there was a crack and a flash in his head, and everything switched off.

13

The basement room that was the transit mortuary was coloured light green – the lino on the floor and the gloss paint on the walls – and smelt of formaldehyde. Hallmets heard Kadakas gasp and cough behind him as they came through the double doors from the staircase. A man with thinning white hair and thick lenses in his glasses came to meet them. He wore a white coat spattered and stained with body fluids and pink rubber gloves, and he walked with a limp.

"*Tere, Härra Professor*," said Hallmets, offering his hand.

"Chief Inspector Hallmets! It's been a while – good to see you again." He pulled off his right hand glove to shake hands with Hallmets. "And who's our young friend from the military?" Hallmets introduced Kadakas to Professor von Stallenborg and explained that he was providing support for the investigation. Kallas was already looking pale.

"I knew you wouldn't want to watch the whole business right through, so I've done it. But the fellow's still on the slab so that we can take a wee look at him while I tell you what we've got. Is that OK?"

"That's fine by me," said Hallmets. He knew one or two policemen who had become fascinated by the life of the body after death and the mechanics of extinction, and attended every PM they could. He could see the value of the knowledge they gained but had no desire to do it himself.

The professor led them over to a table on which lay a body covered in a grey cloth. He whipped the cloth with the dexterity of a magician. "*Et voilà!* Nikolai Vaher, former Chief Inspector and general pain in the ass!"

"I take it you worked often with him," said Hallmets.

"I worked in his vicinity. Nobody worked with him. He worked with them, that is to say, he made use of them for his own purposes."

"What was he like as a man?"

"As a man? Who knows? Not me anyway. I knew him only as a policemen and a corpse. I can tell you a few things about the latter."

"Fire away."

The professor grabbed Kadakas' arm and pulled him towards the table. "Come on, lad, get a bit closer, he's not going to bite you. Well, let's hope not, anyway." Kadakas hung back. "Don't worry," went on the Professor, "Even electrocution won't wake him up again. Now, lieutenant, what's the most noticeable thing about him. Apart from the fact that he's dead, of course."

Kadakas opened his mouth and then shut it again. "I don't feel too well," he whispered.

"Maybe you could wait outside, lieutenant," said Hallmets. Kadakas nodded and hurried out, hs hand to his mouth.

"They don't make 'em like they used to," said the professor, "And here am I trying to teach the poor boy something. Alas, poor Yorick." And he patted the top of Vaher's head. Hallmets could see a line of stitches round the skull. Had the professor removed Vaher's brain? "Well, as I was saying, before our young friend made his exit, the obvious thing about our former colleague here is that there's a hole in his middle. What you want to know is, how did it get there? Did somebody make it, with perhaps a shotgun, or did he fall from a height onto something sharp, or at least slightly tapered?" He paused, for theatrical effect. "I'm happy to announce that it was the latter. If we were to roll him over, we'd see that the spine was broken and pushed out through the back by a sudden impact. Nothing like a shotgun wound. And we'll see there's a whiplash effect on the vertebrae of his neck, and one side of his head has sustained serious damage from being bashed onto a wooden surface. So there's your good news – he did fall onto that roof, he wasn't just set up to look like that."

"Thank you," said Hallmets, "Was he dead or alive when he fell?"

"That's a good question, Chief Inspector, one that our friend here" – he poked the corpse's shoulder with a rubber-gloved finger – "didn't think to ask too often himself. Now, from the blood-flow afterwards, not that there was very much of it, I'd say yes, he was still alive. But here's an interesting thing: he didn't break as many bones as he might have done. On landing that is. In fact I'd say he was very relaxed as he fell."

"Unconscious?"

"Possibly. Or just relaxed."

"Drugged?"

"I can see you've got a few brains, Chief Inspector. For a policeman, that is. Look over here, on his left arm. You might need the magnifying glass." He pointed to Vaher's right upper arm. Hallmets took up the magnifying glass and peered at the zone the doctor had indicated.

"Needle marks?"

"Exactly. Two of them. Probably inflicted prior to his fall. Maybe morphine or something similar. I've sent a blood sample off for tests."

"OK. That's interesting. Anything else?"

"There's a few things, but they mostly date from some time prior to his death. A couple of old wounds which I suspect date back to the war, if not even before. Flesh wound in the right thigh, and what looks like a sabre cut on the upper left arm. Both long healed, although there are scars left. Oh, and his false teeth are missing. I always suspected they weren't his own. Wonder what he used to keep them in place. There's a chemist on Vene Street sells some adhesive stuff I've heard people swear by."

"Could this be the top part?" Hallmets, opening his hand to reveal the upper plate sitting on his palm.

"One way to find out, isn't there?" The professor pulled open Vaher's mouth and shone a torch inside. "Hmm, As I said, the side of his face took a bit of a bash, but we might be able to see if they fit. Pass them over, please." He took the teeth and eased them into place. "Yup, nice and cosy. Now he just needs the bottom bit."

Hallmets was relieved. He wouldn't have to ask Vaher's widow about his teeth. "Thanks, Professor. Anything else?"

"I think that gives you plenty to think about. If you want to look at him again you'll have to go out to the hospital at Juhtental, that's where he's off to this evening, where they have a nice chilled drawer waiting for him." The Professor spread the grey sheet over Vaher, plucked off the rubber gloves, and shook hands with Hallmets again. "You can find your way out, I've got to get *Härra* Vaher packaged for his trip, and then get home for tea. I think we're having pig's trotters tonight. Võru style, very tasty."

Hallmets found Kadakas sitting on the steps outside the front entrance, taking deep breaths. "Perhaps you're not cut out for the military," he said, as the lieutenant hurriedly got up, "Why are you there anyway?"

Kadakas hesitated. "My father, he thought …"

"Say no more," smiled Hallmets. "Just remember, we don't always need to do what our fathers want. Come on, let's visit *Härra* Sepp and see what he's got for us."

Einar Sepp's laboratory occupied two rooms on the second floor. A middle-aged man with mousey hair and a generally shabby appearance, Sepp was slumped in a chair, by a table cluttered with files and papers, reading a book. He looked tired, thought Hallmets, or unwell. Hallmets introduced himself and Kadakas, and came straight to the point. "The Vaher Case."

"Did you read my report?"

"Yes. Tell me about the scene – I mean where the body was discovered."

"Well, he was off the flagpole and laid out on the ground by the time I got there."

"What did you find on the roof of the kiosk?"

"Blood, that was all. The only prints I found belonged to the patrolmen who'd got there first. They'd got him down. I had a look round the area. Plenty footprints, but the ground was solid; it was impossible to tell how recent they were."

"Did you find anything on the ground, that might have fallen with him?"

"Nothing. Unless you'd count a load of cigarette butts, oh, and half a pair of false teeth, probably left by some drunk who coughed them out and didn't notice." Sepp sniggered.

"Top or bottom?"

"What?"

"The teeth, top or bottom half?"

"Bottom, I think, why?"

"I believe the lieutenant here found the other half. Can you get those down to Professor von Stallenborg immediately after we've gone."

"Yes, yes, of course. Sorry, I mean, I should have thought ..."

"Tell me, *Härra* Sepp, why didn't you examine the viewpoint. Didn't it strike you as likely he'd fallen from there?"

Sepp looked worried, or more unwell. "Yes, naturally it did. That's what I said to *Komissar* Sõnn. He said there was no point, the place would be crowded with tourists, and in any case it seemed clear to him it was suicide. I protested, but ..." His voice trailed away.

"But what," Hallmets persisted.

"Well, that's how things were done with Vaher. He didn't set much store by forensic evidence. Said it was a waste of time, if you had a confession in your pocket."

"And you went along with that?"

"What was I supposed to do – he was in charge."

"You could have reported it to Captain Lind."

"You must be joking. He's just counting the days to his retirement. And I think he's scared of Vaher too. Sorry, was scared of Vaher."

"Alright. What about Vaher's clothes?"

"His clothes. Yes. They were, em, best quality. The suit would have cost two hundred crowns at least. Also the overcoat, fine wool, silk lining. The shoes were an Italian brand. His shirt was made in Paris.

Even his underwear was top quality."

"Anything on the clothes – stains, marks, tears?"

"Well, er, clearly there was a rip where the post went through him, and some bloodstains. They were consistent with the landing on the pole. That's about it." Sepp swayed slightly, wiped his forehead with his handkerchief, and sat down.

"Are you OK?"

"No, actually I'm feeling quite rough, and I've got a temperature. But Aino – she was my assistant – left to get married, and they haven't replaced her yet. So someone has to hold the fort. Excuse me." He whipped out the handkerchief again, sneezed explosively into it, then blew his nose loudly.

"Well, I won't keep you much longer. What about his gun?"

"Oh yes. I mean, no. It wasn't there. He didn't wear a holster, must have carried it in his jacket pocket."

"Alright. What did you find in his pockets?"

Sepp rummaged amongst the chaos of paper on his table, and produced a typed list. "Here we are. Wallet, packet of cigarettes – English – eleven left, and a book of matches. Nothing out of the ordinary, in terms of what people have in their pockets."

"I'd like to have a look at it."

Sepp sighed, stood up, with evident effort, and shuffled into the next room, coming back in a couple of minutes with a cardboard shoe box. "They're in here. If you want to take them away you'll have to sign for them."

Back in his office, Hallmets and Kadakas looked the items from the box. The wallet contained nothing unusual – police ID, Vaher's business cards, photograph of a rather attractive blonde, and 200 crowns in notes. "Quite a lot to be carrying around," commented Hallmets, "What do you conclude from that, Lieutenant?"

"Robbery wasn't the motive, Sir?"

"That's what it looks like. Unless they stole something a lot more valuable from him. We'll check out the wife tomorrow, see if she matches this picture. Now let's have a look at the other stuff. What do you think about them?"

Kadakas looked closely at the cigarette packet. Bright red with the name 'Craven A' in a white oval in the centre. "Craven A. That's a woman's cigarette, isn't it, Sir. Cork tips rather than the cardboard holders that ours have. They're quite expensive here, you don't get them everywhere." He opened the packet and took out the remaining cigarettes and the folded cardboard interior of the packet. "Nothing written here."

"OK, what about the matches?"

"Ah! This could be useful. The pack's from that tobacconist just off Raekoja Plats. Tempelmann and Klebb. Maybe he bought his cigarettes there. Should we visit them?"

"Good idea. Anything inside?"

"Oh yes. Let's see. Aha, he's written something. 'Three Monks' That's all. Mean anything to you, Sir?"

"No, but I don't know Tallinn that well, we'll need to run it past someone who does. It could be a lead. Sounds like a tavern, or even a night club. By the way, there's something missing. What does every policeman carry?"

Kadakas thought for a moment. "Of course! A notebook!"

"Exactly. Even a senior officer carries one. I do myself. So what does that tell us?"

"Somebody took it off him."

"Good. That suggests that his pockets were searched and some things removed. So we don't know what else might have been in his wallet."

"Why didn't they just clear everything from him?"

"If his pockets were empty we'd immediately smell a rat. By putting some things back, we won't be so suspicious and might even believe he'd killed himself. Right, it's nearly six, let's put the stuff back now and see if we can get some coffee and a sandwich before Larsson and Maslov arrive."

14

They sat round the table in the workroom. Hallmets asked Larsson and Maslov whether they'd picked up any vibes in the canteen.

"Yes, boss," said Maslov, "I found a couple of guys who were happy to talk. Seems people weren't as much behind Vaher as you might think. They agreed he was successful, but when it came to his methods, there were some who didn't approve. They said no-one really trusted him. He had a small group whom he worked regularly with; they included Inspectors Lepp and Sõnn. Nobody knew much about his private life. One guy said his wife was a film-star. They both agreed he kept himself to himself. Not a big drinker either, he turned up at all the dos but never drank much and always left well before the end." Maslov shrugged and grinned.

"I sat with a few of the secretaries, in the women's corner," said

Larsson. "They all agreed he was tremendously attractive, and could be very charming when he wanted to be, but also very unpleasant if he didn't get his way. They described his secretary – her name's Raina Laar – as an old battleaxe. He seemed to prefer her to somebody younger, probably because she knew how to keep her mouth shut. I asked them to point her out to me, but they said she wasn't in today."

"Had he had any liaisons with anyone they knew?" asked Hallmets

"Not at all. One girl who tried to flirt with him got the sack the next week. Some people apparently reckoned he was, er, not interested in women. But he did have a wife. Lara or Laura, they said, she'd been in a couple of movies, silent ones, before she married him. I'll check that out. Very attractive, they said, from a posh family. Germans."

"What about his working methods?"

"They knew they weren't appreciated by everybody, but the women weren't hostile. 'You've got to put the villains in jail,' said one, 'It doesn't matter how you catch them.' The others seemed quite happy with that."

Hallmets thanked them, gave a brief report of the post-mortem, then summarised what Einar Sepp had told them, and what had been found in Vaher's pockets.

"So here's where we are," Hallmets concluded. "He certainly fell from the viewpoint onto the kiosk. He was still alive when he fell, but may not have been conscious. He wasn't robbed. We can place him on the viewpoint if the teeth are his, and maybe the pen too. And we've one or two interesting finds from his pockets. Some of these things we'll chase up tomorrow. But right now, I think we need a trip down to the archives. We need to check out the people Vaher put away, see if any of them had enough connections to be worth avenging. Somehow I doubt it – if Vaher's method was to fit up a low-level villain for any crime, then they'd all be pretty disposable, certainly not worth a revenge attack. Nevertheless we need to take the possibility seriously, even if it's only to eliminate it."

They went down in the lift to the basement, where the archives were situated next door to the transit mortuary. A tall slim woman with short brown hair and glasses sat behind the counter knitting. She looked up as they came in but her knitting needles kept moving. "Ah. Good evening. Chief Inspector Hallmets, I'm guessing? I've been expecting you."

Hallmets introduced Larsson, Maslov and Kadakas, and learned that her name was Helve Hamann. Well, *Proua* Hamann, why were you expecting us?"

"This is a police station, so one does pick up hints on how the job is done. It seems a reasonable initial step is to check out the people whom Chief Inspector Vaher caused to be incarcerated. His death may be a simple act of revenge. No, that's not quite true, revenge is not always simple. For example, even today in those countries where the blood feud still reigns ..." Hallmets sensed that a lecture was about to begin, but she checked herself, glanced at her knitting, adjusted her glasses. "Anyway, you'll find all the files on the table over there, Chief Inspector. I got them all out for Inspector Lepp this afternoon, so there was no point putting them away again."

"Lepp? Was he on his own, or was there anyone with him?"

"Just him and Sergeant Kleber."

Hallmets was not encouraged by this. He had feared that some of the cops might decide to do this on their own, and it irritated him that they were ahead of him on this at least.

There were two piles of files on the table, about forty altogether. This could not have been all the cases Vaher had been involved in, so Hallmets guessed that the Tallinn detectives must have made a selection, based on their own knowledge.

"Did Inspector Lepp ask for specific cases?" he asked *Proua* Hamann.

"Yes, he'd already made out a list."

"Do you still have it?"

"No, the inspector took it back. But you can see which files he ordered, they're the ones on the table. Do you want to see the index entries?"

"Yes, please."

The archivist fetched a large ring-binder from a shelf behind her, and looked through it until she found the correct entry. Then she extracted several sheets, and handed them to the Chief Inspector. "Please be careful with those. Let me know if you want any of the files, other than those on the table, of course." She took up her knitting again.

The list was in chronological order, covering Vaher's period in Tallinn, from 1920 to 1925, and then from 1930 onwards. There were several hundred altogether. Hallmets understood why Lepp had made a selection. He led Larsson, Maslov and Kadakas over to the table on which the files were piled. "Let's get this done. Kadakas, you make a list of all these files. Then each of you take a third of them, and start going through them. We're looking for somebody who had connections with big gang leaders, or who looks crazy enough to try something himself, and is out of jail. Meanwhile I'll go through the list here and identify any others we might want to look at."

"How are you going to tell, Sir?" asked Kadakas.

"Good question, lieutenant. Well, I'm suspecting that it's probably not something from his first period. In the first two or three years, as an ordinary detective, he'd only be following orders. As a sergeant, he'd have more initiative, especially with minor cases. But anything more complicated would be led by a more senior officer. So our focus should be on cases since 1930, when he came back to Tallinn. But I'll check the earlier lists, just in case there's something interesting."

They got to work. Hallmets wasn't surprised to find that all the files on the table were from the period after Vaher's return to Tallinn. He started checking the list. The earlier cases could be moved through fairly rapidly. But things became interesting when he got to 1924, and the attempted coup. A group of communists, some local, some just arrived from the Soviet Union, had attempted on the early morning of 1st December – it was a Monday – to seize control of key points in Tallinn. The plan was to declare a People's Republic and summon more support from Russia. But there was no support on the streets from the relatively prosperous Estonian proletariat, and rapid reaction from the authorities disrupted the intended course of events. For instance, General Põdder, the victor of Võnnu, passing the telegraph office, which had been seized by the insurgents, learned what was happening, and with a few officers entered the building and captured or shot those who were trying to send the summons to Petrograd.

Vaher was not involved in the events of that night – he had been visiting his parents. But he had returned immediately to Tallinn and played an enthusiastic part in rounding up supporters of the coup in the subsequent days. Most of the suspects arrested by Vaher confessed to being supporters of the coup, and were given long prison sentences. Vaher had received a special commendation for his diligence in these activities, and had been moved to Narva soon after the coup. The move could easily be seen as a promotion rewarding his success. But what if Vaher had gained a reputation which made it prudent to move him out of Tallinn, at least for a while? Hallmets asked the archivist to bring him all the files relating to the coup and its aftermath. He had no intention of reading them all, but wanted to pick out a few at random to get a feel for how Vaher had proceeded. There could well be a revenge motive in there, and he wondered why Lepp had not selected any of these.

The question was soon answered. *Proua* Hamann informed him that all files relating to the coup were restricted, and that to access them, special authorisation was required.

"From whom?" asked Hallmets.

"From Prefect Rotenbork, or Colonel Reinart at the Ministry."

"That's OK. I am working directly on the orders of the colonel," said Hallmets.

"I'm afraid I need something in writing, specifically allowing you access to these files. I'm not being obstructive, but these are the rules."

Hallmets remembered the letter from the colonel. He pulled the envelope from his inside pocket and took out the letter. "I think this will suffice," he said, showing the letter.

The archivist studied it very carefully. "Well, it's not very specific, I mean it doesn't refer to those particular files, but it does say 'any resources required', so I suppose that covers it. Are you sure you want to see all of them?"

It was a tedious job. Maslov was a slow reader, muttering the words as he followed his finger along each line. Kadakas was also moving slowly, because he was getting interested in the contents of every file he looked at. He was also not familiar with the procedures and jargon used in the reports, and had to keep asking the others. Thankfully Larsson was getting on much faster – at least she knew what she was doing. But the job was going to take ages. As Hallmets suspected, the files from 1924 didn't throw up any surprises. They only confirmed Vaher's skill in extracting confessions.

At eight Hallmets phoned the switchboard and asked them to call his wife. Five minutes later the phone in the archive rang, and he was through to Kirsti in Tartu. He made it a point when away to phone home every day. He knew enough policemen who'd got so immersed in the job, they'd lost touch with their families, even when they weren't out of town. He also made a point of sharing what he knew on cases with Kirsti. He knew she would keep it to herself, and besides, often enough she had suggested another way of looking at a case which had enabled a breakthrough.

Hallmets admired her creativity and her intellect; that had drawn him to her when they'd first met in Edinburgh, where he'd been sent for CID training in 1920. At that time Kirsty McRae, as she was then, having completed her degree in German and History at the University, was training to be a librarian. He'd been there for six months, and in the middle of the final month they'd got married, at Greyfriars Kirk. Kirsty had made a point of learning Estonian. And soon she amended her name: the 'y' at the end confused people. It's not in the Estonian alphabet, and people didn't know how to pronounce her name when they read it. They often pronounced the 'y' as in Finnish, so her name came out in Estonian as Kirstü. That didn't sound at all right, so the easiest thing was to replace the 'y' with an 'i'; then people could read it just like it sounded. Later, after the children had gone to school, she'd got a post at the University Library in Tartu. That was one of the reasons he had turned down the second-in-command job in the capital.

He couldn't speak to her this evening about the case – you couldn't guarantee that one of the switchboard operators between the house in Tartu and the counter in the police archives room wouldn't decide to listen in to the call. But this evening the news was Kirsti's: "Jüri, guess what? Edasi, the publishers, want to read my novel. Well, they want to see the first thirty pages and a synopsis, at least." That was encouraging. He'd been pleased when Kirsti told him she was writing a novel set in mediaeval Estonia. He felt more positive after the call, and went back to the table determined to prevent the investigation getting bogged down in its first task.

By ten the job was done, though the results were not encouraging. All four were tired, and it seemed they had little to show for their efforts. As Hallmets had suspected, most of the many criminals Vaher had put away were small fry. It looked like revenge for being put away by Vaher was not the motive for the killing. Several of those convicted through Vaher's efforts were now free again, and Larsson had made a list of them. They would have to be interviewed, if only to eliminate them from the inquiry. "OK," he concluded, "Let's leave it there for tonight. You've all done well. We'll meet again tomorrow at eight."

15

Artur Simm came to. It was dark. His head was sore, but when he tried to feel it, he found his wrists were tied to the arms of the chair he was sitting on, and his ankles bound to its front legs. The cords were tight. As his eyes focused, he could see dim light coming under a door. He felt very afraid. This wasn't supposed to happen to reporters. They demanded the truth, and got it. Not like this. His mouth was dry. He could hear himself breathing rapidly. He was beginning to panic.

The door swung open, a dark figure was briefly outlined in the low light from outside, and the light came on. He shut his eyes, and then opened them slowly. A man had come into the room. It was the man he'd seen talking with Kallas earlier, the man he'd followed to the church. The powerful smell of Cologne came with him, filling the tiny room. For now he saw the space was only big enough for the chair he was sitting on, and another one. The man sat in the other chair. He took from his pocket a wallet – Artur recognised it as his own.

"That's mine," he said, without thinking.

"Yes, Mr Simm, it's yours." He spoke with a slight Russian accent. "But I'm being impolite. I know who you are – and plenty more about you – but you don't know me. You can call me Mr P. I think you followed *Härra* Kallas to his meeting with me, and then you thought you'd follow me too. Isn't that right?"

"This is ridiculous," said Artur with as much bravado as he could muster, "Untie me at once, and then we can talk. I'm a reporter for the *Pealinna Uudised*."

"Yes, I know that. Your wallet is very informative. I liked especially the picture of your wife. Marju. She looks very pretty. It would be a shame if anything nasty happened to her. I mean, with you here, who'll be able to protect her from, say, somebody who might break into your flat during the night, using your own key, and, well, you can use your imagination, what would any man do if he found a beautiful woman, helpless and vulnerable, completely in his power. I know what I would do." Mr P. smiled and licked his lips.

His technique was effective. Artur was frightened. "Wh-what do you want?" he stuttered, "I was only following you to find out what you knew about Vaher. I need sources too."

"I'm sure you do," purred Mr P. "But you see, right now, I'm not going to be your source. Your colleague *Härra* Kallas knows what he wants, and pays a fair price for what he gets. I'm just a businessman, *Härra* Simm. And it's you who's going to help me. You see, my business is collecting information, and selling it on. And for that, I need informants, lots of them. Now you're going to be one of them. Here's how it works. When I need something from you, I'll contact you and tell you what I need. Then you'll go and find it, and send it to me. That's very simple, isn't it?"

"I'm only a reporter. What information would I have?"

"Oh, you'd be surprised, *Härra* Simm. You can find all sorts of things out in a newspaper office. From your colleagues, from the archives. You can go out yourself, too, and interview people, ask questions. People like talking to reporters, don't they. I'm doing it myself. I like talking to you."

"What if I refuse?"

"Oh, now that wouldn't be so good. You see, then I'd have to give my friend Vladimir your front-door key, and send him round in the night to visit Marju. I regard myself as quite civilised, *Härra* Simm, but Vlad, well, he's a different kettle of fish altogether. He's not very well educated, but on the other hand, he's very strong. Oh, and he has a penchant for beautiful women, and violence. Often both at once. Of course, they aren't beautiful once Vlad's finished with them. Such a waste. But I wouldn't want you to be unaware of what's happening to poor Marju, so my other friend Igor will take along his camera to take a few snaps. Maybe they'll take turns at entertaining Marju. I'm sure you can imagine it." He paused theatrically, as if struck by a new thought. "Ah, but how can you imagine it if you haven't met Vlad." He leaned towards the doorway. "Vlad, can you come through for a moment."

Another man squeezed into the room, and stood next to Mr P. He wasn't tall, but his width made up for that, and Artur could see that it wasn't fat. Everything about him was solid and chunky, from the large meaty hands to the bull neck and shaven head. Apart from his nose, which had at some point in the past been bashed flat by a fist or club. He carried in one hand a dark brown rubber cosh – it looked like a toy in his huge paw. Vlad smiled, showing teeth like broken gravestones.

"Yes," whispered Artur, "OK. I'll do whatever you want. Just don't harm Marju. Please."

"Now, *Härra* Simm, I like a man who's co-operative," said Mr P, "It avoids so much trouble, don't you think? I'm sure we'll get on very well. But just to make sure you don't forget, I'll hang onto your house key and your wallet. Oh, and there's just one other thing."

There was a sudden explosion of pain in the little finger of Artur's left hand. Vlad had hit it, very accurately, and with considerable force, with his cosh. Artur screamed. He knew bones had been broken, and pain pulsated into his hand and up his arm. "Why the hell did you do that?" he shouted. "I agreed to work for you, didn't I."

"Of course you did," said Mr P softly, "But you see, *Härra* Simm, or may I call you Artur, now that we have a working relationship, I wouldn't want you to think this is all talk. I want you to see that I'm serious, that I won't hesitate to add deeds to my words. That finger will always remind you. Well now, I'll be in touch soon. I have all your contact details in your wallet here. Goodbye for now." He nodded to Vlad, and this time the explosion was in Artur's head.

Jaan Kallas looked at his watch. Eight o'clock. Finally his article was done. He scrolled it out of the typewriter, separated the top sheet from the carbon copy, and read it through once more.

Underworld denies Vaher killing!

The mystery of top cop Nikolai Vaher's spectacular death plunge deepens, writes chief crime reporter Jaan Kallas. Confidential sources deep within Tallinn's criminal underworld have revealed to me that the city's crime bosses vigorously reject any suggestion of involvement in the horrific murder of the capital's best-known detective. After several clandestine and very risky meetings with spokesmen of the gangs that control illegal activities of all sorts in and around our country's biggest city, I came away with a clear message. The big cheeses declare, 'It wasn't us!'

And do I believe them, dear readers? Yes, I do. Why, you ask, should I take the word of the spokesmen of the dark fraternity? They are hardly men of their word. And I agree with you. But what they say makes sense. Why should they kill Vaher? They know that it would bring down trouble on all their operations, that there will be raids, searches, arrests, questioning, in short, lots of poking into corners they would rather remain dark. Killing a policeman – any policeman, let alone one of the best – is simply bad for business. From the criminal point of view, it just doesn't make sense.

But what if the killer was an individual, someone Vaher put away, eager for revenge, acting on his own, unbeknown to the criminal barons. Well, I've spent hours examining every single case involving Vaher, and I have to say, as a seasoned crime-watcher with some knowledge of the psychology of criminals, that none of those who are now free look like the type to carry out such a ghastly assassination. The worst killers felt the fatal squeeze of the hangman's noose – for them revenge is not an option. Some are still locked away for long sentences. Those who have been set free are lesser creatures, without the imagination or the will to seek out and kill the architect of their incarceration. Indeed a few have even set out bravely to make for themselves new and blameless lives.

And so I throw out this challenge to the bosses. See if you can find who perpetrated this atrocity. And tell me, through the secret channels that we have. Meanwhile I will keep searching. No stone will be left unturned until the mystery is solved and the killer brought to justice. Keep watching the pages of this newspaper. Remember, Pealinna Uudised is always ahead of the game!

He liked it. A clear and simple heading, which should get plenty of attention. And his article sharp and to the point. Not too long, and not a word wasted. He picked up the top copy and headed for the editor's office.

16

Hallmets walked through the Old Town to his hotel. Light and noise spilled onto the streets from restaurants and taverns. Estonians were happy with their country – small, yes, but free, and prosperous, and theirs. Hallmets was proud of his country too. But he feared for it. This case was unusual; it might be just a one-off. Yet he wondered if it marked the beginning of something new. He'd seen the Nazis in action in Germany, before Hitler had come to power, and feared that the spirit that underlay Nazism was not confined to Germany. Theatre as a substitute for reason, violence instead of argument. And this case had both of those.

From an open door came the notes of a piano, and a woman's voice, singing. He recognised the song as a setting of Lydia Koidula's poem, *Mu isamaa on minu arm*, and paused to listen to the words.

My country is my love,
To whom I've given my heart,
To you I sing, my greatest joy,
My blossoming Estonia.
Your anguish burns in my heart,
Your happiness makes me rejoice,
My country, my country!

He and his comrades had fought to bring Estonia its freedom from the Russian overlords and the German barons who had controlled it for centuries. He knew that they would fight for it again, against any odds. He hoped they would not have to.

The Imperial Hotel was on Nunne Street, not as large an establishment as the name implied, but it looked comfortable enough. Hallmets was relieved to find that he had indeed been booked in, and that his luggage had been delivered to the hotel and installed in his room. "And one other thing, Sir," said the young man at reception, "There's a gentleman waiting for you in the lounge. He arrived about fifteen minutes ago, said he'd just wait." Hallmets thanked him and went through the door on the right of the reception area into the lounge, a dimly-lit room with a several armchairs and coffee tables, and at one side a crackling fire of logs. Only one armchair, in the corner of the room, was occupied. Hallmets went over.

"Evening, chief," said Henno Lesser, standing up to shake hands.

"Good evening, Lesser," said Hallmets, and sat in the adjacent chair, "I take it this isn't a social call."

"No, chief. I've been speaking to a few of my regular informants this evening. It's curious – it was as if they were just waiting for me to call. But they're all saying the same thing. Vaher's death was nothing to do with the local crime bosses."

"Question is, are they just trying to distract us to get the heat off themselves, or are they genuinely not involved? What do you think?"

"I think it's genuine. If it were one of them, the others would soon point the finger, not directly of course, but they'd leave enough clues. That sort of killing is just not their style. A knife in the back or a corpse floating in the harbour, yes, these are messages within the criminal community. But not throwing people off Toompea. That attracts far too much attention. And killing a policemen – they're just not that stupid. By the way, I've made a list of the crime bigwigs for you. There are only a handful anyway, this isn't Chicago." He handed Hallmets a sheet of this paper.

"Thanks. Could it be a new gang trying to muscle in. Russians or Ukrainians maybe, less restrained than our own villains? Wanting to make a big impact with a spectacular killing."

"Possible, but again, I think if that was it my sources would have been eager to tell me."

"Lone criminal on a revenge mission?"

"Again, that's possible, but why chuck him off Toompea. An ex-con would be more likely to stab or shoot him. The MO's too dramatic."

"Lunatic?" suggested Hallmets.

"That's always a possibility, but it would need two of them to throw him off the viewpoint."

"So where do you think we are with this, on the basis of what you've heard?"

"Well, chief, you always used to say to us, there's three possible aspects to a case: domestic, criminal and something else. And in that order, too. I'd say, this doesn't look very criminal. If it were me I'd be looking hard at the other two."

"As it happens, it is you. I want you on my team for this. I need somebody who knows the Tallinn scene, and whom I've worked with before. Are you up for that?"

"My pleasure, chief. It'll also give the other guys a lift to know that one of us is involved."

"Good. What about a drink? There's something else I want to ask you." Lesser asked for beer, and soon two half-litres of Saku appeared.

"*Terviseks!*" said Hallmets, and Lesser returned the toast.

Hallmets continued. "Inspector Sõnn. What's he like?"

"Off the record?" asked Lesser. Hallmets nodded. "I'd say competent but unimaginative. Makes up his mind about a case far too soon, then looks for evidence to support his view. Of course, that was Vaher's style too. Sõnn was really cut up when he found Vaher dead."

"What about Lepp?"

"Hmm. I'd be careful in dealing with him. He's clever and sly with it. I wouldn't trust him. Ambitious too. He was very close to Vaher."

"Could he decide to take his own revenge for Vaher's killing?"

"It's possible. And there are others who'd be happy to help him."

"Like Kleber?"

"Kleber? You've been doing your homework all right. He's a nasty piece of work. If Vaher wanted somebody done over a bit, to soften them up for a confession, Kleber was his first choice. I don't think the work 'detection' is in his vocabulary. But yes, I can see him with Lepp, and some others too. Pilvik, Hernes, Mölder. I'd say they're the ones to keep an eye on."

"Thanks, that's helpful. Can you be at my base on the fourth floor at eight tomorrow? I'll introduce you to the team. Oh, sorry, one other thing. Three Monks? That mean anything?"

"Not immediately. Not one of the joints I've come across. Out of town, maybe. Leave it with me."

Hallmets showed Lesser to the front door of the hotel. As they came out into the cold fresh air of the street, a man staggered round the corner from the direction of the railway station and bumped into Lesser. A short, thin, youngish man with fair hair and a toothbrush moustache. He smelt of cheap brandy. He mumbled an apology and looked around, as if he wasn't sure where he was. Then he seemed to recognise the street and crossed the road to an entrance to the tenement block facing the hotel. He fumbled for a while before managing to get the door open, and disappeared inside. "Drunks," said Lesser, "the least of our worries." And he bade Hallmets farewell.

By the time Hallmets got to his room, he was exhausted. As was his habit, he made a to-do list for the following day. Then he got to bed, and only then remembered he'd not spoken to Kadakas about his report to Colonel Reinart. He'd have to speak to the lad in the morning. He was just beginning to think what he'd say to him when he fell asleep.

Day 2. Thursday 23rd March 1933

17

Hallmets was dressed and breakfasted by 7.30. He decided to visit the crime scene again; it was, after all, just round the corner. As he left the hotel he noticed, on the other side of Nunne Street, a hairdresser's shop. The sign said 'M. Simm.' Before the war few women would think of paying somebody to do their hair. Now, thought Hallmets, there were hairdressers all over the place. That must be a positive sign. Women with more confidence in their appearance, and the money to afford it too. And time too, to meet friends in cafes. He remembered how pleased Kirsti had been four years previously when he'd bought her an electric vacuum-cleaner for her birthday. A Lux XI, imported from Sweden, an amazing machine. He'd even used it himself on occasion.

In a few minutes he was at the kiosk. He bought a copy of *Pealinna Uudised*, and introduced himself to the proprietor, who confirmed that he was Kaarel Rebane. He asked Rebane what he'd done when he arrived and found the body.

"Er, well, I had to get the police, of course. I thought of going over to the railway station, but there isn't always a copper on duty there. I could have run down to Pikk Street, but I didn't want to leave the body by itself. I was afraid I was just seeing things, and it might have disappeared by the time I got back. Then I thought of Artur. Artur Simm. His wife's a hairdresser, in Nunne Street, and they live in the flat over the salon."

Hallmets remembered the shop opposite his hotel. "Why did you think of them?"

"Oh, sorry, didn't I say, they've got a telephone. I was there, at their flat, in two minutes, and Artur said he'd phone the police right away. So I went straight back and waited. But it was that photographer who got there first. From the paper. Artur's a reporter, see, for *Pealinna Uudised*, and I think he'd called the snapper before he called the police. He denies it of course, but I don't see how the guy had time to take so many pictures before the cops arrived."

Hallmets thanked Rebane, and headed for Pikk Street. He'd have to have a chat with Artur Simm at some point, made sure he hadn't interfered with the scene, or noticed anything that the police might have missed.

The meeting started promptly at eight. Henno Lesser was there as well as Larsson, Maslov and Kadakas. Hallmets was relieved to see that Kadakas was not in uniform; he was clad in grey trousers, well-pressed, and an immaculate blue blazer with brass buttons, and a badge on the pocket which Hallmets did not recognise. Beneath the blazer was a gleaming white shirt and striped tie. And his brogues gleamed, as did his blond hair, combed and creamed to perfection. A contrast to Lesser, in a shabby and well-worn grey suit, Maslov, with his baggy black trousers and peasant-style tunic, and Larsson, who was wearing a grey polo-necked jumper and olive green skirt. Hallmets would have to have a word in private with the young man; whilst Kadakas may have put aside his uniform, he would certainly not blend into the crowd, unless he was at a posh tennis club, or sauntering along the promenade at Pärnu looking at the girls on the beach.

He introduced Lesser, and asked him to repeat the information he'd brought the previous evening. Then he summed up where he thought they were. "It looks like the criminal fraternity is denying any involvement in this. But we need to eliminate that possibility. Henno, can you and Oleg check out all the folk Vaher put away who are now free again. Visit them. Get alibis for Tuesday night. See if they know anything. Henno, can you take Lieutenant Kadakas with you, show him how it's done.

"What about me, chief?" said Larsson.

"There are three possible aspects to this case. Tell them what they are, Lesser."

Lesser smiled. "Domestic, criminal, anything else."

"Exactly. We're well on the way with the criminal aspect, although it may not lead us anywhere. However the majority of murders are domestic in origin. The killer and the victim are married, related or friends. So we need to see whether that wasn't the case here. Larsson and I will visit Vaher's widow, and try to get some feeling for his life other than as a policeman."

As soon as the meeting concluded, Marta came in to tell Hallmets he had a visitor. Dr Luik, the examining magistrate. Dr Luik was younger than he'd expected. Not as tall as Hallmets, with a jutting chin, Roman nose, and dark glossy hair swept straight back from his forehead, he reminded the Chief Inspector of a predatory crow.

Luik wasted no time. "You need to get this solved, Hallmets. My reputation's on the line here too, so I won't have any dilly-dallying. We need action, and fast. Why didn't you contact me yesterday?"

"I hadn't been informed you'd been assigned this case."

"Hm." Luik wasn't impressed by this response. "Well, as I said, this one needs to be settled promptly and decisively. Some criminal is cocking a snoop at the authorities – that's you and me, Hallmets – and can't be allowed to get away with it. They need to be arrested and severely dealt with."

"For that we'd need to know who it is."

"That's your job, Chief Inspector, and I assume you're not a Chief Inspector for nothing. Now, what progress have you made so far?"

Hallmets summarised what had emerged the previous day. He said as little as possible, as he knew that some examining magistrates weren't above discussing their cases with their pals over brandy and cigars.

With Luik, this did not seem to be a problem, as listening was not his strong point. As soon as Hallmets had mentioned that police informants indicated that the major crime syndicates were not involved, the lawyer cut in: "Nonsense. This is obviously some crime boss showing he's above the law. I'm surprised you pay any heed to these 'informants'. They're simply trying to mislead you. Maybe down in Tartu all your informants are more honest. Let me tell you, up here in the big city, everybody lies."

"Everybody?" asked Hallmets innocently.

Luik looked startled. "I'm talking about criminals, Hallmets. I'm surprised you haven't started interrogating them immediately."

"Which one would you suggest I start with?"

Luik looked darkly at Hallmets. "Why are you asking me? What are you implying?"

"Nothing at all, *Härra Doktor*, but you know Tallinn better than I do." He opened his notebook, where he'd put the list Lesser had given him the previous evening. "For instance, what do you think of Mihkel Härg or Endel Heapõder?"

"No, no. Heapõder is hardly a major operator, and I wouldn't even call Härg a criminal."

"What would you call him?"

Luik frowned in irritation. "He's a businessman, that's all. I know him myself. I don't even understand why you mentioned him. Where did you get his name from?"

"Just one of our informants."

"Shows you can't trust them. Russians, Hallmets, that's where you should be looking. Not bothering our own people."

"Thank you for your guidance, *Härra Doktor*. By the way, what can you tell me about Chief Inspector Vaher?"

"He's dead. That means you should be thinking less about him and more about who killed him. He was a credit to this city, if you really want to know. He knew who the crooks were, and did what he had to do to put them behind bars. I don't know how we'll replace him."

"I'm sure Captain Lind will be able to ..."

"Lind! He's well past it, should have retired years ago and let Vaher take over. This is a historic time, Hallmets, a time for younger men to take over, men who can see the future and take steps to make it happen. This is the Age of Action, Resolution, Will. The Age of the Young, the Strong, the Determined. The old need to step aside before they're pushed out of the way. Believe me, it'll happen. The future belongs to us. Look at Germany – it's happening there already." Luik paused, as if imagining the future. "So, what's your plan for today?"

"My colleagues are checking out known criminals, and will certainly not exclude Russian residents. This morning I need to interview the Chief Inspector's widow."

"Yes, I suppose that has to be done. Go easy on her, Chief Inspector, Laura has a sensitive soul. This must be such a tragic and exhausting time for her. I'm sure she has nothing to do with this awful business."

"You've met her, *Härra Doktor*?"

"Yes, of course. I've played bridge with the Vahers often. He was devoted to her. She'll miss him terribly." After a pause, Luik shook himself. "However, Chief Inspector, we must keep moving. Here's my card. Keep me up to date on this."

18

Hallmets phoned Captain Lind and suggested a press conference that afternoon at six. Then he asked Marta to summon the car provided by the Ministry, and in five minutes a familiar black Volvo slid up to the main entrance of Police HQ. The driver sprang out to open the rear door for Hallmets, who waved Larsson, now wearing a black leather jacket, in first before getting in himself.

"Where to, boss?" said the driver, a man in his forties with a pock-marked face, light brown hair cut short, and a ready smile.

"It's Lembit, isn't it?" said Hallmets.

"That's right, boss. Lembit Osav. Skilled by name, skilled by nature."

"Were you in the war?"

"Too right, boss, I only hear in one ear now, but there's plenty came off a lot worse than me. I were in the armoured trains."

"You did well, those trains were crucial. We couldn't have beaten both the Reds and the Germans without them."

"I heard you did not so bad yourself, boss. Down at Võnnu."

"We all did our bit. By the way, this is Sergeant Larsson. We're going to Nõmme – here's the address, I'm not sure where that is."

"No worries, boss, we'll find it."

As the car made its way out of the Old Town, Larsson turned to Hallmets. "Did you say Nõmme, chief?"

"That's right. Do you know it?"

"Not really. I stayed with a cousin in Tallinn last year, and she took me out there on the electric train – it only takes twenty minutes or so – just to look at some of the posh houses. They had a new market hall too, and a cinema. It's certainly an attractive place to live, with all those trees. But houses there aren't cheap. Maybe we should look at Vaher's financial situation."

They were now out of the cramped streets of the Old Town and making rapid progress down the Pärnu Highway. They passed some as-yet-untouched fields, but it was plain the city was growing, with plenty of house-building going on.

In ten minutes they began to spot, discreetly located amongst the trees, the custom-built houses of the wealthy, ranging from wooden buildings in the traditional style, with steep red roofs, to modern box-like dwellings with flat roofs and lots of glass. Hallmets noticed too, that the inhabitants were not all businessmen and gangsters. Smaller wooden houses, and apartment blocks were there too, and occasionally they could see older, more modest dwellings, dating from the previous century.

"We're near the centre now," Lembit called back to them, and soon they arrived at a cross-roads, by an open plaza, overlooked by a striking modern block in white concrete, with shops on the ground floor and offices in the three floors above. As they turned to the right, they saw a cinema on the corner, and a hundred metres further on, on the right, the new market hall. Many of the other buildings looked new too; this was a suburban township on the way up.

Five minutes later, they were in a street in which the houses were well-spaced, discreetly veiled by trees, and each one unique. As they turned through an open gateway into the drive, Hallmets realised that looking at Vaher's finances would certainly be necessary. This house was well beyond the means of a policeman. Two storeys and probably four or five bedrooms, the house was of whitewashed plaster over brick, and had a steeply pitched roof enclosing the upper floor.

They drew to a halt by the front porch. Before getting out Hallmets leaned forward and touched Lembit on the shoulder. "Lembit, whilst we're inside, take a look around. See how they live here. Can you do that?"

"No problem, boss, there's a limit to how much polishing you can do." He sprang out and deftly opened the door for Larsson to exit. Meanwhile Hallmets let himself out the other side.

As Lembit hung around the car, ostensibly checking the tyres, Hallmets and Larsson approached the front door. It opened, framing an apron-clad maid, blonde and freckled, probably a girl from the countryside. Hallmets introduced himself and Larsson, and they were invited in. The maid took Hallmets' overcoat and Larsson's jacket, and led them through a spacious hallway, and into a bright and airy lounge. The walls were primrose, with framed watercolours of rural scenes, the furniture was modern and uncluttered, a cheerful log fire burned in the fireplace. The maid announced them and retreated to the doorway.

A woman in a long black dress rose from an armchair to greet them. She was slim with black hair cut to a fashionable bob, blue eyes, and a solemn expression. She was playing the part of the grieving widow very competently, suspected Hallmets. She eyed each of them up and down, her gaze passing after a cursory appraisal of Larsson to linger longer on Hallmets.

"*Proua* Vaher," said Hallmets, with a bow of the head. "I hope this is not a bad time for us to be here, but I'm afraid we do have one or two questions. The answers will help us track down the criminals who perpetrated this atrocity. It will not take long."

"Please, do sit down." The woman indicated a sofa opposite her armchair. "Of course I will do the best I can to answer your questions. It was such a shock." She sat down again, fished a white lace handkerchief from the sleeve of her dress, and dabbed the corners of her eyes, although they didn't seem to Hallmets to be watering. Then, as if pulling herself together with an effort, she said to the maid, "Hella, can you bring coffee for our guests, and my usual." The maid made an awkward curtsy and retired.

"So difficult to get good staff," commented *Proua* Vaher, "with the right attitude, don't you think so, Chief Inspector? By the way, do you mind if we speak German. I find Estonian rather uncouth, and at this time of trial, I'm finding everything so draining."

"*Naturlich, gnädige Frau,*" said Hallmets, switching to German, "We are of course very sorry for your loss. Your late husband was a highly valued member of the police force. You may rest assured, *Frau* Vaher, that we shall not rest until the person or persons who ended his life so tragically are brought to justice."

Laura Vaher smiled condescendingly. "*Vielen Dank, Herr Hauptkommissar.* I'm sure you will do everything you can." She frowned and in a moment her expression was one of irritation. "Where is that girl?" she muttered, and jabbed her finger repeatedly at the bell-push on the wall.

In a moment the maid appeared with a tray on which were a coffee pot and teapot, cups and saucers, a small jug of milk, a sugar-bowl and a plate of slim brown biscuits. She poured Hallmets and Larsson a cup of coffee, placing them on small tables, one by the armchair and the other in front of the sofa, then poured tea for *Proua* Vaher. Then she curtsied again and withdrew.

"Please, help yourselves to the milk and sugar," said her mistress, "And do have a biscuit – they're all the way from Paris. You can't get them anywhere here. Please excuse my not taking coffee. In the morning I only drink sea-buckthornberry tea; it's so good for my complexion."

Hallmets took milk and one lump of sugar in his coffee, and a biscuit. It tasted sweet but rather soft; he wondered how long ago it had last seen Paris. He noticed Larsson took no milk and avoided the biscuits.

Before Hallmets had finished chewing, Larsson began the interview, clearly trying hard to get her German correct. "I'm sorry if this seems inappropriate at this moment, *Frau* Vaher, but I think you had a very successful career in films."

This question took Laura Vaher by surprise, but pleasantly so. This time her smile was genuine. "Yes, my dear, you're right, I was really a film star. Yes, those were the days." Her voice had a rather hoarse and gutteral character. Hallmets wondered whether she had a discreet penchant for alcohol. "Of course," she went on, "that was when the movies were silent. Everything had to be conveyed by gesture and expression. That called for real acting, you know. With sound, well, you don't need to act at all."

"*The Princess of Livonia*, I remember that one," said Larsson, with some enthusiasm, "The one where the Estonian princess falls for the German knight. The knight has to choose between the vow of obedience he has made to the crusading Order, and his devotion to the woman he loves. The ending was so sad."

"Ah yes, I'm so glad my work is still remembered."

"It must have been so hard to give all that up. I mean, the fame and excitement. How could you manage to do that?"

"Ah, my dear, there are two answers to that. I met my husband, and he preferred that I withdraw from such a hectic lifestyle and devote myself to him. He believed that a woman's place is in the home, and who was I to say otherwise. And when the talkies came in, well, to be honest, I felt that my talents were ill-served. It's always better to get out when you're on top, isn't it. Since then I've devoted myself to my husband, and of course, to charitable works."

"You have a wonderful house," Larsson went on, "You must have made so much money from the movies."

"Ach, sadly not, I don't know where it all went. But we managed, Nikolai and I, to scrape together a few crowns, to get the place built. Land was cheaper here, back in the twenties. And I inherited some money from my father. He died ten years ago. He never really recovered from the terrible injustice of the land reform."

She paused in studied wistfulness, and Hallmets took up the questioning. "*Frau* Vaher, I'm sorry to come directly to the point here, but how was your husband behaving over the last week or two. I mean, did he seem more concerned than usual?"

"He was always concerned about his work, Chief Inspector, he never relaxed. Such was his devotion to order and justice."

"Do you think he had any particular enemies?"

"I suppose that every criminal he sent behind bars was his enemy. And many who were still free but knew he had his eye on them. Captain Lind had already told Nikolai that he would be chief of CID when he retired. In just six months. But now, it's all to ashes. From the dust we came, and to the dust we must return. Isn't that what the good book says?"

"Who do you think killed him, *Frau* Vaher?"

"Goodness, I have no idea, none at all. Some gangster, I suppose. If you arrest them all, and question them forcefully enough, I'm sure the guilty man will be found. I look forward so much to seeing him hang. It's what Nikolai would have wanted. Perhaps even in public. A public execution would give such a strong message, wouldn't it?"

Hallmets paused, and Larsson came in again: "Are you all alone now, *Frau* Vaher? Surely you have family to comfort you."

"Thank you so much for asking," said the lady, with a sniffle, "Sadly we had no children. But yes, I have two brothers and a sister. I don't speak to my sister any more, but my brothers have been very supportive."

"Are they here in Tallinn?"

"Albrecht was in Germany for a long time, Dresden – a beautiful city you know – but he's just come back, it was so nice to see him again. Heinrich stayed on the estate. His place is not far from here, and his wife is so sweet. They keep me in good spirits. And of course I have my charitable work. We are raising money to build an orphanage."

"How wonderful!" gushed Larsson, "Here in Nõmme?"

"You must be joking. This is far too good a neighbourhood for them. No, somewhere more suitable for their status. I think we have a site earmarked behind the plywood factory. Herr Schellenberg is the chairman of our little group. A wonderful man. So full of human spirit ..."

Hallmets had had enough. "Sorry to butt in, *Frau* Vaher, there are just a couple of routine questions I need to ask. First, can you remember what your husband did the day before yesterday?"

"Of course. He went to his work at seven, as usual. He phoned me at about two, to say he was going to be late home – that happened quite often – so I didn't worry when he wasn't back in the evening. I went to bed at about ten – too little sleep is bad for the skin, you know - and I was wakened quite early, when Captain Lind phoned to say they'd found him." She sniffed again. "Poor, poor Nikolai."

"Thank you. Finally, there are a couple of items here, I wonder if you recognise them." He took the cigarette holder from his jacket pocket. "What about this one?"

Laura Vaher took it very gently from him, turned it over, and looked carefully at the engraved initials. "Yes, that's my husband's. Albrecht gave it to him for his birthday last year. It's ivory, you know. From an elephant. Albrecht shot it himself, and had some gifts made from the tusks. May I keep it?"

"Sorry, I'm afraid we need to hang onto it, for the moment, as evidence. But it will certainly be returned to you as soon as we're finished." She gave the holder back to him. He pocketed it and brought out the fountain pen. "And this?"

Frau Vaher started, but quickly controlled herself. She made no attempt to take it, just peered at it and frowned. "No, I don't think I've seen that before. It looks like a nice pen. What make is it?"

"It's a Pelikan Toledo. The best you can get. Someone would have been proud to own one of these."

"I'm so sorry I can't help you there, Chief Inspector."

Hallmets rose. "That's no problem, *Frau* Vaher. Thank you so much, you've been most helpful. Oh, just one other thing. Can you give me your brother Heinrich's address. I'd like a chat with him too."

Laura Vaher looked dubious. "Why? I don't know what he can tell you."

"It's a formality, *Frau* Vaher. Routine elimination of people who didn't do it, so that we can home in on those who did. It will only take me five minutes."

"Well, I suppose so. I can hardly refuse, can I? You'd lock me up for not co-operating. I have his card here." She opened a little drawer in the coffee table next to her chair and took out a card, which she passed to Hallmets. He and Larsson made their farewells.

Lembit was waiting for them by the car. Once inside, Hallmets said to Larsson, "That was some good work in there. I'd never have thought of starting with the films."

"Thank you, Sir, I did some poking around in the library last night."

After a few minutes, Hallmets leaned forward. "Lembit, can you stop here." When the car stopped, he went on: "Did you manage to have a look round?"

"Sure thing, boss. I'll tell you one thing right away, there's plenty dosh swilling around there. There's a couple of buildings round the back. One's a garage, and you'll never guess what was sitting inside. A Rolls-Royce Phantom II, polished bronze, all the way from England. Absolutely fantastic! Makes this car – and it's not a bad one – look like a farm cart."

"Did you get inside the garage?"

"Er, yes, the door wasn't quite locked. Anyway, there's another building next to it, same sort of size, I guess they're a pair. Door to that one was firmly locked, but I peeped in the window. Looked like wooden boxes stacked in piles. Couldn't see what was in 'em though. So then I knocked at the back door, asked for some water for the radiator. Had a good chat with the cook – Anna's her name. She says the Vaher woman is a real pain in the ass. Never satisfied. Spends a lot of time shopping. Dresses, coats, shoes, bags, hats, you name it. Keeps going on about her charity work, but all she does is give away the clothes she's got bored with, and has slap-up meals with the rest of her so-called committee. What a poser, eh? But here's something interesting, boss. Anna says there's all sorts of comings and goings, in the night as well. Mind, she goes home at seven, it's only Hella, that's the maid, who lives in, but she's told Anna too. Mostly cars, but even the occasional lorry. That's definitely dodgy, isn't it?"

"That's very helpful,Lembit, I think you found out more than we did. Right, back to Pikk Street then."

19

Artur Simm woke up on the sofa with a bad headache. Things didn't look good. When he'd found his way up the stairs to the flat the previous evening, Marju had not been amused. She assumed he'd been out drinking with his colleagues, and no doubt made a fool of himself. She knew he couldn't handle alcohol, that even she could drink him under the table any time. And she was furious. At the state of him, at how she imagined he had behaved, and at the money wasted.

But he could hardly tell her the truth. That he had been coerced into serving a criminal, who had threatened to have his thugs rape her if he didn't co-operate. That his little finger had been broken, probably in several places. That he'd then been hit over the head and dumped outside the Baltic Railway Station, with a bottle of cheap brandy poured over him. Had then managed to find his way home. And had then staggered into a man right outside the Imperial Hotel, across the road from the flat. He hoped the man wouldn't report it to the hotel management, who would swiftly deduce his identity, and perhaps inform the police. No, he couldn't tell Marju all that. Better to endure a tongue-lashing and be banished to the sofa for the night. Maybe things would be better in the morning.

His hopes were soon dashed. As soon as Marju came into the living-room-and-kitchen, he knew it was going to be bad.

"Artur," she began, "What the hell do you think you are doing? We're trying hard to save up, remember, to buy a place further out, so that we can bring up children in fresh air and peacefulness. Why are you trying to destroy everything?"

This was the worst thing about Marju's anger. If she'd just shouted abuse at him, he could keep quiet and eventually she'd run out of steam and give up. But this interrogation – yes, that's what it was, interrogation – was unbearable. Particularly as his answers wouldn't make any sense. "Look," – he tried to stay calm – "I'm sorry about it. I guess I got talked into it by Jaan or one of the others, and then I had too much. I'm not trying to ruin our plans. I don't do this all the time, do I?"

"Once is enough. We can't afford it. And if you get a reputation as a drunkard, you won't last long at the paper. And what in God's name have you done to your finger?"

With some effort he raised his hand and looked at his finger. It was black and blue, and had swollen to twice its usual thickness. He tried to move it. Nothing happened except a wave of pain shooting up his arm. He winced. "I caught it in a door."

"It looks awful. You might have broken it. Now we'll have a bill from the doctor and the hospital too. What are we going to do, Artur? What are we going to do?"

He laid his good hand on her arm, but she pushed him away. "I can't live like this, Artur. Every time you're late, I'll think this is happening again. I've got to be able to focus on my job, even if you don't care about yours. Now, get washed and shaved, and then go to work. You're probably late already. And get that hand seen to, I don't want you whining about it for the next week." Then she turned her back on him and started making some coffee.

He took the hint. Getting out as fast as possible sounded like a good idea – he'd buy some flowers from the vendors by the Viru Gate on his way home and offer to take her out for a meal. He washed, grimacing as his little finger caught on a tap, shaved, changed his shirt and trousers, grabbed his other jacket, and headed for the door. Marju kept her back resolutely to him.

It was eight by the time he got to the office, and he was summoned to the editor's room as soon as he arrived.

"What sort of time do you call this, laddie?" barked Hunt, "Do you think the news waits until you've decided to drift in here. This is a bloody newspaper, that means we wait on the news, do you understand that?"

"Yes, Sir."

"Why do you think I noticed you were late, Artur? Do you think I waste my time checking on everybody?"

"No, Sir."

"No, I was waiting for you to come in because this folklore piece you wrote is rubbish." Hunt waved a sheet of paper at him.

"But it's all genuine material. It's in ..."

"Yes, I know where it's in, I can read too. And I don't pay reporters to copy stuff out of books. What have you been doing with your time?"

"Well, I thought there was a lead on the Vaher case, and you said ..."

"I said you had to get that folklore piece done first. That means exercising your brain and your imagination. Yes, you can take the occasional bit of illustrative material out of a book, but mostly you write it yourself. If it's about weather forecasting, you find somebody who does it, and interview them. Talk to people in the street, see what they think. Produce something original and above all, entertaining. This is about selling papers, laddie, and whether it's crime or folklore it has to be interesting. This stuff is shite. Now forget about Vaher – Jaan has got that well in hand – and do this folklore piece again. And once you've done that, I want you to get out to that new farm community the government has established in the forest near Vaida on the Tartu road, and see how it's going. Have they got the roads and services in, have they got enough volunteers for the new farms, what are they giving them to get up and running, that sort of stuff. That should take two or three days. By the way, what the hell have you done with your finger?"

"I got it caught in a door."

"It looks like you've broken it. Get to the bloody hospital before you do anything else, get it seen to. You're no good to me with blood poisoning or gangrene. And shut the door behind you!"

Jaan Kallas sat at his desk, wondering where to go next on the Vaher case. It was too much to hope for that some gangster would phone him up with a clue, despite his appeal. If they did find out who did it, they were more likely to torture him until he wrote a confession, then leave his corpse outside police headquarters with the confession nailed to his chest. But his gut feeling was that the criminal world wouldn't be a lot of help here.

So what else was there. He'd need to talk to the widow first. An ex-film star, that was worth a bit of coverage. He could start with a sympathy piece, the grieving wife left bereft by her husband's brutal slaying. Of course, it was quite possible she'd done it. Not personally – he didn't see a lone woman throwing Vaher off Toompea in the middle of the night. Maybe she'd paid a couple of heavies to do the job. He glanced at his watch. Not even nine yet. No good turning up too early; he suspected she wouldn't be an early riser. So, time for a coffee before he set off. Nice day for a trip on the electric train.

20

When they got back to Pikk Street, Hallmets sent Larsson to check out Tempelmann & Klebb, the tobacconists, whose shop was only a couple of streets away. Now he took out his notebook, to jot down what he'd learned from the visit to Laura Vaher. First, that she didn't seem particularly distressed by her husband's sudden demise; second, that she wasn't a very good actress; third, that she'd confirmed the cigarette-holder was Vaher's; fourth, she'd recognised the fountain pen, but pretended not to; fifth, that the amount of money available to the

Vahers seemed suspicious, given that Vaher's salary seemed to be their only source of income; and sixth, that the nocturnal comings and goings at the Vaher house needed some clarification. He went through to the workroom and asked Marta if she could get hold of Ilmar Hekk for him.

A few minutes later Larsson was back. "Been to the tobacconists, talked to Mr Tempelmann. Vaher was a regular customer. He mostly bought Craven A. An English brand. 'Easy on the throat' is the slogan. Patent rubbish. Nobody can tell me smoking is good for you."

"Anything else?" Hallmets didn't want a discussion about the dangers of smoking. Otherwise he might have to admit she was right. Then he'd have to try and stop. "Did Vaher buy cigars?"

"No. Just cigarettes. He also got the matches from them. They hand them out to regulars."

"OK. Thanks, Eva. Now lets have a look at Vaher's office. Captain Lind had it sealed, but I've got the keys here. Let's see what we can find."

They'd almost reached the door when there was a rapid knock, and before Hallmets could respond, it opened and Ilmar Hekk came in, somewhat out of breath. "Sorry to barge in, chief, I got the message from Marta. But on my way up I heard another body's just been found, below the viewing platform."

"Change of plan," said Hallmets. He quickly introduced Hekk to Larsson. "Now let's see what's going on."

As they hurried along the corridor, he wondered why he had not been informed of the new body immediately. It must have been obvious that it was connected to the Vaher case. "Who's dealing with it?" he asked Hekk.

"They said Lepp was on it."

21

As the electric train cruised smoothly out of Tallinn, Jaan Kallas watched the factories and warehouses slide past, then clusters of houses and two- or three-storey apartment blocks. Then green fields and cows. And then Nõmme. Designer dwellings discreetly lurking amongst the trees. After a 25-minute journey, the train slid to a halt by the new station building, itself resembling the comfortable family home of a lawyer or accountant. He came out of the station, passed the grey stone building with the round gothic tower, which had once been the post office, and the brand-new fire station, with three wide doors behind which he assumed were fire engines of the latest design. He came to a cross-roads with an open plaza and a modern office block with shops at ground level.

He went into a chemist's shop, and introduced himself as a reporter covering the death of Chief Inspector Vaher. "But I want to get the human angle, what it means for his poor family. He was married to a film star, wasn't he?"

"Oh yes," said the plump lady behind the counter, "Laura Steinberg was her name. I saw her in *The Princess of Livonia*. I wept at the end, it was so sad. She gave it up when she married the Chief Inspector. They've a lovely house, you know. I think the architect was German."

Twenty minutes later Kallas was standing outside the house. It had started to rain as he walked there, and he was glad he'd worn his overcoat, although he felt himself sweating from the unaccustomed exercise. He straightened his tie, and made for the front door.

A maid answered the bell. Kallas gave her his card and asked if he might talk with *Proua* Vaher. He was soon ushered into the bright lounge. He explained to *Proua* Vaher that he was covering the death of her husband, and wanted to convey to his readers the depth of grief which affected his family. Would she be willing to give him an interview?

The lady kindly assented, but asked that the interview be in German. Although, like everyone in Estonia who'd been to grammar school, Kallas could manage passable German, it would put him at a disadvantage in the interview, so he explained that he didn't speak German, but would endeavour to make his Estonian understandable. He would also give her plenty time to answer, so that he could get the gist of her words into his notebook in shorthand.

His first questions were deeply respectful, inquiring into the sense of loss which the family had suffered, and nodding thoughtfully as the lady played her part. He couldn't remember having seen any of her films – he suspected they were all romantic tosh – but concluded fairly quickly that she was hardly a great actor. Time for the gloves to come off.

"*Proua* Vaher, ..."

She smiled sweetly. "Please, call me Laura."

"Thank you, Laura. Tell me, the Chief Inspector's death must also have affected you financially. I mean, how will you be able to support yourself now that he's gone?"

She looked down at the thick pink and green carpet with a serious expression. "I really don't know, Jaan – if you don't mind me calling you that – It was hard enough to make ends meet while he was alive. But now..." Her voice drifted away.

"And yet you live in a big house in an expensive suburb, you have servants and expensive furniture. Forgive me for being blunt, Laura, but where did all the money come from? Sure not from a Chief Inspector's salary."

She frowned. "That's a rather impertinent question!"

"I'm sorry Laura, but it's what our readers will demand to know. And I'd rather give them your answers than have to make something up which might be wildly inaccurate." He smiled apologetically.

"Well, if you must know, my family is not poor. I inherited money from my father. Our manor is near Harku, so it's not far from here. My brother Heinrich is still there. Of course the family was badly affected by the so-called land reform. It was just theft. All the care devoted to our peasants over the centuries, and that was what we got in return – most of the land, and all the best bits too, seized and handed over to those feckless idlers."

"You must have had quite a lot of assets salted away, to come out of it so well, then."

"My father had been well-advised in his investments. Can we move on now?"

"Of course. How did you get on with your husband?"

"What do you mean by that?"

"I've heard you argued a lot." Kallas hadn't heard anything, but it was worth a shot.

"Who told you that?" she snapped. "Was it that nosey-parker next door? Well, whatever that cow says, it's not true. Absolute nonsense. Nikolai and me, we were as close as ... " She groped for a suitable metaphor.

"Chalk and cheese?"

"Yes. No! What are you suggesting? I don't want to say any more. Now please leave."

"*Proua* Vaher, did you commission your husband's death?"

"*Raus! Sofort!* Get out immediately!" She jabbed at the bell push furiously, but Kallas was already on his way to the door.

Outside, in the street, he noticed the house on the left of the Vahers' was quite close, whilst the one on the right was separated by a hedge, a wide lawn, and a row of poplar trees. He turned left.

22

They hurried through thin rain, and saw the crowd of spectators half way up the Patkuli Staircase before they reached the scene. Pushing through the crowd, and ducking under the railing, guarded by a uniformed policeman, they picked their way carefully across the steep scrub-covered slope. A man's body lay as if resting against a projecting rock. The photographer was still at work, and Einar Sepp stood to one side, talking to a tall, thin man with short ginger hair. His face was almost skeletal – skin stretched over the bone of his skull. As Hallmets approached, he stared at him with a blank, emotionless gaze. Hallmets noticed he had green eyes.

Hekk whispered to Hallmets, "It's Inspector Lepp."

Hallmets held his hand out to Lepp. "I've not met you before, Inspector," he said politely.

Lepp paid no attention to the hand. "What do you want?" he said, "This is my case."

"If this death is relevant to Inspector Vaher's death, I have a right to be here. I'm disappointed that you didn't let me know yourself."

"You learned soon enough. What do you want to know? You're interrupting my investigation. And whoever this woman is, a crime scene is not the proper place for her."

"Sergeant Larsson is working with me on the Vaher case," said Hallmets coldly, "She has every right to be here. You should keep your opinions to yourself, Inspector, they cheapen your rank as well as your person."

Lepp's eyes blazed with anger, and his fists clenched, but he said nothing.

"Now," said Hallmets, "Please tell us what we've got here."

"Isn't it obvious," sneered Lepp, "A body. Anything else?"

"Do you know who he is?"

"Not at the moment."

"His name's Eino Lehmja," said Hekk, who was peering down at the corpse. "He did time for armed robbery. Vaher put him away. I think he was released late last year."

Lepp glowered at him.

"Do you know what he's been up to since his release?" Hallmets asked Hekk.

"No. I guess he'd not got himself into any trouble, or we'd have heard."

"I don't think he's got rich," said Hallmets, "His jacket's worn, there are dirt and grease stains on his trousers. And one of the soles of his shoes is worn through. How did he get here?"

"I don't think it takes a university degree to work that one out," said Lepp, in a tone that oozed contempt. "Fell from the platform, landed here, hit his head on that rock."

"There was a note," said Sepp, "Clipped to the dead man's jacket. 'The killers will die.' That's all it said. I took it off the victim as soon as I got here, in case the rain damaged it. I'm going up the viewpoint now to see what's there."

"Good," said Hallmets, turning to Lepp, "Inspector, did anyone see him come down?"

"No," replied Lepp, "It tends to be dark during the night."

"People saw him earlier this morning, assumed he was sleeping rough," added Sepp, "From a distance, it's not obvious he's dead." He glanced past Hallmets. "Ah, here comes the doc."

Professor von Stallenborg, wrapped in a heavy Ulster and a tweed cap, clambered very gingerly across the steep slope, assisting himself with his walking stick. "Well, good day, gentlemen, and lady." He bowed shortly to Larsson. "And what have we got here? Don't tell me, it's a body! But we mustn't presume he's dead, even though, I must say, he looks it." He waved the photographer aside and knelt over the dead man. After a few minutes, he got up again, with some effort, and, taking out a small notebook, made notes as he spoke. "Definitely dead. Injuries consistent with a fall from a height. Main cause of death a severely fractured skull, probably caused by this rocky outcrop – you might find a bloodstain on it, if the rain hasn't washed it off. Probably several other bones broken – again, consistent with a fall. Also bruises to his face which might have had the same cause, though I'm inclined to think they were already there, but fairly recent. He may have other injuries but they're not visible at the moment. More details after the PM."

"One thing I must know, *Härra Professor*," said Lepp coldly.

The doctor looked at Lepp with distaste. "Ah, the ever-impatient Inspector Lepp. Yes, the perennial question, how long ago did he die? Well, all I can say now, and this is not to be taken as a definitive statement, is that he's been dead for more than six hours, but probably not more than ten."

"So sometime after one or two in the morning, and before it got light?" said Hallmets.

"Precisely," said the doctor, "The hours of darkness. No doubt the preferred time for a dastardly crime. Well now, Inspector Lepp, can you get somebody to cover him up, keep the rain off. I'll send some chaps to collect him. PM sometime this afternoon, while he's still fresh.

All welcome. Now I must rush, got a lecture to deliver. Good to see you again, Hallmets. Cheerio." He nodded vaguely in Lepp's direction, smiled at Larsson, and set off back towards the staircase.

The rain was getting heavier, and one of the uniformed officers produced a cape, which they draped over the body.

"Well, Inspector, what do you make of this?" asked Hallmets.

Lepp exhaled, suggesting he had better things to do with his time. "The criminal fraternity are giving us the people who did it. That's what the note says. All you have to do is read."

"That's certainly possible. But it makes more problems for us, doesn't it?"

"I don't think so," sneered Lepp, "If the bosses are identifying the killers, and executing them, they're doing our job for us. All we have to do is pick up the corpses."

"Sadly, Inspector, it's not as simple as that. The Vaher case is very public. How does it look if we let criminals behave as if they're the law? And there's another problem. We need to prove that these are the men – and the note suggests more bodies are on the way – who did in fact kill Vaher. What's to stop the bosses rounding up a few guys who are out of favour at the moment and throwing them off Toompea? Then telling us they're the killers. Get us off their backs, and let things get back to normal, eh?"

Lepp gave a short, bitter laugh. "Are you saying they should get the guys to write confessions before they kill them?" He shook his head as if trying to explain something to a simpleton.

"That wouldn't help, I'm afraid," replied Hallmets calmly, "As I'm sure you're aware, people will write anything under duress. No, if these men are alleged to be Vaher's killers, we, the police, have to prove it. We have to say why they did it and how they did it, and support that with convincing evidence. Please alert me to any evidence you find that links Lehmja to Vaher's death."

"What if there isn't any? Apart from the fact that he's dead in the same spot."

"Then maybe he didn't do it. And here's another thing. The people who killed this man – and we can assume it took at least two to get him off the viewpoint – are, as far as we are concerned, murderers, and we need to find them too. Even if Lehmja killed Vaher, it doesn't give anybody out there the right to kill him. Does it, Inspector?"

"You're inventing pointless complications. Maybe that's what you do in Tartu, discuss it like you're in a seminar at the university. But we don't waste our time in that sort of crap here. We should be out there looking for the rest of Vaher's killers. Although I suspect the crime bosses will have done it for us before too long. They don't waste their time talking."

"Perhaps if you investigate Lehmja he may lead you to the others."

"Are you joking? He's dead. How can we investigate him?"

"Inspector, investigation means more than just beating somebody up. Look for evidence."

Hallmets tipped the rim of his hat to Lepp and turned away. Hekk and Larsson followed him back to the staircase, where with the onset of the rain the crowd had diminished. He led them up to the viewing platform and passed through the police cordon.

Hallmets asked them what they thought of the latest development.

"Lepp is certainly a nasty piece of work," said Larsson. "But there's also something fishy about him. He kept fiddling with his wristwatch all the time you were talking to him. I wonder if he knows who did it. Was he poised to get over here as soon as the body was reported?"

"Maybe they tipped him off," said Hekk.

"That's possible," said Hallmets, "Things are going to get very confusing round here, so let's see if we can find any witnesses to Vaher's death before everybody starts focusing on last night, and forgets about the one before." He glanced at his wristwatch. "It's now almost twelve. Let's get round the houses up here on Toompea. A lot of the buildings are government offices which were shut overnight. Others are foreign embassies, where they'll just tell you to bugger off. But there are a few flats here and there. Eva, you go to the left. Hekk, you go to the right, and I'll do the bit in the middle. We'll meet at the *Alt-Revaler* once we're done. I'd guess between one thirty and two."

23

The house was a large cube of brick, with windows stuck in apparently at random. Kallas wondered how long the flat roof would last; roasting summers and freezing winters would soon screw up whatever trendy and no doubt grossly expensive roofing material the architect had recommended. There was still an unfinished look about the garden, if the scrubland around the house could be so described. He rang the doorbell.

The woman who opened it had her hair in rollers and was wearing a pink silk dressing gown. She looked too old to be living in such a modernistic house.

He introduced himself, and asked for the lady of the house.

"Oh, that'll be my daughter," said the woman, "Maarika Frantsen. She's working at the moment. She's on the staff of *Today's Estonian Woman*, you know. I'm Renata Kass, by the way."

It occurred to Kallas that this might be the person he really wanted to talk to. "Actually, *Proua* Kass" he said, "I believe you might be able to help me. We're doing a human interest piece on your neighbour – her film career and so on – after the tragic death of her husband. It would be really interesting to get some insights from one of her neighbours."

Five minutes later he was sitting at the kitchen table with a cup of coffee and a piece of apple pie in front of him. *Proua* Kass had explained that her son-in-law and daughter didn't like her using the lounge whilst they were out. "And, to be honest, those chairs they've got in there, you can't sit in them for more than ten minutes before you feel all the hard bits poking into you." Kallas thought she had plenty of padding, but nodded sympathetically. "They don't like me smoking in there either – I'm only allowed in here. And in the garden, of course. I'm out there quite a lot. I've got a little patio round the back, where I sit when it's warm. I can have a cigarette or two and a coffee. Karl always has the best, he imports it, you know, for the cafes and hotels. And that's not all, we have …"

"Your patio sounds lovely," cut in Kallas, "Does it overlook the Vahers' house, by any chance?"

"Well, as it happens, it does."

"So you must catch sight, accidentally, of course, of the Vahers now and then?"

"Yes. I mean, when I've done the washing up and so on, there's always time to sit out. In the evening, too, I like to give the young ones time on their own together. That's when I tend to catch sight of them. The Vahers, I mean."

He could see she was keen to share. "What were they like, as a couple. Very romantic, I suppose. I mean, what with her being a film star."

"Hah, you're joking," exclaimed *Proua* Kass. She could keep it in no longer. "Anything but. Believe me, they were at it hammer and tongs. I mean, of course, you couldn't help but overhear. If they were in the garden, or had the windows open. They knew how to argue, those two. I suppose her being an actress that's what they're like, you know, ready to explode with passion all the time. And him, well, I know he looked like a film star himself – maybe that's what she saw in him – but he could be quite vicious too."

"I suppose all couples have their ups and downs."

"Yes, that's true enough. Sometimes they could be very lovey-dovey. Some of what they got up to, even out in the garden, where anyone could see, well, I was disgusted, I can tell you. Other times, as I said, they'd be yelling and shouting at each other. They both wanted their own way. Lack of discipline as children I'd say. And he beat her too, you know. I saw her one day, with a black eye as plain as your nose. Didn't even try to cover it up. And the way she looked at him sometimes. I thought to myself, one day she'll get her revenge. She'll poison his mushrooms all right. That's what a Roman emperor's wife did, wasn't it, I mean, poisoned him with mushrooms? Funny what you remember, isn't it. I think that was in a novel. But I'm sure she wouldn't push him off Toompea. I suppose he had lots of enemies. I mean, dealing with criminals all the time, stands to reason. Now, my friend Anna, she says …"

"What were they like as neighbours?" asked Kallas, "Did they have much to do with yourselves, or anyone else?"

Proua Kass paused for thought. "Not much, kept themselves to themselves. I think she thought we were all beneath her, you know, 'cause she's an aristocrat."

"Is she really?"

"Oh yes, von Langenstein, that's the name she was born with. Not that she called herself that when she was in the movies, no, then she called herself, what was it now? Stein? No. Steinberg,

that's it. Laura Steinberg. I guess she thought it was snappier than von Langenstein. Her brother still lives on their estate, you know, in a manor house."

"Does he come often, to visit the Vahers?"

"Oh yes, all the time. Even in the middle of the night sometimes. His car, you see, you can easily recognise it. One of those big German ones."

"Why does he come in the middle of the night? That does seem a bit odd."

"Well, that's too true, my friend Anna, she says, well, I won't say, it's too disgusting, and I don't believe it anyway. But there is something weird going on there. Cars, vans, even lorries, all times of the night. I mean, that's not right is it?"

"Do you think it could be anything illegal?"

"Well, it's got to be, hasn't it? Why else would you want to be creeping around in the middle of the night."

"Have you managed to catch sight of them?"

"Unfortunately, they go round the other side of the house. Mind, you, I did once creep out onto the road and went round there – I couldn't sleep – and tried to get a bit closer. But that dog – they had a dog then, a sort of poodle, not very big, but always yapping – and it must have seen me and, well, I had to scarper, I can tell you. Want some more coffee, by the way?"

Kallas took that opportunity to scarper himself. He'd learned enough to be going on with. There were a few nuggets here. Which one would he pick up first?

24

Today's Special at the *Alt-Revaler* was 'Meatballs cooked to an old German recipe with potatoes,' and that was good for Hallmets and Hekk, with beers alongside, whilst Larsson had a salad with cold sliced pork, and a glass of orange juice.

Hallmets summed up the possible witnesses. "So, it looks like no-one saw very much. There's the man in the flat near the cathedral who thought he saw a black car pulling up in the square, and some people getting out. But he couldn't say whether they were dragging somebody, or just going to a party. And he couldn't say what time it was, just that it was dark and that he couldn't sleep as he'd had so much to drink that evening."

"A bottle and a bit more of vodka, he said," confirmed Larsson.

"Then there's the woman who was walking back to her flat when she passed a crowd of what she thought were drunken Germans, on the other side of the road. That was about 1 am. But she only heard a few words, she was keen to get past them. And finally the man who thought he heard Russian voices out in the street at 4.15 am. But he's Dutch, and admits he doesn't speak Russian, so it could have been any Slavic language."

"So we're not really much further forward," said Larsson. A thoughtful silence ensued.

"What about the wife?" asked Larsson, "Could she have hired some thugs to kill him? Her grieving seemed to me mostly play-acting. And what was going on at their house – those comings and goings in the night?"

"They do need looking at," commented Hallmets.

"Want me to keep an eye on the place overnight, chief?" asked Hekk, "It may be that after Vaher's death they stop whatever it is for a while, but you never know."

"Thanks, Ilmar, give it a shot. Can you take Kadakas with you. Time you taught him the skill of staying awake when it's dark and nothing's happening. Take the rest of today off, and get some rest. I'll get Kadakas to meet you at the workroom at eleven."

25

Artur Simm was struggling. He was having a difficult day, and it was about to get worse. After waiting an hour to be seen at the hospital, they told him he'd broken his finger in two places. It would probably be stiff for the rest of his life. A nurse bound it tightly to the next one, and then gave him some aspirin. Despite that, the finger kept throbbing, as if to keep reminding him of his stupidity. Once back at the paper, he'd phoned up the National Museum, in Tartu. Someone there told him the man whose seaweed saved all the people on the boat had died in 1913, but did point him towards another old man, who lived at Randvere, on the coast not too far from Tallinn. He'd gone out there and found the old guy, but couldn't make any sense of what he had to say, as he used a lot of dialect words Artur didn't understand. He'd just got back, but reflected that no-one else would be able to make sense of the old duffer, so he might as well just make it all up. He was feeling hungry, and noticed that it was already one o'clock. But he'd better get this out of the way first.

As he began to compose his fictitious interview with 'The man who saved a hundred lives', the phone, on a shelf at the other end of the room, rang. Someone nearer to it than he was picked it up, then called him over. "Artur, for you, says he's your Uncle Peeter."

Artur's heart stopped, and he suddenly found himself short of breath. He didn't have an Uncle Peeter. But he did know a Mr. P.

"Artur, how are you?" The oily voice made him want to scream. "I hope your finger's not too sore. And I hope Marju wasn't too sore when you got back last night." When Artur didn't answer, the voice went on. "I've got a little job for you, Artur. Are you listening carefully?" Artur still said nothing. "This is the bit where you need to say 'yes', Artur. Because if you don't, you know what'll happen. I'm going to count up to three, and then ..."

"Yes, alright, I'm listening."

"That's a good boy. They usually find it hard to respond the first time. Now you've done it, it'll be a lot easier next time. Now, here's what I'd like to know. Who's on the police team investigating Vaher's death?"

"How do you expect me to find that out. I'm on folklore and agriculture, not crime. Why don't you ask Kallas?"

"*Härra* Kallas is a customer. I serve my customers. You are my employee. I use my employees. Now Artur, don't be pathetic. You're a reporter, so I'm confident you'll find a way."

"But how do I get you the information?"

"That's a good question, Artur, it shows that you're focused on the task. But don't you worry about it, one of my people will contact you. You have until noon tomorrow. Goodbye."

Artur sat for a while, thinking. He decided to get the article done first, then chase up the information for Mr P. At least he had until tomorrow. An hour later the piece was done. Hunt stared at it for a long time before grunting and throwing the paper back to him. As he got up to go, Hunt growled, "It'll do. But too long. Take a hundred words out."

Another half hour, and he was free, for the moment. He didn't need to go to the farm settlement till tomorrow. Now he could chase up the information. The direct approach might work. After all, he was a reporter. And he might pick up something he could use himself.

He was soon at Pikk Street. He went up to the uniformed female officer at reception, and introduced himself as a reporter, showing his press card. He asked who was handling the Vaher case, and discovered it was *Ülemkomissar* Hallmets, from Tartu. "And who's he got on the team?" asked Artur.

"I'm not allowed to release that information," said woman, whom Artur could easily imagine as a prison guard. "You'll have to talk to the Chief Inspector himself if you want any further information."

"That's fine," said Artur, "Where do I find him?"

"You don't," said the woman, expressionlessly, "I'll see if he is willing to give an interview. Wait over there." She pointed to a steel and canvas chair by the wall."

"Thank you. Tell her I also have important information for the Chief Inspector."

Without changing her expression, the woman picked up the phone. After a brief conversation, she turned back to Artur. "He'll give you two minutes. But that's only because you've got information for him. Wait until you're called."

As he waited, Artur considered what information he had that might interest the Chief Inspector. He could, of course, tell him about his interview with Mr P the previous day, the police would certainly be interested in that. He could even ask for their help, to arrest him, and save Marju. But he reflected that Mr P may have anticipated that his informants would go to the police, and have plans ready for such an eventuality. He suspected the plans would involve Vlad and Igor doing what they enjoyed doing.

He noticed a tall thin, grey-haired woman coming towards him. "I'm Chief Inspector Hallmets' secretary," she said, "Come with me." She led him through the double doors next to the reception desk, and to the left, where a lift awaited them with open doors.

As they entered Room 422, he realised this was the base for the Vaher case team. A large table sat in the centre of the room. A slim woman, plainly dressed, sat there, reading papers, and making notes.

Artur went over to her. "Tere! Artur Simm, *Pealinna Uudised*. Pleased to meet you. You're ..."

She looked up him for a moment, and he felt her eyes appraising him. "I'm working," she said, "and don't want to be disturbed. Thank you." She returned to what she was doing.

Artur felt a sharp tap on his shoulder, and turned. It was the secretary. "This way," was all she said. She led him to a door in the left-hand wall of the room, knocked twice, and opened the door. "Artur Simm, from *Pealinna Uudised*," she announced," and as he went in, closed the door behind him.

The man who faced him was a little above average height, and looked fit. His light brown hair was beginning to go grey at the edges, and it was getting a bit thin on top, too. He was wearing a dark grey suit. The suit matched his eyes, which seemed to be looking straight through Artur's own and into his brain, evaluating everything in there. His face showed slight surprise. Artur wondered what he'd seen inside his head.

"Please, sit down, *Härra* Simm. Your name is familiar to me." He opened a paper on his desk and glanced at it. "Yes, *Härra* Rebane told you about the body he'd found on his kiosk, and you were at the kiosk not long after. Inspector Sõnn noted here that you had left the scene before he arrived. Why was that?"

Shit, thought Artur, this wasn't what he'd expected. But at least he could say that was the information he had for them. "Well," he said, trying to sound as concerned as possible, "I offered to wait until the detectives arrived, but the patrolmen told me they didn't need me, since I hadn't discovered the body. But when I read about who it was, I thought I'd better come here anyway."

"I'm most grateful," said the Chief Inspector, "Perhaps you could begin by telling me why you didn't report the discovery of the body to the police yourself."

"But I did!"

"No. It was a woman who phoned us. Our switchboard staff are clear about that. The call was carefully logged. Your wife, I suppose? But that would have been after you'd called your paper, to get a photographer round, wouldn't it?"

Artur squirmed, and tried to put on a brave front. "I'm a reporter. What do you expect me to do?"

"Sometimes you have to do your duty as a citizen." Hallmets peered more closely at him. "I believe I've met you before, *Härra* Simm."

"No, I really don't think so."

"On Wednesday evening, quite late. I was outside the Imperial Hotel with a colleague. You staggered towards us from the direction of the station, bumped into my colleague, didn't seem to know where you were, then went across the road, and into the building where your flat is."

"That can't have been me. I was somewhere else."

"Shall we go round to the salon and ask your wife what time you came in that night? And what state you were in? We can do it right now, before you have a chance to prompt her. I'll just call a car." He leaned towards the telephone on his desk and picked up the handset.

"No, don't do that. Yes, all right, it was me. I'd had a bit too much to drink, that's all. It happens now and then."

"And you hurt your finger, too, I see. How did that happen?"

"I caught it in a door. It was very painful."

Hallmets was tempted to give Simm's bandaged finger a good squeeze, but restrained himself. Instead he asked Artur to describe exactly what he saw when he came upon the body. Artur's description added nothing to what he already knew, but the way in which he presented it gave the impression of a man who had something to hide.

"What is it you're not telling me?" he asked at last.

Simm seemed to shrink in front of him, and looked around furtively, as if seeking a way to scuttle out of the room, like an insect caught in the light when a stone is lifted. "Honest, I've told you all I know. I'm sorry I delayed over the phoning. I didn't really think it would make any difference."

"What about last night? What were you doing before we saw you."

"Nothing. I mean, I'd just had too much to drink, that's all."

"You're a reporter, Mr Simm. Are you working on the Vaher case?"

Simm hesitated. "Among other things. But I can't tell you what we've got. That's confidential. We have to protect our sources." Now he seemed to relax. He'd realised this mantra could be repeated any time he was questioned.

"Well, thank you for coming in to see me. I'm afraid I have a great deal to do now." Hallmets concluded the conversation, and stood up to shake hands with his visitor.

Artur stood up too. He was relieved this was over. But he still had to do what he came for. "May I ask one thing, Chief Inspector? With my reporter's hat on, as it were." He forced a smile. "Could you tell me who's on your team for the Vaher case?"

Hallmets paused only for a moment. "There's going to be a press conference at six. Whoever represents your paper at it may ask any question they like."

26

Hallmets looked down into Pikk Street from his window. A horse-drawn cart loaded with milk-churns was plodding along, holding up a string of cars. He glanced at his watch: three thirty. Time for a quick look at Vaher's office.

Larsson was in the workroom drinking coffee. He asked her to come along. They made their way down the stairs to the second floor and along the brightly-lit corridor. Each door had a name written in a neat hand in black ink on a small white card fitted into a metal frame attached to the door. Near the end of the corridor, they found the door marked 'Vaher N'. Hallmets tried the door; it was locked. He unlocked it, and they went in.

The room was large, with three tall windows in the wall opposite the door. A desk was positioned so that light from the right-hand window fell across it, and behind it one of those fancy leather-upholstered office chairs that could rotate. Facing the desk were two upright wooden chairs, with neither upholstery nor arms. No-one who visited Vaher would sit comfortably, thought Hallmets. By the left wall were a filing cabinet and a set of bookshelves. To the right of the door stood an empty coatstand, and a dark wooden cupboard about a metre high.

The desktop was empty, apart from a blotting pad at the left hand side, and a telephone on the right. There were no loose items on any of the other surfaces.

"Looks like Vaher was well-organised," observed Hallmets. "Eva, can you check the filing cabinet and the cupboard, and I'll have a look at his desk. I expect they'll be locked. Here are the keys."

Larsson tried the cupboard door. It opened. Then the filing cabinet. "They're already open, chief."

"That doesn't sound good," muttered Hallmets, as he leaned over the desk. The desk drawers slid open easily. "No-one leaves all his desk drawers unlocked. Unless he's very careless, and I don't think that was Vaher."

He looked at the contents of the three drawers, which were on the right hand side of the desk. The top one contained only stationery items: blank sheets of writing paper with the police crest at the top, envelopes, a bottle of Pelikan black ink, four pencils, perfectly sharpened, and an eraser. The second drawer contained a Tallinn telephone directory, a booklet containing contact details of government departments and a duplicated sheet listing police stations in other parts of the country.

In contrast to the first two drawers, which were in perfect order, the papers in the bottom drawer appeared to have been stuffed in willy-nilly. There were receipts, bills, letters, and scraps of paper with pencilled notes. Hallmets scooped everything out and piled it on the desk.

"Somebody's been through all this," he said, "We'd better take it away, and look at it upstairs. What's doing over there?"

Larsson was peering into the top drawer of the filing cabinet. "Files on cases he was working on currently. And the second drawer, let's see, this looks like his own files on cases he'd worked on. The third seems to be more of the same – some of them go back to the 20's – and the bottom – ah, this is different – there are, let's see, eight bottles of vodka."

"That's interesting," said Hallmets, coming over to have a look. "There's been no suggestion Vaher was a heavy drinker." He picked one up and looked at the label. He recognised it as the brand Captain Lind had offered him. '*Leikari*' There was a picture of a stylised figure playing a lute on the label. "He must have used these as sweeteners, or rewards. Not a brand I've seen in the shops.

Anything in the cupboard?"

Larsson opened the door and knelt down to look in. "Pair of handcuffs, knuckleduster, couple of shot glasses, box of ammunition for his pistol, but no pistol, and a few other bits and pieces. And a shoe box. Feels light. Let's see what's inside. Ah. Nothing." She sniffed inside the box. "Slight smell of oil. robably kept his pistol in it."

"Well, let's use the box for these papers," said Hallmets. He took the box and started stowing the papers from the bottom desk drawer into it.

"Can you go through this stuff once we're back upstairs. We might have to check the filing cabinet at some point, though I suspect someone has already removed anything that might have interested us."

Hallmets spent the next hour writing a brief report on the progress made so far. Then he gave it to Marta to type up. In triplicate – one for him, one for the files, one for Dr Luik.

He heard voices in the workroom, and went through to see what was happening. Maslov, Lesser and Kadakas had got back from tracking down the ex-cons whom Vaher had put away.

"Anything promising?" Hallmets asked.

"Not much," replied Lesser. "Mostly little guys who've had the worst of life. Some of them trying to go straight, some will be back inside soon, others just trying to survive. None of them we could see going after Vaher. Maybe folks got wind of what we were doing, a few of them seem to have cleared off."

"Oh. Who was missing?"

"Let's see." Lesser consulted his notebook. "Grigori Jesinev, Arnolds Kauščis, and Eino Lehmja."

"Well, we found Eino Lehmja. Dead. Half way down Toompea."

"Thrown off?"

"Looks like it. Seems like somebody thinks he was involved in Vaher's killing. Are those three connected at all?"

"No. Not part of the same gang. But they're all hard types. Thugs rather than thinkers."

"Perhaps a third party hired the three of them to kill Vaher," suggested Larsson.

"That could work," said Lesser, "Each of them would certainly kill his granny for a hundred crowns. And the three of them could easily overpower Vaher. And chuck him off Toompea. But the drugging – I don't see any of them doing that. They'd be more likely just to beat him to a pulp. So even if they did do it, there's somebody else behind them."

"Could this somebody else be getting rid of his hired killers now, to keep us happy and remove any witnesses who might incriminate him?" continued Larsson.

"That's a hypothesis we can't dismiss," said Hallmets. "It's also possible the crime bosses don't actually know who did it, so they're just killing plausible villains, to make us think it's all been sorted out."

"What about cops?" asked Maslov. "Killing known villains just in case they did it."

"Sadly, that's also a possibility we can't overlook," said Hallmets.

"Who's handling the Lehmja case?" asked Lesser.

"Lepp."

"You won't find him very co-operative."

"So I've noticed. OK, Henno and Oleg, see if you can track down Jesinev and Kauscis. Ants, I want you to take the rest of the day off. Get some rest, come back here at eleven tonight. Ilmar will take you over to the Vaher house to do some overnight surveillance. Let's meet again tomorrow morning at eight. Just one other thing. Bashed little fingers. That ring a bell with anyone?"

"Oh yes," said Maslov, "That's Vladimir Krilenko, aka 'Vlad the Despoiler'. Ukrainian hard man. Came here after the Reds took over, like all the other Russian villains. Clever with a cosh, cruder with everything else. The little finger job is his speciality, his signature effect. You never forget it. He was down in Petseri when I last saw him, that was maybe eight years ago. So it wouldn't surprise me if he's moved up in the world. Is he involved in this?"

"I don't know. Just something I noticed today. By the way, our friend Dr Luik has suggested the killers must be Russians. Is there a reason for that?"

"Luik's believes all our criminals are Russians, "answered Lesser. "And that all Russians are criminals." He paused. "But he has reasons. His parents were in Tartu when it was occupied by the Reds in 1918. They were both killed. He had to identify them. Bayonetted to death in the police station basement. Then the bastards threw all the bodies down the well."

27

Just after five thirty Hallmets' phone rang. Professor von Stallenborg.

"Ah, Hallmets, there you are. Thought you might like to hear the results of the PM on that chap found below Toompea this morning. Lehmja. Killed by the fall all right. But beaten up pretty badly before that. A few ribs already broken before he fell. And signs of recent torture on the body – cigarette burns, scald marks, small cuts, unsophisticated stuff. That's it, really. I don't trust Lepp to pass anything on to you. Oh, by the way, re Vaher: morphine in his blood."

The ground floor room at Police HQ was full, and a pall of cigarette smoke already hung over the crowd of impatient journalists. At six Captain Lind and Hallmets entered. The Captain began by confirming that Vaher's post-mortem had established that he had come down from Toompea, and, given the point at which he had landed, it seemed that he had been thrown. It was clearly a case of murder. Then he introduced Hallmets as the senior officer brought in to handle the case.

Hallmets indicated that their inquiries were at an early stage, and therefore, beyond what Captain Lind had already said, there was very little to report. However, he assured them that once some progress had been made, he would call them together again. He appreciated how much the public were concerned about the murder of a prominent polioce officer. Meanwhile, he was happy to answer any questions.

Several hands went up. Hallmets indicated an overweight and timeworn man in the front row.

"Jaan Kallas, *Pealinna Uudised*. Wouldn't you agree that the discovery of Eino Lehmja's body earlier today tells us the underworld has heeded my call for them to find Vaher's killers?"

So this was Kallas, thought Hallmets. "Thank you *Härra* Kallas. However, we have as yet no evidence to tell us that Lehmja was involved in Vaher's death. Maybe he was, maybe he wasn't. Maybe someone else thought he was. We must avoid jumping to conclusions. Inspector Lepp will no doubt examine all possibilities."

"Lepp says he thinks the underworld is handing Vaher's killers to you on a plate."

"If the underworld knows who did it, I would suggest they deliver them to us alive, so that we can interview them and establish the truth."

"Was this a communist gang gaining revenge for Vaher's actions in 1924?" asked another reporter.

"We're exploring every avenue," answered Hallmets, "We have not, as yet, established a motive for the killing." He repeated this statement when others raised the possibility that the culprits were anarchists, gypsies, or freemasons, or that Vaher had fallen foul of Jewish moneylenders. It seemed the reporters were more interested in airing their own theories about the murder than trying to find out what the police already knew.

Finally, when it looked like no more questions were forthcoming, a voice from the rear of the room asked "Can you tell us who are the members of the team investigating the case?"

Hallmets recognised the voice and saw Artur Simm in the back row. He also noticed Kallas turning round in his seat, a look of annoyance on his face. "I'm not sure I see the relevance of the question," he said, "I'm assisted by very able officers, both from the capital and from other parts of the country."

"Is it true that one of your team is female?" asked Simm. Hallmets realised that Simm had seen Larsson when he'd come up to his office.

"Yes, that is correct."

"Would that be Eva Larsson?" called someone else. This was not a difficult guess. There were very few women police officers in Estonia, and only one detective.

"Yes. Sergeant Larsson is assisting us."

There was some muttering in the audience, and somebody laughed at a muttered remark from his neighbour. Captain Lind raised a hand for attention. "We have every confidence in Sergeant Larsson. Sergeant Maslov has also joined us from Petseri. And our own Inspector Lesser. We will bring in further officers from any part of our country if necessary. Take it from me, gentlemen, this case will be solved."

Lind invited Hallmets up to his room. They began as before with a shot of Vaher's vodka. It was, as he'd thought, '*Leikari*' brand. The name was not a word he recognised, and the picture of dark figure playing the lute was no help. He noted also that the level of liquid in the bottle had sunk significantly since his meeting with Lind the previous day.

"Thanks for talking to the journalists, Jüri. Even if there's not much to go on yet, we have to show we're being open on this one. What do you think about Lehmja?"

"Just what I said back there, Peeter. There's no hard evidence connecting him with Vaher's death. Just because he's been dumped off Toompea doesn't prove he killed Vaher."

"But it would wrap up the case neatly if we could assume it were him, wouldn't it?"

"Why would we want to do that?"

"Let's face it, Jüri, you're not going to find any real evidence about who killed Vaher. I can tell that already. It's the obvious solution, I mean, an ex-con that he put away, maybe even two or three acting together, decide to get revenge. Then the bosses get worried about a police clamp-down, round up the guys who did it, and hand them to us."

"Dead, therefore not much use."

"After your appeal today, they may supply more information. But as a scenario, it's very plausible. Maybe Lehmja even told someone what he was going to do, or bragged about it afterwards. After all, what criminal wouldn't want to be remembered as the man who killed Nikolai Vaher?"

"I'll certainly be interested in whatever Lepp turns up," observed Hallmets.

Lind poured himself another generous measure of vodka, and drank it in one. "All those cranky ideas – anarchists, gypsies, moneylenders – they're all just fantasies. Even Reinart and his paranoia. He's talking about closing down the German Club in Tallinn, you know. Thinks some of them are Nazis."

"You don't think that's a problem?"

"He's making a mountain out of a molehill. The Nazis aren't a threat. They'll bring order to Germany, and put a stop to all the fighting in the streets, and the strikes, and Red plots. I'm sure once Hitler has settled in things will calm down. And all that marching around with banners and bands, it's just the sort of pageantry the Germans lap up. It's harmless enough. And don't forget that Hitler was chosen by the people – he didn't seize power in a coup. Care for another drink?"

Hallmets excused himself. As he climbed the stairs, he was reminded of Artur Simm's question. Was he asking because he knew there was a woman on the team? In some respects, Estonia had made huge leaps forward. But other things would take a lot longer to change, and that included the attitude to women.

28

Artur Simm made for the door as soon as the conference finished, and hurried back to his corner of the room in the offices of *Pealinna Uudised*. He grabbed from the shelf the *Yearbook of the Ministry of Agriculture* for 1932, opened it at the page he'd marked on new agricultural settlements, and made every effort to read it. But his mind was awhirr. He had the information Mr. P. wanted. But were the three names he had enough? After all, Larsson, Maslov and Lesser's names would be in every newspaper well before the noon deadline.

The door burst open and Kallas marched in, an angry look on his face. Apart from Simm, there were three other junior reporters at their desks, and they all looked up. Kallas came over to Artur's corner, pulled over a chair from the next desk, and sat down. "What the fuck do you think you're doing, Simm?" he snarled. "Just who do you think you are? I permit you, against my better judgement, to give me some assistance in the archives, and the first thing you do is piss off somewhere else. Now you gatecrash a press conference, pretending no doubt to be a crime reporter. And you even have the cheek to ask a question."

"Look, er, Jaan, it's not…"

"I'm not interested in your excuses! Just let me tell you one thing. I'm the crime reporter on this paper. Not you. And if I so much as smell you near any work that I'm doing, or suspect that you're doing your own thing on this, I'll personally break all your other fingers." He grasped Artur's left hand tightly, so that he gasped with the pain. Then he got up. "Oh, and by the way, I've already reported your conduct to the editor." And he left.

Artur stared at his book, seeing nothing. He didn't want Kallas for an enemy. For one thing, he really did want to learn from him. And for another, Kallas had influence with Hunt. And if Kallas had reported him, his job would be well and truly on the line.

"Shit," he said to himself, "Shit, shit, shit, shit."

He could sense the eyes of the others on his back, and thought he heard a whispered conversation and a snigger. He felt tears welling behind his eyes. He tried to concentrate on the book, but it was no good. He slammed it shut, stood up and walked out of the room without looking at the others. He made for stairs at the end of the corridor. He knew he could not escape Hunt's wrath for ever, but he just wanted to put it off for a little while. He had just turned into the stairwell, when he heard heavy footsteps coming down the flight above. He pressed himself against the wall and peeped around, to see the bulky figure of Eirik Hunt stomping down the corridor towards the room he'd just vacated. He ran on tiptoes down the stairs to the ground floor, gave Kristiina a quick wave and a smile, and strode as quickly as he could out the front door.

He wanted to get away from the usual reporters' haunts, and soon found that without thinking about it he had arrived at the *Alt-Revaler-Café*. A vague thought crossed his mind that Mr. P. might be there, sitting placidly in one of the high-backed armchairs, waiting for the reports of his minions. But he wasn't. So Artur sat at one of the plainer tables near the front window, and ordered a shot of vodka and a coffee. The vodka was strong, he could feel it burn his throat and force its way down his gullet, but that was followed by an immediate sensation of warmth and calm. He let time pass for a few moments with nothing at all filling it except his own breathing, and he watched his hand as it laid the empty glass carefully back on the table. Then he lifted the small coffee cup to his lips and sipped the thick, sweet, black liquor. Comforting and stimulating. Now he could try to think. He closed his eyes.

But a few seconds later, he felt his sleeve being tugged, and opened his eyes to see a street-urchin, perhaps ten or eleven years old, clad in brown shorts and a woollen jumper of uncertain colour. The boy thrust a scrap of paper onto the table. "Mr. P. says to write down the names 'ere," he announced, "Quick as yer can, I ain't stoppin here long." He fished a stub of pencil not quite three centimetres long from his trouser pocket and placed it on the table.

Artur swallowed. Had they been following him all the time? Or did they somehow know he would be drawn back to this café? He took the pencil – it had a greasy feel to it – and wrote on the paper 'Sgt Larsson, Sgt Maslov, Inspector Lesser'. "There," he said, pushing the paper and the pencil back towards the boy, who seized both without another word, and rapidly exited the café.

Artur breathed a sigh of relief. At least he'd got some information to Mr. P. before it became generally known. But at the same time he felt deeply ashamed, that the Artur Simm who'd dreamt of becoming a fearless crime reporter, who'd uncover the evils of the modern age and the villains who lay behind them, was reduced to a messenger boy for a low-level criminal. And that he had been so naive and simple as to walk into it. And now because of that he'd lose the career he'd wanted. And what would Mr. P. do then? Would he continue to use him, as a tiny and disposable cog in his information machine? A petty criminal. Without his job he'd lose Marju too. She wanted children, and wanted to be able to hire someone part-time to look after the salon while they were young. He wasn't that keen, but he'd gone along with it. However, that needed him to be in a job, one that paid a regular income. He could lose everything that made life worthwhile.

He sat up and tried to pull himself together. What would Kallas have done in this situation? That was easy, he wouldn't have got into it, he would have been more careful, bided his time, not pushed his luck. He knew he'd been a war correspondent – the war had been the making of many of the men of his generation. Hallmets he knew had been some sort of hero, against the Germans in Latvia. Had peace and prosperity condemned his own generation to weakness and cowardice?

Then he remembered why he'd agreed to work for Mr. P. – his fear for Marju. He thought back to their wedding day, five years previously. The happiest day of his life. His father had told him it would make a man of him. And given him a present fit for a man. The old man had said, "A man must defend his woman," and gave him the bundle wrapped in sacking. As he unwrapped it later the smell of oil came through first, and then the weapon lay before him: the Luger pistol his father had taken from a German officer who'd surrendered to him. "One day you might need this," said the old man, "Don't be afraid to use it if you have to."

He got up, and left the café. He wanted to go home now, to hold Marju tight and not think of anything else. It had started to rain, and was getting dark.

As he made his way along the dim alley that took him towards Pikk Street, he saw a figure come round the corner and walk towards him, a blind man, tapping a walking stick on the wall beside him. The man's hair and beard were unkempt and dirty, his clothes ragged and patched. He wore small round glasses with dark lenses, but he didn't seem to be looking on front of him, but rather over Artur's head. Artur feared the man would bump into him, and moved into the centre of the lane. As the old man came past, he smelt him, sweat and mustiness, and pointlessness.

But the man without warning lurched towards him, and grabbed his arm, pulled Artur towards him with a relentless strength. "See here," he whispered, and his breath smelt of cigarettes and urine, "Three names ain't enough. Mr. P. wants more. By noon tomorrow."

Artur tried to back away but the man's grip held him firm. "Get off me," he gasped, "He's got all that I could find out!"

"Didn't you hear me, boy?" hissed the man, and Artur felt the flecks of spit on his face. "I reckon you need a little reminder, eh?" All at once he kicked Artur's legs from under him, so that he fell on his back onto the wet cobbles. Then the man spun his stick expertly in the air and seized the tip end, so that it became a cudgel, and Artur noticed the heavy and knobbly handle arcing towards him, and then a blow in his side and a sharp pain. He rolled over and tried to squirm away, and the next blow caught him on his thigh.

But now, to his own surprise, his fear was supplanted by a growing rage. What right did these people have to do this to him? To threaten him, and his Marju. Another blow caught him on his leg again, and a fourth missed him completely, whacking the cobbles. The blind man cursed, and peered around. Artur realised that the man was not blind at all, but in the dim light of the nightbound lane his dark lenses were making him so.

"Where are you, you little bastard?" muttered the man, raising the stick again. Artur kept quiet, and began to crawl away. Then he saw, lying in the gutter at the edge of the lane, a bottle, long since drained of its vodka, and cast away by some drunk. He grabbed the bottle by the neck, and felt it thick and heavy. The base clunked on a cobble and the man was at him again, with a vicious blow on his back. He cried out and swung the bottle in desperation. By chance the bottle's heavy base connected with the man's ankle, the force of Artur's rage giving it enough momentum to cause damage. The man yelped, took a step forward onto the damaged leg and fell over, dropping the stick. "You fucking bastard," he shouted, "I'll bloody kill you for that."

Artur scrambled to his feet and now his anger drove him. As the man began to push himself up again, and groped for his stick, Artur, with all the force he could muster, swung the heavy bottle down onto his head. There was an audible crunch. The man's movement was arrested, and he seemed to be working out what to do next. Artur didn't waste time and, standing over him, brought the bottle down again with all the power of his shame and his hate. Again the crunching impact, and this time the man slumped to the ground.

"Hey! What's going on there?" came a shout from the lower end of the lane. Artur glanced over and saw a dark figure in the light from the street lamp on the corner. A policeman! He limped as fast as he could up to the top of the lane, throwing the bottle aside before he emerged into the square. He raised himself as straight as he could, and made himself walk calmly around the edge and into the lane at the opposite corner.

29

When Hallmets got back to the workroom Larsson was still there, looking through the pile of sheets from the shoebox.

"I've separated this stuff into three piles, case-related material, personal material, and financial stuff. The case-related material is mainly just memos to himself and to-do lists, nothing that seems relevant. The financial stuff is mostly old bills and receipts. A couple of chairs he ordered from a furniture-maker, a stone bird-bath for his garden, and so on. But one bill did look interesting." She picked up a single sheet which lay on the table to one side, and handed it to Hallmets.

"'Services rendered' – that doesn't tell us much. Who are Sjoestedt & Pfinster? Lawyers?"

"Accountants."

"Hmm. So Vaher had an accountant. That's hardly usual for a police officer. People usually hire accountants because they want to avoid paying tax, their sources of income are complicated, or they can't add up. Why did he need one?"

"We'll need to talk to them. But they may be reluctant to help."

"Go and see them tomorrow morning. What about the personal stuff?"

"Mostly letters of appreciation from relatives of victims. For instance, the widow of a man who had been beaten up when he interrupted a couple of burglars in his house. He had later died from his injuries. The widow thanks Vaher for catching the killers and persuading them to confess. With their execution, she feels a sense of closure. Vaher's work was certainly appreciated by some. But there was one interesting item. This note."

It only took seconds to read, but it opened up a host of new possibilities. It was written in a small neat hand in dark red ink on otherwise blank paper. The paper was expensive: smooth and firm and coloured a pale shade of lilac. The message was simple: 'The time is now. We have to act.' It was signed with a simple 'K'. Hallmets knew at once it wasn't a thespian offering Vaher a change of career. The obvious conclusion was that it was from a woman other than Vaher's wife, that they were having an affair, and that the woman was urging Vaher to leave Laura and go off with her. But Hallmets knew that the obvious conclusion wasn't always the correct one, that nothing can be assumed. Indeed, he still remembered, in early 1920, during his six-month police training course in Scotland, a senior officer telling the class, 'Never assume – it makes an ass of U and me.' His English wasn't good enough for him to get it right away; it was only when he wrote it down that he understood. But he hadn't forgotten it, and that simple piece of advice had stood him in good stead since then.

"That's another lead," he said. "Plenty to do tomorrow, I think. Let's leave it there for today."

Back in his office, he realised that he was late making his phone call to Kirsti. He put the call through, and asked her how the submission to the publishers was coming on.

"I'm going through the first thirty pages again. I don't think they're exciting enough. I'll have to move the bit where the bishop is poisoned nearer to the start, so that it happens not long after the new minstrel arrives at his castle. What do you think?"

It was a while since Hallmets had read his wife's novel, *The Bishop's Gold*, a story of murder and romance set at a time when Estonia was divided between the bishops and the Teutonic Knights, and no love was lost between the two. It had everything: a murdered bishop, dramatically falling dead at the altar in his cathedral after drinking the wine at mass, a minstrel newly arrived from foreign parts possessing some strange and useful skills, a rapacious vassal of the Knights, keen to expand his own lands at the expense of the Church, a beautiful girl from the country who turns out to be the bishop's daughter, and a scheming merchant who wants to marry her to his dim-witted son. And it moved at a good pace too. He'd been impressed.

"Yes, great idea. In fact, why not start with the bishop's death. It's a great scene, and it'll really grab the reader's attention."

"But what about the minstrel arriving at the harbour. That happens first."

"Maybe you could have that bit as a kind of introduction."

"A prologue?"

"That's the word."

He was tired now. It had been a long and tough day. He hoped the hotel kitchen would still be open. He'd just put his coat on, when there was a knock at the door. A uniformed sergeant entered, and saluted. "Sergeant Renn, Sir. A patrolman has found a body, name of Rudolf Pottsepp, otherwise known as Blind Rudi. I wonder if you can assign someone from CID to the case."

Hallmets asked why Captain Lind hadn't already done that. The Captain was at home, he was told, and didn't want to be disturbed. Hallmets wondered what state the captain was in by this time in the evening. He asked the sergeant to tell him what was known so far, then asked him who the duty CID officer was, and was told it was Inspector Sõnn. He asked the sergeant to send him up.

Five minutes later Sõnn arrived, looking rather apprehensive. He'd also made an effort to look his best, his shoes shining and his tie pulled tight.

"You sent for me, er, Sir?" he said. Clearly the S-word was not an oft-used element in his vocabulary.

"Yes, thank you coming up so promptly, Inspector, I want you to handle a murder case. Rudolf Pottsepp."

"Blind Rudi. Who did he top, then? Some other beggar, I'll bet."

"No, he was the victim."

Sõnn's eyes widened. "What! Why would anybody kill him?"

"That's what I want you to find out."

"What happened?"

"Seems there was a fight, in an alley, near Raekoja Plats. Someone bashed his brains out with a bottle. That's all I know at the moment. Sergeant Renn has the details, and the patrolman who reported it is with him. He found the bottle, so there's a chance there are fingerprints."

"Right oh, chief, I'm on it. Thanks." Sõnn nodded to Hallmets and turned to go.

"Just a moment," called Hallmets.

Sõnn froze, and turned back, as if he feared Hallmets had some new sting to hit him with as he left.

"Tell me more about this Blind Rudi. He seems quite well-known."

Sõnn relaxed. "Well, of course, he's not blind at all. But he pretends to be. Uually sits at the edge of Vabadus Plats, near the War Memorial, begging. Claims he was blinded in the war by poison gas."

"Did he fight in the war?"

"He was in jail when it broke out. GBH, seven years. But they let him out when he volunteered for the army. So yes he did, I'm not sure where. He came up with the blind beggar thing afterwards."

"Is there any more to him than that?"

"Nothing we've picked him up for. But there are rumours he works for Boris Popov. As an enforcer."

"Popov?"

"A Russian. He sells information. To anybody who'll pay for it. So he has informants to supply him, and muscle, to keep them in order."

"OK. Let me know as soon as you get something."

"Will do, chief." Without thinking, Sõnn saluted, then left the room.

30

Jaan Kallas was in a bad mood. He'd been thoroughly annoyed by Artur Simm's performance. Jaan had given him the hand of friendship, offered to teach him a few things, and what did he get in return? The little turd thought he could elbow his way into Kallas's job. Did he think being a crime reporter was something you could just prance into whenever you felt like it, just because you happened to come across a body? And Simm hadn't even found the body – a pal had led him to it.

Kallas remembered some of the bodies he'd seen over his fourteen years as a crime reporter. And that was not counting all the corpses he'd seen during the war, when he was reporting from the front. He'd seen enough of death not to be excited by it, just saddened by the waste. The worst things he'd observed had been the atrocities meted out by the Reds to the civilian population – mediaeval cruelty that the Estonians could scarcely comprehend. This primeval savagery seemed embedded in the Russian soul. Perhaps one day they would get past it, but he suspected it would take generations. Simm had no idea. He'd seen one corpse, tidily pinned to a kiosk roof, and thought he knew about crime.

He remembered the time he'd spent, before the war, as a cub reporter. He started off in trade and industry, making new factories sound like palaces of manufacture, copying out the market prices for cheese, pork, fish, oil, wood, and everything in between, and listening to the German merchants and industrialists, who regarded the Estonians as inherently dull, and therefore in need of constant supervision and occasional corporal punishment. Then he was moved – he couldn't call it a promotion – to Social and Family. That meant attending funerals and other public events, kowtowing to the Baltic German aristocrats, who regarded themselves as the sole bearers of civilisation in that part of the world. They would only talk to him in German, and treated him as some sort of insect, necessary but nevertheless rather disgusting. Then he was moved again – this was a promotion – to Official Events, and had to stand around for hours at turgid ceremonials, noting the doings and decisions of the Russian rulers of the provinces of Estonia and Livonia, men without any understanding of or sympathy for the people they ruled. The war had freed him from that. Plus his natural abilities as a writer; he had to admit that was a factor too. It was a long and hard apprenticeship, but it made him a good reporter. And Simm thought he could just skip all that.

What made it worse was that he suspected Hunt had put Simm up to it. He knew Hunt preferred to encourage competition rather than co-operation among the paper's staffers. What game was he up to now? Sure, he had complained to the editor as soon as he got back from the press conference, and Hunt said he would talk to Simm. But what did that mean? That's why he felt he had to give the rat a few words of his own before Hunt got there. He didn't like doing it, he knew the other cubs would soon spread their accounts of it around, naturally increasingly embellished as they spread, and he would end up as a monster picking on the poor innocent young man. You couldn't win.

And to compound it all, when he got angry, he couldn't write properly, his words got mixed up and he lost perspective. Just when the Vaher case required him to be at his best.

He stared at the typewriter, trying to calm himself down, to focus on his piece for the next day. His first thought had been to go with Lehmja's death, and declare it to be the Tallinn underworld's response to his appeal to uncover the murderers of Vaher. He knew this was not the case; the killing had been carried out before his appeal appeared in print. But few of his readers would bother to work that out. It was too good a story, and if the story is better than the truth, they would tend to go with the story.

However, there was an alternative story, just as appealing and with more human interest, opened up by his visit to the not-so-grieving widow and his conversation with her nosey neighbour. A murder commissioned by an angry wife would make a more gripping story than the one about crime bosses eliminating Vaher's killers. The fact she was an ex-film star was a godsend too. The gangsters tended to be faceless, and when they appeared occasionally in court, turned to be rather ordinary men who rarely showed any emotion, and always had a lawyer sitting next to them when they opened their mouths. But a murderous movie star, that would sell a lot of papers. And he was the only one who'd got it, he felt sure of that.

Nevertheless, taking the credit for the crime bosses' execution of Lehmja was the one he knew Hunt would want to run with, if only to get one over the other papers. They would certainly run it, but only *Pealinna Uudised* could claim the credit for calling for action from the criminal world. Nevertheless, he'd keep the other story up his sleeve, and he knew it wouldn't be there for ever.

Three paragraphs later, the phone rang. Kallas recognised the voice of one of his contacts, a officer based at Police Headquarters.

"Tiberius here. I've some information. Usual rate?" Kallas never used the real names of his ears, in case of eavesdroppers or phone-taps. Their aliases were selected randomly from Suetonius' *Twelve Caesars*, a favourite of Kallas's. Suetonius would have made a good journalist, he had a good sense of what sold papers.

"Fire away."

"Blind Rudi's been murdered."

"Well, well. Not thrown off Toompea, by any chance?"

"No, no, nothing like that. Found in an alley not far from here. A patrolman passing the end of the lane thought he heard the sound of a fight. When he went to investigate, one of the men involved ran away. Then the patrolman found Rudi's body. Bashed over the head with a heavy bottle."

"Any idea who did it?"

"None at all. We got fingerprints on the bottle, they're going through all the cards now to see if we can get a match."

"Who's running the investigation?"

"Hallmets asked Sõnn to handle it."

"Doesn't Lind make any of the decisions there?"

"He seems to be leaving everything to Hallmets now."

"OK, thanks. That's good stuff. Anything else doing on the Vaher case?"

"Not that I'm aware of. I'll get back to you when I hear something."

Kallas had to think about this. Blind Rudi pretended to have been blinded in the Independence War, and would talk at length, for a donation, about the horrendous effects of poison gas. If anyone raised the point that chemical weapons had not been used during that particular war, he would simply say, "There's lots went on then that no-one talks about now." And who could argue with that?

But Kallas was also aware that there was more to Rudi than that. In particular, he suspected Rudi was connected to Popov in some way, either as a messenger or as an enforcer. He had form before the war as a thug, and was never without a nasty-looking cudgel masquerading as a walking stick.

But why kill him? There was no obvious reason. Sõnn, being rather unimaginative, would come up with a stock motive, perhaps an argument over a begging spot or a drunken spat which got out of control. Kallas wondered if there was more to it, and if it were connected to the Vaher case. What if Rudi had found something out? Or, more likely, someone else had found something out, and Rudi was on his way to Popov with it. A key piece of information might be out there, perhaps even the name behind Vaher's killing.

However, after his visit to Nõmme, Kallas had begun to doubt the gangsters-did-it theory. It could easily be that the gangsters were simply chucking a few known thugs off Toompea in the hope that the case would be closed and things could return to business as usual. He recognised that, by making his appeal to them in the paper, he had himself contributed to the plausibility of the gangsters' narrative.

He wound the paper out of the typewriter and placed it carefully on his desk, then took up a new sheet, fed it in, and started again.

31

Artur needed a drink badly. But not too near the scene of his encounter with the blind man. He crept past his own front door and made his way to the railway station. The station bar was as anonymous as you could get. The walls were of dull wooden panelling, hung with faded pictures, and lit by weak electric bulbs. The clientele were travellers, the majority single and male. They were largely silent, staring into their glasses, occasionally gazing at the faded face of the big clock over the bar. Some were reading cheap paper-bound novels or crumpled newspapers. At one table two tired men talked in sad low voices. At another sat a young man and woman, whispering to each other earnestly, the young man looking around him apprehensively every few minutes. By their table rested a cheap cardboard suitcase, off-beige in colour. There was a hint of mustiness in the air which the cloud of cigarette smoke hanging beneath the invisible ceiling failed to cover up. The ceramic stove in the corner served to take the chill out of the atmosphere, but not to warm the room. There was no incentive to linger there, and no-one was there because they liked it. Artur bought a small cup of black coffee and a glass of cognac from a surly barman, and sat down at a table near the corner.

What the hell was happening to him? Only the previous morning he was facing a great opportunity, a reporter's dream gifted to him by a generous fate. Since then he'd been kidnapped, threatened, beaten up, forced to work for a criminal mastermind, fallen out with Marju, been denounced by Kallas, and then attacked in the street. Now he had probably lost his job and was being hunted down as a murderer.

For he knew he'd killed the supposed blind man. He hadn't been able to check if he were really dead, but he remembered with a vividness that was palpable the sickening crunch of the heavy bottle crashing into the man's skull. He knew he'd hit him more than once, enough to smash his head to pulp. He could imagine the face, reduced to a mess of blood, bone and brain. He had fled the scene as fast as possible, tossed the bottle aside on his way. He realised now that had been a mistake; it would be covered with his fingerprints. He didn't know whether the policeman who disturbed them had seen him. If so he didn't have long. He tried to put aside the feel of the hangman's rope around his neck. He loosened his tie, took a swig of brandy, almost cried out as the crude spirit burned its way down his throat.

He heard an announcement echoing from the platforms: the train for Valga was going to depart in five minutes, and passengers were urged to board at once. He was tempted to get on the train. His papers were in his pocket, so when the train reached Valga he would be able to cross the border into Latvia. If he made his way to Riga, he could take a ship to Denmark or England, or even the USA. But reality soon intervened. He only had twenty crowns in his pocket. That might get him to Valga on the train, and across the border, maybe even onto a bus to Riga. Then he'd have nothing. And where would he be without Marju?

He finished off the brandy, the spirit acrid in his throat, and felt again the anger which had driven him to fight back, to kill. How dare they threaten him, threaten his Marju, who waited at home for him, and made him feel worthwhile, threaten his job, which he had wanted more than any other job. Bastards who tried to push his life this way and that, like a billiard ball, forever being poked hither and thither at someone else's whim.

As the anger subsided he felt a lightness fill his being, he felt that he could float up towards the ceiling and swim through the thick smoke cloud and out of the building. Out of the building and back home. Because he also knew that somehow, and soon, Mr. P. would know of the blind man's death and of who had killed him. And would seek revenge. Not just on him, but on his Marju too. And he couldn't let that happen.

He drained the strong, sweet coffee and made his way out of the building. As he came out, he could see before him the dark silhouette of Toompea – black roofs, black spires, black towers, black cliffs – against the dark blue, tinged with purple, of the night sky. He breathed the cool smoke-free night air, and set his steps to home.

Marju wasn't pleased to see him.

"Just what's going on, Artur? Something's obviously happening to you, and it's clearly something very bad. I'm not exactly stupid, despite my Dad being a farmer. And the worst thing is that you're not telling me. And don't say you're keeping it from me for my own good. If you can't share this with me, what's the point of us being married? Please, Artur." She was angry, but she was also desperate. Two nights running her husband had come home late and looking as if he'd been beaten up, and wouldn't say anything about it. All sorts of possibilities ran through her head.

Artur looked at floor, and then at his wife. He couldn't lose her, he knew that. "Let's sit down," he said, "I'll tell you everything." And he did.

Half way through his account, Marju wiped her eyes and got up. She brought from the cupboard below the sink a bottle. "This is some fruit wine from Põltsamaa. I was keeping it for a special occasion, but I think we should drink it now. I'll just get the glasses."

When he'd finished, he'd expected her to break down and sob uncontrollably, not knowing how to deal with a situation so far beyond her imagining. But the opposite was the case. Bad news was the norm for farmers. It wasn't just that they could always find a negative aspect to anything that happened. It was that terrible things did happen. Marju had heard the stories her grandfather told of the old days, when the German landowners could do whatever they wanted, and often did. Any means of getting money or goods or free labour out of the peasants was worth trying. Any improvements a tenant made only resulted in his rent being raised. A new calf or piglet could be seized on the grounds that everything on the estate belonged to the baron. Some barons even declared that this applied to the farmers' daughters. Any attempt to resist could result in the farmer and his family being ejected from their farm. Then, as landless labourers, things were a whole lot worse.

Thankfully, the land reform after the War had got rid of most of these parasites, and redistributed the land to the Estonians. But the stories remained, and would not be forgotten.

"So," said Marju, "We need to decide what to do next. You've been a real fool, Artur, I hope you realise that. I didn't think you could be so stupid. And all because you wanted to get on in a hurry, to get one over Jaan Kallas. Only froth rises fast, Artur. Anything good needs time to grow, isn't that obvious?"

"I just don't know what to do," mumbled Artur.

"Well, for a start, you've got to stop feeling sorry for yourself. That's not helping anybody. You've admitted that you were stupid, and that's a good place to start, because you have to recognise that stuff's behind you. And that's where we've got to keep it."

"But …"

"No buts, please, Artur, try to be a man. Now, you were foolish letting yourself get drawn in by this Mr. P, whoever he is. But I guess he realises now that you're not working for him any more."

"Yes, but now he'll send his thugs after us."

"So, where's that pistol your Dad gave you when we were married?"

"It's under the bed, I think, in a cardboard box, but …"

"I said no more buts, Artur! The first thing we need to do is be ready if these thugs come after us. Go and get it."

Ten minutes later the Luger had been unwrapped from its sacking, oiled, and loaded. But it still looked to Artur a puny weapon, which would hardly damage thugs like Vlad and his associate.

"We don't know how long it will take for Mr. P. to learn of the man's death …" said Marju.

"Not long," replied Artur.

"… and then to connect it to you. He may not realise you have anything to do with it. From what you've said, it doesn't sound as if the policeman saw you. Could anyone else have?"

"It's a lane, there are hardly any windows."

"That's good."

"What are we going to do, Marju?"

"Let's think about that in the morning, Artur, things are always clearer in the daylight. For now, you need to get cleaned up. Then we should eat something. All this wine on an empty stomach isn't good."

32

Back in his room at the Imperial, Hallmets took off his shoes and his jacket, and sat on the bed. He was exhausted. He'd had a mushroom pie and a beer in the hotel restaurant. But he wasn't finished with the day yet.

He started to make a list of things he needed to do the next day. The investigation was like some mythical sea beast, sprouting three new tentacles every time you cut one off. No doubt the morrow would bring a host of new possibilities. It occurred to him that he'd not talked to Kadakas about his report to Reinart. But what bothered him more than anything else was the suspicion that other cops may have been involved somehow, either in killing Vaher himself, or in supplying fall-guys to take the rap, posthumously.

His room, on the second floor, faced the front of the building, and looked onto Nunne Street. He turned off the light, and opened the curtain. The street light just outside the hotel's entrance cast a dim pool of light onto the pavement, still wet from the rain earlier that day. No-one was in the street. Across the road was the building with the hairdresser's shop which he had seen Artur Simm entering. The Simms must live in one of the flats in the building. It was a narrow building, he thought there would only be room for one flat on each floor. And there were only three floors. With the shop at ground level, it made sense that the first floor flat went with it. Looking directly across, he could see there were no lights on in the second floor flat. But when he looked down, he could see a light was on in the first floor flat. He could even see, through the window, for the curtains were not drawn, two people sitting at a table, talking. One he recognised as Artur Simm. The other, a plump blonde, must be his wife, the hairdresser. The two were clearly having an animated discussion, for Artur frequently put his hands to his face. He noted a bottle on the table too.

But Hallmets was tired, he needed to sleep.

Day 3. Friday 24th March 1933

33

Artur Simm woke up with a start. Light streamed in the bedroom window. And he was still alive. So was Marju, lying alongside him, sleeping peacefully. They had taken preparations before they went to bed. Of course, they made sure the door to the flat was locked, and the bolt on the inside fastened. Artur didn't think that door would be much of a problem for Vlad – he'd just kick it in. But surely kicking the door in would create and enormous racket. So who would hear, said Marju. There would be few passers-by in the street in the middle of the night. And old Mrs Tamm upstairs would hardly intervene. She'd be hiding under her bed if she heard any sort of noise. And she didn't have a phone, so she wasn't in a position to summon any help.

So they carried the table into the narrow hallway, and pushed it up against the door. Then they wedged a chair under the bedroom door handle. That would give them another few seconds. But they needed sleep, urged Marju. Sitting up all night in the living room in case the thugs came would leave them unable to cope in the morning.

Nevertheless, they kept their clothes on, and lay on top of the bed. The loaded pistol lay on the bedside table at Artur's side. On Marju's little table, beside the alarm clock, was the electric torch they'd got as a wedding present from her brother. It was a chunky and solid cylinder which produced enough light to avoid falling over things in the night. She had no thought of dazzling any invaders, but at least she could try to hit them with it.

At first sleep would not come. Every noise from the street seemed to presage the arrival of the two enforcers. But gradually the strong fruit wine had its effect, and eventually they both had drifted off.

The clock told him it was 6.50 am. He knew the alarm would go off at seven, so he allowed himself to lie back for a few minutes and savour the thought of still being alive. Then he gently blew in Marju's ear. She giggled and rolled over towards him, putting her arm round his chest. "Now, my boy ....," she murmured.

Then she opened her eyes and froze. "Dear God," she gasped, "Are we still here?" She sat upright and seized the clock, throwing the switch before its deafening clatter would fill the room. "Artur, that stuff you told me last night. Was that real?"

"Yes it was," he said, "I'm sorry."

"No good feeling sorry for yourself," she said, "Time to get up. I'm opening as usual at eight."

"But ..."

"I told you, Artur, no buts. We're not going to live the rest of lives in fear. The thugs didn't come in the night. That tells me that Mr. P. hasn't connected you to the blind beggar's death. Maybe he never will. So our best bet is to act normally, and try to get on with our lives."

"But ..."

"Please, Artur, stop whining. Let's get on with today. I'm working as usual and that's that. After all, these guys are not going to burst into a ladies' hairdressing salon, now are they? There are always people waiting in the chairs at the side, and there's Riita too, at the sink. Too many witnesses. Neither are they going to burst into the newspaper office, so you'll be OK there too."

"But ..."

"Yes, I know, you're going to get the sack, etc., etc. You told me all that last night. However, you don't know that for sure, so you'd better go and find out. Go straight in and see Mr Hunt. Apologise for annoying Kallas. Promise you won't do it again. But don't be pathetic. Nobody likes a man who's pathetic. If he says you're fired, tell him he doesn't deserve you, and walk out. Now, get yourself out of bed, then go downstairs and get the heater going in the shop. The water needs to be hot by the time I open."

At ten to eight, having seen Marju into the shop, and seeing that her apprentice Riita was already there, Artur reluctantly set off for the newspaper office. Each moment he expected the two thugs to appear out of nowhere, take each of his arms, and drag him away to some torture chamber, where Mr. P. would preside over activities he dared not imagine.

But nothing happened. As he passed the reception desk, Kristiina said to him with a smile, "*Tere*, Artur! The boss wants to see you again. Two days running. You must be getting something right."

Artur went directly to the Door of Doom and knocked, entering at the summoning word. Hunt sat staring at him, as if thinking what he was going to do. Maybe he had a torture chamber too, thought Artur.

"Sit!"

Artur sat.

"Kallas tells me you've been getting in his way."

"Yes, Sir, I ..."

"Did I ask you to speak?"

"No, Sir."

"As I understand, you obtained an interview with Chief Inspector Hallmets, managed to spot one of his team, a female CID officer, whom we can identify, and then attended a press conference and asked a question which no-one else had thought to ask. Is that a correct summing up of the events of yesterday?"

"Yes, that's ..."

"Yes is all I need. Explanations are usually bullshit. You think Kallas is getting too complacent, so you decided to show what you could do. Is that it?"

"Well, I ..."

"That's a good attitude. You don't get anywhere in this business sitting on your ass. And you did it with actions rather than words. That's good too. A good newsman has to be active. Ever-active. Perpetual motion. Of course, you've got to be able to write, need the gift of the gab, but without getting out there where it's happening, the words are just hot air, speculation, fantasies. Kallas knows a thing or two, he's got some good contacts. But you're right, Simm, he's not out at the coal-face enough. Maybe you can show him a thing or two, give him a bit of a prod. So, here's what I want you to do. Forget the agriculture and folklore for the moment. I've already told Raudjas he's on it now. I'm giving you a special assignment. The Vaher case. I want you out there chasing up the facts, following the investigators on the spot. Interview everybody connected with it. Then report it each evening. No speculation. No theories. Just the facts. And useful quotes. Leave the speculation to Kallas – he's good at that. That way your reports complement his. Well, are you up for it?"

"Yes, Sir, I ..."

"I thought you would. Right, clear off and get to work. Glad you got the finger seen to, by the way." Hunt picked up a pencil and turned his eyes to a sheet of paper on his desk.

"Er, Sir, does Mr Kallas know that ..."

"Of course he does! I told him half an hour ago. Close the door on your way out."

Artur dashed down to the Juniors' office, grabbed the notebook and a couple of pencils from his desk. He was about the dash out again, when he noticed Emil Raudjas at another desk. He took the *Encyclopaedia of Estonian Folklore* from his desk and laid it front of Raudjas. "This may come in useful," he said. And left the room. And the building.

He needed to sit and process what had just happened. He headed as if by instinct for the *Alt-Revaler-Café*. He ordered a large coffee and a doughnut with whipped cream. He put two spoonfuls of sugar in the coffee, and another on the whipped cream, in its little ceramic bowl. He cut the doughnut in half, into two semicircles, then dipped one into the cream and took a bite. Delicious! And a sip of strong sweet coffee, the perfect complement. Maybe a tad too sweet, but nevertheless, a moment to savour.

After a moment of savouring, however, it was time to confront reality. First the good bit. This was indeed good news, he'd been gobsmacked when the offer came. Next, the not so good news: he had to deliver the goods, and do it every day until the investigation was over. Finally, the bad news: Mr. P. was still around somewhere, and, he had no doubt, would make further demands on him.

He knew what Marju would say: forget the negative stuff and get on with the job. So what to do next. He could seek another interview with Chief Inspector Hallmets. Or even with Sergeant Larsson, the only woman in CID. That would make a good human interest piece. But that wasn't what Hunt wanted, he wanted facts. Snippets of the reality at the coal-face. He remembered Lehmja – his death was surely connected with the Vaher case, so a word with Inspector Lepp was in order. He took out his notebook and began to jot down a few ideas.

34

At eight Hallmets met his team. Everyone was there: Larsson, Maslov, Lesser, Hekk, and Kadakas, the latter looking very tired. Hallmets brought them up to date on the previous days' events. A lot had happened, but most of it seemed to be peripheral to the Vaher case itself. Lehmja had been killed either because someone thought he was involved in the Vaher killing, or because they were looking for a plausible fall-guy. And was there any connection at all with the murder of Blind Rudi? "It seems," he concluded, "that Vaher's death is triggering all sorts of other activity, but the other stuff is threatening to swamp the original event."

"Maybe that's the intention," said Lesser, "Maybe whoever's behind Vaher's death is orchestrating all these events."

"I'm not so sure," said Larsson, "When people see a threat or an opportunity, they take action. And the actions people take don't always have the consequences they thought they would. Thinking through all the possibilities that might arise is too hard for most people."

"Ah so," said Maslov, affecting a Chinese accent, "Even Fu Manchu, with doctorate from Edinburgh and Harvard, make error sometimes."

"And real people make more mistakes than fictional ones," added Larsson.

"I still feel there's somebody behind it all," said Lesser.

"Such as?" Larsson asked him. "Fu Manchu, or Professor Moriarty? I don't think we have any criminal masterminds here in Estonia."

"Mind you," said Hekk, "I think Boris Karloff was better as the Mummy than Fu Manchu."

"I don't think this is taking us anywhere," Hallmets intervened. "Ilmar, any luck last night at the Vaher place?"

"Some hints, I'd say," said Hekk. We watched the place the whole night. Unfortunately a lone car sitting outside the house would have aroused suspicion – everybody who lives there has a big drive, and they're all paranoid about burglars – so we had to park some way away and creep around in the undergrowth a bit. However we did see a couple of vehicles arrive. A one-tonne truck arrived not long after midnight, and left about half an hour later. Then an unmarked van came at about 5 am; it left twenty minutes afterwards. And at ten past six, a large Mercedes with diplomatic plates arrived; it was still there when we left at seven. Registered to the German Embassy. Probably Laura Vaher's brother, Albrecht von Langenstein. He works there."

"What does he do?" asked Hallmets.

"Third Secretary. I'm not sure what he actually does."

"We'll need to follow him up. What about those other two vehicles?"

"We got the van registration number. Belongs to a liquor shop down near the harbour. I'm afraid we didn't get the number of the truck. ..."

"That was my fault," muttered Kadakas, "I fell into a pond. Sorry about that."

"Can't be helped," said Hallmets, "You two should get some sleep."

"I'm OK, boss," said Hekk, "but Ants here could do with a bit of shut-eye. And a shower."

Hallmets sniffed the air. "Good idea. Here's what we'll do today. Henno, can you and Eva call in at Sjoestedt & Pfinster, and then see if you can get any further with Vaher's finances. Ilmar, can you check out the liquor store."

"Boss, let me go with Ilmar to the liquor shop?" put in Maslov, "I know a few things about booze."

"OK. I think I'll pay a call on Laura's other brother at his manor house."

"What about that note from the myterious K, chief" asked Lesser.

"Let's just keep that at the back of our minds for the moment, and see what happens today. If it's like yesterday, nothing will go to plan."

"What about me, Sir?" asked Kadakas.

"Ants, you get off now, get a shower and some sleep, and come back after lunch."

"Just one problem. I haven't done last night's report for the colonel yet."

"Don't worry, I'll give him a ring, I need you fresh for this afternoon, there's plenty to do. Oh, and just for this afternoon, put your uniform on. By the way, Henno, anything on that place, The Three Monks?"

"Not a sausage, chief. Can't be around these parts. Sorry."

"Three Monks!" laughed Maslov, "It's not a place, it's brandy. Good stuff, too. Made in Georgia. Used to be very popular before the revolution. They kept going for a few years afterwards, but imports here were very sporadic, and it stopped coming in altogether about six or seven years ago. I met someone from down that way last year. He reckoned they were still making it, but all the output was being sent direct to the Kremlin. Comrade Stalin's personal choice."

Back in his office, Hallmets phoned Colonel Reinart. He explained that the colonel's order to Kadakas to give him a nightly report was unsustainable. Kadakas was needed full-time on the investigation. Thus, the previous evening he'd been on all-night surveillance at a suspect's house.

"Whose house?" asked the colonel.

"*Proua* Vaher."

"Interesting. What makes you think she has anything to do with it?"

"The Vahers' lifestyle didn't correspond to their apparent income. And there were some odd comings and goings at night reported by an informant. That was true enough, we kept an eye on the place last night. Night-time visitors included a car with diplomatic plates."

"Now it's getting interesting. Who was that?"

"Probably Albrecht von Langenstein."

He could almost hear Reinart sit up even straighter than usual. "The third secretary at the German Embassy? What's he got to do with it?"

"He's Laura Vaher's brother."

"I thought Vaher's wife was called Laura Steinberg."

"That was her stage name. When she was in films."

"Is this Albrecht related to Heinrich von Langenstein, the one with the estate near Harku?"

"Yes, they're both Laura's brothers."

"Well, well, well," said the colonel, "I see I'll need to get our files updated. So, Albrecht must have German citizenship. That's an easy matter for the Baltic Germans, of course. So many of them went to Germany after the land reform. The Baron – their father, that is – was one of the few landowners who stayed. On a much reduced estate, of course. So, one son stays here, one goes back to the Fatherland. Keeping their options open, eh?"

"Is the third secretary post significant?" asked Hallmets.

"It could well be. The ambassador is a figurehead, a messenger who parrots what he's told in Berlin. The consul is just a bureaucrat. But the secretaries, they're the ones you've got to watch. They make friends with politicians and businessmen, fund organisations which favour their country or study its culture, go around on fact-finding trips to report back, and, of course, run spy-rings. So we'll need to keep an eye on Albrecht von Langenstein."

"There's something else I want to ask you about. An incident with a Doctor K is mentioned in one of your reports on Vaher. Can you elaborate? Something's come up which may be linked to that."

"Hmm. It was in early 1925, not long before Vaher was moved to Narva. In fact, it was that incident that got him moved out of Tallinn. Vaher raided a night club in the Old Town, there was a tip-off they were selling opium under the counter. Among the people seized there was a Dr Krummfeldt, owner of an engineering factory – they made parts for tractors, I think, something like that. Krummfeldt gave Vaher some cheek, demanded to be released, got a broken nose for his trouble. Next thing somebody from Berlin phones for a chat – that was with my predecessor, of course – seems Krummfeldt was quite well connected with the German military. He was even pally with Ludendorff. Well, we got him to the best hospital, and fixed his nose, apologised to him profusely, and gave him a compensation payment. It was also decided to get Vaher out of his way. Funny thing was, when we told Krummfeldt that Vaher was being moved out to Narva, he said he hoped the matter wouldn't spoil his career. He appreciated Vaher's technique, he was just unfortunate in being on the receiving end of it."

"But he was moved anyway," observed Hallmets.

"Oh, yes. Not just for Krummfeldt's sake – we had to keep Berlin happy too. Anyway, what has all this to do with Vaher's death. Are you suggesting Krummfeldt's involved?"

"I don't know. We found a note in Vaher's office. It read 'The time is now. We have to act.' Signed 'K.' That's all."

"Could easily be a woman he was involved with."

"Possible. But I remembered the reference to 'Dr K' in the file you sent me. Probably nothing to do with this, but you never know. Is Krummfeldt still around?"

"Oh yes. He's still here, seems to be doing very well, exporting stuff to Sweden, Finland and Latvia. Nothing sinister about him that we can see."

"One other thing. Kadakas and his reports? Isn't it easier if the two of us just talk when necessary? Like we just have."

"Yes, that might be best, especially if we stray onto sensitive ground. I'll relieve Kadakas of his reporting duties, as long as you keep me up-to-date."

35

Artur decided to talk to Lepp first. A phone call from a booth in Independence Square established that the Inspector would be willing to talk to him, but preferred to meet outwith the police station. Artur suggested the *Alt-Revaler*. On reflection he wondered if that was such a good idea, but it was the first thing that had come into his head, and he didn't want to sound indecisive on the phone. They were to meet at ten, which gave Artur time to sketch out an introductory paragraph for his first report.

Crime is the spectre which threatens our freedom. And the police, our brave and noble police, are the vanguard who stand for the people, at the very head of the battle against evil. Back in the days of our subjection to the German landlords and the Russian tax-collectors, we Estonians were too poor to be the victims of crime. But now, in the days of freedom and new-found prosperity, crime has entered our lives. Now that we possess things worth stealing, someone will try to steal them. Those who live in the gutter of our society, many of them aliens, think they can break our laws and prey upon the hard-working majority. They may try, but, out of nothing, our state has nurtured a group of men, and even the occasional woman, who say to these dregs of humanity, 'No! You shall not succeed. We will stand against you, and law and order will be maintained.'

He read it to himself. Yes, this was good stuff. He began the second paragraph: *Yet even one of our top policemen, the best of the best, was not beyond the satanic ambition of the criminals.*

Ah, there was a problem here. He'd just said the criminals were the dregs of society, so how could they get at the best of the best. The answer struck him like a blow. It was so obvious now. Just as God and Satan confront each other, great good is challenged by great evil. This was not the work of ordinary criminals, but a mastermind!

One evening last October, he'd taken Marju to see *The Mask of Fu Manchu*, with Boris Karloff as the fiendish oriental genius. Over the next week he'd gone himself during the day three times to watch it again. Once was enough for Marju, who found the torture scenes distasteful, and noted with disapproval Artur's keen interest in Fu Manchu's daughter, played by Myrna Loy. But for him, the persona of Fu Manchu was irresistibly gripping. How he wished he could attain some of the qualities of the master of evil: the inscrutable look, which rendered all humble before it, the breadth of knowledge which encompassed all the Arts and Sciences, and the ages-old wisdom, which enabled the master to plan his schemes with both vision and practicality. It was only by pure luck that Commissioner Nayland-Smith and his bumbling associates managed to foil Fu Manchu. Why did evil underlings always tie such bad knots? But even though the master was seemingly killed at the end of the film, Artur knew he would be back.

Of course, Vaher's death was not the work of Fu Manchu. Artur was fairly sure Fu Manchu was fictitious. Someone had told him there were books written by an Englishman, but they weren't available in Estonian. No, this was the work of some other genius of the underworld, a satanic doppelganger of Nikolai Vaher, stepped out of a darkened mirror. But who was he?

His thoughts were interrupted by a shadow crossing his table. His heart leapt to his mouth, and he sniffed hurriedly to try to catch the odour of cologne. But there was nothing on the air, only the skeletal form of Inspector Lepp, as if condensed out of the smoky air of the café, materialised at a chair by his table.

Lepp stared at him with unblinking green eyes.

Artur could not hold his gaze. "Artur Simm, *Pealinna Uudised*," he said, holding out his hand. Lepp stared at it as if it were a piece of rotting meat. His narrow, pointed nose twitched, as if he smelt the putrefaction emanating from it. Artur saw that Lepp was wearing black gloves of a fine leather.

"Why you?" asked Lepp, in a hoarse voice. The tone was somehow out of tune, grating on the ear. "Where's that shit Kallas?"

This sounded positive, thought Artur. "I've been assigned as special reporter for the Vaher case. I want the police get the credit they deserve."

Lepp gave a hint of a nod. "Have you talked with Hallmets?" He almost spat the latter's name out.

Artur took his cue. "Yes, I have. And been to his press conference. He said virtually nothing. I got the impression his team wasn't making much progress."

Lepp sneered, with a contempt so tangible that Artur felt it settle on his face and his hands like a humid membrane. "Team! Lesser, a man who's afraid to take the action that's needed, Hekk, a nothing, Maslov, a fat Russian from onion-land, Kadakas, a toy soldier. And a woman. What sort of team is that?"

Artur waited for him to continue.

Lepp's eyes bored into him. "I asked you a question."

"Er, not a very good one, I suppose, the team, I mean. As an experienced police officer, why do you think they're not making progress."

Lepp's thin lips curled at one end. Was this a smile? "Because they're waiting for the solution to fall into their laps. They're not out there looking for it, because they don't know where to look."

"And you do?" Artur immediately felt he'd overstepped the mark, and Lepp's eyes blazed.

"Don't try to be clever with me, Simm. I don't like people who try to be clever. The answer to your question is yes. I do know where to look."

"Lehmja?"

"Obviously."

This wasn't going to be easy. Lepp was a man of few words.

"Do you think Lehmja did it?"

"Yes. And others."

"Others?"

"You heard me, I think."

"Which others?"

"My information suggests Grigori Jesinev and Arnolds Kauščis. Both hardened criminals. Both caught, at one time or another, as Lehmja was, by Vaher."

Artur wrote the names down. "Are you looking for them?"

The eyes blazed again. "Ask me a sensible question."

OK, thought Artur, go for it. "Is there a new devilish genius on the scene, who has decided to take on the police at the highest level."

Lepp stared at him. For a long time. His expression remained fixed. He became very still, like a statue made of grey granite, for his suit was grey and his face was grey. Only his hair remained a strange gingery shade, as if some creature that was also part of him had scurried up his back to perch on his head.

"No comment," he whispered at last.

So, he knows something, thought Artur, but he's not going to say. Another thought crossed his mind. "The man known as Mr P.," he said, "What do you know about him?"

Lepp's eyes widened so much that Artur feared his eyeballs would fall out, roll down the taut grey skin of his cheeks, then drop onto the table. "Popov! Why do you ask that? What do you know?" he hissed.

Artur thought fast. "An informant mentioned his name. In confidence. I can't say any more. Do you have a quote you'd like to give me, for the paper."

Lepp stared again, his eyeballs twitching back and forth, as if he were reading some tiny script hovering before him. "Yes," he intoned, "The killers will be caught. If someone is behind them, he also will be taken. They will receive their just deserts. Law and order will be enforced."

Then he stood up, took a slip of paper from his pocket, and put it on the table. "This is my home telephone number. If you want to talk again, and I'm not at Pikk Street, try me here. Goodbye." And he left.

Artur ordered another coffee and tried to pull his thoughts together. It seemed clear that Lepp agreed with him that there was some big wheel behind Vaher's killing. "Someone is behind them" – Lepp's very words. And Lepp's reaction to his mention of Mr P. Mr. Popov. Artur hadn't realised. But Lepp was an experienced officer, he'd worked closely with Vaher. He'd not dismissed Popov as simply an information seller. It struck Artur that being a purveyor of information would be a clever front for a man who knew everything that was going on, not because he collected scraps of it from an army of tawdry eavesdroppers, but because he was orchestrating it all. It was as if the scales had fallen from his eyes. This, then, was the kind of breakthrough which the great detectives experienced, as they peeled away the skin of the everyday to feel for the red flesh and the pulsing blood beneath.

Wow! He said to himself. Time to write some more.

36

Hallmets bought a copy of *Pealinna Uudised* on the way back to Pikk Street. In his office, he laid out the paper on his desk. On the front page was a headline, '*UNDERWORLD FIGURE SLAIN*.' The sub-heading was '*Brains Beaten out with a Bottle*.' The report was by Jaan Kallas, and revealed that Rudolf Pottsepp, otherwise known as 'Blind Rudi' a feared underworld figure who posed successfully as a blind beggar, had been brutally murdered in a dark lane in Tallinn's Old Town. *'This slaying,'* the report went on, *'illustrates as can no other exemplar, the fervid chaos into which the criminal community has been thrown by the killing of Chief Inspector Vaher. The criminal fraternity seeks to exorcise the stain of this killing, which violated the deep respect those on either side of the law have for each other. First to meet the fatal judgement of his peers is local hard man Eino Lehmja. Rumour has it that other thugs are also suspected. Now in a new twist Rudolf Pottsepp has been executed in the most brutal manner. Police believe he was ambushed in a lane near the Old Town by his assailants, who proceeded to viciously beat him, finally using a heavy liquor bottle to smash in his skull and spatter his brains onto the cobbles.'* The article continued in the same vein, with no new information, for another two paragraphs, concluding with the injunction, *'But are they barking up the wrong tree? Turn to page 4 for another reading of this week's tragic events.'*

Hallmets did as he was bid, to find the headline 'The Black Widow.' He read on:

The deaths of Eino Lehmja and Rudolf Pottsepp lead us to think that Chief Inspector Vaher was killed by underworld figures, seeking revenge for their incarceration at the his hands. The criminal barons themselves may also believe this, and are trying to put their own house in order by offering up those they believe to be guilty of the crime.

But what if that were not the case? What if we are simply looking in the wrong direction, seeing what we want to see. Because Vaher was a policeman, we assume his death was related to his work. But it is a simple statistic, known to every policeman, lawyer, judge and even newspaper reporter, that the majority of murders are family affairs. Statistically, the most likely murderer of a man is his wife.

So let us apply this simple principle to the Vaher case. What do we know about the widow of Chief Inspector Vaher. First that she is a Baltic German. Her name before marriage was Laura von Langenstein. Her father was the late Baron August von Langenstein, owner of the estate of Heinaküla, near Harku, not far from this city, and her mother was Countess Agnethe von Drzinski, daughter of Baron Drzinski, owner of a large estate in East Prussia. Her elder brother Heinrich von Langenstein now owns the estate, or at least what was left of it after the land reform. Her younger brother Albrecht von Langenstein spent much of his life in Germany, remaining there after attending the

University of Jena. However, he has recently re-appeared here in Estonia, being appointed third secretary in the German Embassy in Tallinn.

Another important fact about the widow Vaher. Proua Vaher, or should we say, Laura Steinberg, for that was her stage name, featured in a number of silent films, her most memorable role that of Princess Aino in The Princess of Livonia.

However we would draw the reader's attention to one of her less-well-known films, Death by Tramcar. *In this film, Laura Steinberg plays a scheming and unfaithful wife who hires two criminals to kill her husband, so that she may marry her lover. They achieve this by pushing him under a tram as it rushes past. In the end, of course, they are caught, and her part revealed. Her end can be imagined. Did this film suggest an idea for a real-life plot? Who knows, dear reader.*

According to our film critic, her acting abilities were limited, and her films only moderately successful. It is also said that her voice was not suitable for talking pictures, being of a timbre unsuited to the demands of the microphone. And thus she gave up the pursuit of stardom.

What does a lady do, then, when she has no career? She marries, of course. And so, leaving her filmic fame behind her, Laura fell into the arms of Nikolai Vaher. Maybe they were attracted to each other. He was a handsome, ambitious and successful policeman, who had just been appointed deputy chief of the CID in Tallinn. She was a film star and an aristocrat. Who knows? Maybe it worked for a while. But we have it on good authority, from witnesses, that their marriage was a rocky one. Nikolai Vaher was the son of a farmer in the north east of our country. Maybe, despite his looks, he did not have the refinement which an aristocratic lady required in her spouse? Maybe her brothers disapproved of her marrying a man who was an Estonian, as well as a commoner. When I interviewed Proua Vaher yesterday, she did not deny that the Vahers had been considering divorce.

I also could not help noticing, when I visited the Vahers' opulent mansion in the exclusive suburb of Nõmme, that they were surrounded by the trappings of wealth. Proua Vaher claimed this money was inherited from her father, who died in 1923. Finally, I did not form an impression of deep grief in Proua, or should I say Frau *Vaher. Maybe that is not the way of aristocrats or film stars.*

I would suggest the police, who at the moment look as if they have no ideas at all, take a closer look at this 'Merry Widow.' Perhaps then we will all be surprised.

He considered these articles. The first told him that Kallas had an informant within the police headquarters. That was worrying, but there was not much they could do about it right now. He was not passing on highly confidential information that was only known to a few people. Nevertheless, it was irritating, and they'd have to be careful about who knew what.

Kallas' suspicions following his meeting with *Proua* Vaher echoed his own, though he had not gone so far as to suspect her of murder. And Kallas was right to suggest that her role should be looked at more closely. However, his crude insinuation that she was a murderess was not helpful to the investigation. Anything Laura Vaher had to hide would now be buried twice as deep. He also feared that hotheads incited by Kallas's invective might try to cause trouble at the Vahers' house.

He asked Marta to connect him with the police station in Nõmme. He spoke to an inspector, and warned him there might be trouble at the Vaher house. He was told it had already started. A group of people had come out from Tallinn by bus, located the house, and started shouting insults and throwing stones at the windows. The police had been called immediately, and the house now had round-the-clock protection. *Proua* Vaher had been advised to stay elsewhere for the moment. It would be easier to protect the house if she were not resident.

Hallmets turned over the first page of the paper to see the foreign news on page 3. 'Hitler takes full powers' was the headline; the article described how the previous day a bill had been passed in the Reichstag giving Hitler's government power to rule by decree. So Hitler had not wasted time in setting up a dictatorship. Although the new powers were to last only for four years in the first instance, he had no doubt that before that period expired some excuse would be found to extend them, perhaps indefinitely. This wasn't a good sign. So far dictatorships had been confined to smaller European countries, such as Lithuania and Portugal, Italy being the only major power to adopt an authoritarian regime. But Germany lay at the heart of Europe, it was a modern country with an educated electorate; and still the people turned away from controlling their own destiny. Where would it end? He feared for Estonia's fragile democracy.

37

Going through to the workroom, he saw that Larsson and Maslov were there, Larsson reading through some papers, and Maslov chewing a pencil whilst staring down at a blank piece of paper. They both looked up when Hallmets came in.

"Glad you're both here, he said, "How did it go. Eva, ladies first."

"Very useful, chief. We saw Pfinster. Sjoestedt died a few years ago. First he denied Vaher was a client. Then we showed him the bill, so he said Vaher had only wanted some advice. Then Henno said would he rather talk down at Pikk Street, and we'd make sure all his posh clients would find out, and wonder what he'd been pulled in for. So he admitted they'd done Vaher's accounts for him, because he had some 'complicated investments.' His very words. Henno asked for a copy, he said they were confidential, Henno told him to put his coat on, he handed them over – 'Under protest,' he said – and demanded a receipt. So now I'm going through them."

"Good. Anything interesting so far?"

"As the man said, they're complicated." She indicated the sheets spread out on the table.

"OK. Thanks Eva. Oleg?"

"Well, boss, we went down to the liquor store – 'Alkohol' the place is called, certainly couldn't be clearer, started looking round the shop. Some interesting brands I'd never heard of before, so I asked about them. The guy running the place, name of Idla, Arno Idla, he started looking worried and asked who we were. Then he got a lot more worried, said he just sold the stuff, didn't know anything about it. When we asked to see round the back, what he had in store, he made a run for it. Sadly he tripped over Ilmar's foot, landed on his chin. Quite an Ali Baba's cave back there, all sorts of interesting stuff. Lots of duty-free that hasn't seen a boat, if you know what I mean. We called in the excise people then, they're still there, I'd guess. We brought him back, and Ilmar's keeping him on ice downstairs, thought you'd like to talk to him."

"Sounds good. Let's go."

Hallmets and Maslov made their way down to the ground floor, where the interview rooms were situated, along a corridor with grey walls and grey lino on the floor. At the end they could see Hekk sitting on an upright wooden chair by a door, reading a newspaper. As they came up, he folded the paper up and thrust it into his pocket, and stood up.

"Hi, chief," he said, "We thought you'd like to take a look at this one."

"Thanks," replied Hallmets, "you two can talk to him, I'll watch."

"There's a viewing room; the next door along." He pointed along the corridor to an unmarked door.

Hallmets found himself in a small room. He turned on the light, but the bulb was very weak. The reason for that was clear. A couple of chairs faced a window through which the well-lit interview room was visible: a two-way mirror. He sat down to watch.

He saw a thin man with thinning hair and a thin moustache sitting behind a worn table. His sad expression changed to fear when he saw Maslov come into the room. He calmed down somewhat as Hekk came in after. Maslov and Hekk sat at the table.

Hekk began the interrogation. He smiled encouragingly. "*Härra* Idla, can I confirm that you own the shop known as 'Alkohol?'"

"Well, I don't own it, I mean, it's my shop, yes, but I don't own the shop, it's rented."

"Ah. So the premises are rented. But you own the liquor-selling business?"

"Yes, like I said, it's my shop."

"Could you explain to us why you tried to run out of the shop when we asked about some of your stock?"

The man had worked out his answer whilst he was waiting to be questioned. "Yes, I thought this man" – he nodded at Maslov – "was a criminal, and he was going to attack me and rob my shop. You hadn't told me you were police." He smiled at Hekk.

"You know that's not true, *Härra* Idla," said Hekk quietly, "Now, I'd like to ask a few questions about some of the items you stock in your shop. What about the product called *Sandtsteiner* which the label declares to be a herbal liqueur imported from Germany? We know there is no such product in Germany. So where do you get it?"

"I didn't know that. The guy who supplies me told me it was German."

"And his name is ...?"

Now Idla was challenged. He had used up all his creativity. He thought hard. "I don't remember."

"Please, *Härra* Idla, don't waste our time," said Hekk, "Or we might stop being friendly." Maslov grinned, and winked at Idla. Hekk went on, "We know from the paperwork in your shop that you yourself collect your stock, you don't have a supplier. Most of it you collect from legitimate sources – Saku and Viru beer, Põltsamaa fruit wine, and so on. But there doesn't seem to be any paperwork for *Sandtsteiner*. And one or two other products. Tell us about *Sandtsteiner*."

Idla said nothing. He was sweating. His hands lay on the table and all at once Maslov seized one of them in his large fist, and squeezed, so that Idla winced, and tried unsuccessfully to pull it away.

"I'm getting frustrated," said Maslov to Hekk, "I want to snap his fingers off, one by one, and then stuff them down his throat. Why don't we take him downstairs?"

Idla looked frightened. "Please," he gasped.

"I don't think that's going to be necessary," said Hekk, unpeeling Maslov's hand, "not yet, anyway. *Härra* Idla, talk to me, please."

"All right, all right," said Idla, "Its not as if it's a big deal. I don't know why you're making such a fuss. All the shops do it, and your people know that too."

"*Sandtsteiner?*" pressed Hekk.

"All right. It's a guy out on a farm towards Rakvere, he makes it. It's good stuff, forty-two percent."

"And he doesn't pay duty on it?"

"What do you think?"

"You're absolutely right, *Härra* Idla," put in Maslov, "It is good stuff. I tried it. So why the hell doesn't the guy sell it legitimately and make a virtue of the fact that it's Estonian. He'd sell loads of it, make a fortune. You tell him that from me, when you meet him in jail."

Idla paled. "Look, I can settle any duty that's due. I don't want to go to jail, just for selling a few bottles of moonshine."

"OK," said Hekk, "That's better. What about this vodka, *Leikari,* where do you get it from?"

Idla frowned. "I don't know who makes it. Could be made from anything."

"Beet," said Maslov, "It's made from beet."

"How do you know?" said Idla, "It's just vodka, it all tastes the same."

"I can smell it," said Maslov. "Beet."

"Why don't you know who makes it?" asked Hekk, "Don't you go to his farm to collect it. You've got plenty of it in your storeroom, you must have been there quite recently. In your van, perhaps."

"In the van, yes, but I don't go to the producer. I collect it from an address in Nõmme. A big house. There's a shed at the back, and I collect it from there."

Hekk slid a piece of paper across the table. "Is this the address?"

"Yes, how did you know ...?"

"We've been watching you, *Härra* Idla, for quite a while. Your van was observed as recently as last night going there. So who do you deal with there?"

"I don't know his full name. He's German, I think. Calls himself Ingvar. All the business is done in cash of course."

"Don't you think it's odd that you don't go directly to the producer?"

"No. According to Ingvar, the distillery is in the south, near Helme somewhere, so the producer uses the shed in Nõmme for distribution in the Tallinn area. Makes sense when you think about it." He looked at Maslov, still fearfully, but his curiosity overcame him. "You seem to know your vodka. What's your opinion of *Leikari*?"

Maslov smiled, and patted Idla's hand. "Very tasty, my friend. You're going to miss it."

38

Artur Simm was enjoying his new role. He read through his first on-the-spot report again. It was gripping stuff, he had to admit. He had captured the lack of progress by Hallmets, referring to the noncommital responses to most questions. He named Hallmets' team, and wondered if these were the right people to be on the case. He contrasted their uncertainty and indecision with the dynamism and vision of Lepp. This was the man, he argued, who should be leading the case. '*Inspector Lepp believes,*' he concluded, '*that a criminal mastermind is behind the killing of Chief Inspector Vaher, an evil genius who has spun his web in Estonia. Where did this man come from? Perhaps from the depths of the Soviet Union, a country so vast and disorganised that evil flourishes at its heart, and runs rampant through the endless primeval wastes of Siberia. We may surmise that a man of dark brilliance arose there, built up his devilish edifice of criminal empire, but found the pickings too poor, the laws no challenge, the underworld too unsophisticated, too dull to match his vision. And so he has moved towards the West, towards the old centres of civilsation and culture. Not for him the savage onslaughts, the chaotic and temporary conquests of Genghis Khan or Timur, when the empires of Alexander or Napoleon may be his exemplars. And his first step into the West is here, in Estonia. We are the first bastion of the civilised world. And so we must hold firm, we must unveil and defeat the dark Caesar who seeks to make Tallinn his Rome.*'

His mention of Genghis Khan reminded Artur again of Fu Manchu. In *The Mask of Fu Manchu*, the oriental mastermind had presented himself as a kind of reincarnation of Genghis Khan, seeking to lead the Asiatic races in a murderous crusade against the West. 'You can kill the men, and take their women for yourselves,' declared Fu Manchu to the crowd of baying oriental chieftains. Myrna Loy in her shimmering oriental costume flickered before his eyes again. He realised he was hungry. Time for lunch. He waved the waitress over and ordered a cheese and leek pie and a bottle of beer.

He had just taken the first bite of his warm pie, and closed his eyes to enjoy the feel and taste of the food, when all at once he felt a shapeless fear grow in his stomach. Then the odour that stirred it reached his brain. He opened his eyes, and by him sat the man he least wanted to meet in the whole city, and yet the man who may, he thought, hold the key to everything.

"You enjoy your lunch, my friend?" said Mr P., his voice almost a whisper. It reminded Artur of Peter Lorre, whom he'd seen as the child-killer in *M*.

But now Artur was careful. Mr P might be the mastermind.

"Good afternoon, *Härra* P.," he   said, attempting a measured and neutral tone, "How are you today?"

"The better for seeing you, my friend. I think you have some names for me."

"Yes, of course. Hallmets' team. Larsson, Maslov, Lesser, Hekk, Kadakas."

"That's good. I like a man who knows what I want."

"But you knew that already, didn't you?"

"One should always set one's new employees an exercise which enables them to demonstrate their worth. Don't you agree, *Härra* Simm?"

"I'm hardly your employee. You're forcing me to do this."

"Dear me, no. But a good employer needs to, how can I put it, incentivise his employees."

"If I'm your employee, what are you going to pay me?"

"Well now, that's the right approach, Artur, the businesslike approach. Too much emotion gets in the way of good business, don't you think? So what do you think you're worth?"

"I've been assigned to the Vaher case. I'll give you information, but I want information I don't have in return." Artur could hardly believe what he was saying. Who was this tough guy who had borrowed his mouth?

"An interesting proposition. And you say you've been assigned to the Vaher case? What about our friend *Härra* Kallas? Is he doing the weather forecast with seaweed now?"

"No, he's still the main crime reporter. But they want someone down in the trenches, so to speak, reporting on the minute-by-minute activity that makes up the investigation, capturing the feel of it, the excitement of the chase, interviews with the front line people, that sort of thing."

"Hmm. Yes, I think you and I can do business. It's such a pity you weren't so reasonable when we first met. Your finger would still be in one piece. So who have you spoken to so far?"

"Hallmets and Lepp."

"Hallmets. What did you learn from him?"

"Nothing much. The usual 'no comment till we've something to tell you' stuff. I don't think they're making a lot of progress, to be honest."

"What do you know of Hallmets?"

"Not a lot. He's in charge of the CID in Tartu. Before that I think he was in Viljandi. Got a medal in the War – that's where he lost a few fingers."

"See if you can find out more about him. His past, his family, personal details. Why not do a feature on him? Give me all you get on him. Now, what about Lepp?"

"He's the man who should be running the show. He's dynamic, and knows what he's doing."

"And what is he doing?"

"Looking into Lehmja's death. But he believes there's some criminal mastermind behind it all. You don't know who that is, do you?"

"Me? Come, come, Artur, you'll have to bring me some very useful information before you can expect an answer to a question like that. To start with, you could find out for me who Lepp thinks this person is."

Mr P. got up to go, then seemed to be reminded of something, and sat down again. "Just one more thing. One of my employees, known as 'Blind Rudi', met with an unfortunate accident last night. I'd sent him to have a word with you, as it happens. Do you know anything about it?"

Artur tried to give the impression of thinking back to the previous evening. "Er, no. No-one spoke to me after I left here yesterday. I went to the station and had a drink then went home. No-one approached me."

"Well, no need to worry about it, Artur. I'm carrying out my own inquiry. You see, I really don't like it when one of my employees is brutally murdered. They are all dear to me, so if they are attacked, I always seek to be revenged." He smiled, and left.

Artur remained sitting, staring at his now cold leek and cheese pie. He took a gulp of his beer. What the hell was he doing? He'd agreed with Marju that he'd get out of all this, and now he was in it deeper than ever. However, he reflected, it seemed Mr P. was still in the dark about who killed Blind Rudi.

39

The black Volvo swung off the road between two tall stone gateposts – there was no longer a gate between – and onto a narrow drive edged on either side by a line of poplar trees.

"Here we are," said Lembit from the front, "Heinaküla Manor. I guess that gateway used to be the border of his Lordship's land. Before the Land Reform, that is."

On either side of the drive, other tracks led off at intervals towards, Hallmets presumed, the houses of the farms created when the land was divided after the War.

"Excuse me, Sir," said Kadakas, sitting beside him in the back, "How do we address the owner? Do we call him Baron or what?"

"No," said Hallmets, "These titles don't exist here now. If he wants his servants to call him *Herr Baron*, that's up to him. But for us, he's plain *Härra* von Langenstein. How's your German, Ants?"

"OK, I think, Sir."

"Good. This guy may not have bothered to learn any Estonian, so we may have to talk with him in German. We'll see. And Lembit?"

"Yes, Guv?"

"Same as you did at Vaher's place, eh?"

"Understood, Guv. No problem. Oh, here's the old place now."

The car swung to the right and there was the manor house. A two-storey building in the neoclassical style, built of light-coloured stone. The central section resembled the frontage of a Greek temple, Ionic columns reaching the full height of the building, supporting a wide pediment; and there were matching wings on either side. A staircase at the centre led up to the main door. The building had been recently whitewashed, and looked in good condition, in contrast to many of the manor houses, which, since the land reform, had become rather dilapidated.

"I'll drop you gents here at the front and take the car round the back," said Lembit, "Get a better look round that way."

Kadakas had come in to Police HQ at lunchtime, after a few hours sleep, looking like the smartly-uniformed young officer that he was. Now Hallmets led him up the stone stairs. He had asked Marta to phone ahead and alert Heinrich von Langenstein that they were coming, and a gentleman in a dark burgundy smoking jacket and black trousers came out of the main door to greet them. He was perhaps in his early forties, of average height though somewhat running to fat, with blond hair and moustache, and a ruby complexion. He smiled amiably.

"*Guten Tag, meine Herren*," he said, clicking his heels, and bowing slightly, then held his hand out to Hallmets. "*Hauptkomissar* Hallmets, I presume. Heinrich von Langenstein, at your service."

Hallmets shook hands, "I'm pleased to meet you, *Herr* von Langenstein." Then he indicated Kadakas. "And this is *Leutnant* Kadakas, on secondment from our armed forces." Kadakas stood ramrod-straight and saluted. Von Langenstein made to salute back, but stopped himself, and instead offered the lieutenant his hand. "I'm sorry," he said, "Old habits die hard. I was in the Imperial army during the War."

"Ah, yes, which one?" asked Hallmets innocently.

"The Russian, of course," smiled von Langenstein, "Yes, I know, there were many in the Empire who, as war approached, worried about the loyalty of us Baltic Germans. But we proved on the battlefield that our oath to the Czar meant something to us. Of course, after the revolution, with no Czar, the oath was, in effect, annulled."

"And what did you do then?"

"I returned here to the estate. Things were of course in turmoil. My father was still alive then. He advised me to join the forces of General von der Goltz."

"Seeking to make a new German Duchy of the Baltic provinces?"

"I prefer to think of it as seeking to establish a stable state here, in the face of the bolshevik menace. Had the local populations joined us, this would now be a powerful and unified Baltic state, able to resist the communist menace when it next arises. But alas, they wanted their own little countries. Short-termism, I'm afraid. They'll come to regret it."

Hallmets felt that the local populations deserved to determine their own fate, but did not wish to fall out with the *Herr Baron* so early in their conversation. "Then I think we fought on opposite sides at Võnnu."

"*Ach.* You are that Colonel Hallmets, who outflanked our offensive. I congratulate you, Sir. It was a bold move. And I hope there are no hard feelings."

"Not at all. By the way, do you prefer that we talk in German or Estonian? We are happy with either."

"German, if you don't mind. Of course, I've learnt some Estonian since the War, but my vocabulary is mostly concerned with running the estate. Or what's left of it. But do come in, gentlemen, may I offer you some coffee?"

He led them into an airy, and rather chilly, hallway, in which a marble staircase curved up to a balcony, then through a door on the left to a cosier and warmer room, the walls lined with books. "My library. I've asked Hans to serve our coffee here." He indicate three padded chairs, of a colour matching his jacket, grouped round a low table.

In a moment a servant entered, a muscular young man with cropped hair on a bullet-shaped head, and an impassive expession. He put the tray down on the table and silently poured the coffee.

"*Danke, Hans,*" said von Langenstein.

"*Herr Baron,*" said Hans, bowed, and left.

"Well now, gentlemen, what can I do for you. My sister told me I should expect a visit from you, *Herr Hauptkommissar,* so it is not a surprise. A routine matter, she believed."

"That's correct. In a case of murder, it's necessary to check the whereabouts of everyone connected to the victim. This enables us to eliminate those who are not under suspicion, and to focus on those who are. It's often simply a matter of routine, but, I'm afraid, necessary."

"Of course. I understand completely. And thank you for coming in person. Please ask whatever you like. But first, do have a marzipan fruit. Our cook made them this morning. I can't resist marzipan, myself."

After sampling a marzipan potato, dusted with cocoa powder, moist and flavoursome inside, and sipping his coffee, Hallmets began. "Please, *Herr* von Langenstein, compliment your cook for me. These are superb. You are the eldest sibling of *Frau* Vaher?"

"Yes, that's right. She's the second child of our father. Then there is Albrecht, who works now at the German Embassy here. And finally Lucia. I believe she lives somewhere in the south of France now. She married an artist. A Jew she met in Germany when she was studying."

"Is he well-known?"

"I've no idea. We have no contact with her."

"And are you yourself married?"

"Yes. Of course, the von Langenstein line must be continued. My wife has gone with the children to visit her parents in Saxony. Her father is not well, and we felt some more company would cheer him up, help him to recover. Before you ask, they've been there for a week now, and will probably stay another couple, depending on how things go with her father."

"So it's just you at the moment?"

"And the house servants, of course. There's Hans, and the cook, and one of the maids, the other is with my wife. Hans will confirm for you that I was here on the night of poor Nikolai's death. And so will the gardeners."

"You have several?"

"Usually none at all. But we have a group of young people here at the moment. From a voluntary organisation in Germany. Like the Boy Scouts. They come here for a holiday, and work on a project while here, in this case, tidying up the garden and rebuilding the garden house, which was badly damaged during the War. They're staying in the stables. I spoke to them that night too, they'll all vouch for me."

"That's most helpful of you, Sir. May I ask, since the land reform, you have a much smaller estate than previously. How do you manage to live?"

"I'm glad you asked me that. Most people here have no sympathy for us former landowners at all. They think we deserve to be poor. When my father decided that we would not flee from our ancestral land – the von Langensteins have been here since 1322 – we considered seriously how to support ourselves in our new and much straitened circumstances. My father sent me to Agricultural College in Germany for two years, and the farm we have left is run very efficiently, using the latest techniques and materials. We also breed horses, and that's been very successful. There's a lot of demand from newly wealthy Estonians. Fine horses have become a bit of a status symbol."

Hallmets remembered his daughter Liisa begging for a horse for her thirteenth birthday. They got her a dog instead. "Yes, that's true," he said. "Would you say your sister's marriage to Chief Inspector Vaher was a happy one?"

"Absolutely. Obviously they had their differences now and then, I mean, what couple doesn't, but yes, I would say they were happy together. And well-matched too."

"I'm not sure what you mean."

"She was always a spirited girl. The whole film thing was done to defy our father, that's all it was. That she happened to be quite good at it was a lucky coincidence. She needed someone who could control her, channel her self-will, keep her on a sensible path, if you know what I mean. Vaher was just the man to do that. I don't know what she will do without him. I really don't."

"I guess you'll soon find out," said Hallmets, "Well, now we must be going. Thank you so much for your time, *Herr* von Langenstein." He stood up.

"Not at all, Chief Inspector. The pleasure was all mine."

A couple of miles down the road from the manor, Hallmets told

Lembit to stop. "OK, Lembit, what did you find?"

"Interesting place, Guv. Some nice gee-gees in a field behind the house. I had a chat with one of the stable lads, he's very proud of them. Must earn his lordship a bob or two. But there's something else. A big barn, the lad was very reluctant to say what they did there. And a truck parked there, they're shifting stuff around. Not the sort of truck you'd use for hay or any sort of farm produce, more the sort you'd put boxes on, then strap them round and put a tarp over the top."

"Did you see any boxes?"

"No, not here. But I did at his sister's place, in that shed round the back. Bit of a coincidence, eh?"

"We certainly need a closer look at that barn."

"Can't Dr Luik give us a search warrant?" asked Kadakas.

"I doubt he'd be very willing," said Hallmets. "We'll have to be a bit undercover, as they say in the spy business. Fancy a bit more creeping around in the dark, Ants?"

"I'm up for it, Sir. Right away?"

"You'll have noticed that it's not dark. And you're in uniform."

"I didn't quite understand why you wanted that, Sir, I mean, me in uniform."

"These people appreciate uniforms. I hoped it would relax him a bit."

40

Jaan Kallas put down the phone. He'd just received a tip-off, anonymous of course. Be at the kiosk at four. Which kiosk? he asked. Don't be stupid, said the voice, and hung up.

Kallas called in on Tõnu the photographer on his way out of the building, and the two soon reached Kaarel Rebane's kiosk. Ten to four and nothing happening. He stared up at the viewpoint. A man was leaning on the railing, looking down on them. They couldn't throw somebody off at this time of day, in broad daylight. Maybe a car would drive past and the body would be tossed out. He assumed there would be a body somewhere. Why else be at the kiosk – the killer was hardly summoning people to a press conference. There were several men hanging around whom he recognised as fellow hacks. His tip-off hadn't been exclusive then; that was a disappointment. At least that creep Simm wasn't there. He wondered what crap the little twerp would produce for the morning's edition. He noticed some of the hacks had tin mugs of steaming coffee. Kaarel Rebane had a little kerosene stove in his kiosk and was doing a healthy trade in coffee and pastries.

Almost four. Kallas could sense the expectancy in the air. The photographers who were there checked their cameras, held them ready to grab the first shots of whatever was going to happen.

A black car screeched to a halt by the kiosk. The photographers rushed forward as the passenger door swung open. But the cameras were lowered again as Inspector Lepp stepped out. The Inspector stood by the car, taking in the press gathering. One of the hacks shouted, "So you got a tip-off too, eh?" Lepp ignored him.

They all waited another five minutes, each man looking anxiously around, keen to be the first to spot whatever was going to happen. Lepp took out a set of field glasses and began to peer up at the viewpoint. "Shit!" he said loudly, "He's up there." The hacks and snappers swung like a synchronised gymnastic display to stare up at the viewpoint. All that Kallas could see was a man leaning on the railing, looking down at them.

Then, as if the spell was broken, they made for the steps, every man for himself. Kallas didn't join in the race. He knew Tõnu would get the picture. Lepp shouted at them, "Don't touch anything!" but made no attempt to hold them back. As they charged up, one of the photographers was given a sharp push in the back and tripped over, dropping his camera.

Kallas and Lepp followed them up at a more dignified pace. "Who is it?" Kallas asked the inspector.

"Kauščis," said Lepp.

Arnolds Kauščis. Kallas knew of him. A Lithuanian hard man who'd made his home in Tallinn, no doubt when Kaunas got too hot for him. Hired muscle for whoever could pay. Like Lehmja. Kallas could see the flashes, as the snappers got to work.

Even before he reached the viewpoint Kallas could see that the man leaning on the railing was dead. He appeared oddly dwarfish, little more than a metre high, and stocky, with a bushy brown moustache and brown hair cut military-short. Then Kallas realised he'd been propped with his knees on the ground, his chest against the railing, and his arms over it. He could even see the exit wound in the front of the man's throat. Shot in the back of the neck, then. Execution-style.

As Kallas reached the viewing platform, he saw the group of journalists crowding round the body, no doubt trampling any footprints the killers might have left.

"Get back, now!" commanded Lepp, and the crowd receded slightly. Lepp pushed his way through, violently shoving aside one man who was slow to give him room. He looked carefully at the corpse, surveying him from head to toe, then ducked under the railing, and holding on to it, leaned back to look at the corpse from the front. Then he returned and gently lifted the man's jacket, first at one side, then the other.

Kallas noticed that two other plain-clothes officers had now appeared – they must have been in Lepp's car, and followed them up. Kallas recognised them as Kleber and Pilvik, both big men, Kleber identifiable by his heavy eyebrows and thick moustache, Pilvik by his shaven head and broken nose. They pushed the journalists back with ease and some relish, until they were a couple of metres from the body. Lepp faced them, and waited for silence. He indicated the body. "This man is Arnolds Kauščis, a Lithuanian national currently resident in Estonia. He has a prison record, both here and in his country of birth, for crimes of violence."

"A thug?" someone asked.

"You said it," answered Lepp. "*Härra* Kauščis is dead. Death appears to be due to a gunshot wound in the neck, entering at the rear and exiting through the throat at the front."

"OGPU style?" came a comment from one of the group, "So the Reds were involved."

Lepp ignored the remark. "It is not possible at this point to say how long *Härra* Kauščis has been dead, nor whether there are any other injuries. Further information will be available after the post-mortem, which will take place either this evening or tomorrow morning. Any questions?"

"Did you get a tip-off, Inspector?"

"I can confirm that at approximately three forty-five, I received an anonymous telephone message requesting that I attend *Härra* Rebane's kiosk. I came there as soon as I received the message."

"Who did it?"

"If I knew that, I wouldn't be standing here wasting my time with you people."

"Who do you think did it?"

"It's not my place to speculate. However, one theory might be that the same people who pushed *Härra* Lehmja down from here yesterday may be to blame."

"Do you think Lehmja and Kauščis killed Vaher?"

"That is one line of inquiry which the police are following. We are also seeking to interview one Grigori Jesinev, an Estonian citizen of Russian extraction."

"Another hard man," came a comment from the crowd.

"Assuming these men killed Vaher," asked Kallas, "Who do you think was behind them?"

"What makes you think there was someone behind them?"

"Come on, Inspector," said Kallas, "These guys aren't hired for their intellect."

Lepp looked coldly at Kallas. "You mean some sort of criminal mastermind? Like Professor Moriarty or Fu Manchu?"

"*Doctor* Fu Manchu," shouted somebody else.

"Someone was behind them, wasn't he?" Kallas persisted. "Maybe now he's getting rid of the evidence."

"Or she," came another shout, "Revenge of the black widow!" There was laughter.

"This is a scene of death," snapped Lepp, "It is no place for jocularity. Please leave this area now to allow our investigation to begin." Kleber and Pilvik began shoving the newsmen back towards the stairs.

"Someone killed Vaher," Kallas called to Lepp, "And got away with it, didn't they? How do you feel about that, Inspector?"

Lepp's eyes narrowed. "I won't forget you, Kallas," he snarled, "Now piss off!"

41

Hallmets rubbed his eyes. He must have dozed off whilst writing his report. He remembered being told of the discovery of Arnolds Kauščis' body. He would have preferred someone other than Lepp to have handled the case, but Lepp having got to the scene right away, thanks to his invitation, it wouldn't look good if the case was then taken off him, so he okayed it. He supposed that the tip-off had been directed to Lepp because of his involvement in the Lehmja case. But it wasn't good that that Lepp was handling both cases. At least Jesinev might still be alive. If so, there was always the possibility that they could reach him, and find out who'd paid him. If indeed he was involved at all in Vaher's death.

He put a call through to Colonel Reinart, and brought him up to date with developments. The colonel was particularly interested in Hallmets' impressions of Heinrich von Langenstein.

"He would welcome the return of German control over the Baltic states," said Hallmets, "Quite sympathetic to the Nazis, I would guess. Cut off his sister when she married a Jew."

"That doesn't surprise me. Guess who was one of his pals when he was young. Alfred Rosenberg."

"The one who wrote that book about the Jews. What was it called?"

"*The Myth of the Twentieth Century*. Heinrich's a bit older than him, but his brother Albrecht was in the same year as Rosenberg at the Petri-Realschule here in Tallinn, and they were very close. I'm told the book is unreadable, but its one of the key Nazi texts, and Rosenberg is very high in the party. We think when Albrecht went to Germany after the land reform, he met up with Rosenberg again."

"Do you think he's working for Rosenberg?"

"We don't know. It's not even clear what Rosenberg's job is in Berlin at the moment. But Albrecht must be pretty close to the Nazis to have got the embassy job."

"Hmm. Heinrich said he had some German Boy Scouts, or something like that, staying with him, helping with his gardening."

"They're more likely to be Hitler Youth. I wonder what they're really up to. Thanks for that, Chief Inspector, Do keep me up to date."

Hallmets went through to the workroom to see how Larsson was getting with Vaher's finances. As he came in he noticed she was wearing glasses. She looked up quickly and made as if to take them off, then realised there was no point. "I only wear them for reading," she said. Hallmets understood right away. Many in the police were opposed to the idea of women officers. Even a touch of long-sightedness might be enough excuse to get rid of Eva Larsson.

"That's not going to be a problem here," he said, "Now, what have you got? Apart from eyestrain."

She laughed. "Most of it is perfectly normal. But he seems to have had a couple of extra sources of income, over and above his police salary. First, there's a regular monthly payment into his bank account of 2,000 crowns from the August von Langenstein Stiftung. That's a trust set up by Laura's father for the benefit of his descendants. That may be to keep Laura in the style to which she's accustomed. And second, there's a payment of 2,500 crowns a month from a company called Astiz AB, based in Norrköping, Sweden. In the accounts it's marked only as 'consultancy fee.'"

"What does the company do?"

"They buy and sell things. Mainly machinery and weapons."

"Vaher can hardly have been making weapons in his back garden. Can you contact them, see if they can tell you what it was all about. Where are Maslov and Kadakas, by the way?"

"They've gone down to the canteen for something to eat."

"Ask them to see me when they get back. I've a job for them."

42

The news of Kauščis' death came as a surprise to Artur, and he had to rewrite his article slightly, to take it into account. He was glad Lepp was in charge of the case, knowing Lepp's opinion of Kallas. He would talk to Lepp again tomorrow, get a few more quotes. He went down to Pikk Street, only to be told Hallmets was busy and couldn't see him. He sauntered into the police canteen, and noticed Sõnn sitting in one corner, with a plate of blood pudding and fried potato. But Sõnn was not willing to talk about the Pottsepp case, or indeed anything else. He invited Artur to leave the building before he was thrown out. Artur took his advice.

He went back to the paper, finished off his piece, and sent it to Hunt. half an hour later a message came back, saying the article was accepted. He was relieved. His first crime piece would be published. Goodbye to seaweed and folktales. Time to go home.

He bought a bottle of fruit wine on the way. By the time he got there Marju had finished her day at the salon, and was making the evening meal, a casserole of beans and sausage. She was pleased to see the wine, and was keen to reassure him that no-one had disturbed her at her work. He also assured her that the problem had been solved, that his connection with Mr. P. was at an end, and that his first crime article had been accepted. They had a very pleasant evening indeed. But before going to bed, Artur wedged the chair under the handle of the front door. "Better to be on the safe side," he said, "We don't want to be disturbed now."

Jaan Kallas wasn't so satisfied. He was pleased that it was he and not Simm who had been invited to the display of Kauščis' body, but Kauščis' death had not really taken things forward. Just another thug eliminated. However, he was puzzled that Lepp had been tipped off, rather than Hallmets. Even if Hallmets was an unknown from Tartu, he would have thought that, as the officer in charge of the Vaher case, it would have been important to whoever was killing off the thugs to get their message direct to him. Yet whoever was behind it wanted Lepp to be there. Why? Was it someone who had had previous dealings with Lepp. Or someone who knew him personally. Like Laura Vaher. Lepp, as one of Vaher's close circle, could well have mixed with the Vahers out of work. Was Laura arranging for the thugs whom she had paid to kill her husband to be disposed of, and having Lepp at the scene to link the deaths with the crime bosses? It was ingenious in its audacity.

But how could he prove it? Any direct approach to either of them would get him nowhere, and they would be alerted to his suspicions. Now he needed evidence, something undeniable that could be splashed across the front page of *Pealinna Uudised*. He phoned his colleague, gossip columnist Angelina Horovits. Angelina confirmed that there had been other men in film star Laura Steinberg's life before she had married Vaher and given up her film career. Unfortunately none of them was called Lepp, but he hadn't been expecting that – it would have been a real bonus.

Finally he made his way up to the next floor, to the dimly-lit room where Tõnu Raudsepp lurked amongst his chemical jars, developing trays and photos hanging up to dry. Thankfully Tõnu was in his outer room, reading a novel, and not in his inner sanctum, the developing room. He put the book down hurriedly as Kallas entered.

"Well, Tõnu, what have you got for me?" asked Kallas.

Tõnu checked briefly through the photos hanging on clothes pegs from a cord tied to hooks high on opposite walls of the little room. He took one down and passed it to Kallas. "I think you'll like this one. I ducked under the railing and got a shot looking up at Kauščis' body. What do you think?"

"Yes, it's good," replied Kallas, "We'll use it. How about one of Lepp?"

Tõnu fished another three pictures down. "Have a look at these."

The thing that Kallas liked about Tõnu was that he didn't just record the facts. He had an artist's eye for a composition, and could often capture a crime scene in a way none of the other snappers did. And yes, here was one of Lepp looking suitably arrogant, with a contemptuous sneer in the twisted ends of his thin mouth.

"Yes, this one's good, Tõnu. Do you mind if I see what else you've got?" The other admirable trait that Tõnu possessed was that he didn't stop shooting, and he shot a scene from every angle. Sometimes he'd produce an amazing picture that didn't include any of the main features of the scene, but somehow summed it all up. At the scene of a fire in an apartment block, which had killed three people, Tõnu's shot of a woman who'd escaped the blaze holding the body of her dog was the one which everybody remembered, capturing the tragedy of the event in a way no picture of the raging flames or the black smoke ever could.

Kallas walked over to the line of hanging photos, and took a brief look at each one. Then he unclipped one of them and took it down. He took it over to Tõnu's reading lamp and held it in the pool of bright light. "Shit!" he said.

"Something up?" asked Tõnu.

"Not sure yet, Tõnu, look, do you mind if I borrow this one. I need to check something out. By the way, when did you take it?"

Tõnu glanced briefly at the picture. "Not long after we got to the viewpoint. Whilst Lepp was examining the body."

"Yes, that makes sense. We were all watching him. Except you, Tõnu. Thanks for this. I'll get back to you."

Back in his room, Kallas laid the picture on his desk, smoothed it flat, and stared at it. Whilst everyone had been watching Lepp, Tõnu had turned away and taken a shot of the intense and eager expressions on the faces of the reporters. But that was not what had gripped Kallas. Behind them was the archway leading from the viewpoint to the narrow lanes of Toompea. Two men were caught in the archway itself, coming into the viewing area. They were not completely in focus, but Kallas had recognised them at once: Kleber and Pilvik. They had not come up the stairs, as everyone assumed; they had been there all the time!

The implication of this was clear to Kallas. They, and by extension their master, Lepp, knew in advance of the placement of the body. Yet, instead of immediately investigating it, they had allowed the theatre of discovery to be played out. Lepp had delayed the forensic and other examinations in order to be the star of his own detective story. The anomymous caller must have alerted him before the reporters, and not after them, as he had claimed. The thought struck him that Lepp may have known who Kauscis' killers were, or who was behind them. After all, he and they were accomplices in presenting the narrative of a crime boss delivering to the authorities the bodies of Vaher's killers.

But as he stared at the grim faces of the two men in the archway, a third possibility struck him, with even more force. What if Pilvik and Kleber, were in fact Kauscis' killers? They had themselves placed the body on the railing, then retreated behind the arch, to emerge later at an opportune moment. And if with Kauscis, why not also with Lehmja? If this was the case, then surely Lepp was the moving spirit, the puppeteer pulling the strings, catching the thugs then killing them one by one to create a fake narrative.

Whichever of these scenarios was the truth, Lepp was up to no good. Kallas decided to keep his deductions to himself for the moment. He slid the picture into the top drawer of his desk, and locked it. Then he turned to his typewriter.

43

As evening came, Hallmets considered how he could tie up one of the loose ends that was distracting him from the Vaher case. It was clear from Arno Idla's evidence that illicit vodka was being trafficked via the Vahers' home. But was this with or without their knowledge? It was just possible that some servant was responsible, and the Vahers ignorant of what was passing through. However, the nightly visits by commercial vehicles could hardly have gone unnoticed by a sharp-eyed cop like Vaher. Therefore he knew about it. Perhaps he simply took a percentage for allowing the stuff to pass through his shed. Would his wife then know of it too? Again, the noise of the vehicles at night meant she must be aware.

But they needed to find where the stuff was coming from, and where else it was going. Accordingly, at eight Maslov and Kadakas were waiting in the workroom, Maslov almost invisible in drab garments of muddy brown, and Kadakas in camouflage gear with army boots on. Hallmets instructed them to watch the Vaher house again. This time, if the delivery truck came, they were to get the registration number, and follow the truck when it left. With luck, it would lead them back to the source of the shipments. If not, it would at least give them another link in the chain.

When they left, he put a call through to his home, and felt the cares of the day recede as he heard Kirsti's voice. Hearing her was enough to tell him what was important in his life.

"Jüri, how are things, love?"

"The better for hearing you, Kirsti. What about yourself? How was today?"

"I changed the story last night, the way you suggested. You're right, it works better that way. Then I got Liisa to read the first thirty pages after tea this evening. She was gobsmacked, wants to read the rest of it now. We had a really good discussion about it. I think she'd imagined what I'd write would be like those stories you get in magazines like *Estonian Housewife.* You know, midwife Anni gets sent out to one of the islands where she can't understand a word people say. Then she meets the new doctor at the cottage hospital. And so on. Anyway, it's my turn to work Saturday this week, so tomorrow I'll let Erna Viiding in the History section have a look. She'll put me right if I've made any historical blunders."

They talked for another fifteen minutes. Hallmets didn't say much about the case, but indicated that things were progressing, and he hoped he'd be back soon.

As soon as he put the phone down, it rang again. Doctor Luik.

"Hallmets, what the hell's going on on? I've been trying to call you for the last half hour!"

"I don't think so. I was on the phone for twenty-one minutes."

"Well, that's unreasonable. Who were you talking to?"

"That's my business. What do you want?"

"You haven't reported to me today."

"That's correct. I'm still writing up today's events. Would you like a summary now?"

"I expect reports from policemen on my desk by six pm, so that I can take them home with me."

"Writing reports is not my priority, so I do them when I have the time."

"Chief Inspector Vaher was always very punctilious with his reports."

"Ah yes, those were the days, eh? Well, where did being punctilious get him?"

"Look here, Hallmets, this is no joking matter. I …"

"No. It's not. And we should be focused on solving the case, not quibbling about reports. Do you want to know what's been happening, or not?"

Luik was silent for a few moments. "All right," he said finally, "But make it brief. I'm already late for dinner with Judge Klements."

Luik found it hard to relate the different strands which were now developing. "This is getting absurdly complicated," he finally admitted. "But I'm sure most of this has nothing to do with Vaher's death. This murdered beggar, that sounds like some squabble between low-life elements over a bottle of vodka. The sooner strong alcohol is banned here the better, it's the cause of so much misery. And I'm not talking simply about crime. Lives ruined, Hallmets, good lives. People who could be productive reduced to the gutter. The Finns are certainly correct to ban the stuff, we should be doing the same. The Swedes make people pay through the nose for it. I'm not sure that's working, people still manage to get hold of it. But here, where it's freely available and not that expensive, I tell you, Hallmets, it'll destroy our society. I'm glad you caught this illicit alcohol dealer. But I don't see how he's relevant to the case."

"Only in that he collects illicit vodka from an outbuilding at the Vahers' house."

"That's not possible. Surely he's making that up. He's trying to embarrass us so that we don't charge him. I know these black market merchants. Sly devils."

"I don't think so. We noticed the building he described when we went to see *Proua* Vaher."

"Then the Vahers were no doubt unaware of what was going on."

"That's quite possible. We'd like a warrant to search the place, *Härra doktor*. Just to be sure."

"No, certainly not!" snapped Luik. "This alcohol business is not central to the case. Focus on catching the killers, though it seems the crime bosses are doing your job for you. Two are dead, where's Jesinev. Have you got him yet?"

"Not so far. He may be dead already. If he saw what happened to the others, he may well have fled the country."

"Hmm. Alcohol and Russians, two plagues on our country. Vaher had no time for them, Russians I mean, he saw them for what they were: scoundrels, thieves, drunkards, parasites. He was a man who loved his country, Hallmets. A true Estonian. Anyway, I've got to be off now, but I want to see some signs of progress. The gangsters and the newspapers seem to be making all the running. And if you can't do that, we'll get someone in who can."

Back in his hotel room, Hallmets glanced across the road at the window of the Simms' flat. The curtains were firmly shut. He was going to put a call through to Kirsti, when he remembered that she was on the late shift at the library that evening. He'd have to wait till after ten. By 9.30 he was fast asleep.

Day 4. Saturday 25th March 1933

44

Hallmets was in his office by 7.30. He'd bought a copy of *Pealinna Uudised* at Kaarel Rebane's kiosk before walking down to Pikk Street, and now spead the paper out on his desk to read. The first thing he saw was the dramatic picture of Arnolds Kaus̆čis looming over the railing at the viewpoint on Toompea, his dead eyes glowing eerily, reflecting the light from the photographer's flashgun. But the headline then arrested his attention: '*Another Thug Dies. Are the Police Complicit?*' The article, by Jaan Kallas, gave an eye-witness account of the discovery of Kaus̆čis' corpse. But it went on to accuse the police of having prior knowledge of the event. '*This newspaper possesses cast-iron evidence,*' the article went on, '*that two CID officers were already concealed at the scene when journalists, summoned by anonymous telephone calls, arrived. We believe that a senior policeman, Inspector Lepp, knew in advance of this killing, and stationed his underlings at the scene, presumeably to keep sightseers away before the selected journalists arrived.*' There was a photo of Lepp at the scene, wearing a very unpleasant expression and pointing a finger threateningly at the camera.

But this wasn't the only piece on the Vaher case. Near the bottom of the page was another report, headed '*Vaher Killing the Work of a Criminal Mastermind?*' Hallmets was surprised to see that this piece was by Artur Simm, described as '*Our roving reporter in the frontline of the fight against crime.*' The article seemed to be based on an interview with Lepp, and took the opposite line from Kallas' piece. Lepp was presented as the man who was taking action to solve the case, while others were doing nothing. The main thrust of the piece was that Lepp believed some new criminal mastermind had moved into the Tallinn area, and was seeking to demonstrate his power by eliminating a senior policeman. Simm insinuated that the mastermind had the services of a widespread network of informers, which included members of the police. His conclusion was dramatic: '*We stand at a crossroads. Our society faces the greatest threat since the arrival of the so-called crusaders in the thirteenth century ended the quiet and happy lives of the peace-loving Estonian tribes. This criminal genius who has come from the East to seize control of our society must be stopped.*'

Hallmets wasn't so worried about this piece, as it was clear to him most of it was simply fantasy. He knew that if there were a new crime boss on the scene, the police would have picked up rumours of it. But it did suggest that Lepp had an agenda of his own.

He was about to phone Captain Lind when there was a knock at the door, and Inspector Sõnn came in. He looked reluctant to be there. "Thought you'd want a report on the Pottsepp case, chief," he said, and it was plain from the tone of his voice, or rather, the lack of it, that he had in fact nothing to report.

"Take a seat," said Hallmets, "I guess you're not much further on."

"No, Sir, sorry. No witnesses at all. The patrolman who disturbed the killer didn't get any sort of sighting of him, though his impression was that the killer was thin and wiry, and not as tall as Rudi. That might suggest a drug-addict or thief, and supports the notion that it was an opportunistic killing, perhaps even unintentional."

"A robbery gone wrong?"

"Yes. We got some prints from the bottle, but they don't match any that we have on the files. Short of taking prints from the entire population of the city, there's nothing we can do with them."

"What about our usual informants, haven't they heard anything?"

"Nothing at all. Whoever did it is obviously lying low and keeping his mouth shut. Our only hope is that sooner or later he gets hold of another bottle of vodka, and starts blabbing to his pals. Then the word will surely trickle out."

"You think he drank the vodka, then used the bottle on Rudi?"

"That seems the most likely sequence of events. I'd say he drank the stuff, decided he wanted more, had no money, then by chance, in the alley, comes across Rudi, whom he believes to be a successful beggar and moreover, blind, and therefore an easy target. So he threatens Rudi, and demands his cash. Rudi doesn't take too kindly to this, maybe takes a swipe at the guy with that stick of his. The guy gets annoyed, or desperate, whacks Rudi over the head with the bottle. Rudi's a big lad, so he doesn't go down right away, and there's more of a fight. Our man finally comes out on top and by this time his blood is up, so he beats Rudi's brains out. Then the patrolman spots them, so the guy scarpers pronto, doesn't even get the chance to take Rudi's cash. We found 62 crowns and 34 cents still in his pocket. Begging seems to be quite lucrative, if that's how he made it."

"I must admit, Inspector, that does seem a reasonable explanation. And I guess you're right, we'll just have to put this one on the back burner, and hope that sooner or later we pick up something on the grapevine. Or we find a set of prints that match. On the plus side, this looks like one murder that's not connected to Vaher's death. Good work, and thanks for taking it on."

"Pleased to be involved, chief," said Sõnn, smiling hesitantly, "Anything else I can do?"

"What do you think of this idea in today's paper, that there's some new crime boss taking over the city, and he had Vaher killed?"

"I don't buy it, chief. We'd hear about it right away. And if you don't mind me speaking off the record, you'd hear about it pretty quick, from Doctor Luik."

"Luik! How on earth would he know? Does he have informants too?"

Sõnn laughed. "Not him, chief. But he's best pals with Mihkel Härg."

"The gangster?"

"Shh! We're not supposed to say that. Luik gets very angry if anyone suggests there's anything dodgy about Härg. He's *just an honest businessman* as they say in New York. But he and Luik are big golf enthusiasts. They often play at the club over beyond Kadriorg. Luik also visits Härg, he's got a big place out at the coast. Apparently he had a course constructed between the house and the cliffs. The story goes, some Englishman was visiting, said the course was just what they call a 'pitch-and-putt' over there, not a challenge to a real golfer. Härg wasn't pleased, but he gave the Englishman a five-course dinner before having him thrown off the cliff into the sea."

"How do you know all this?"

"Chief Inspector Vaher had a file on Härg. Had him under surveillance, when who walks into the frame but Luik. Vaher wasn't daft, only a few of us saw what was in that file. And it wasn't just Luik that Härg was pally with."

"Could Härg have had Vaher killed?"

"That's certainly a possibility. If he found out what Vaher had on him."

"Where's that file now?"

"Should be in Vaher's office. He kept it in his safe."

"I took a look round his office on Thursday. I didn't see a safe."

"No, chief, it's well hidden."

"But you know where it is?"

"Yes, only I don't know the combination. You want me to show you?"

"What are we waiting for?"

When they got to Vaher's office, Sõnn made straight for the bookshelves behind Vaher's desk. "Let's see," he muttered, kneeling down to reach the bottom shelf. "Here we are, works of Fyodor Dostoyevsky." Kneeling beside him, Hallmets saw a row of eight chunky volumes, bound in red leather, with the titles in gold on the spines. "Right, where's *Crime and Punishment*?" went on Sõnn, "I have to say, *Härra* Vaher did have a sense of humour." He pointed to the spine of the last book in the set, then slid his finger over the top and back, and they both heard an audible click. "Ah! That's it," said Sõnn, and the spine popped out a few millimetres. Sõnn put his finger in the gap and swung open a secret door fronted by the spines of the Dostoyevsky volumes, revealing th door of a compact safe, a recessed dial in the centre, and a recessed handle at the right. "Looks like it's locked. Like I said, I don't have the combination."

Hallmets leaned over and took hold of the brass handle. He twisted it 90 degrees clockwise and then pulled. The door opened. "Seems it wasn't locked," he said grimly, "That's not good." As the door swung open they saw that the safe was empty.

"Shit, it's been cleaned out," said Sõnn. Sometimes what was obvious needed to be put into words, just to make it real.

By the time Hallmets got back to the workroom, the team had assembled.

"Sorry to keep you all waiting," said Hallmets, "I had to check Vaher's safe."

"Don't tell us, boss," said Maslov, "Let me guess. Empty?"

"Got it in one, Oleg," smiled Hallmets, "But I learned of one thing that was in it. And keep this strictly to yourselves. A file linking Dr Luik to Mihkel Härg."

There was silence in the room for a few moments.

"Tricky," said Hekk.

"Right, everybody," said Hallmets, "Now we need to get moving. Things are getting pretty crazy out there. You'll have seen the papers." Nods all round. "We need to start coming up with results, and action, before Joe Public declares us a waste of space. Not to mention Prefect Rotenbork. Maslov, Kadakas. Last night, any results?"

"Yes, boss," said Maslov, "I think you're going to like this one. You tell him, Ants."

"Er, yes," said Kadakas. "This is my first report, Sir."

"Then just get on with it, Lieutenant," invited Hallmets, "We're all waiting."

"Yes, well, we decided that hanging about in the street would look suspicious, so we made contact with a Mrs Kass, who lives next door, explained who we were, and interviewed her about the Vahers. She was very forthcoming. Seems the nightly comings and goings are a regular occurrence. So then Oleg asked if we could park the car in her drive, and observe the Vaher house from her garden. No problem at all. Her husband is at a conference in Riga about catering supplies for the tourist industry, so she has a free hand. So after dinner ..."

"She gave you dinner?" said Larsson.

"Only a plate of meatballs with fried potatoes and gherkins home-pickled in cider vinegar and honey," said Maslov, "oh, and some cheesecake to finish. Let him tell it, he's more literate that I am. Far too bright to be in the army."

"So," continued Kadakas, "we concealed ourselves in the bushes by the fence between the Kass place and the Vahers. At eleven Mrs Kass brought us a cup of coffee and a pastry. She was very thoughtful." He opened a notebook, newly purchased by the look of it. "At twelve thirty, we observed a lorry arrive at the Vaher property, and disappear behind the house. About one tonne capacity. We moved to the bottom of the garden, and climbed over the fence into an orchard, from where we could see the outbuildings. The double doors of the shed had been opened and two men were moving wooden boxes into it from the lorry. You could hear bottles clinking in the boxes. Oleg estimated twelve 70 centilitre bottles per box. They must have shifted at least 120 boxes – it took about an hour and a half altogether. In the light coming from the shed I was able, using binoculars, to read and note down the registration number of the vehicle. Finally one of the men began to shut up the back of the lorry, so we moved rapidly back to our car."

"He's good, isn't he?" said Maslov.

"The lorry left at 02.20 hours. We followed at a discreet distance, sometimes without headlights. Oleg was driving, in case anyone wondered. The vehicle took a circuitous route, aiiving finally at ..."

"You'll never guess this," put in Maslov.

"The Heinaküla estate!" Now everyone was paying close attention. "To be precise, to the farm complex beyond the manor house. We couldn't get very close, but with my army issue binoculars – German quality, Karl Zeiss Jena – I was able to see that the lorry was driven into a tall rectangular building. After an hour the vehicle had not re-emerged, and there were no lights or signs of movement, therefore we decided to conclude our surveillance and get some sleep. That concludes my report. Thank you."

Applause from the team greeted Kadakas' conclusion. "Well done, Ants," said Hallmets, "An exemplary report. Make sure you copy it out for the file. So it looks like someone on the von Langenstein estate is supplying illegal hooch via the Vahers' place."

"Which could imply," added Lesser, "that both Vaher and his wife's family were involved in the racket. So where were they getting the booze from?"

"They weren't," said Maslov, "They're making it, at Heinaküla."

"How do you know?" asked Larsson.

Maslov touched the side of his nose. "I smelt it. There was a light movement of air, I wouldn't even call it a breeze, but enough to carry the odour of the mash over. Beet mash, I'd say."

"You think they've got a distillery there?" asked Hallmets.

"I'm sure of it. We only need to raid the place. You can't hide a distillery. Especially if this is on the scale that it looks like."

"But why all the secrecy?" asked Lesser, "Having a distillery on your estate is perfectly legal. There's nothing to stop von Langenstein producing his own vodka and selling it on the open market."

"Then you have to pay duty," said Maslov, "And your vodka ends up costing the same as everybody else's. Cheaper vodka, more customers, more profit."

"I think there's more to it," said Larsson, "The money coming into Vaher's account is too much to be simply a pay-off for letting them use his garden shed."

Maslov frowned. "Hmm. To make more money, you'd have to smuggle it abroad. The obvious choices would be Finland and Sweden. In Finland it's banned, in Sweden it's only obtainable in the state shops, and very expensive. In both places you'd have to sell it on the black market, but you can charge a lot more than you can here."

"How would the smuggling operation be carried out?" asked Hallmets.

"If the amounts are small, all you need is a motor-launch, and you can put in at a landing-stage anywhere along the southern coast of Finland, or in one of the inlets up the Swedish coast. But it's a risk. The Finns and Swedes are constantly on the lookout. The other alternative is send it on a regular cargo ship, but pretend it's something else. You might label the cases as Saaremaa Cheese and send it to an importer who'll pass it on to your black market retailers."

"OK," concluded Hallmets, "I think this is the best lead we've got at the moment. So we need to keep an eye on the lorry again and see if it leads us to a little ship in a small harbour somewhere. Henno, can you organise that? Eva, can you stick with the finances, follow up this Swedish company. They could be involved. And Oleg, can you get down to the port area and have a look around the wharves and warehouses. Keep an eye open for that lorry, you've got the number. Or for anything to do with Astiz AB. And use your nose."

In his office, a telegram awaited him, from Hanover, Germany:
Sehr geehrter Hauptkommissar, Es freut uns, Ihre Frage zu Antworten. Der Füllhalter, Modell Toledo 4B, Einzignummer HC1434, gehört dem Albrecht von Langenstein, Karlsstraße 27, Dresden, Deutschland. Hochachtungsvoll, G. Schmidt, Pelikan AG

So, the pen belonged to Albrecht von Langenstein. No wonder his sister recognised it. There were probably very few of them in the whole of Estonia. She must have realised that if Hallmets had it, that was bad news. The pen was not conclusive evidence of Albrecht's involvement in Vaher's death. It could have been stolen by someone else, who was then involved. Or he could have lost it himself whilst at the viewpoint sometime prior to Vaher's killing. Nevertheless, the most likely explanation was that he was party to the murder. Questioning him was going to be tricky though. As a diplomat he was effectively immune from prosecution, and could simply refuse to co-operate with the police.

He was thinking of coffee, when the phone rang. Captain Lind, sounding flustered. "Look, Jüri, can you come down here right away. Something urgent."

In five minutes Hallmets was in Lind's office, and had turned down a shot of vodka.

"Look, Jüri," the captain began awkwardly, "We've had a complaint about the investigation."

"Oh yes? Who from?"

"The German Embassy. Apparently the Third Secretary ..."

"Albrecht von Langenstein?"

"Yes, that's him. How did you know?"

"Vaher's brother-in-law."

"Ah. Well, this morning he sent an official note to Prefect Rotenbork, claiming that the von Langenstein family is being harassed by the police, and treated as if they are suspected of crimes. They are also being vilified in the press. He draws the prefect's attention to the responsibility which the German Government feels towards German minorities in whichever country they might live. He asks that: 1. The von Langenstein family and other ethnic Germans are left alone; 2. You are taken off the Vaher case and replaced by someone with a more 'balanced' approach; and 3. Any journalists slandering the von Langenstein family be arrested and appropriately punished."

"As far as I'm aware, Peeter, Hitler's dictatorship only applies to Germany."

"Yes, yes, of course. I have to say, the Prefect takes the same view. He has made it clear to von Langenstein that he has every confidence in you as senior officer on the Vaher case. He has emphasised that there is a free press here in Estonia. Finally, however, he has indicated that the von Langenstein family will be treated with the respect due to any citizen, or resident, of Estonia. In other words, please handle them with care. We don't know how far this new German government will take this notion of 'responsibility' for ethnic German minorities." Lind poured himself another vodka. "Surely the von Langensteins aren't involved in Vaher's death anyway. They're hardly criminals."

"I happen to think it's criminal to exploit the Estonian people for six centuries," said Hallmets, "But, aside from that, I'm afraid there is evidence that may connect Albrecht von Langenstein to Vaher's death. We found his fountain pen at the viewpoint."

"Ah. That's not good. Maybe it was stolen from him."

"Maybe. But there's more, I'm afraid. There's also a possibility that Heinrich von Langenstein is involved in illegal alcohol production on his estate. It might be linked to smuggling. That will have to be followed up. As you know, the government is very sensitive to the alcohol question. They don't want Estonia to be seen as the Baltic vodka fountain."

Lind groaned. "Yes, yes. But can you be discreet about it. Do everything by the book. Avoid anything they might seize upon as proof of harassment."

"I'd better avoid beating him up, then. Don't worry, Peeter, I'll be diplomatic. But I'm not going to treat the family more leniently than the law requires, just because they're Germans. And Herr Hitler doesn't rule Estonia, thank goodness."

As Hallmets left the Captain's office, he heard the clink as Lind retrieved the vodka bottle.

45

Jaan Kallas read Artur Simm's article very carefully. He hadn't seen it until the paper was printed. He didn't like the fact that Hunt had put Simm onto the Vaher case. But that was how Hunt operated, creating rivalries that he hoped would stimulate each side to greater efforts. And if each day's paper was going to carry a piece from both of them on the Vaher case, he'd have to make sure his was the best. At least he had one advantage, that he knew what he was talking about, and made up his own mind. It seemed to him that someone was feeding Simm the stuff he wrote. He didn't see Simm getting much out of Hallmets, but he'd clearly been talking to, or rather listening to, Lepp. And Lepp's plan seemed clear enough, to distract attention away from himself and *Proua* Vaher, and invent some new crime boss. He was pretty sure there wasn't a new big cheese rolling round the town, he would certainly have heard about it. Besides, if a new boss wanted to make a point, he'd be better chucking Mihkel Härg off Toompea. But maybe Härg was next.

And he knew that his own material was based on evidence, exclusive evidence, rather than speculation. He now had enough material to produce another piece on the possible link between Lepp and Laura Vaher. He'd learned from the gossip columnist that Lepp had been married and divorced, not once, but twice. Both his wives had been of the empty-headed wannabe-starlet type. However, she knew of no scandal surrounding Lepp. Maybe he was planning to get married again. That would be advantageous if he was in line for Vaher's post. The high-ups preferred married men in the top jobs.

He could get a short piece into the lunchtime edition. That would get him one up on Artur – he didn't see Simm as enough of a grafter to get something out that quickly. Then he'd have to dig up something more.

After a twenty-minute walk, from the bus stop at the village, on a lane running gradually uphill through untended woodland, Artur Simm reached the gates of the Rüütlimäe estate. The sun was shining and he could hear birds singing. Just the day for a woodland walk. An old wall stretched away on either side of gleaming black-painted wrought-iron double gates. The large brass padlock and steel chain suggested there was no point trying to open them. However, beside the left-hand gatepost was a single narrow gate for pedestrians, and this swung open easily on well-oiled hinges, to admit him to a well-maintained gravel drive leading further uphill through tidier woodland. Five minutes later the drive emerged from the trees to run alongside a well-manicured lawn, beyond which stood a large and attractive house of dark red brick, built in a tasteful rural style, probably sometime during the previous decade. Beyond that was the open sea, and over it a wide and empty sky.

As he approached the house, Artur noticed a man standing on the lawn. He was tall and solidly built, but not fat, dressed in a tweed jacket and plus-fours, and was standing upright bent slightly forward at the hip, concentrating on his putt. Artur paused, so as not to disturb the man's concentration. He noticed now that the lawn was laid out as a putting green, with painted metal flags marking the holes. After what seemed a long moment, the man completed the putt successfully. Then he straightened up and Artur took in his long face and high forehead, short white hair and moustache. He looked every centimetre the retired military officer. Now he seemed to notice Artur, and turned ice-blue eyes on him, appraising him.

"Ah. Hello. I think you would be *Härra* Simm?" There was no accent in his voice, a perfectly neutral expression on his face.

"Yes, that's right."

The man approached him, smiled, and shook hands. The handshake was firm and, Artur felt, somehow welcoming. "Mihkel Härg. Pleased to meet you. Do come this way and we can have some coffee and a chat." He pointed with his putter in the direction of the house.

The previous day Artur had spent some time in the archive, looking through old articles by Kallas, and had recognised the name of Mihkel Härg several times. Kallas never made specific allegations against Härg, but alluded to connections between Härg and known criminal figures. There was one piece commenting on Härg's construction of a modest golf course on the estate he owned on the coast near Tallinn. Kallas referred to 'rumours' that an English visitor – a man not long previously released from prison in London – had met with an 'accident' after commenting negatively on Härg's golf course. Apparently he had tripped whilst on a cliff path and fallen into the sea. Other articles in the archive, not written by Kallas, took a different line. The business pages presented Härg as a successful businessman, although it was not clear what his business was, whilst the social and gossip columns highlighted his friendship with prominent public figures and celebrities, and the sports pages focused on his sponsorship of golf tournaments, and attempts to develop the sport in Estonia.

From all this, it seemed to Artur that Härg could well be aware of any new criminal boss moving in to Tallinn. Artur resolved to try and interview him, but suspected it would be hard to get close to such a key figure in so many areas of Estonia's life. Imagine his surprise then, when his phone call that morning was put through to Härg's private secretary who, ten minutes later, returned his call to inform him Härg would be happy to see him that very day. He was given details of how to reach the estate, and told to be there around eleven o'clock.

Härg led him round the house to a terrace with a fine view over the sea. Here a garden table with two chairs awaited them, and as they sat down, a servant was already emerging from the house with freshly-brewed coffee and expensive-looking pastries.

"This spot is perfect, is it not, *Härra* Simm?" said Härg, "Completely isolated, yet not far from the capital, a house designed to harmonise with the traditions of our country, and yet possessing every modern convenience, and an outlook that is without parallel. The breeze brings me the smell of the sea every morning, the air is fresh and stimulating, I hear the birds singing in the woods. Here I can work hard, or I can relax. I have my own vegetable garden, at the other side of the house, to give me healthy food, and my own golf course, where I can take exercise. This is the perfect environment for today's man of business. Now, please, take some refreshment."

The coffee was strong but well-rounded, much better than what was served at the *Alt-Revaler*, and the pastries divine, the pastry light and fragrant, whilst the filling of cream and ground almonds with a hint of some exotic liqueur, was indescribable with a normal vocabulary. After two, Artur felt it would be rude to have another.

"You like my pastries, *Härra* Simm? No need to answer, I can see it. I have them made to my own taste, and freshly baked every morning. I shall give you a box to take away with you. It will make a lovely present for your wife. Now, how can I help you? I must confess that I'd not heard of you until I saw your article in this morning's paper. Most interesting, and above all, positive. This is the right attitude, *Härra* Simm, be positive at all times. You are newly appointed as a crime reporter, I take it. Good. Your work will be a welcome contrast to the reports of Kallas. He's always looking at people with such suspicion, everything he sees is corrupt. I really pity him, he seems unable to appreciate the beauty that's all around. Please, tell me, what is it you'd like to talk with me about?"

"Well," began Artur hesitantly, "I've been asked by my editor to cover the Vaher case on the ground, so to speak, to talk to the man in the street, rather than speculating myself." Artur had worked out this form of words on the journey out to Härg's estate.

"Yes, I understand. You leave the speculation to your colleague." Härg smiled. "But I'm not sure how my opinions can be relevant to this. I'm only a businessman."

"I want to show how it's not only the police who have a view on these events. They reverberate out into our society. I'm aware that you're a significant and successful member of our business community, and I'm wondering how it affects you." Artur took out his notebook. "By the way, do you mind if I take notes?"

"Not at all. Please, do go on."

Artur cleared his throat. "First, then, how do you think Vaher's death has affected the business community?"

"An interesting question. I would say that they're horrified by it. Ours is not generally a violent society, and such a barbaric occurrence as this is far outwith our normal expectations of behaviour. But it's also deeply worrying. No-one is safe if a senior policeman can be murdered so publicly. This will have a negative effect on business. You see, business gets along best when there are peaceful, safe and secure conditions. I mean, if you send a consignment of say, watches or wireless sets or even live cattle, you want to be sure that they will reach their destination. If they don't, it's you who's out of pocket. So, in less secure times, you have to hire more guards, take more precautions, check the consignment regularly, and so on. And naturally that puts the price up. So anything that makes people feel insecure is bad for business."

"Do you think this event shows our society is becoming more violent, or is it just a one-off?"

"Hmm. Well, as a statistician once told me, one instance does not make a trend. I personally think this is more likely to be a one-off event, engineered by some maniac with a grudge against Vaher, or the police in general."

"You don't give any credence to the theory that there's a new criminal mastermind moving into the Tallinn area, seeking to intimidate both the police and other criminal gangs."

"Your article suggested that was *Komissar* Lepp's view?"

"Yes. I think he fears there's a real danger of violence between this new gangster and others."

Härg nodded thoughtfully. "Hmm. Well, I personally have not heard of any new criminal figure moving in. As a businessman, naturally I keep my ear to the ground. But of course it's not impossible. Does Lepp have any idea who this person might be?" Härg poured himself some more coffee while he waited for Artur's response.

Artur needed a moment to think. It wouldn't look good to appear too ignorant. Härg offered him more coffee and he paused as his cup was filled, before thanking his host, and answering his question. "Yes, actually he did confide to me his suspicion, that he suspected a man known only as Mr. P. He didn't want me to print that, as it would alert the man to the fact that Lepp was onto him, so I'd appreciate it if you didn't mention that to others."

Härg sipped his coffee, and nodded. "Of course not. But this Mr. P.

sounds very mysterious. Can you tell me a little more about him?"

Artur warmed to his story. "According to my sources, he's a Russian called Popov who's built up a pretty extensive criminal network. He has a number of violent henchmen and specialises in infiltrating other organisations." Härg raised his eyebrows at this. "Lepp believes that now Mr. P., as he calls himself, wants to be top dog."

"You do seem very well-informed," said Härg, with a concerned expression, "I really hope this doesn't mean there are going to be violent confrontations on our streets. The business community needs peace and stability, and fully support the forces of law and order. And we are right behind courageous journalists such as yourself, who are prepared to report exactly what is happening."

With that he stood up. The interview was over. "Well, thank you for coming to see me, *Härra* Simm, feel free to quote anything I've said today. I look forward to reading your report tomorrow."

As they walked back towards the putting green, a middle-aged woman intercepted them to give to Härg a white cardboard box with a red ribbon round it. She then curtsied and returned to the house.

"Your pastries, *Härra* Simm. I'm sure you'll enjoy them. It's been a pleasure to talk to you. Come again any time."

Artur thanked Härg profusely for his time as well as his pastries and coffee, and smiled to himself as he made for the gate.

46

The Krummfeldt factory was beyond the harbourarea, so Hallmets decided to go by car. As on previous occasions, he briefed Lembit to take a good look round whilst he was making his call.

Attached to the factory was a small brick building which served as the administrative centre. Dr Krummfeldt's office was on the second floor. Dr Krummfeldt reminded Hallmets of Boris Karloff, as himself of course, rather than the mummy or Fu Manchu. But at least he could speak Estonian. The doctors seemed to have done a good job on his nose, as any discontinuity in its noble Romanness was not visible. He explained to Hallmets that he would do anything which would help capture the killers of Chief Inspector Vaher.

"Thank you, *Härra Doktor*, I appreciate that. I'm just exploring any aspect of Chief Inspector Vaher's life that might have given rise to any motive to kill him. I'm aware that there was back in 1925 an incident involving yourself and the Chief Inspector."

"And you're suggesting that I killed him eight years later in revenge for having my nose broken?" Krummfeldt smiled faintly.

"No, not at all. I believe afterwards you expressed approval of his methods. As long as they didn't affect you."

"Quite so."

"And did you keep in touch with *Härra* Vaher?"

Krummfeldt frowned. "Why do you ask that?"

"I'd like to know if he may have antagonised any particular group, who may have sought revenge. This is why I'm talking to people who knew him."

"I see. In that case, I can say we did keep in touch. I discovered that his views were very similar to my own. He certainly was aware that the Reds were the biggest threat to our society, but he was also wisely suspicious of socialists – simply closet Reds – and of course Jews and gypsies, though there are precious few of them here in Estonia, thank goodness."

"I believe he had strong views on law and order."

"Yes, I know. I'd agree with him there. What Estonia needs right now is discipline. You see, when a society becomes sick, it needs strong medicine. This is what *Herr* Hitler will bring to Germany – a cure for the loss of the nation's self-respect."

"I've not been to Germany for a while. Do you know what the public mood is like there now?"

Krummfeldt nodded. "I go there often on business. The last time was about three weeks ago. There was a mood of real excitement. People knew great things, unprecedented things, were about to happen. Then, in a sudden and dramatic move, the government showed its vision and courage: hundreds of the communists and their sympathisers were arrested, as well as other enemies of the German people. The purification had begun. Now you should watch Germany, see how she will grow and prosper, see how she will revel in finding herself again!"

"I'm obliged to you, *Härra Doktor*. I can read about these events in the papers, but it makes so much difference to hear an eye-witness account."

"Not at all, *Härra Ülemkomissar*, it's a pleasure to be able to share my experiences. I wish you success in finding the murderers. I'm sure it will turn out to be Reds or Jews." Krummfeldt stood up, clicked his heels, and bowed stiffly to Hallmets.

As Hallmets exited the building, his car swept round to pick him up, summoned from a parking area somewhere to the rear.

"Get me away from here, please Lembit, I need some fresh air."

"No problem, boss," said his driver, as the car swung onto the main road, and headed east. They passed the harbour and reached Narva Street. They were held up here a short while – a van had broken down on the road, the bonnet was open and lots of steam issuing from the radiator. Two men were peering into the bonnet and scratching their heads. As they waited, a well-built man in a black suit with his shirt collar open walking past in the opposite direction gave him a cheery wave. It took him a while to remember who he was, but it finally dawned: Jaan Kallas, the reporter. Once past the obstruction, they soon passed the office of *Pealinna Uudised*, and a little further on turned off left onto the Pirita Road, and soon they reached the promenade by the sea. Here in summer the Tallinners took the sea air, enjoyed the sun, and ate ice-cream. But this wasn't summer. The car coasted to a stop by the Russalka monument, erected in 1902 by the Tsar to mark the sinking of a Russian warship, and surmounted by an exquisite bronze angel carved by Estonian sculptor Amadeus Adamson.

They got out and walked onto the promenade. Standing by the low wall, they could look out over the modest beach to the bay. To the left they could see the ships crowding the harbour, to the right, the little harbour of Pirita, home to yachts rather than cargo boats, and the onward curve of the coast running north into the distance. Despite the sunshine, there were few people on the beach: an old woman with a small child enthralled by the movement of the waves, an old man shuffling after an old dog, a young couple walking hand in hand. The ice-cream seller's booth was closed. Hallmets would have welcomed a cone, to take the taste of fanaticism out of his mouth. He turned to Lembit.

"See anything back there?"

"Lots of lorries coming and going. Plenty of export stuff. I chatted with one of the drivers. He takes the stuff down to the docks. Germany, Sweden, and Finland seem to be the main destinations. He says their parts go into all sorts of things – tractors, harvesting machines, mobile cranes, even tanks. Lots of stuff coming in, too. Must be raw materials and so on. One thing I did spot, though. That lorry you gave me the number of. It was parked round the back. No sign of the driver, though, and it was too public for me to get a peep inside."

"I wonder what they were up to."

"The plot thickens, eh, boss?"

47

Kallas leaned back and sighed. The piece had been written and submitted in time to make the lunchtime edition, which came out at twelve. So, time for lunch. He left the building and walked along Narva Street the short distance towards Viru Square. The traffic was slow – a van had broken down, steam was billowing from the open bonnet – and amongst the cars waiting to pass it he noticed Chief Inspector Hallmets sitting by the driver of a black Volvo Pv652 sedan. Nice car for a policeman, thought Kallas, he must have borrowed it from the Prefect. He waved to Hallmets. In Viru Square, he turned right and passed the Valgesaar department store and Rosen's Vodka factory, heading towards the harbour. He had almost reached the corner where he would turn to reach the café, and was already thinking about whether to have meatballs or blood sausage, when he felt each arm being seized and found himself held between two unsmiling men in overcoats. At the same time a car slid to a halt beside him, one of the men swung open the door with his free hand, and he was bundled in, followed by the two men. "Hey!" he managed to shout, before a black canvas bag was thrust over his head and a moment later a heavy blow to the head knocked him into unconsciousness.

When he woke up, he found himself tied to an upright chair, his legs bound by cords to its legs, his wrists to its arms. His mouth was gagged. His jacket, shoes and socks had been removed. He was in a small room with dark stone walls. A tiny and grubby window high in one wall let in a dim light. The closed door was a heavy wooden one, painted black, but there was a small hatch at eye height and a wider one near the bottom. A cell door! The Patarei Prison came to mind, the former Tsarist barracks on the coast near the harbour. But the occasional passing of shadows across the grimy window suggested he was in a basement adjacent to a street. That might mean the notorious basement at Police Headquarters in Pikk Street. He looked for any scratches or carvings on the walls. Sure enough, there were a few, dates and names: M RIIKS AUG MDCCCCII; J MAGI 1905; P ДЕНИСЕВ IV-22. He listened for sound: there was none. He sniffed the air: urine, with a hint of cigarette smoke. There was a bucket in one corner, and a wooden chair in the other, similar to the one he was attached to.

After a while – perhaps it was only minutes – he heard a bolt sliding on the other side of the door, and the eye-level hatch opened outwards. He saw an eye and a thick eyebrow. The hatch shut, more bolts slid back, and the door creaked open. Two men came into the room. Kallas recognised them at once as Kleber and Pilvik, Lepp's henchmen. The two men stood looking at him. Kleber smiled, and smoothed his moustache; Pilvik grinned, showing yellow teeth randomly scattered, and scratched his bottom. Kleber took off his jacket and hung it carefully on the back of the chair in the corner. Pilvik took off his and laid it over the arm of the chair, but he had misjudged the position, and it slid off onto the stone floor. He left it there. Then he removed Kallas' gag.

"Well *Härra* Kallas," began Kleber, "Welcome to Pikk Street. Inspector Lepp asked us to have a little word with you about what you've been writing in the paper."

"Yeah," rasped Pilvik, "He don't like it."

"Which bit in particular?" asked Kallas politely.

"What you wrote this morning," answered Kleber, "See, Inspector Lepp thinks that making them sort of insinuations ..."

"Yeah, insinuations," echoed Pilvik.

"Suggesting that we were involved in them killings, see, that undermines people's respect for the forces of law and order, don't it?"

"Yeah," responded Pilvik.

"But you did kill them, didn't you?" said Kallas to Pilvik.

"Yeah," Pilvik grinned again.

"Shut up, you cretin!" shouted Kleber. Then turned again to Kallas, "He don't know what he's talking about. And whether we killed them low-lifes or not, well, that ain't your business. See, your job is to report the news, not add your own speculations."

"Yeah, speculations," growled Pilvik.

"If you want theories," Kleber went on, "Inspector Lepp can supply them. He provided lots of information yesterday, but you didn't use it. Now, that wasn't reasonable was it?"

"It was perfectly reasonable," said Kallas, who was getting fed up with this. He was also irritated by Kleber's breath, which carried a mixture of onion and beer, and some indefinable cooked animal product. "What's the point of all this? Let me go at once, and I'll forget this happened."

"What's the point? Well now, the point is to show you what happens to reporters who write stuff that undermines the forces of law and order."

"Law and order," echoed Pilvik.

Kleber slapped Kallas' face with the back of his hand. After the blow, Kallas felt a stinging just below his right eye. "Oh dear," said Kleber amiably, "You're starting to bleed. Forgot to take my ring off, didn't I?" And he punched Kallas in the ribs. Kallas gasped. Kleber did it again. Then Pilvik kicked him in the shin. Now the blows came faster. Pilvik, in particular, was beginning to enjoy himself. Laughing, he flung Kallas' chair over, and started kicking him in the ribs and stomach. "Not his head," warned Kleber, "We don't want to kill him, not just yet anyway." He pushed Pilvik away and pulled the chair upright again. "Oh dear," he smiled, "You're going to have some nasty bruises tomorrow. Something to remember us by, next time you put pen to paper, eh? See, if you write bad stuff about us, we'll do bad stuff to you. That's only fair, isn't it?"

"Yeah!" said Pilvik.

They had left the cell door ajar behind them, and someone looked in. Kallas couldn't see who it was. The figure soon moved away, unseen by Kleber or Pilvik.

"You won't get away with this," mumbled Kallas. There was blood in his mouth and one of his teeth felt loose. And lots of other parts of him were very sore.

"You're going to have to do better than that if you want out of here," said Kleber. "Or you could be stuck down here for a long time. And nobody knows where you are."

"They'll look for me," said Kallas. But he wasn't so sure.

"They may look. But they won't find. Then one day you'll turn up again. Oh, but you'll be dead. Your shirt'll be soaked in vodka, the empty bottle will still be in your pocket. When you were drunk, you must have gone up to that viewpoint and just fallen off. And all that bruising as you fell down the cliff. What a mess."

"Let's kill him now," suggested Pilvik, "Keep kicking till he shuts up, eh?"

"No, no," chided Kleber, "We're just asking him to change his approach. But his answers aren't helpful. We'll have to leave him here till the Inspector decides what to do with him. Come on, let's go. I need another beer, that exercise has made me thirsty."

"Yeah," said Pilvik, "Beer."

They picked up their jackets, and made for the door. In the doorway Kleber turned and smiled at Kallas again. "We're off for a little refreshment. But we'll be back soon. Don't get up to any mischief whilst we're away, now." He laughed as he shut the door. Kallas heard the bolts slide to on the other side.

Now there was peace and quiet again. So much for standing up for free speech. If he kept this up, they'd just kill him. Was it worth throwing away his life on this? No-one would thank him, no-one would even appreciate what he'd done. Hunt couldn't care about him, he didn't care about anyone. And Simm would be happy to take over his job, and write whatever crap Lepp spouted at him. He wasn't made to be a hero. That reminded him of some of the stuff he'd seen during his years as a correspondent in the Independence War. Atrocities that made a beating up by a couple of thugs seem child's play. Tortures and disfigurements that could only be described as demonic. Crucifixion, impalement, disembowelling, cutting off of a whole range of body parts. Actions not of maniacs, but of coldly calculating men in Petrograd, whose aim was to create a terror which would deter anyone from opposing them. Yes, he'd also seen the Whites' attempts to emulate the Red Terror, but they were amateurish by comparison, driven only by cruelty. And he was wingeing about a few cracked ribs and a loose tooth.

48

Back in Pikk Street, Hallmets had a light lunch in the canteen, then went back up to his office. He looked into the workroom. Marta was on her lunch break, but Larsson was still there, poring over the papers.

"Any luck?" he asked her.

"Yes, I think so. I've been looking at this Swedish firm Astiz AB. They act as middlemen for many of the Swedish arms manufacturers. That could enable them to relabel arms as, say, 'machine parts', and send them to recipients the Swedes don't want to be seen doing business with. Chinese warlords, repressive military regimes, that sort of thing. I've checked the shipping registers and noted that Astiz do business with a number of companies here in Estonia."

"Have you got a list of them?"

She flicked through the pile of papers and pulled out a single sheet. "Here we are."

Hallmets ran his gaze down the list. "Krummfeldt. Now that's interesting. Can you find out what kind of business they do with him?"

"That should be fairly straightforward. I just need to…"

There was an urgent knock at the door, it was thrown open, and Sõnn dashed into the room. He had to get his breath back before he could reveal why he had come.

"Sorry," he gasped, "I've just come up the stairs from the basement."

"You're out of condition," said Hallmets, "Don't overdo it. Take your time."

Sõnn took a few more breaths. "Thanks, chief. Every so often, I check out what's doing down in the basement, mainly to see who we've got in there. Normally it's the usual crowd of drunks and pickpockets, but every so often there's somebody interesting who's been pulled in. This information doesn't get shared, so going down there regularly is the only way to find out. I've just been down, and caught sight, in one of the cells, of Jaan Kallas, you know, the journalist. Kleber and Pilvik, Lepp's guys, were in there, and it looks like they'd been knocking him around a bit."

"What sort of condition was he in?"

"Not good."

"We'd better go and get him out. Are you with me, Inspector?"

"Yes, Sir. I wouldn't be here otherwise."

"Count me in too," called Larsson from the table, "I need a break."

A few minutes later they were making their way along the dim corridor in the basement. Near the end, Sõnn stopped. "It's this one," he said, and slid back the two bolts securing the door.

Inside, they saw a bloodied figure slumped in a chair.

"Untie him," Hallmets ordered. Sõnn and Larsson were immediately by the man. They freed him, and tried to get him onto his feet, but he was barely conscious and it was necessary to let him rest in the chair.

Noiw they heard footsteps in the corridor, and in marched Kleber and Pilvik.

"What the fuck's going on here?" said Kleber, "This is our prisoner, Sõnn, so put him back and clear off."

Hallmets turned to face Kleber. "Chief Inspector Hallmets. And you are?"

Kleber became more wary. "Sergeant Kleber, er, Sir. There seems to be a mistake. This is our prisoner."

"His name?"

Kleber hesitated. Hallmets could see that he was trying to decide whether to give Kallas' real name or make one up. "Sepp. His name is Victor Sepp, I think."

"And what's he charged with?"

"Drunk and disorderly behaviour, and assaulting a police officer."

"He doesn't smell very drunk."

"That was last night. We came to let him out this morning and he attacked us. We had to defend ourselves."

"He was tied up."

"Yes, Sir. That was after he attacked us. We tied him to the chair for his own safety."

"Yeah," said Pilvik, "His own safety." He grinned.

Hallmets turned to Pilvik. "And you are?"

"What's it to you?" said Pilvik, and belched loudly.

"This is Officer Pilvik," said Kleber.

"I'm sure he can speak for himself," said Hallmets, "Officer Pilvik, have you been drinking?"

"Only four beers," said Pilvik, "I don't like you. It's rude to ask a man how much he's been drinking. I'll have to teach you a lesson." He swung a fist at Hallmets.

Hallmets easily dodged the blow, and his own punch sent Pilvik reeling across the room until he hit the wall, and slumped to the floor, blood pouring from his nose. Then he turned again to Kleber. "You've been misinformed about the prisoner's name. It's not Sepp, it's Kallas. And we've been looking for this very man, in connection with an ongoing inquiry. So we're going to take him up to my office now to ask him some questions. If you want him back after that, send me a completed charge sheet, and I'll think about it."

Kleber glared at Sõnn and Larsson, then assumed a more wheedling expression as he turned to Hallmets. "I'm afraid it's not possible to release him to you, Sir. Inspector Lepp made it expressly clear that under no circumstances should he be let out of this cell. He's very disturbed." He paused as a new idea came to him. "In fact, Sir, the inspector wants to question him regarding the murders of Eino Lehmja and Arnolds Kauščis. He thinks he knows something about both murders."

"Ah." Hallmets seemed to be softening. "I see. Is he a career criminal then?"

"Yes, Sir, I'm afraid so. Violent crime since his teenage years. You wouldn't believe how often he's been in jail. He knows the Patarei Hotel better than his own home."

"Which is where?"

"Out towards Kalamaja somewhere, near the plywood factory. In fact, he often works there."

"Funny, he doesn't look like a working man. But then, he isn't one, is he, Kleber. I must say, I admire your facility in bullshit, and I'm sorry I don't have the time to listen to more of it. But, as I said, we'll take Mr Sepp, as you call him, up to my office for a little chat. Perhaps you could send his file up to me as soon as possible."

"He's not leaving here!" Inspector Lepp was standing in the doorway. "He's my prisoner and he's going nowhere. Once I've finished with him, you're welcome to do whatever you like, Hallmets, but right now he's staying here. Now take the fat man and the floozy, and get out."

"Inspector Lepp," said Hallmets quietly, "I'm your senior officer."

"Not for much longer, I think," countered Lepp.

"This man's name, as you and your subordinates know perfectly well, is Jaan Kallas, and he's a journalist for *Pealinna Uudised*. I believe he recently wrote some pieces that were not particularly complimentary of you. That's his privilege in a country where the press is free. And it's no reason for you to drag him down here and beat him up. If he decides to press assault charges against these two, I will personally take the witness box to testify against them. This is the sort of behaviour that gives all of our police a bad name, and it needs to be stamped out. Now, Inspector Sõnn and Sergeant Larsson are going to help *Härra* Kallas up to my office."

By now Pilvik had got himself back on his feet, and stood by Kleber and Lepp, wiping blood off his nose with the back of his hand.

"And I told you to leave him!" snarled Lepp,

"Yeah," growled Pilvik. Then he launched himself at Hallmets. This time Sõnn's foot in his stomach arrested his forward progress, and sent him to the ground doubled up.

"Fuck you, Sõnn," rasped Kleber, pulling a truncheon from his trouser pocket. This time Larsson appeared to spring into the air, and kicked Kleber in the shoulder, with such force that he was sent staggering backwards through the open door of the cell and fell into the corridor.

"That's enough!" Lepp had his pistol trained on them.

Hallmets stood in front of him. "Please, Inspector, this is not a very grown-up attitude, is it? First your underlings try to attack fellow-officers, and now you point a gun at us. I suggest you shoot me first, simply because I'm the oldest. But that's as far as you'll get, isn't it. So calm down and put the gun away." He reached out his hand and pushed the gun barrel aside.

Lepp stepped back a couple of paces, into the doorway, and lowered the gun. "You haven't heard the last of this, Hallmets, believe me," he sneered. "I don't forget any slight on myself or my men." Then he turned on his heel and stalked off down the corridor. Kleber got to his feet and staggered after him.

"Let's go," said Hallmets.

"What about Pilvik?" asked Sõnn. "He's none too clever. You're more likely to get the truth out of him than Kleber or Lepp. If we question him now while he's still a bit dazed, you never know what he might tell us."

"Good idea. Take him up to one of the interview rooms on the ground floor. Keep him there and don't let anyone in till I get back."

Up in the workroom, Marta did her best to patch up Kallas' cuts. But it did look as if he'd cracked a couple of ribs, and Hallmets offered to send him immediately to the hospital. However, a couple of aspirin tablets and a glass of plum brandy seemed to have a positive effect, and he eventually croaked, "No, no, I need to talk to you first, before they try to silence me for good. I'd appreciate a ride to the hospital after that, though. And another glass of *snaps* would help matters too."

In Hallmets' office he went through what had led him to his conclusions about Lepp and Laura Vaher, and about Lepp's possible involvement in the killing of Lehmja and Kauscis. Hallmets asked him to wait till he returned from interviewing Pilvik. Meanwhile Maslov had arrived back, so Hallmets asked him to make sure no-one tried to seize Kallas. Then he headed down to the interview rooms.

Pilvik was slumped in a chair, to which he was handcuffed. Hallmets sat down at the table next to Sõnn and Larsson, facing Pilvik. He took out his note book and flicked through a few pages, then looked up at Pilvik. "Officer Pilvik, you're going to be charged with assault on *Härra* Kallas, attempted assault of a police officer, oh, and murder."

"Murder? Don't understand."

"Pilvik, we know you killed Lehmja and Kauscis."

Pilvik looked blank. "Who?"

"Those two thugs you killed. One of them you pushed off the view point and the other was shot in the neck. That was a neat shot, by the way."

"Kleber killed him! I just carry. Ask Lepp. He say so. He say, Kleber shoot, Pilvik carry."

Hallmets leaned back. They'd got enough, and three witnesses to that statement. He noticed that Larsson was writing it down

Sõnn leaned forward. "Konrad, listen to me." His tone was soothing, encouraging, confidential. "I know you like westerns."

Pilvik nodded. "Yeah."

"Remember *Gunfight at Cactus Ridge?*"

Pilvik smiled. "Yeah. Cactus Ridge. Gunfight. Good film."

"Remember the scene at the beginning, in Deadwood City."

Pilvik nodded, smiling. "A hanging."

"That's right. The man who helped with the bank robbery. All he did was hold the horses while the others mounted. What happened then?"

Pilvik frowned, then grinned. "Yeah. His horse not so good. He got caught."

"Yes, that's right. And even though he just looked after the horses, he was part of the gang who robbed the bank, so what happened to him."

Pilvik looked sad. "He was hung up, died."

"You see, Konrad, that's what's going to happen to you."

"No! No! I just carry!"

"Remember how they put the rope round his neck, then yanked him up in the air, and his feet were swinging all over the place and he couldn't breathe, and just before he died he thought about how he'd disappointed his mother."

"Killed herself." A big tear rolled down Pilvik's cheek and dropped onto the table.

"That's right. She threw herself into the creek and was drowned. She couldn't bear the shame."

"Poor mama." said Pilvik, and another tear fell.

"That hanging, Konrad, that's going to happen to you."

"No! No!"

"And what do think your mother will think?"

Pilvik began to sob loudly.

"But this is the twentieth century," Sõnn went on. "You don't have to be hanged. We know that Lepp and Kleber did the killing, you just carried. But you have to tell us exactly what happened. Then the judge will know that you weren't the real criminal."

"Not a criminal." Pilvik moaned. Then his eyes lit up with fear. "They get me! They kill me!"

"No, they won't. They'll be hanged. Then they won't be able to hurt you. So please, Konrad, just tell us what happened."

And he did. He described, in sentences of simple words, how Lepp and Kleber had told him they were going to punish some bad guys. These guys had killed Chief Inspector Vaher, and were going to get away with it. They would make sure that they didn't. No, he didn't know where the others found the men, all he had to do was help carry the bodies. Well, he'd helped beating them up too, but only because that was fun. Where did the beatings up take place? In a basement, somewhere he thought, near the Patarei Prison. No, they hadn't got the two together. First the Estonian. He thought Lepp and Kleber had already hurt him, there were red marks on his hands, looked nasty. Then he and Kleber had beaten him till he was unconscious. Then they took him up to Toompea, to the viewpoint, and threw him off. It was almost the same with the foreigner, except Kleber shot him before they brought him to the viewpoint, and then they propped him on the railing. Then he and Kleber hid behind the archway so no-one would see them.

That was fun too. All the people came up and looked at the dead man. Then he and Kleber came out and herded them, like cows. Lepp had thought of that, it was clever wasn't it? He was going to be the top man one day, he'd told them. Then he, Pilvik, that is, would get the chance to beat lots of bad guys up. Kallas, he'd said bad things. Lepp said so. Bad men deserved to be beaten up. Women too, if they were bad. But he didn't beat women up, just slapped them around. That was fun too.

They brought Pilvik up to the workroom, cuffed him to the radiator by one wrist, and got him a glass of beer and a pie, while Larsson dictated her handwritten version of his statement to Marta, who typed it up. Kallas was quickly hustled through to Hallmets' office, and Sõnn came in too.

"Well done, inspector," said Hallmets, "This is a breakthrough. You did the right thing in the first instance by warning us Kallas was here."

"Thanks, chief. It's Hjalmar, by the way."

Hallmets turned to Kallas. "I think you deserve a scoop here, *Härra* Kallas. Pilvik has told us all he knows. Lepp, Kleber and Pilvik killed Lehmja and Kauščis. Obviously I can't give you his statement, but I'll drop you a few hints which will no doubt help you with your article."

"I'm grateful to you, Chief Inspector."

"Sõnn's the one you should really thank. If he hadn't noticed you were there, and alerted me, who knows what would have happened? But we don't have a lot of time. Lepp and Kleber will do whatever they can to get themselves off the hook. So we need that film your photographer took. Can you phone him right away and ..."

"It's done! While you were downstairs. The same thought had occurred to me, so I phoned Tõnu and asked him to send the whole roll here, addressed to you."

"Good thinking! The other priority must be Pilvik. They'll want to get him back and either get him to retract his statement or maybe just kill him."

"I don't think he's safe anywhere in this building," commented Sõnn.

"Let me make a call," said Hallmets,

Hallmets dialled the internal number for Colonel Reinart. The colonel answered after two rings.

"Hallmets here. Can you do me a favour, in connection with the Vaher case? I've got a witness, and I need him in a safe house for a few nights."

"Have you got the people who killed Vaher?"

"Not yet, but I've nailed the people who killed the two thugs, Lehmja and Kauščis. Three police officers. One of them's confessed, but I need him safe till the other two are under arrest."

"Police officers! That's not good. When can he be ready?"

"As soon as he's signed his statement. It's being typed up now. I'd say twenty minutes."

"OK. A car will pick them up in thirty minutes in Lai Street, opposite St. Olav's Church. Your guard should give him the password 'Casablanca.' The driver will reply 'Vienna.' I'll call you back when they're installed in the safe house."

"Thanks."

"Don't mention it."

As Hallmets put the phone down, he thought, now I owe him one. What might he ask me to do? He turned to Sõnn, "Hjalmar, I've arranged a safe house for Pilvik. Do you have two reliable men who can keep an eye on Pilvik at the safe house, and keep their mouths shut afterwards?"

Sõnn thought for a moment. "We can use Ilves – he's sharp as a lynx – and Mürakas – if Pilvik gives any trouble he'll just sit on him. I'll see if I can find them." He went off.

Marta popped in to say she'd had a call from reception to say a package had arrived for the Chief Inspector.

"Can you fetch it now," said Hallmets, "And take Eva with you, just to be on the safe side." Marta looked at him as if to suggest that she could look after herself perfectly well, but nevertheless nodded and went out.

Kallas winced and groaned.

"Are you OK?" asked Hallmets.

"No, this is bloody painful. But I'm not going to miss any of this. The scoop of a lifetime. Almost worth being beaten up for it. What do you think your pals downstairs are up to now? I don't see Lepp giving in quietly."

"They'll be weighing up their options, I'd guess. Should they go to the newspaper office and try to seize the film? Should they come up here to try and get hold of Pilvik? Or maybe go to Captain Lind and claim they've been framed?"

The phone rang. Hallmets picked it up.

"Jüri, it's Peeter. I've got a difficult situation here. Inspector Lepp has made some serious allegations against you and your team. That you abducted a prisoner they were interviewing, and assaulted Officer Pilvik and Sergeant Kleber. They also claim you're now forcing a false confession out of Pilvik. You'll need to come down here and explain what's going on."

"Sorry Peeter, I'm afraid I'm rather busy now. These allegations are false. Lepp and Kleber killed Lehmja and Kausčis, Pilvik has confessed to his part in it, without any pressure. The so-called 'prisoner' was Jaan Kallas the reporter. If I hadn't got him out of the basement, they'd have killed him."

"Oh. Well, you'd best come down now and put your side of the story. I've asked Dr. Luik to come over too. This not a request Jüri, it's an order."

"Sorry, Peeter. I'm not coming down without the evidence I need to arrest those two. Marta's almost finished typing up Pilvik's statement, so I'll be down as soon as he's signed it. Then you can be the judge. Fifteen minutes." He put the phone down without waiting for an answer. "Lepp and Kleber are claiming we've framed them."

"All the more reason to get hold of those pictures," said Kallas, "Look, I'll come down with you, tell them what happened, show the bruises."

"OK. Having an outside person in there might not be a bad idea. Sõnn's not officially on my team, so he'll be useful too. If Luik's there and we can persuade him there's a *prima facie* case against Lepp and Kleber, we might be able to arrest them on the spot."

They heard the outer door of the workroom open and a moment later Marta came in and handed over the package from the newspaper. "No-one ambushed us," she said, "I'll get the statement finished now."

Tõnu was not stupid, and he had included both a contact print of the complete roll of film, so that the sequence of events was clear, and a larger print of Pilvik and Kleber in the archway.

As Hallmets and Kallas were studying the contact print, the phone rang. Hallmets picked it up, expecting it to be Captain Lind, but it was Marta, saying there was a call for Kallas. He passed the phone to Kallas, then went through to the workroom to see how things were progressing. The statement was typed and Pilvik was now reading a copy of it, with some difficulty, and with Larsson going through it with him and reading out the longer words. Hallmets wondered how Pilvik had got into the police, and even made the CID. He'd clearly got some help from higher up.

49

Hallmets remembered Maslov was back from the docks, and asked him for a report.

"I had a good look round, and then had lunch with some of the

Russians who work there. They reckon they've seen that lorry down at one of the warehouses. I checked the place out, and it's used by a couple of firms." He consulted his notes. "One is Astiz AB of Nörrkoping, Sweden, the other is Krummfeldt of Tallinn. I took a little peep inside. Cases labelled 'machine parts' from Krummfeldt heading for Nörrkoping, Turku, and Riga. I gave them a little sniff too, and I'd bet you a kilo of onions there's alcohol in some of them. If we raided the place now ..."

"We'd find evidence of smuggling. But that's not what we want right now, until we've a clearer link with von Langenstein. Besides which, if this is a regular business, even if we miss this consignment, we can intercept a later one."

"OK, boss. One other thing. I persuaded one of the guys to give me a ring if there's a lot of activity at that warehouse. Can I give him a modest reward?"

"Yes. Put it on expenses. Good work, Oleg."

The door opened and Sõnn came in with two other men, one who looked like a museum curator, with unruly brown hair and round glasses, and the other wider even than Maslov, puffing at the exertion of mounting the stairs to the top floor. "Lukas Ilves and Evald Mürakas," announced Sõnn. Hallmets shook hands with the men, thanked them for being willing to do the guard duty, and assured them that he'd sign for the overtime. They seemed happy with that.

By now Pilvik had finished reading his statement, and signed the top copy and two carbon copies. "Can I go now?" he said, "You're going to keep me safe, please?"

"Don't worry, Konrad, old buddy," said Sõnn, "Lukas and Evald will look after you. They're going to take you to a safe place now. I'll phone you up and see how you're getting on, and let you know when it's safe to come back."

"Tell Mama I'm OK," said Pilvik, and sniffed, "Can we go now?"

Hallmets explained the where the car would wait, and the passwords.

"Casablanca," said Sõnn, "I went there once. Got horribly ill. Bad dates."

"Ah, Vienna," put in Ilves, "Now there's a city. So many magnificent buildings. But it's too big, you know, too grand. I was glad to be back in a place that's small enough that you know it."

"I'll go with them to the rendezvous," said Sõnn, "And see they get away OK. We'll go down the staircase at the rear end of the building and out the side exit into the lane." He led Pilvik, handcuffed to Mürakas, and Ilves out into the corridor.

Hallmets went back to his office. Kallas had finished his call. "That was Eirik Hunt," he explained, "Kleber turned up at the offices demanding to be taken to the photographic room. Waved an envelope, said he had a warrant. Marched past reception without waiting for a reply. Kristiina – she's the receptionist – alerted Hunt right away. In fact, because he stuck out as police by a mile, no-one would tell him where Tõnu's base was. Hunt, along with a couple of the despatch handlers, who are heavy guys, caught up with Kleber on the third floor, reading the signs on every door. He was only three doors away from Tõnu's. When Hunt asked Kleber what he was up to, he said he was on essential police business to do with a murder enquiry, and he had to search the photographic room for 'essential evidence'. When Hunt asked to see the warrant, Kleber waved the envelope in front of him. He didn't expect Hunt to snatch it from his hand. The envelope turned out to be empty. When Hunt told the handlers to throw Kleber out the building, he decided to go, but swore he'd be back with reinforcements. 'Come back with a warrant then,' said Hunt, 'The Nazis aren't in charge here.' Once he'd gone Hunt ordered the doors bolted and phoned me – Tõnu had told him I was over here."

"We'd better go down and see Lind then," said Hallmets.

When Hallmets and Kallas, who found walking very painful, got to Lind's door and Hallmets knocked, there was no answer. He opened the door. The large office was empty, apart from Captain Lind and a bottle of vodka. The captain, slumped behind his desk, had evidently had plenty of it. He looked up at the newcomers with little interest.

"Where's Lepp?" demanded Hallmets.

"He's gone," muttered the captain, "Said he couldn't wait, too much to do."

"When did he go?"

"Not long ago. Ten, twenty minutes, I don't know. Kleber arrived, said he had to speak to Lepp urgently. Lepp went out to talk to him, said he had to go."

"What about Luik?"

"Never showed up."

There was an urgent knock on the door, and Sõnn came in. "Sorry I'm late – oh, where is everybody?"

"They're off," said Hallmets, "To rethink. What are they likely to do?"

"If Lepp's got the file linking Luik to Härg, they could go to Luik."

"What's that?" muttered Lind, "Luik and Härg?"

"Luik could sign a warrant to seize the photos," said Hallmets, "Could even issue arrest warrants for Sõnn and Larsson for assault. That would muddy the waters enough for them to dispute Pilvik's confession, even claim that we wrote it and forced him to sign. I would be suspended, and Lepp would be in line to take over the Vaher case. And Vaher's job."

"Then you need get hold of this file," said Kallas, lowering himself painfully into one of the chairs. "If you don't mind, Captain, I'll take a little of your vodka."

"Peeter, pull yourself together," urged Hallmets, "Do you have pass keys for this building?"

Lind sat up straighter, pushed the bottle towards Kallas. "Help yourself." Then he took a small key from his waistcoat pocket, unlocked the bottom drawer of his desk, and extraced a bundle of keys on a ring, perhaps fifteen or twenty. He handed these to Hallmets. "I don't know which one's which, but between them they'll open all the rooms here. What are you going to do?"

"Lepp's got a file that links Luik to Härg. We need to get it." Hallmets picked up the phone. "What's Lepp's number?"

"231," said Sõnn.

Hallmets dialled. And listened. "OK. Sounds like he's not in. Can you get down there and see if you can find that file. That OK with you, Peeter?"

Lind nodded, trying to concentrate. "Yes, whatever you say, Jüri."

Sõnn left. Kallas produced a small bottle of aspirin pills Marta had given him from her first aid box. He took two and washed them down with a swig from the vodka bottle. He glanced at the label. "*Leikari.* Good stuff. Never seen it in the shops, is it imported?"

"No, it's quite local actually," said Hallmets. "Peeter, we need to tell you what's happened."

By the end of the account Lind was wide awake. "This looks pretty persuasive, Jüri, but if Luik won't look at it ..."

"Then we need another magistrate."

"Right. Yes, of course. I'll try Dr Kellassepp, I've always found him open-minded. Vaher didn't like him, thought he wasn't proactive enough, wasted time examining the evidence for himself. I'll give you a call when he gets here."

Hallmets ushered Kallas into his office. Marta popped her head in to report that Colonel Reinart had phoned to confirm that Pilvik was at the safe house.

171

"Thanks for your help, *Härra* Kallas," Hallmets began.

"Please, it's Jaan."

"Thank you. Jüri." They shook hands.

"Jaan, I need to ask for some discretion here. I need to know you're not going to write everything you've heard, before it's all been sorted out. After that you can write a book if you like, but for now..."

"I understand. You don't need to worry. I'm not going blow all this stuff in just one article, that would be a terrible waste. Besides, I can't tell all till you've got Lepp and Kleber in the bag. Just don't tell all the other papers everything until I've had a chance to use it. If it's OK with you, what I'll write for tomorrow's paper is how I was grabbed off the street and beaten up. Then rescued by your team. Only what I witnessed myself."

"That sounds good. If you don't mind, I'll hang on to the photos. You won't need them for your article; maybe before and after shots of your face would do! And once we've got this sorted out, you'll get the first interview with me. I promise. Now I'm going to order a police car to take you to the hospital."

50

Artur Simm sat in the tiny single office which marked his raised status at *Pealinna Uudised*. He needed something dramatic for the next day. He'd thought he'd get a good piece from his interview with Härg, but when he went through his notes, he found Härg hadn't said anything very substantial. However, an article covering the deaths of Lehmja and Kauščis, Lepp's achievements, further mention of the mysterious criminal mastermind, and comment on the case from a prominent businessman looked okay. Time to take it to Hunt.

As he came out of the office, on the fourth floor, he sensed a certain commotion amongst those in the corridor. He asked someone what was going on. "They're saying there was a cop downstairs, trying to get into the photography room."

Artur headed for Tõnu's office, and went in. Tõnu and his assistant Ernst were taking rolls of negative film out of boxes and hanging them up. "Give us a hand, Artur, will you," called Tõnu, "We had to get all these out of sight, even though they're not quite dry." He passed Artur a pile of small boxes. "You missed all the excitement. He was almost here, when Hunt and a couple of heavies intercepted him. Then threw him out. No warrant. He had an envelope, but it was empty. Can you imagine that. The cheek of it."

"What was he looking for?" asked Artur, taking a film out and hanging it from one of the clips attached to a cord stretched across the room near the ceiling.

"A whole roll. I shot it for Kallas, up at the viewpoint. *That* viewpoint. When they found Kauščis. In fact, it wasn't here, but the cop didn't know that."

"Who was the cop?"

"Kleber. Lepp's crony. Nasty piece of work. He'd have made a real mess if he'd got in here."

"Where's Kallas?" asked Artur.

"I'm not supposed to say. But take it from me, it's all happening."

Artur put the boxes on the counter by the cupboard. "Sorry Tõnu, got to go." He made his way to Hunt's office, puzzling over this incident.

Hunt seemed preoccupied, and barely looked at his piece. "Yes, that'll do fine," he said, putting it onto the pile already in the tray labelled 'TONIGHT'S EDITION.'

Artur coughed politely. "Er, Sir, should I write something about this incident with the policeman here? I could interview you about it."

"Eh?" said Hunt abruptly, then seemed to replay his memory to remember what Artur had said. "No, no, that won't be necessary. Kallas will be back soon, I'll need to hear what he has to say. He'll have a pretty good piece, I imagine. But thanks for the offer, Simm, that's positive thinking. Good."

Back in the corridor, Artur didn't feel so good about it. He had no idea what Kallas had been up to, but it sounded dramatic. Maybe he was doing it just to show Hunt he was better than Artur. He reminded himself that Kallas speculated from his office, while he, Artur Simm, got down to the nitty-gritty and captured the facts as they happened.

51

By the time Hallmets got back to the workroom Larsson, Maslov and Lesser were seated round the table. Kadakas had just brought coffee up from the canteen for everyone, when there was a knock at the door, and Sõnn came in. "Bingo!" he said to Hallmets, handing over to him a brown folder tied shut with faded yellow ribbon.

Hallmets untied the ribbon and flicked through the contents, then closed it again. "Well done, Hjalmar, where did you find it?"

"Top drawer of his desk. False bottom."

"Take a seat, have some coffee," said Hallmets. With interspersed comments from Sõnn and Larsson, he brought them up to date on what had happened with Lepp and Kallas.

"What happens next, chief?" asked Lesser.

"The file will have to go straight up to Prefect Rotenbork."

"What if he's a pal of Härg's too?" asked Maslov.

"He's not," said Lesser, "Rotenbork is a bit stiff, but he's OK."

"Could Härg or Luik, have had Vaher killed? Because of the file," asked Larsson.

Lesser continued. "Well, Härg doesn't draw the line at killing people. But off Toompea, that doesn't fit, he's more discreet. Even the Englishman who fell off the cliff, that was on his own estate, not in the middle of town. And I'd guess Vaher was using the file mainly to pressurise Luik, so Härg could live with it. With Luik, no, I don't see him setting up a killing. At heart he's a coward. Plenty of hot air but no guts."

"Thanks, Henno," said Hallmets, "Now the alcohol racket. Oleg has located the warehouse where stuff is stored for both Astiz AB and Krummfeldt. He's sure there's alcohol in some of the crates there. And Lembit spotted the lorry from Heinaküla at the Krummfeldt works. Henno, anything from your surveillance today?"

"Not much, chief. The lorry set off about half past ten, and went to the Krummfeldt place. We couldn't get round the back to see it, but it was there for a couple of hours – that's when Lembit must have seen it – then went back to the estate. The same thing happened this afternoon. Ilmar is still out at Heinaküla, keeping an eye on the place."

"Eva, anything to add from the paperwork?"

"Yes," said Larsson, "There's a ship, it's called *SS Dimitrios*, Greek-registered, sails every Thursday afternoon at five from Tallinn to Nörrkoping, Sweden, gets there at about mid-day on Friday; then off at five from Nörrkoping to Turku, in Finland, where it arrives about 10 am on Saturday. Then on Monday afternoon from Turku to Nörrkoping, and on Tuesday from Nörrkoping back to Tallinn, arriving here about mid-day on Wednesday. That ship handles the the Krummfeldt and Astiz shipments in and out of Tallinn. I'm wondering if the alcohol from Heinaküla is being shipped in Krummfeldt crates to Sweden and Finland. That would suggest that it's delivered to the Krummfeldt works from the distillery in plain boxes, then transferred to Krummfeldt-branded crates at the works for onward shipment in amongst the real crates of machine parts. The deliveries seem to be going on all week, since Oleg noticed stuff already in the warehouse today. Quite a big operation, then."

"If that's right, we've only one more link to make," said Hallmets.

"Is anything coming back to Heinaküla? The alcohol's going out, but is something else coming back in?"

"That would be a good way of smudging the money trail," said Larsson, "Sell the alcohol and use the money over there to buy something to bring back, then turn that back into money by selling whatever it is over here."

"Right. So if we see stuff going from the harbour to the estate on Wednesday, after that ship's arrived, that's when we'll raid the estate."

"Will that help with the Vaher case?" asked Larsson.

"If we can get inside the house, we may find something incriminating. Or somebody on the estate could be persuaded to talk. Vaher can't have been unaware of the distribution activities in his own back garden. I suspect the payments Eva found are part of his cut. Maybe for just keeping quiet about it."

"Albrecht's pen at the viewpoint," said Larsson, "That does suggest a connection."

"He'll say it was stolen or lost long before the killing. But it's too much of a coincidence."

"Could the German government be involved?" Larsson continued. "Albrecht being a diplomat."

"Let's hope not," said Hallmets, "That's the last thing we want."

"What about the wife, then, boss?" asked Maslov, "Should we bring her in for questioning?"

"No, not yet. We've got to tread very carefully there."

"What about Kallas' theory that she's involved with Lepp?" put in Lesser, "I think it's a bit far-fetched myself. But Kallas isn't stupid, there may be something in it."

"I'd agree with that," said Hallmets, "Right, tomorrow's Sunday. We'll keep watching the movements from the estate, and hope we see a clear link to the warehouse. Then I can get a warrant for a raid sometime in the week."

Hallmets gave everyone the evening off, and retired to his office to read Vaher's file on Luik and Härg. It made interesting reading. The file began with material referring to the murder of a businessman in 1928, before Vaher's arrival back in Tallinn in 1930. Luik was then a lawyer, and represented Härg, who was suspected of involvement in the affair. Luik's legal role in the purchase of Härg's estate – at a suspiciously low price – was then flagged. His later visits to the estate and participation in social events fronted by Härg were noted, along with his involvement in the project to construct a golf course near

Tallinn. The file concluded with handwritten notes – by Vaher? – on Luik's behaviour since his promotion to the bench in 1929. Vaher suggested that Luik was receiving a regular backhander from Härg, though his evidence was not quoted.

It seemed that Vaher had decided to use what he knew of Luik and Härg to his advantage. Particularly with Luik, who had the most to lose if the material were released. But, although the file would raise a lot of suspicions, Hallmets felt there was not enough hard evidence there to prosecute either man. The most likely outcome, when Rotenbork read it, was a slap on the wrist for Luik. He might even be asked to resign from the bench, 'for reasons of health.' And there the matter would rest. A discreet solution with no danger of a public outcry.

Time to go back to his hotel. He checked the workroom; Maslov was still there, reading a magazine at the table.

"Nowhere to go?" asked Hallmets.

"We thought it might not be safe for you to walk back to your hotel on your own, so I volunteered to see you there."

"We'd better get going then."

They walked rapidly to the Imperial Hotel in the gathering dusk. No-one sprang out of the shadows at them. But Hallmets realised this was a wise precaution on the part of his colleagues. If anything happened to him, the political chaos could escalate, and who knows where that might lead.

Back at the hotel, he offered to treat Maslov to dinner in the hotel restaurant. While his guest tucked into a roast pork knuckle with sauerkraut, potatoes and mustard, Hallmets chose a meat loaf with potatoes, broad beans and gravy. Both took a glass of the Saku beer from the cask.

"How are things down in Petseri?" asked Hallmets.

"Very strange. Life goes on as usual. It's not a big town, but it has its choir and band. I sing bass in the men's choir. Great fun. But there's a tension too. We all know the Reds can roll right through whenever they want to – there's nothing to stop them."

"You think it will happen?"

"Sooner or later. It's bound to, I think. Not just to Petseri, but the whole of Estonia. The Reds are just the inheritors of the Czarist empire, and they want to reclaim all the territories they lost after 1917. Sooner or later there'll be a war between Hitler and Stalin, and then we'll be stuck in the middle. My wife wants us to emigrate. To America. Her brothers are there already – they run a restaurant in Boston. They say there are good opportunities in the police there too, especially for people with experience. So we're taking English lessons now. It's not an easy decision to make. I mean, I like the work here, and Estonia is a great country. It's just a pity it's where it is."

"Your wife's keeping things going at home?"

"Yes. Ekaterina's her name. We've got a little plot of land, so the cow and the pig and the chickens need looking after. And the children too, of course, there are four of them, three at primary, the eldest at secondary school. It would be a big change for them to move so far, but I'm not sure there's a future here. For any of us. I think in the long run Estonia is doomed. And when the Reds do get back here, there'll be a bloodbath, I'm telling you. The cops will be amongst the first to be rounded up and shot. We'll be replaced by Red thugs enforcing political correctness. After all, socialism is perfect, so there can't be any crime, can there? Only treason."

"You sound quite sure about that."

"My mother-in-law reads the cards. She told us all to get out."

They were just thinking about a dessert, when the waiter approached, saying that there was a policeman waiting in the lobby for Chief Inspector Hallmets. It was a uniformed officer, who saluted and explained he had a message from Inspector Lesser. Another body had been discovered, this time in Raekoja Plats, right in front of the Town Hall.

52

It didn't take Hallmets and Maslov long to walk there, in light rain. As soon as they emerged from the lane into the square, even though it was now dark, they saw in the light from the cafes and restaurants the crowd, clustered by the colonnaded frontage of the mediaeval Town Hall. Pushing through the spectators, they came to a police cordon, and were waved through towards a smaller gathering in a pool of light created by a portable electric lamp on a stand, a cable trailing from it towards the door of the Town Hall. In the centre of the light, like a scene from a play, a figure lay, face down on the glistening cobbles. He was dressed in a charcoal grey overcoat, and beside him lay a grey fedora. Under the overcoat dark pin-striped trousers were visible, and his black shoes were polished to a shine. The police photographer was taking shots of the body, and in the bright white of the magnesium powder flash Hallmets could see thinning hair and a small moustache.

Inspector Lesser came forward from the group by the body. "Glad to see you, chief. Another stiff. Is that one a day since Vaher?"

"Who is it?" asked Hallmets, who didn't recognise the dead man.

"Boris Popov. Runs a network of informants, sells to whoever will buy. According to witnesses a car stopped here at about twenty to eight. A minute or so later it drove away. The body wasn't noticed right away because the light here wasn't too good. Einar Sepp is off sick, so once the photographer's done, I'll get some uniforms onto their hands and knees, and see if there's anything to find."

"Where does Popov fit into all this?"

"I can't imagine. Everybody used him, even us sometimes, off the record, of course. The only reason I can think of is that he found some dirt that someone didn't want him to have. Maybe even about Vaher's death."

"Another complication. How was Popov killed?"

"Bullet in the back of the neck."

"Same as Kauščis. Another coincidence?"

"Could even be Lepp and Kleber continuing their drive to clean up the city."

"Just what we need. But then, things can always get worse, as my granddad used to say. OK, Henno, thanks for letting me know. I'll leave you to it. Oleg here can give you a hand."

Back at his hotel, Hallmets phoned Kirsti. Everything was fine in Tartu, even the weather was better. Kirsti wondered if she could come up on Sunday for the day. Hallmets advised her against it. The trains always took twice as long on Sundays, and with another body just discovered, he guessed he'd be pretty busy.

"Well, don't overdo it, will you? And eat sensibly. I miss you. Oh, by the way, you know Dr Levi, in the German department at the Uni, he was in this morning to say goodbye to all of us. He left a lovely box of chocolates, Kalev's best. He and his family are off to America. I asked him why he didn't wait till the end of term. He said since the Nazis were now in power, nowhere in Europe was safe, especially for Jews. He didn't name names, but he hinted that one or two of his colleagues were Nazi sympathisers, and could make things difficult for him."

"What'll he do in the States?"

"He's already been offered a job. Simpson College. It's in a little town near Albany, New York State. He showed me a photo they sent him – it looks lovely. They're getting a boat to Stockholm on Monday, then on Wednesday they sail from there to New York. Shame we're losing him, he was a nice guy, great sense of humour, his students love him. It really feels like there's a change in the atmosphere, and not for the better."

When his call was completed, Hallmets realised that twice in one evening he heard talk of people leaving the country. Was Europe really sinking into a period of darkness? Was the political choice between chaos and dictatorship? Had democracy shown itself to be incapable of dealing with economic crisis? He remembered the panic when the British had left the gold standard the previous year. Because Estonia didn't do likewise, prices started rising, and the trade balance got worse. The politicians seemed paralysed, as if they didn't understand what was happening.

Was his own case a little part of the descent into darkness? The beginning of the end for law and order? It wasn't a good thought to go to bed on.

Day 5. Sunday 26ᵗʰ March 1933

53

Hallmets was in his office at eight, reading the Sunday edition of *Pealinna Uudised*. The front page headline ran, '*Reporter Beaten by Rogue Police!*' It was written by the editor, Eirik Hunt, and described how Jaan Kallas had been seized in the street, taken to a basement in Pikk Street, and viciously beaten by two police officers, Kleber and Pilvik. These men made it clear they were acting on the instructions of Inspector Lepp, whose suspicious behaviour the brave reporter had drawn attention to in the pages of *Pealinna Uudised*. Kallas' ordeal only ended when he was rescued by a dynamic trio, '*Tartu CID boss Jüri Hallmets, Tallinn's own Inspector Hjalmar Sõnn, and attractive young female detective Eva Larsson,*' who had confronted the two thugs and their boss, and got Kallas out. Hunt declared that it was time that, '*the bad apples, or rather, mad dogs, within the police force were winkled out and cast into the abyss. There is no place for them in a free society.*' He went on to say that the attack on Kallas proved that his suspicions were correct, and he concluded, '*it is time for Lepp's possible role in the murder of Chief Inspector Vaher to be taken seriously. We await the arrests of the criminal Lepp and his murderous associate, faded film star Laura Vaher. It is time to cleanse the Augean Stables, and throw the Hydra and his gorgon to the dogs.*'

Hallmets smiled to himself as he read the report. On the one hand, this was bad publicity for the police. On the other, it made it clear that there were good policemen (and women), as well as bad ones. The report would certainly not help Lepp if he was intending to hit back at Hallmets.

A line at the bottom of Hunt's piece advised the reader to turn to page 2 for Jaan Kallas' own account of the event. Here Hallmets found the whole page devoted to Kallas' description of his experiences, varying in style from dramatic to lurid. The beating scene in particular had brought out Kallas's most colourful prose. Pilvik was described as '*drooling with pleasure as his bloodstained fist smashed again and again into my face,*' while Kleber was '*sneering and manic, like some crazed inquisitor of the Middle Ages,*' and Lepp, when he finally appeared, was '*a cold and demonic mastermind, an orchestrator of violent death.*' Pictures accompanying the article included Lepp pointing at the camera with an angry expression, Hallmets lookin calm at the news conference, and one of Larsson in a short-sleeved shirt holding a rifle, presumeably taken during a shooting competition. Before and after shots of Kallas were not included – perhaps the hospital had done too good a job patching him up – but the paper's artist had drawn the scene of the beating in a manner worthy of the best cinema posters.

There was more of interest in the paper. At the bottom of page 4 was a piece by Artur Simm, based on an interview with Mihkel Härg. The article was full of praise for Härg, described as '*a model for Estonian businessmen, open and hospitable.*' Apart from that, however, the piece was fairly content-free. Härg's views on the Vaher case were mostly bland platitudes. Hallmets expected the piece to conclude with a repetition of Simm's view that Lepp should be taking over the Vaher case, but it wasn't there. He guessed it had been taken out, probably by Hunt, and that *Pealinna Uudised* would now cease to champion Inspector Lepp.

As he closed the paper he glanced at the Stop Press column on the left of the front page, where breaking news could be added right up the point where the presses began to roll. A short item reported the discovery of a body identified as one Boris Popov in Raekoja Plats the previous evening.

He looked into the workroom. Kadakas, in his blending-into-the-background clothes, was reading a book. He jumped to his feet as soon as Hallmets came in. "Good morning, Sir."

"Morning, Ants, what are you reading?"

"Oh, nothing really. A detective story. *The Man who was Nobody.* Edgar Wallace. Just published in Estonian."

"Is it any good?"

"It moves fairly quickly, but the characters aren't very realistic."

"Yes, I've read one or two of his. *The Four Just Men*, that was quite good."

"Sad that he died just last year. He was working on the script for *King Kong*. It came out in America at the beginning of this month. They say it's the greatest horror film ever made."

A few minutes later, Marta informed him that Captain Lind had arranged a meeting with Dr Kellassepp at two o'clock that afternoon in his office.

By half past eight Maslov, Larsson and Hekk had arrived. Maslov reported that nothing more had come up on Popov's killing the previous night. The post-mortem was set for that afternoon, but it didn't seem it would tell them anything more than they'd already seen.

Unfortunately, since Popov had been shot somewhere else, then dumped in Raekoja Plats, there was no bullet. So they couldn't link his death to any of the others. Lesser was working on the case.

"Now we've got five unsolved murders," said Hallmets, "Though it looks like we can put two of them down to Kleber and Lepp. Oleg, can you and Hekk go over to Heinaküla and keep an eye open for any movements? We don't want to be caught out of anything dramatic happens."

54

Artur Simm frowned as he sat in bed reading the Sunday edition of *Pealinna Uudised*. Once again Kallas had grabbed all the headlines. It was so irritating. So he'd been roughed up by the police, but what did he expect after virtually accusing Lepp of being a murderer as well as having an affair with Vaher's wife. Nevertheless, cops beating up a reporter was never a good idea. If they got away with it, it could easily happen to others too, even himself. He shivered at the thought. But splashing the front page with it, and Hunt himself writing it, was a bit much. And then all the stuff from Kallas on page 2. Artur was green with envy. He had to admit, Kallas could write. If only he'd gone straight to Hunt when he'd first been threatened by Mr P, he would probably have been asked to write a piece like this. He could write about his encounter with Blind Rudi too, but then he'd probably be arrested for murder, and that wouldn't help.

Then, glancing at page 4, he caught sight of his own piece at the bottom. He read it quickly, and realised it had been heavily edited. Half the stuff he'd put in about Lepp had been excised, as well as some remarks he'd made about Hallmets' handling of the Vaher case. Of course, Hallmets was the hero now, having saved Kallas. He'd have to think carefully about what he wrote next.

As he closed the paper, he saw the notice about the body found in Raekoja Plats. Boris Popov. Artur sat up straight. Mr P. His persecutor was dead. Now he smiled. His bondage was over, and he didn't have to worry about Marju or his other fingers again.

"What are you looking so happy about?" asked Marju, sitting next to him, with the latest issue of *Today's Estonian Woman.*

"Remember that man I told you about, the one who threatened us. He's dead. His body was dumped in Raekoja Plats last night."

"Like in *Scarface*? You know, when Keach's body is thrown out of the moving car onto the street right outside the gangsters' headquarters.

Do they know who did it?"

"No, just a brief notice in the Stop Press." Artur suddenly had a picture in his head of Mihkel Härg, smiling over coffee and pastries – Marju had loved those pastries, they'd had some for breakfast – and asking if he'd heard who the criminal mastermind might be, and himself naming Mr P. The penny dropped – he had himself had condemned Mr P to death by giving Härg his name. Now he knew something the others didn't: he knew who had killed Mr P. But then again, it wasn't information he could make much use of, or Härg might just finish him off too.

"Artur, you're not listening!"

"Sorry, dearest, I was thinking over what this all means. What did you say?"

"I said, what about those two thugs of his, were they killed too?"

"Well, there's nothing about it here."

"I mean, they may try to take over his business. You know, like in the film. The underlings always think they can do it better than the boss."

Artur hadn't thought of that. It was true, yesterday's henchmen can be tomorrow's bosses. "OK. We'd better take care, and keep the door secure at night."

And the more he thought about it, the more likely it seemed that Vlad and Igor might want to take over their former boss's business. Maybe it was even them who killed Mr P, and not Härg.

"The weather looks nice," said Marju, "We could go the park at Kadriorg. There's always a band playing there on a Sunday afternoon."

But Artur was still thinking. What would happen to Lepp now? Maybe he could contact the inspector, get his side of Kallas' story. "Must make a phone call," he said to Marju, then jumped out of bed and went to the living room, phoned Pikk Street. But Inspector Lepp wasn't in his office. Then he remembered the slip of paper Lepp had given him. He went back to the bedroom, groped in his trouser pockets, and there it was. Lepp's home number. It puzzled him that Lepp wasn't at the station, given the important cases that were in progress, but maybe Hallmets was keeping him out of the loop, isolating him out of jealousy no doubt. He gave the operator the number.

Someone picked up on the second ring. "Who is this?" Lepp's voice, urgent, stressed.

"Artur Simm here. I wondered if we might have another chat."

"I'm busy at the moment," snapped Lepp. Then paused. "No, wait, the bar at the Baltic Station, be there in fifteen minutes." And he hung up.

The bar was virtually empty when Artur arrived, but he saw Lepp at once, at the darkest corner table. He went over. A single glass of cognac sat on the table in front of Lepp.

"Sit!" hissed the inspector, "I don't have much time."

Artur sat. "What's going on?"

"Just listen! I've only got a few minutes. This is just for you. There's a conspiracy. I think Lind's behind it. He never liked Vaher, and as soon as Vaher was dead, he got his old pal Hallmets in. Now the pair of them are trying to frame me for killing Lehmja and Kauscis. It's all part of a purge to get rid of anyone who worked closely with Vaher. There's probably a political motive. Those liberals keep mouthing on about justice and equality, when they should be taking out the bad guys."

When he paused to draw breath, Artur got in a question: "So who did kill Lehmja and Kauscis?"

"What? Who knows? Some crime boss."

"You must have some idea? I can't write that you haven't a clue."

Lepp frowned. "All right. I'd say the main suspect would be Härg. He's the Mr Big around Tallinn. But there's no proof. And he always has an alibi – having dinner with an MP or a businessman, at the theatre or some sporting event, whatever. But you can't write that. He'd have his lawyers onto your paper right away, and probably take you out too."

Artur gulped. "So where does Popov fit into all this? Was that Härg, do you think?"

Lepp smiled. "Ah yes, Popov. Yes, here's what I think. Popov was the middleman Härg used to organise the killings. He probably hired Lehmja and Kauscis to kill Vaher, and then got some other goons to kill them. Now Härg's had someone else rub out Popov. Neat. But it might be better for you to leave out Härg's role. Suggest Popov was the mastermind. And that other underworld bosses were so horrified by his killing of Vaher that they got rid of him. End of story."

"What are you going to do now, then?"

"I'm keeping a low profile until Lind and Hallmets run out of steam. Hallmets has got all his pals on the main cases now, they don't want people like me there, who might show them up. But I'll be back, believe me. And here's another thing. Those liberals, their influence won't last much longer. Things will be changing. Our day will come." He knocked back the brandy in one gulp, and stood up. "I've got to go now."

"But ..."

"Stay loyal to me, Simm, and you won't regret it." And he was gone.

Artur had to work hard to get everything he could remember Lepp had said into his notebook. Then he walked back to the flat. This was useful. No other journalist had a link with Lepp. He started writing his article in his head. He'd get a bit done this morning, and finish it after they'd been to the park. He even whistled a tune, the one from *Scarface* that Tony Camonte whistled before he killed someone.

55

At two Hallmets went down to Captain Lind's office. The captain was drinking coffee with another man, a tall gentleman with a white moustache and beard, dressed formally in a style that made Hallmets think of the time before the war, when the Russian Empire seemed like a settled part of the world's furniture. He wore a white shirt with a winged collar and bow tie, black waistcoat and tailed coat, grey trousers and shiny black shoes, with spats. His black top hat sat upside down on top of a cupboard near the door. Hallmets recognised Dr Kellassepp, one of the senior magistrates, and greeted him. Lind offered him another seat round his desk.

Hallmets took both of them through all the evidence he had relating to Lepp, Kleber and Pilvik. He also mentioned Vaher's file on Luik and Härg. Kellassepp listened carefully, leaning forward slightly as if his hearing was not good. He studied Pilvik's statement for so long that Hallmets wondered if he were going to fall asleep. There were also typed witness statements from Sõnn, Larsson, Hallmets himself and Kallas, which Kellassepp studied too. Finally he laid them carefully on the desk.

"Yes, Chief Inspector, I would say there's a clear *prima facie* case there against Kleber and Lepp. Stronger against Kleber than Lepp, would be my judgement. Kleber was clearly involved, along with Pilvik, in the assault on Kallas. There is no excuse for this sort of behaviour, and both men must be punished severely for it. However, as regards Lepp, the evidence is weaker. In relation to the assault, he could argue that Kleber and Pilvik exceeded their orders, and he was reluctant to take them to task in front of an outsider, especially a reporter. That would of course be a lapse of professionalism, but no more. The charge that he and Kleber murdered Lehmja and Kauščis is weaker. Apart from Pilvik's confession, you have nothing substantial. Lepp could argue that Pilvik had some sort of grudge against him, and made it up, or that you and your colleagues intimidated him into confessing, and then wrote the statement for him. The photograph of Pilvik and Kleber at the viewpoint certainly suggests they were already there, but Lepp could claim that he sent them up there as soon as he got the anonymous call, to protect any possible crime scene. And you have no forensic evidence linking Lepp to either Lehmja or Kausčis. So, as far as Lepp goes, it all hangs on Pilvik's confession."

"So how do you propose we proceed?" asked Hallmets.

"Don't get me wrong, Chief Inspector, personally I'd agree with you that Lepp is the leader of this nasty little bunch. I also don't like his attitude to the business of policing. The law is there to be respected, not just pushed aside when you think you know better. Sadly Vaher was the same, and I suspect Lepp wants to take his place. But, and this is a big but, I'm afraid, as a magistrate I have to be ruled by the evidence. I will gladly give you a warrant for the arrest of Kleber on an assault charge, and the police will be able to say goodbye to him and Pilvik. He can also be questioned about the murders of Lehmja and Kausčis; and if you're lucky he may incriminate Lepp. As far as Lepp himself is concerned, I can order you to question him, and for him to be arrested if he fails to present himself voluntarily. I can also advise Prefect Rotenbork to suspend him whilst he is under investigation. I'm sorry, but that's as far as I can go."

They were silent, as Hallmets thought through Kellassepp's decision. Finally he nodded. "Thank you, *Härra Doktor*, I can see your reasoning. What about the file Vaher had prepared on Luik and Härg?"

"In relation to Lepp, his possession of the file does not advance the case against him. He can simply argue that Vaher had given him access to it as a sort of insurance for himself, and that he didn't know what was in it."

"The existence of the file could point to Härg as Vaher's killer," observed Hallmets.

"I'd have to read the file before answering that," answered Kellassepp gruffly. "It depends how much evidence there is in there of any crime on Härg's part. In order for the existence of the file itself to be significant, you'd have to show Härg either knew or had reason to think that there was something in it which incriminated him. There are a lot of ifs there, I'm afraid."

"And Härg has never been convicted of any crime," added Lind. "We suspect he's behind a lot of stuff, but there's never anything linking it directly to him. To all intents and purposes, he's just a businessman. We'll only get him if one of his aides decides to spill the beans, and that's unlikely, as the guy's life wouldn't be worth much after that."

"Chief Inspector," asked Kellassepp, "You've read the file. Do *you* think there's clear evidence there of anything illegal on Härg's part?"

Hallmets frowned. "That's not easy for me to answer. Unfortunately, much of it is hearsay. It certainly suggests a relationship between a businessman and a magistrate that's too close for professional detachment on Luik's part, and from which Härg may have gained some advantage. It also certainly raises a lot of questions, and if it got into the public domain, the newspapers would have a field day."

"I'll have to read it, and talk to the minister. If it's as you say, Luik will either get a slap on the wrist and maybe moved to another part of the country, or he could be asked to resign from the magistracy, and go back to being a lawyer. I'd appreciate it if you both kept the existence of the file to yourselves, until it's sorted out."

Hallmets needed some fresh air and exercise after that. Otherwise he was liable to beat up his waste-paper basket or coatstand. He understood entirely the magistrate's reasoning, and the limitations of what the law allowed them to do. Nevertheless, it was deeply disappointing. He'd thought that at least they'd got the men who killed Lehmja and Kauscis, and maybe a lead into Härg as well. Now it seemed that, even if they nailed Kleber and Pilvik, Lepp was going to wriggle away, and they'd nothing on Härg. The only positive sign was that it might get Luik off his back for a while.

It was cold and clear out on the streets. He walked briskly past the Interior Ministry and onto Lai Street, then up to Raekoja Plats. He noticed that there was now no sign remaining of the discovery of Popov's body in front of the town hall. He walked on to Vabadus Plats, where the memorial stood to those who'd died in the war. He took off his hat, and stood for a few moments with head bowed in front of the monument. He'd lost friends and colleagues in the war. They'd fought for a free Estonia, and, although there were problems, the infant republic was, he felt, succeeding. And yet, with Hitler's Germany to the west and Stalin's Russia to the east, the outlook was worrying. Both had a historical claim on Estonia – the Germans through the barons who had owned the land and the people, and the Russians through the Czar's political control up to 1917. Even if they ended up fighting each other, the Baltic states would probably be the battleground.

Hallmets moved on to a café on the square, to reflect, over coffee and cake, on his meeting with Kellassepp. It was clear that if they wanted to put Lepp clearly into the frame for the murders of Lehmja and Kauscis, they'd have to hope that Kleber could be persuaded to talk, at least to corroborate Pilvik's statement, and hopefully to add more detail.

With regard to Härg's involvement in Vaher's murder, he had to admit that it didn't look very plausible. It seemed Vaher and Härg had achieved a happy equilibrium, by which Vaher didn't bother Härg's operations as long as they remained out of sight, and arrested low-level members of the gang when the public needed reassurance that the police were not slacking.

But if Härg hadn't ordered Vaher's death, who had? Lepp? It might enhance his chances of promotion. But if Vaher had become Head of CID, he would surely have promoted Lepp to his number two. Or could it have been about something entirely different. This brought him to Kallas' view that Lepp and Vaher's wife had been having an affair. He'd have to question Laura Vaher again. But that would have to wait. He wanted the von Langensteins to think the police were no longer interested in them, so that the raid would catch them unprepared.

56

Artur and Marju had taken the bus out to the Russalka monument. It wasn't warm, but the sun was shining, and they had their coats on. They walked along the promenade and bought ice-creams from a vendor whose cart promised 'ice-cream in the real Italian style.' After the ice-creams, they walked back to Kadriorg Park. They walked past the palace where the prime minister lived when in town. There were a couple of soldiers at the main door, but not much sign of life otherwise.

Beyond the palace, they heard music playing and went on towards the bandstand by the ornamental lake, where a wind band from one of the city districts was in full swing. Swing being the appropriate word, as they played arrangements of some of the latest American favourites. Artur and Marju sat on a bench to watch, Artur tapping his feet. He put his arm round Marju, and she rested her head on his shoulder. They lost themselves in the music.

All at once Artur sat up straight. "Dammit!" he said.

"What's wrong?" Marju asked.

"Over there. Towards the lake. It's Mr P's thugs, Vlad and Igor. And they're looking this way. Let's go, quick." He dragged Marju up to her feet. "Come on, towards the kiosk." The kiosk sat at the entrance to the park from the main road, and it didn't take long for the Simms to get there. Artur glanced back, to see the two men pushing their way through the crowd gathered round the bandstand. "The tram-stop!" They ran towards the stop, although Matju's tight skirt and fashionable shoes limited her speed.

The stop was the terminus for the trams coming out to Kadriorg, and there was a tram sitting there. They got there, climbed aboard gasping, and threw themselves into a seat.

"You just made it," said the conductor, "Well, actually I saw you running, so we waited." He tapped the driver on the shoulder. "Come on, Paavo, we're half a minute late now."

As the doors shut and the tram began to move off, the two men reached it and ran alongside the door hitting it with their fists. The tram slowed down. Oh no, thought Artur, they're going to stop and let them on.

"Come on, Paavo," said the conductor, "We can't be waiting for everybody. There's another tram in ten minutes, and we're running late now." The tram picked up speed again. The two men waved their fists and shouted at the conductor, though it was hard to hear through the closed doors exactly what they were saying. "Anyway, they look like a couple of troublemakers," said the conductor, "Just as well we didn't pick them up."

Artur and Marju didn't say anything to each other for several minutes. When the tram passed the Viru Gate, leading into the Old Town, Artur said, "I don't think we should go home just yet. They know where we live, so maybe we should stay away from the house for a bit."

"Do you think they were after us, Artur, I mean, had they been following us, or did they just see us by accident?"

"I don't know. Whatever it was, it looked like they wanted to talk to us. And not just to say hello, I'm sure."

As they approached Vabadus Plats, Artur said, "Come on, let's get off here. There are plenty people about, so we won't stand out."

They got off the tram. A crowd had gathered to watch a band playing, next to the War Memorial. Just as they arrived, however, everybody stood still as the musicians started played the national anthem. Artur kept moving. "Come on, Marju," he hissed, "There's a café over there. Let's get inside."

As they reached the door, a tall man, leaning on a stick, was coming out. Artur skidded to a halt, and just avoided bumping into the man. He apologised.

"Have you no respect for your country, young man?" said the man, "When the anthem is played, you stand still, don't you understand that?" He turned to Marju and made a stiff bow of the head. "I'm sorry to speak unkindly to your husband, my dear lady, you were no doubt merely following him, as a good wife should. But he must learn to respect our country, which our anthem represents. I hope you will remind him in future." He inclined his head to her again, and walked off, moving one leg stiffly,

Artur and Marju made for a table right at the back of the cafe and sat down, sensing that there was silence in the café, and all eyes were upon them. Gradually, as the couple sat staring down at the table, interest waned, the eyes turned away, and conversation began again.

Artur ordered coffee and cake, and glanced round at the other customers. "Shit!" he said again to Marju.

"Oh, God, no!" she gasped, "How did they get here so fast?"

"No, no, dear, it's not them, we're OK. It's the guy sitting on his own at the table near the window. That's Hallmets."

"Chief Inspector Hallmets?"

"Yes."

"Do you think he recognised you?"

"I don't know. He's not looking this way, looks as if he's watching the people out in the square."

"Shouldn't we tell him? I mean, about those men following us?"

"No, no, then we'd have to tell him everything. Let's just keep quiet."

"At least with him there, those two men wouldn't dare come in here. Oh, have you noticed, he's missing two fingers from one hand. How awful. I suppose it was in the war. He's quite handsome, you know, I can imagine him in a uniform, waving a sword. I bet he was a general."

"Hmm. They say he got a medal from the Latvians. He led a charge, or something."

"I knew it! Maybe he comes to the War Memorial every Sunday afternoon, to remember his fallen comrades. How sad. Should we go and talk to him?"

"What? Are you mad?"

"No, not to tell him anything, just to chat. You're a reporter, don't you want to get to know him. If he knows you, he's more likely to give you information, isn't he?" Before Artur could say anything, she got up and walked over to Hallmets' table. Seeing her approach, the Chief Inspector stood up. "Chief Inspector, I'm sorry to disturb you," said Marju, offering her hand. "I'm Marju Simm. I think you may know my husband there."

Hallmets shook her hand politely. "I'm very pleased to meet you, *Proua* Simm. But I hope your husband isn't looking for an interview.

I'm off-duty at the moment."

"No, not at all," said Marju, "I just said to him that it's rude to dash past people you know without greeting them and exchanging a few words. If people talked more to each other, I think the world would be a much happier place. Don't you think so?" She gave her most charming of smiles, and it seemed to do the trick.

"Of course," said the Chief Inspector, "Please, do join me."

By this time Artur had reluctantly come over. Hallmets offered him a neutral expression and a handshake, and motioned him to sit alongside Marju. The waitress now arrived with the coffee and cakes, having spotted the couple changing tables. Artur offered to buy Hallmets a coffee.

"Thank you. I will have another. But this is my table, so please allow me to pay for everything."

Artur opened his mouth to protest but felt Marju's hand squeeze his arm, and shut it again.

"That's so kind of you, Chief Inspector," said Marju. Like most Estonians, she had been brought up to be courteous and to respect courtesy in others. Turning down an offer from a host would be extremely disrespectful. She sometimes wondered how Artur had been brought up. "Do you come here regularly? To the memorial I mean. You must have lost so many good friends."

"No, I don't even live here," said the Chief Inspector with a hint of a smile, "My home is in Tartu. And yes, I did lose many good friends. That's what happens in war. It makes you appreciate what's really important. Without that war, we wouldn't be sitting here, with coffee and cakes on the table, and nobody listening to what we're saying. Anyway, what about yourselves? You seemed to be something of a hurry when you arrived."

"Er, yes," muttered Artur, "Actually it was because I was desperate to go to the bathroom. Please excuse me." He jumped up and hurried through to the rear of the café.

"Is something wrong?" Hallmets asked Marju. "You looked frightened when you came in. Both of you. I can sense it in you still. Fear clings, you see, like a sort of sticky mist. If you need help, *Proua* Simm, please tell me."

Marju bit her lip. She felt like bursting into tears and telling this man, who seemed so understanding, everything. He would know what to do, she knew that instinctively. He wouldn't have run from those thugs either, she felt. He would have known how to deal with them. "No, no," she stuttered, "It's, um, just a personal matter."

"Of course," he said. "Let me change the subject. I think you own a hairdressing salon."

Marju was puzzled. "How do you know that?"

"Nothing sinister, I can assure you. I just happen to be staying at the Imperial, and noticed your name on the window of your salon. It amazes me how hairdressing has become so popular. Before the War there were hardly any, and now, well, not quite on every corner, but there are certainly a lot more of them about. How did that happen?"

Marju relaxed. "Yes, there are lots more salons than there used to be. Partly, people have more money, so they can afford little luxuries like having their hair done for them. But also, I think women are coming into their own too. They want to assert their own identities, and not just be slave labour on the farm or in the home. One way of doing that is to have their hair styled. Not just the plaits or bun that all women wore before the War. After all, why look like an Estonian peasant when you can look like Jean Harlow. Well, a bit like her. And if you look a bit like Jean Harlow, maybe it helps you feel a bit like her too. Some of my customers leave the salon as if they're different people, their whole manner changes. I think it makes them feel happier too. I'm sorry, I seem to be hogging the conversation." She blushed, looked down, grabbed a forkful of cheesecake. Delicious. Where the hell was Artur?

She looked up again. Hallmets was looking out of the window.

"Are you watching somebody?" she asked, "You know, a surveillance operation."

"No. As I said, I'm off-duty at the moment. And my face is probably a bit too well-known now – I couldn't disappear into the anonymous crowd any more."

"Tell me, Chief Inspector, are you married?"

"Yes, I am."

"Do you have children?"

"We have two, a boy and girl. And yourselves?"

"No. Not yet." She looked down again. She felt like she would cry.

"Please, *Proua* Simm, I know there's something you want to tell me. It's burrowing around inside you. Let it out before it eats you up. I'm not your enemy, you know."

She had to tell him. Everything. "Yes, there is something. It's about Artur. He ..."

And suddenly he was there, looming over her, his face pasty white. "I'm sorry, Chief Inspector, I'm not feeling too well. I'm afraid we'll have to go home now. Thank you for the coffee and cake, I'm sorry I didn't manage much."

"Oh dear," said the Chief Inspector, "I hope it wasn't the cake made you ill."

"No, no, in fact I hadn't even touched it."

"It's really delicious," said Marju. She felt her voice quavering. Artur looked at her meaningfully, but she wasn't sure what meaning he was trying to convey.

Artur was putting his coat on, she stood up and put hers on too. Hallmets also stood.

"Goodbye, *Härra* Hallmets," said Artur, and turned for the door.

"I'm sorry about Artur," said Marju, "Thank you so much for the cake."

"My pleasure." He held out his hand and she shook it. It was a firm, warm hand. A friend's hand. It reminded her of her father's hand. She let go and rushed for the door.

Hallmets watched her as Artur hustled her away from the cafe doorway. She knew something. He was sure of that. They both did. Artur's alleged illness was simply an excuse to get away. She was the stronger of the two, he guessed. Artur was an opportunist, a shallow thinker. His wife was deeper. And whatever it was they were hiding, it would hurt her more than him to keep it hidden. He would go and have a chat with them in the next day or two.

He contemplated Artur's untouched cheesecake. It would be a pity to let it go to waste. He picked up the fork.

57

He was back in his office in good time for Maslov's call at five. He was at the harbour police office at the docks. He reported that at mid-morning the lorry had made one trip from the estate to the Krummfeldt works, which he and Hekk had followed; it had returned early in the afternoon. Then they moved to the docks, and saw two Krummfeldt lorries arrive at the warehouse at around four, and unload a large number of crates. Hallmets thanked him and told them to leave it there and take the evening off.

He looked into the workroom to see Larsson still there.

"Some interesting news from the tax police," she said, "The Heinaküla estate haven't declared any alcohol production. There's no distillery registered there. They claim their main source of income is horse breeding."

As they were talking, a messenger brought an envelope from the court office. It contained a warrant for Kleber's arrest, along with formal permission from Kellassepp for Hallmets to invite Lepp to be interviewed. Checks downstairs however showed that neither Lepp not Kleber had been in the building that day.

Hallmets called Lesser, and asked how things were going with the Popov investigation.

"Nowhere so far, chief. No-one got the car number, no-one saw the occupants, nothing found at the site, nothing on Popov except a bullet hole."

"Hmm. Any thoughts?"

"My guess is Härg. He's always very meticulous. The others are sloppier. That's why they get caught. Our only hope is that an informant might drop us a hint. That won't help us prove anything, but at least we'd know who was behind it."

Lesser was about to go home, but when he heard about the warrant, he offered to take some uniformed officers to their respective dwellings, to arrest Kleber and inform Lepp that he was to attend the Pikk Street headquarters at 9 am the following morning to be interviewed.

Hallmets told Larsson to go home, but she insisted on waiting until he himself left, to escort him to his hotel. "Kleber and Lepp are out there, chief, we need to be careful. If they take you out, this whole operation will be thrown into chaos."

Half an hour later Lesser phoned from one of the suburban police stations. As they had feared, neither Kleber nor Lepp were at home. It looked like they were both lying low, perhaps fearing a summons to Pikk Street for an interview, or even arrest. A call was sent out to all police stations in the country, and to frontier posts, to apprehend Sergeant Kleber if there was any sight of him. They could do nothing about Inspector Lepp until it was clear he wasn't going to turn up for his interview.

It was nearly eight, and Hallmets had just made his nightly call to Kirsti, when he had a visitor. Colonel Reinart was as well-turned-out as the previous time they'd met, his uniform brushed, his creases perfect, his shoes shining, despite the lateness of the day. Hallmets was relieved however that, unlike many other senior officers, Colonel Reinart did not dress as if he'd just got off a horse.

The colonel put his cap on Hallmets' desk, took his brown leather gloves off and laid them on it, and took the seat facing the desk. He accepted a coffee and made sure the door to the workroom was closed before he got down to business: "Good evening, Chief Inspector. We need to talk about Kleber and Lepp. I had a meeting with Dr Kellassepp a couple of hours ago and have seen all the material you gave him. I've also spoken on the phone to Prefect Rotenbork and to *Härra* Anderkop."

"The minister too?" said Hallmets. Ado Anderkop, Minister of the Interior and Minister of Justice.

"Just so. The public perception of the law-enforcement agencies is in danger here. We are all agreed on what should be done. Pilvik and Kleber should be made examples of for their treatment of *Härra* Kallas. That is quite clear, and the evidence is indisputable. They were caught red-handed. Their punishment will show that we are committed to a police force which is worthy of the complete trust of the population."

Hallmets frowned. He could see where this was going. "That's all very well, Colonel, but the biggest criminal in all this is Lepp. He's the one who needs to be made an example of."

"I'm sorry, Hallmets, that's not on. He's too prominent. Any action against him would damage people's faith in the police. And especially in this case, where the evidence is hardly conclusive."

"Pilvik will testify against him."

"Any lawyer worth his salt will tear Pilvik to pieces. You know that as well as I do."

Hallmets had to admit that was true. "What if we catch Kleber, and persuade him to testify?"

"That would give you more of a case. But from what I've read of him, Kleber's not likely to talk, even if we find him."

"So Lepp will get away with it?"

"No, not altogether. Your suspicions will go in his file, along with Pilvik's statement. He'll know we're watching him, and that he has to behave himself. And he'll be moved away from Tallinn. Maybe one of the islands."

"Lepp is a murderer."

"I won't argue with that. But no-one will miss his victims. We can blame 'unknown underworld elements' for the killings. We could even put Vaher's killing down to them as well."

"I don't have any evidence yet of who killed Vaher."

"Well, do keep at it. The sooner we have someone behind bars for it, the better. One other thing, do you know anything about Vaher's funeral?"

"No. I assume it'll be a family event out at Sonda, and he'll be buried in the graveyard there. We'll send someone, just in case the killer turns up to gloat. I wasn't aware the body had been released."

"It hasn't. And you're right about the funeral. But we need something here in the capital to commemorate him. I've had a word with the Prefect and with Captain Lind, and we've arranged a memorial service for Tuesday morning. Ten o'clock. In St. Olav's Church. Sorry about the short notice. The minister felt it should be sooner rather than later. Especially after this business with Kallas. Refocus the public mind, eh?" And the colonel left.

Hallmets felt the case slipping away again. All he had now were a couple of thugs who'd beaten up a reporter, and he only had one of them in custody. If Kleber and Lepp had fled together, they were clever enough to make themselves very scarce. He could see what would happen. Pilvik would go down for the assault on Kallas. A few weeks later Lepp and Kleber would reappear, claiming they'd lain low because they feared for their lives. Lepp would be moved to Hiiumaa or Muhu Island. Kleber would confess to the assault, say that Pilvik made him do it, and nobly offer to accept whatever punishment was meted out to him. He might lose his sergeant's stripes, then he'd be sent off, probably to join Lepp in internal exile. And a few years later, they'd both be back.

And he was no nearer finding Vaher's killer. The only pointer he had was Albrecht von Langenstein's pen, and that could be disputed. He hoped that they'd at least get the illegal distillery. That would enable them to get a warrant to search the mansion, and that might reveal something more. He'd not mentioned the raid to Colonel Reinart, as he felt the political sensitivity caused by Albrecht von Langenstein's intervention might prompt him to veto it.

It was time to give up for the day. Larsson walked back with him through the darkened streets to his hotel. Heavy clouds filled the sky. He offered her a coffee, but she thanked him and declined, said goodbye, and went off. He wondered if she was meeting the others somewhere. That was the drawback of being the boss – you weren't one of the gang any more.

He had a light meal and went to bed. He glanced out of the window to the flat across the road. The Simms were facing each other across a narrow table. Artur was talking, waving his hands around. He couldn't quite see Marju's face. Not a happy couple, thought Hallmets. Keeping the lid on something, but what? Marju had almost told him. He remembered Artur's articles praising Lepp. Had Artur seen Lepp again, did he even know where he was hiding? Once the business at

Heinaküla was done he'd have to get back to the Simms. Snowflakes drifted past his window.

Day 6. Monday 27th March 1933

58

Artur stared at the alarm clock. 6.30 am. And it was getting light. They had made it through another night. Perhaps Vlad and Igor were going to leave them alone. He got out of bed quietly, removed the chair from the door handle, and went to the bathroom. Then he put some clothes on, and went through to the living room. He looked out the window; carpeted with new-fallen snow, the street seemed unnaturally quiet, although there were now a good few people, mainly men, making their way along Nunne Street, on their way to work. A trampled path was already forming in the centre of the road. The snow had stopped. Perhaps this was just a belated effort from a winter already on the back foot. The scene reminded him of a film by Fritz Lang, but he couldn't remember which one. Maybe it wasn't even by Fritz Lang.

As he watched, two men came along together from the direction of the railway station, well-built, probably manual labourers. But something about one of them was familiar. The man glanced up at his window and he dodged back. Shit, it was Vlad! He ran through to the bedroom and shook Marju awake. "My God, Marju it's them, they're here!" he gasped.

She was out of bed and flung on her clothes. She rushed through to the living room, and shouted to Artur, "Quick! Help me with the table!" Together they manoeuvered the narrow table into the hall and pushed it up against the door.

They could hear footsteps on the landing, footsteps that weren't furtive, footsteps that were meant to scare you, and then there was a knock at the door. The heavy blow of a meaty fist.

Artur opened his mouth but no sound emerged. He disappeared into the bedroom.

It occurred to Marju that he was going to hide under the bed. "Who's there?" she shouted at the door.

"Police!" came the reply, but the voice had a Russian bent to it.

"What do you want?"

"Just a routine enquiry. Nothing to worry about. Open the door please, Madam."

Marju thought for a moment, then called out again, "We've been warned about burglars pretending to be policemen. If you give me your name and number, I'll just telephone Police HQ to check it's on the level."

There was silence for a few seconds. Then the voice again, "Open the bloody door. Now!"

"No way," shouted Marju, "I'm calling the police station."

"Listen, Simm," the voice shouted, "We know you're in there too. You got Mr P. killed, didn't you? He thought you were involved in Blind Rudi's death. Then that piece in the paper, all about Härg. You made a deal with that gangster, didn't you? You sing his praises, and in return he gets Mr P. off your back for you. You bastard! Well, Mr P. may not be coming back, but we are. We're gonna tie you up so you can watch us fuck your wife to death, then we'll cut off lots of little bits of you, and leave you to bleed to death." There was a pause, then he went on. "Oh, tell you what we'll do, here's a special offer. Just let us in and we'll kill you first, quick and painless like, then you won't have to watch the rest. Think about it."

Artur came out of the bedroom, clutching the Luger. He stood next to Marju. He was shaking. It wasn't visible, but she could sense it. Again a few seconds silence. Marju could hear a few muttered words in Russian from the landing. Then suddenly an immense weight hit the door with a crash. There was some splintering, but the woodwork held.

Marju rushed into the living room and picked up the phone. Then she realised there was no time and put it down. She dashed over to the kitchen end of the room, opened the top drawer, and pulled out a long knife with a wooden handle. She used this knife for cutting meat, and kept it razor-sharp. Only this knife could cut slices from the tough-skinned smoked sausage her grandfather made. She came back to the doorway leading back to the hallway. They waited.

They heard a grunted command, and then the weight hit the door again. This time the lock and the bolt gave way with a crack, and the door burst open a few centimetres, pushing the table towards them. A chunky arm entered the gap and groped around till it found the table. "A fucking table, is that all you've got," shouted Vlad, and he grabbed the table by its edge, and heaved it, so that it flipped over ninety degrees, coming to rest on its edge and the side of its legs, still blocking the hall. The door opened further, and behind Vlad, Artur could see another man, taller and thinner. The man was filming the scene with a 16 mm. cine-camera.

"We're going to kill you," grunted Vlad, "But first the lovely Marju." He laughed.

That hit home to Artur. "No, you won't," he gasped. He raised the pistol from behind the table-top and fired at Vlad. But he wasn't holding the pistol firmly enough, and had forgotten the twitch of the barrel when it fired. The bullet flew over Vlad's shoulder and hit the other man in the throat. He dropped the camera, staggered a couple of steps back and disappeared out of sight.

Vlad turned to see what had happened to his associate, then returned to the doorway. "You fucking bastard," he rasped, then grabbed the ends of the lower table legs and flipped the table onto its back. He shoved the door open and went for Artur, who jumped into the living room doorway and fired again at Vlad. The shot hit him on his left shoulder. He winced and carried on up to Artur, knocking the gun out of his fingers with his right hand as if it were a toy, and grasped him by the throat, pushing him up against the edge of the door frame. Vlad's left arm seemed to be out of action.

"You little scumbag," he growled, "Now I'll ..."

But he didn't finish the sentence, because Marju, with all the strength of a farmer's daughter, thrust the knife into his neck. It sliced the carotid artery, and slid through flesh and gristle to pierce the windpipe, and the point emerged at the other side.

Blood sprayed into the air. Vlad grunted, let go of Artur and turned, fixing Marju with a wordless gaze. He tried to pull the knife out, but it wouldn't come, so, holding his right hand against the spurting wound, he turned and made for the door. He began to stagger as he reached the landing, and disappeared towards the stairs. A series of thuds and bumps told them he had fallen down the staircase.

Artur was still gasping for breath, but Marju could see he was unharmed. She recovered the pistol, and, holding it in front of her, made her way out of the door onto the landing. Here she saw the tall man lying on his back at the top of the stairs, blood pooling under his neck, and then running down the stairs. He was making croaking noises but otherwise not moving. Sprays of blood like bunches of scarlet flowers on the mustard-coloured walls showed Vlad's downward progress, and when she went down a few steps, she could see him at the bottom, curled up in a foetal ball.

"D-do you think he's dead?" gasped Artur.

"Looks like it," said Marju, "but I'm not going down to give him a prod. We'd better call the police."

"But ..."

"Are you mad, Artur, we can't keep this quiet."

"Their conversation was interrupted by a screeching noise from upstairs. Marju led Artur back into the living room and opened the window. The screeching was louder. Their upstairs neighbour, Mrs Tamm, was leaning out of her window shouting, "Help! Murder!

Police!"

"I don't think we need to phone anybody," said Marju.

Chief Inspector Hallmets was sitting in the dining room of the Imperial Hotel at a table by the window, enjoying his breakfast. He was in his shirtsleeves, and would put on his tie, waistcoat and jacket after he had eaten. He had finished his boiled egg and now regarded with approval a slice of dark rye bread laden with cold ham and Saaremaa cheese, and topped with pickled gherkin. But as he lifted the tasty concoction to his awaiting lips he suddenly paused. He could hear a shrieking out in the street. Putting his open sandwich down again, he pushed back the net curtain and stared out. An elderly woman had flung open the window of the second-floor flat in the building opposite, and was yelling at the top of her voice. Hallmets opened the window and caught the words "Help! Murder! Police! They're all dead!"

Instantly he got up, grabbed a swig of black coffee, and made for the door. He noticed the reception desk was unmanned, and, as he reached the street, bumped into the young man who should have been there – he was standing staring up at the woman.

"Get back inside!" ordered Hallmets, "Call the police! Tell them I'm on it already. Ask for an ambulance too, there may be injured people in there."

"Yes, Sir, of course," gasped the man, and hurried to obey.

Hallmets felt for his jacket pocket, but of course, his waistcoat and jacket were in his room, along with his pistol. No time to go and fetch it now. He noticed a older man, well-dressed, with an upright bearing, who had been passing, heard the shouts, and was making for the door.

"Just a moment, Sir!" he called.

The man paused and looked at him. "That woman needs help," he said.

"I'm a police officer," said Hallmets, "Chief Inspector Hallmets. Were you an officer in the War?"

"Captain, with the Fourteenth. Arne Teivas."

Hallmets grasped his hand. "*Meeldiv tutvuda.* Pleased to meet you. I'm going in there. Can you stand by the door here and keep everybody else out. Until more police arrive."

"No problem," said the man, "Give me a shout if you need help."

"Thanks," said Hallmets, as he opened the street door carefully and went into the passage. He could soon see a bulky shape at the foot of the stairs. It wasn't moving, but nevertheless, he approached warily. He passed the door giving access, he presumed, to the shop, trying the handle and finding it locked, then came up to the body, for such it was. It was a big man, curled in a mountainous heap, and he was clearly dead. A knife handle protruded from his neck, and Hallmets bent down to see the point sticking out the other side. A puddle of blood had formed under the neck, and the spray marks on the wall told him the carotid artery had been severed. He didn't recognise the man. He had a carelessly shaven head, and a blank expression, eyes staring into an afterlife that didn't seem too welcoming.

Hallmets stepped over him and made his way up the stairs. At the top he came upon another man, lying on his back with blood still dripping from a wound in the throat. Gunshot by the look of it. But he was still alive. Lying on the floor near him was a black box-shaped portable cine camera. Hallmets stepped around him and came to the open door of the flat.

He could see into the hall. It was empty, apart from a table lying upside down in the middle of the floor. "Police!" he shouted, "Anybody there."

"In here," came a woman's voice, "We're in here. The living room."

"Put your weapons down! We're armed!" shouted Hallmets. No need for them to know at this point there was only him, and he wasn't armed.

He heard a thud, and the voice again, "OK. The gun's on the floor."

Nevertheless he wasn't taking chances. He kept to the side wall of the hall, avoiding the upturned table, and peeped into the living room. Sitting on a wooden bench against the wall next to the window were Artur and Marju Simm. Artur was sobbing, whilst his wife held an arm round him.

She glanced at Hallmets. "It's OK, it's only us. There's no-one else here. Are they dead?"

"One is. The one on the landing here isn't. We'll need to get help for him. Please remain seated where you are, both of you." He strode across the room to the window and opened it. Below him the ex-officer must have ordered spectators to keep to the other side of the street, for there was a group of five or six men, in working clothes, staring up. Amongst them the receptionist from the hotel was conspicuous by his bright red waistcoat. The woman upstairs had stopped screeching; she must have been told by the spectators that the police were there.

He turned to Marju, "Where's your phone?"

Sixty minutes later the scene had changed. Two uniformed officers were stationed at the door. Ex-Captain Teivas, who was the manager of a department store, had been thanked for his services, his address taken so that a letter of thanks from the Prefect could be sent. The tall man, still alive when the ambulance arrived, had been rushed to hospital. His position on the landing had been marked in chalk. A photographer was at work recording the scene. There was no hurry to remove the body at the foot of the stairs – it had been certified as dead. Einar Sepp, apparently in better health, was much in evidence, collecting fingerprints, and supervising two uniformed officers who were on all fours, one in the hall of the flat and the other on the landing, examining every inch of the ground. The cine-camera had been taken to Pikk Street for the film to be developed. The table had been returned to the living room and at it sat Artur Simm, being questioned by Inspector Lesser. On the bench by the window, Marju Simm was talking to Sergeant Larsson. Hallmets had used the Simms' phone to report the matter to Captain Lind.

Marju had told Hallmets the whole story, from Artur's first meeting with Popov, right up the present. He now knew that Artur had killed Blind Rudi, and that the intruders were Vlad and Igor, the late Boris Popov's enforcers. Vlad had been identified as Vladimir Krilenko, aka 'Vlad the Despoiler', and Igor as Igor Glasunov, a jack-of-all-trades henchman. Two thugs who wouldn't be missed. But there would have to be an inquiry into the deaths.

Marju said she knew very little about Artur's work as a reporter. She was aware that he'd interviewed Härg, and mentioned the pastries Artur had brought back. They had left an impression. She told him Artur suspected that what he'd said to the gangster had resulted in Popov's death. Vlad and Igor seemed to have made the same connection and were seeking revenge for their murdered boss. They'd given no suggestion that they were trying to continue his information-gathering business. "Intelligence-gathering would require intelligence," was her comment. But she was unaware of any connection between Artur and Lepp. He'd have to get that information out of Artur himself.

It had taken a while for Artur to recover from his ordeal. A cup of coffee laced with brandy had helped. Hallmets wasn't minded to be soft on him. Artur's actions had resulted in the deaths of three people so far. He made it clear that unless Artur came clean on everything, he'd be charged with Blind Rudi's murder.

"But that was self-defence," Artur whined.

"Maybe, maybe not. So you'll need to tell us everything. It may all be connected. And we can see connections that you can't. Now, start from the beginning."

Artur's account largely matched that of Marju, so at least he'd been honest with her, Hallmets thought. But he didn't mention Lepp.

"Tell me about your contacts with Inspector Lepp," Hallmets asked.

"That's confidential," stuttered Artur, "I'm a reporter."

"So you interviewed him?"

"Yes."

"How often have you talked with him?"

"That's confidential."

"Listen, *Härra* Simm, Lepp is a very dangerous man. He organised the killings of Lehmja and Kauščis, maybe even of Chief Inspector Vaher. And the beating-up of your own colleague. I need all the information I can get about him. So here's what I'm going to do. I'm going to ask you one more time about Lepp. If you don't co-operate, you'll be remanded on suspicion of the murder of Blind Rudi. I'll see that you're sent to the Patarei. Many of the prisoners there will be friends of Blind Rudi, or Popov, or Vlad, or Igor. Maybe even of all four. You won't be a popular little chappie there, will you, Artur?"

Artur had turned white, and begun to shake again. Hallmets filled the glass again and Artur gulped it down, then shivered as the alcohol caught at his throat. "All right," he croaked, "I'll tell you. I've only met Lepp twice."

"When was the last time?"

"Just yesterday. About one o'clock."

"Where?"

"The bar at the Baltic Station."

"What did he tell you?"

"He said he thought you were trying to frame him for the deaths of those two thugs, so he was going to lie low for a while. He thought you'd soon be taken off the Vaher case. Then he'd come back."

"Anything else?"

"Yes, he seemed to think some big political change would happen, and that would benefit him. But it was only a hint, he didn't say any more than that."

"Did he say where he was going to hide?"

"No, not a word. He only told me what he wanted me to know, I didn't have the chance to ask him any questions. As soon as he'd finished his speech, he just got up and left. Please, that's all I know. For God's sake, don't let them send me to Patarei."

Hallmets could only find Artur contemptible. The young man was an opportunist, possibly a liar, and certainly a coward. He didn't understand what Marju saw in him. But then, women were often a mystery. He knew he would never have sent Artur to Patarei – some of the stories he'd heard about the prison were chilling.

"All right, *Härra* Simm, here's what I'll do. For the moment, until the inquiry, we'll put you under house arrest here, and I'll put a uniformed man on the landing, in case anyone else has the idea of avenging Popov, or Rudi, or anyone else you've killed in self-defence. We'll also put a tap on your phone …"

"But that's …"

"Necessary, *Härra* Simm, in case any persons under suspicion of a crime, or wishing to threaten you, attempt to get in touch. I'm afraid you will not be permitted to contact your newspaper, either directly or through a third party. Any visitors you wish to have here must be cleared with us. Any infringement of these conditions will result in immediate incarceration. Do I make myself clear?"

"What about Marju?"

"Your wife is not under any suspicion. Her killing of Vladimir Krilenko looks pretty clearly like self-defence. She is therefore free to come and go as she pleases, although I would advise that she makes no contact with *Pealinna Uudised*, and does not step outside the city limits. She is a brave and resourceful woman, you should be proud of her. Without her prompt responses to danger, you would not be talking to me now. Do you understand that?"

"Y-yes, Chief Inspector. Er, one other thing. Can I write about this, I mean for the newspaper? Obviously not right now, but once it's all over. Like Jaan Kallas did."

"Of course, *Härra* Simm, no-one is taking away your freedom of speech. Right now, anything you write that's printed could compromise our ongoing investigations, but afterwards, there's no problem, provided of course, that your report is truthful. Why not spend your time here writing it up? In doing so you might remember some details that you haven't already told us."

59

He got in to his office at half past nine. Maslov, Hekk and Kadakas were waiting. He explained what had happened at the Simms' flat. "This business certainly clears up Blind Rudi's killing," he concluded, "And has taken three more criminals off the streets. But it doesn't take us any further in solving Vaher's death. We need to get the raid on the distillery set up for Wednesday. Oleg and Ilmar, can you do the same as yesterday, keep an eye on what's doing at the estate and the warehouse.

I'll set a press conference for this afternoon. Lesser and Sõnn can take it. Sõnn can announce the solution of the Blind Rudi case, and Lesser can give an account of what's happened at the Simms' place. That'll give the newshounds plenty to get their teeth into."

At ten Ilves arrived. He didn't look happy.

"It's Pilvik, Sir. He's dead."

"How?"

"Looks like poison. He took a cup of cocoa with him to bed. Next morning we found him dead."

"Who made his cocoa?"

"Well, er, I did. The powder was in a tin in the kitchen."

"Did you search him when you'd got him to the house?"

"We got him to strip naked – not a pretty sight – and went through his clothes very carefully. Nothing there. You'd got all the stuff out of his pockets before he came with us."

"Did anyone visit the house that day?"

"Yes, a couple of Reinart's men came, just to check all was OK they said. I suppose one of them could have ..."

"We need the body."

"That could be tricky. Given that the house was a ministry safe house, the investigation has been taken over by the political police. We were told very firmly that it wasn't our case, we should get back here. Didn't even give us a lift, we had to get the bus."

Hallmets dismissed Ilves, and phoned the colonel.

"Very unfortunate," said the colonel blandly, "Looks like he brought the poison with him, and put it in the cocoa after he went to bed. Pity your men didn't search him more thoroughly."

Hallmets could not disguise his irritation. "Please don't patronise me, Colonel. Pilvik was searched twice, very thoroughly. Once here and again at the safe house. It certainly wasn't my men who killed him. You realise not being able to produce Pilvik as a witness damages our case against Kleber and Lepp."

"Against Lepp, maybe, but the case against him was always going to be difficult, and I know the prosecutor was not keen on pursuing it. But you've certainly enough, given what you and others were witness to, to take down Kleber. He should certainly be made an example of. Well, I must go now. I'll see you at the service tomorrow." The line was cut before Hallmets could answer. He put the phone down and thumped his fist on the desk. It was clear to him that Pilvik had been eliminated, probably at the Colonel's behest. But why? The only reason he could think of was to undermine the case against Lepp. Was there something going on he wasn't privy to?

By eleven Larsson was back from the Simms' flat. She reported that Lesser had everything under control. Vlad's corpse had now been moved to the morgue for a post-mortem later that day.

Hallmets phoned the hospital. They reported that Igor Glasunov was still unconscious. He had been taken to the operating theatre as soon as he was brought in, and the surgeons had inserted a tube in his throat. But the chances of recovery were still slim; throat wounds were very prone to infection. It would probably be a while before anyone could talk to him. Nevertheless, he sent Kadakas to the hospital to keep an eye on Glasunov and report back if there were any change in his condition. Just in case.

With everyone else occupied, Hallmets could get on with writing up his report. There was plenty to go into it, so he was grateful for the peace and quiet.

At five Maslov phoned from the docks. Same pattern as the day before. Hallmets told them to get something to eat. After that they should get up to the estate and keep an eye on the place.

"Through the night, boss?" asked Maslov.

"Yes, take turns at sleeping. Stay there, don't follow the lorry if it goes off."

At half past five, Larsson reported that she'd phoned the harbour authorities in Turku, and they'd confirmed the *Dimitrios* had left the Finnish port on time for Nörrkoping. She asked whether they should contact the Finnish and Swedish police, let them know what they suspected.

"No, they might be too tempted to pounce at their end, before we get a chance. That's the trouble with multi-national investigations: each partner wants the timing to suit themselves."

He phoned home, but when Liisa answered he remembered Kirsti worked an evening shift at the library on Mondays. At least he could assure himself the kids were OK. Which of course they were. Liisa was going out with friends to the cinema – they were showing *Frankenstein*, made the previous year and now supplied with Estonian subtitles. Though Liisa declared she didn't need the subtitles, her English was good enough. Hallmets remembered reading the book by Mary Shelley some years ago. Then he'd found there was a family of Baltic Germans actually called Frankenstein who lived somewhere south of Tartu. He mentioned this on the phone to Liisa, who was suitably impressed. "What! The Frankensteins came from round here. Wow!" Then he spoke to Juhan, who had homework to do. Had they had something for tea? Of course, they'd made sandwiches, did he think they were incapable? Work to do, Dad.

He was wondering what to do next, when Kallas phoned, asked if they could talk over a meal. Hallmets suggested the Imperial, the food was good and he could relax. He asked Kallas to call for him at Pikk Street at six. Then he told Larsson to go home, Kallas would walk with him back to the hotel. She was sceptical until he showed her the Browning was in his jacket pocket.

He was waiting on the front steps of the Pikk Street building when Kallas arrived, still looking a little bruised and wearing dark glasses. They walked up Pikk Street and along Nunne to the Imperial. Kallas winced occasionally but otherwise didn't complain about his ordeal. He was a professional, and wouldn't let that get in the way of the inside story of the day's events.

Hallmets gave him as much as he could. He realised a focus on the events at the Simms' might make the von Langensteins think the police were distracted, and relax. The pork knuckle with turnip and fried potato was delicious, with beer that was dark, strong and full of the fruitiness of the hops. Kallas only had blood pudding with mashed potato and gravy, and explained that he hadn't got to the dentist yet. He also insisted on paying, and didn't stay late. He had to get back to the paper and rewrite his piece for the morning.

At nine thirty Hallmets phoned Kirsti, now home from her late shift. She wanted to talk more about *The Bishop's Gold*. She was beginning to think the title was too melodramatic, and might give the impression the book was a cheap shocker, not a serious work of historical fiction.

"What are the alternatives?" asked Hallmets

"I've been thinking. What about *The Minstrel*?"

"Sounds a bit old-fashioned. Is he the main character?"

"Not really. He's certainly inportant, and he solves the mystery. But there's more to it than that. About the power struggles between the Church and the Order. And how the Estonians survive despite it all. The Bishop's daughter is probably a more significant figure in the story."

"What about *I was a Bishop's Daughter*?"

"Now you're being silly. That just sounds like a scandal-sheet."

"*Survival of a Nation*?"

"Too pretentious. It's not an trilogy."

"*Dead at the Altar*?"

"That makes it seem like a murder mystery."

"*The Shadow of Power*?"

"That sounds like one of those Edgar Wallace stories about a mysterious criminal brotherhood led by an apparently respectable millionaire financier."

"How about *The Bishop's Legacy*? After all, it's the bishop's death right at the beginning that causes all the other things to happen. Like, er, you know, ripples when a stone's dropped in water."

"I like that idea. *A Stone in Water*. How about that? Conveys the main theme."

"Won't sell as many as *The Bishop's Gold*, mind."

Before going to bed, he crossed the road to the building opposite, and went up to the first-floor landing. A uniformed officer was sitting on a kitchen chair reading a dog-eared paperback. When he saw Hallmets he jumped to his feet and saluted.

"Any problems here?"

"None at all, Sir." He consulted his notebook. "*Proua* Simm went downstairs to work at eight thirty a.m., came back for lunch at twelve, out again at one thirty, back at six, with a full shopping bag. No sign of *Härra* Simm at all."

"Good. What are you reading?"

The man looked shame-faced. "Oh, only a detective story, Sir. *The Fellowship of the Frog* by Edgar Wallace."

"Don't tell, me, it's about a mysterious criminal brotherhood led by ... ah, I'd better not say."

"Thank you, Sir. It's quite gripping. Starts with a police inspector being murdered."

"We've got our own case like that."

"Oh. Yes. Sorry Sir, I didn't mean to ..."

"That's OK. At least the ending for that one's already there on the last page. I hope we can have everything tied up as neatly here."

Day 7. Tuesday 28th March

60

Hallmets met with the team at eight. He'd also asked Sõnn to sit in. After bringing them up to date with events, he explained that they'd get very little done until afternoon, thanks to the memorial service for Vaher, which they'd all better attend. He suggested they meet again at two.

Lesser reported that the paperwork for the events at the Simms' flat was done. The prosecutor had not however made up his mind whether to charge the Simms with anything. It seemed a clear case of self-defence.

"Yes," put in Sõnn, "It's the same with Blind Rudi. Though we've only got Simm's word as to what happened. He might be charged with manslaughter, though there's no evidence for it. It would be a waste of time for the courts."

"How's Glasunov, by the way?" asked Hallmets.

"No change," replied Kadakas, "Still in a bad way. I was at the hospital all night. I just came over for the meeting. Mürakas is there now."

"OK Ants, you look as if you need some sleep. Take the rest of the day off. We need you fresh for tomorrow. I'll see the rest of you in church.

At nine fifteen Captain Lind phoned to ask Hallmets to accompany him to the service. Hallmets asked Larsson, Maslov and Hekk to position themselves around the edge of the church, and keep a look out for anything unusual at the service. "I'm not sure what," he explained, "But you never know what might happen."

The captain was dressed in his best uniform, medals and all. He was having a last drink before the event. Hallmets declined. Lind knocked back the vodka, grimaced, then put down the glass and stared at it.

"What's up?" asked Hallmets.

"They want results," said Lind.

"Who's they?"

"The minister. Maybe even higher up."

"Päts?" Konstantin Päts, Prime Minister and Head of State. Leader of a fragile coalition in Estonia's parliament.

"All these killings are making it seem as if the government are allowing things to descend into anarchy. So they want everything tied up fast. A return to normality. They're planning something, over at the ministry. I don't know what, but Colonel Reinart's behind it. Just watch yourself, Jüri."

"I'll keep my eyes open, Peeter, thank you for warning me. Now I suggest we get over to the church while you're still able to walk." He saw the pain in Lind's eyes as the captain slowly got to his feet.

Lind clutched Hallmets' arm. "Listen to me, Jüri. Working with Vaher was hell. Part of me jumped for joy when he was killed. He treated me with contempt from his first day here. He made it clear he wanted my job, that he regarded me as incompetent and above all, soft. If I knew who killed him, I'd thank them. Then I'd hang them. Irrespective of what they say, of what I say, I want you to keep looking till you find him. Come on, let's go."

St. Olav's Church was just around the corner, so it didn't take Hallmets and Lind long to walk round, and Lind managed to stay on his feet. He had not been a soldier for nothing. Uniformed police lined the pavement all the way.

Pews extended the length of the wide nave of the church, and they were shown to the rightmost end of the second row, Captain Lind at the very end. The front row remained empty. A glance behind showed the church steadily filling. Hallmets recognised a number of the policemen, and saw others who by the way they carried themselves he recognised as colleagues. Wooden chairs had been set out in the side aisles, and they were filling too, with members of the public. Looking past Lind, Hallmets recognised Jaan Kallas, who nodded. There was Krummfeldt too, looking bored.

He felt a movement at his side and looked round to see Professor von Stallenborg, who shook his hand before sitting. "Good to see you, Chief Inspector. Looks like everyone's here for the party, eh? Oh, and I see even the late inspector himself is joining us." He pointed up towards the altar, where Hallmets now saw two trestles had been set up.

Now the rest of their row began to fill. Three men in dark suits, whom Hallmets assumed to be from the ministry, a couple of army officers, and, at the other end of the row he recognised Dr Kellassepp and one of the other prosecutors. There was no sign of Luik.

The music of a brass band could be heard faintly. "What's happening outside?" Hallmets asked Lind.

"The coffin's being carried by police officers from Pikk Street, followed by official mourners. That's the police band we can hear – it was at the front."

The music stopped. A clergyman appeared and asked everyone to stand. The whispering and muted chattering ceased and they all stood in silence. A shuffling sound from the main door behind him told Hallmets the coffin was coming in, and soon the six tall and solidly built police officers in dress uniform appeared, bearing the coffin on their shoulders, followed by a senior uniformed officer. At a command from the latter the men lowered the coffin and laid it on the trestle in front of the altar. They stood to attention as the mourners filed to their seats in the front row. Hallmets could see them clearly. First the family: Laura Vaher, demure yet fetching in black; Heinrich von Langenstein, tall, ramrod-straight, looking noble to the core; Albrecht von Langenstein, shorter and shiftier-looking, a small swastika badge on his lapel; and an old lady all in black, led by a younger couple – this must be Vaher's mother, thought Hallmets. Then the official mourners: Colonel Reinart, sharp-eyed as ever; Prefect Rotenbork, stolid and expressionless; Ado Anderkop, Minister of Justice and of the Interior, looking even younger than his 38 years; and beyond him the heavy-set figure of Konstantin Päts, the State Elder.

The final figure to take his place was the leader of the main opposition party, Jaan Tõnnisson, tall, thin, austere. Tõnnisson glanced along the row behind him before sitting, and, meeting Hallmets' gaze, nodded. He knew anyone who mattered in his home base of Tartu, and plenty who didn't. Hallmets didn't live far from Tõnnisson's house, and passed it every time he walked along Tööstuse Street to the railway station. A modest and tidy wooden building. On summer days Tõnnisson could be seen in a deck chair in the garden, always reading.

As the two foremost politicians in Estonia, and two of the men who had led the country to independence, Tõnnisson and Päts were contrasting figures. While Tõnnisson was an idealist and intellectual based in the university city of Tartu, Päts was a pragmatist who had worked his way up to the top. Before independence he'd edited a radical newspaper, and had to flee the country in the aftermath of the traumatic disturbances of 1905. He'd supported the confiscation of the land from the German landlords in 1921, but then moved to the right, as his support base, the small farmers, having got what they wanted, saw no reason for further change. Hallmets thought that while Tõnnisson looked like a schoolmaster, Päts reminded him of a nightclub bouncer. But both men were devoted to their country, and had risked everything to bring it into being.

The service got under way, led by the minister of the church. An opening welcome, a hymn, a prayer, a bible reading – the one about a man being willing to die for his friends – another hymn. Then the clergyman announced that there would be speeches of appreciation of *Härra* Vaher's life and achievements. The first from the man who had been leading the old lady, introduced as Vaher's younger brother Paal. He was stocky and weatherbeaten, a man who lived out of doors, on the family farm. The sheet of paper which he read from shook as he spoke, but his voice remained steady; he talked about their upbringing, hard but fair, of the family's pride at Nicolai's career, and of their sorrow that he died without heirs. He did not mention Vaher's wife.

The second speaker was the Minister of the Interior, Ado Anderkop. One of a rising generation of young politicians, some said he was destined for great things. He spoke with warmth and confidence, outlining the official achievements of Chief Inspector Vaher. He confessed his own personal feeling that Vaher would undoubtedly have gone on to more senior positions, and pointed out that his death left a space in the hierarchy of law and order which would be hard to fill. He finally paid tribute to the great work carried out by the police forces throughout Estonia in making the country a safe and peaceful place to live in.

The clergyman indicated that the final speaker would be one of Chief Inspector Vaher's colleagues in the Tallinn CID, someone who had worked with him on a day-to-day basis. The was a pause before anyone appeared, then Hallmets could see people moving in the seats in the aisle furthest from him, and the officer, in uniform for the occasion, mounted the dais where the coffin stood. Inspector Lepp! Hallmets tried to rise from his seat, but felt a hand grip his right arm tightly. Lind leaned into him and whispered, "Don't do anything silly, Jüri. This has been approved from the top."

Lepp laid his hand on the coffin, appearing for a few moments to commune with the man inside. Then he shook himself back to the present, and introduced himself: "My name is Indrek Lepp. For many years I was a close colleague of Nicolai Vaher. I learned most of what I know about policing from him. He was my trainer and my mentor. He could be a demanding master, but also an inspiring leader. When it came to crime-fighting, he did not shy away from the truth. He knew who the servants of evil were, and was courageous and implacable in his pursuit of them. I think I knew him better than any of his colleagues, indeed, he became a good friend to me. He shared with me his private opinion, that law and order is fundamental to the stability and prosperity of the state. If citizens cannot have confidence in the safety of themselves and their property, the state cannot function, and will surely perish. I hope we will honour his memory by continuing to work as he did, for the preservation of order, which is the basis of freedom. In this way his sacrifice will not have been in vain." He turned to the coffin and bowed solemnly to his departed colleague, then left the dais, and disappeared from Hallmets' view.

It was plain to Hallmets that this performance had been orchestrated by Colonel Reinart. No wonder the colonel had shown no interest in putting Lepp on trial. In fact, by presenting Lepp at this occasion, the colonel seemed to be suggesting that the inspector was going to be back before too long. Maybe even promoted. He felt sick.

During the singing of the hymn that followed, Hallmets whispered to Lind that he felt unwell, and the captain reluctantly allowed him to squeeze past into the passage. Restraining himself to a dignified gait, he left the church. Outside on the street, he took some deep breaths and muttered a few expletives.

A moment later Maslov and Larsson were with him. "What's going on, chief?" asked Maslov, "Are we going to try and grab Lepp as he leaves?"

"I don't think so," answered Hallmets, "We won't get him. He'll be spirited away by the Colonel. And even if we did get hold of him, he'd soon be free."

The church door opened again and they saw Jaan Kallas come out. He came over to them. "Are you folk as disgusted as I am?" he said, "The man's a murderer, and they're presenting him as a noble policeman. It makes you sick!" And he walked off.

"Come on," said Hallmets to Maslov and Larsson, "Let's get some coffee."

61

Over a long coffee that drifted into lunch, Hallmets managed to put aside the anger and disgust he had felt at the service.

"Come on, boss, cheer up," urged Maslov, "Governments always behave like this. And it could be a whole lot worse. If we were in Russia, you'd have been shot by now for not toeing the party line. Whatever you do, don't go shouting at Reinart, it won't get you anywhere, except maybe a transfer to Hiiumaa."

"What's wrong with Hiiumaa?" put in Larsson, "My grandparents came from there. No, chief, the worst that could happen to you is a move to one of those god-forsaken towns down by Lake Peipsi, full of onions and Russians."

Hallmets had to smile. "Hold on, you two, remember you're distantly related. Eva, some of your Swedish ancestors were the *Rus*, who moulded a bunch of savage tribes into what became the Russian state. We still call Sweden *Rootsi* in Estonian. And we're all three of us Estonians, whatever our ancestry. But you're right, Oleg, being bitter isn't going to get us anywhere. We need to focus on the raid tomorrow. Even if all we get's a distillery!'"

That afternoon the plans were made for the morrow. Maslov and Hekk were to watch as the *Dimitrios* unloaded its cargo, then note any lorries which picked up material at the warehouse. If any seemed to be making for Heinaküla, they were to be followed. If all the crates were taken to Krummfeldt's, then the watchers were to wait until any vehicles set off from there, and follow them. The rest of the team, plus a number of uniformed officers, were to follow in unmarked vehicles. The lorry was not to be stopped until it was within the Heinaküla estate. Then they would pounce.

Hallmets knew he was taking a risk. It was possible that in return for the smuggled booze, perfectly legal goods might be being imported to sell on. It was also possible that nothing was brought back to Estonia at all, and the proceeds of the alcohol sales were moved around some other way. However, even if these scenarios were to play out, all was not lost. He trusted entirely Maslov's nose. If the worst came to the worst, they would still uncover an illegal distillery.

Larsson reported that the *SS Dimitrios* had left Turku on time at 5.00 pm on Monday, and reached Nörrkoping at ten that morning. The harbour authorities there promised to phone her as soon as the ship had left for Tallinn. Hallmets sent Maslov and Hekk over to the docks, to keep an eye on the Krummfeldt warehouse just in case something unexpected happened.

At two Sõnn came up. Hallmets asked him to prepare an application for a warrant, and take it over to one of the magistrates who'd not been connected to the Vaher case. It was to be presented under Sõnn's name simply as a routine illicit booze operation. The target address would be given as 'Heinaküla Farm' – this way the judge would hopefully not connect it to the von Langensteins. Hallmets did not want to risk the Ministry telling him to call off the operation just to keep the Germans happy.

By half past two the details were clear. Lesser and Sõnn would run the operation on the ground. Sõnn's focus was to be on the distillery raid. Maslov was to assist him, along with two carloads of uniformed officers. Their objective was to secure the building, and any evidence it might contain, and arrest and interrogate anyone working there. Lesser was to look after the wider picture: watching the docks, following any vehicles from the warehouse, and securing whatever was being brought to the estate. He would have several plain-clothes men at his disposal. Hallmets would be there in a supervisory capacity. His authority would be needed if it was necessary to enter the manor house, or to question Heinrich von Langenstein or Laura Vaher. Larsson and Kadakas would support him, and liaise with the two teams.

At three, without prior warning, Colonel Reinart appeared. He accepted coffee, and got down to business as soon as it had arrived. "Look, Hallmets, I realise you were appalled by Lepp's appearance at the the service, I noticed you leaving. I don't blame you at all, you'd be justified in thinking it was the height of hypocrisy, since we know what he's really been up to. But you've got to appreciate the big picture. Of course, it's all political. We're just the marionettes who have to dance when the politicians pull the strings."

Hallmets wasn't at all convinced that Colonel Reinart was just a puppet, but he let it pass. "All right, Colonel, let me in on the big picture."

"Of course, I wouldn't dream of keeping you in the dark. We need you with us on this, if it's possible. As you know, the political situation is quite unstable. And now Hitler's taking power in Germany has complicated matters further. A lot of the German community here are sympathetic to him. Landowners who've had most of their land taken off them, businessmen who like their support for employers, and poorer folk who like the idea of the master race, and wouldn't mind lording over everyone else. And we mustn't forget that our own Alfred Rosenberg is very close to Hitler."

"Has the German government given any indication of its attitude to us yet?"

"Their ambassador has already been saying that we're too hard on the Baltic Germans. That's why we need the Vaher case sorted out fast. Before anyone can use it to cause trouble. And of course the Reds aren't just sitting over the border snoozing. I'm telling you, Hallmets, the next few years are going to be very tough. We're going to have to work very hard to hold on to our independence."

"So where does the Vaher case fit into this?"

"We need to maintain people's confidence in the police. That's why we had the memorial service for Vaher, and that's why Lepp was brought in. But let me assure you, we're not going to present him as a hero, or give him any promotion. Quite the opposite – he'll be moved to a backwater and told to keep his head down. He'll not gain from this, you have my word on that. Let me be quite clear. The politicians want this case solved. Right now. That's from the very top. And we have a plausible solution ready."

"Let me guess. Vaher was getting too close to a criminal gang, so they got two thugs to bump him off, and did it in a public way to warn the police off. But the police were getting too close, so they decided to give us the killers, nicely pre-executed. Am I right so far?"

"More or less. But as I'm sure you'll say next, that scenario doesn't reveal who was behind Vaher's killing, only who carried it out. So we'll produce documents showing that the gang behind it were Lithuanian, and that because of the effective police response here, they've decided to leave Estonia alone."

"So when is this 'solution' to be announced?"

"The evidence will be ready in a couple of days, and then we'll have a press conference. But it will only make sense if you're part of it. Of course, you'll get the credit. And promotion too. As you know, Captain Lind will soon be retiring, and you would be well placed to succeed him."

"As you already know, Colonel, pinning crimes on plausible villains, and faking the evidence for it, isn't my habit. The whole thing stinks. And before you interrupt me, I understand what you're saying about the bigger picture, and I appreciate that. Policemen can't be blinkered to what's going on around them. But somebody killed Vaher, and for a reason, and we need to find who and why. Surely the truth of the matter would be even more satisfactory to the public."

"That would be fine if we knew what it was. Uncertainty over this case is now contributing to the political instability. We simply don't have the time to get to the bottom of it. Believe me, Hallmets, I really sympathise with you here. But we have no choice. Please help us."

"Alright. You say you'll have this fake evidence in a couple of days. Then give me another two days on the case. If we don't deliver anything, go ahead with the press conference. I'll sit in on it, but I won't take any of the credit, and I won't tell any lies."

Reinart sipped his coffee thoughtfully before replying. "Fair enough, Hallmets, that'll have to do, though it's not the helpful attitude I was hoping for after taking you into my confidence."

"Sharing your confidences doesn't oblige me to agree with your proposals. But I've understood your reasoning, and I won't contradict them. Unless, that is, we discover what really happened."

Once the colonel had gone, Hallmets had some hard thinking to do. He understood the politicians' need for a quick and plausible solution to the Vaher case. But he knew too that faking evidence is like killing people: when you've done it once, it's a lot easier the next time, and the next.

What could he achieve in just two days? It was possible something might come out of the raid at Heinaküla. If not he could pull in Laura Vaher for questioning. She might confess to a relationship with Lepp. But that wouldn't prove Lepp had killed Vaher. And even if it did, that wouldn't go down well with the politicians after Lepp's appearance as their supporting act at the service.

In the midst of his thought, the phone rang. It was Mürakas from the hospital. As the doctors had feared, inefection had set in, and Igor Glasunov was no more. Whilst Hallmets was disappointed that they couldn't inteview Glasunov, he knew that Glasunov's role had been very minor. He'd not even had a speaking part. If anything, his demise left things a little tidier.

Marta knocked on his door. "Someone else to see you, sir."

"Show them in," said Hallmets. He was ready for anyone now. Except Kirsti. He opened his mouth and nothing came out.

"Oh dear," she smiled, "Shall I go out and come in again? This time you could say 'It's lovely to see you.' Or something like that. You might even get up and kiss me." She took hold of the door handle.

"No, no, sorry, dear, I was thinking. No, it is good to see you, really it is." He got up. They embraced.

"I've got the afternoon off, and I'm on the late shift tomorrow, so I thought I'd come up and see you. The kids can look after themselves. And I even managed to get some writing done on the train. How are things going?"

Later, they ate at the restaurant in the Imperial. The food was good, the company better. He'd needed to be reminded of his own life, to be Jüri Hallmets the husband and father again, not the policeman or the political pawn. Having assured himself there were no eavesdroppers, he told her everything about the case. Kirsti asked questions that showed she was listening. At the end she said, "This Laura Vaher, she's the weak link, isn't she? If you throw her in the cells for a night, she'll probably confess to everything to avoid ruining her hairdo. Yes, I know, then you'd get into trouble because her brother's a German diplomat. But don't worry, by the time they've sacked you, I'll have become a best-selling author, and I'll be able to support us."

Hallmets took the hint, and they talked about *The Bishop's Gold*. Kirsti still wasn't sure she had the ending right. "You'd think, having written so much before, it would just fall into place. But somehow it seems the hardest bit. This is the third version, and it still doesn't pack enough of a punch. Maybe it's too much of a happy ending."

Day 8. Wednesday 29th March

62

As Hallmets woke up to find Kirsti beside him, he imagined for a while that he was home in Tartu. It was a nice thought while it lasted.

After breakfast he walked Kirsti to the station and saw her off on the eight o'clock train to Tartu. "Don't worry," he said, "I'll be back in a few days. They won't want me around after their press conference." Then he walked down to Pikk Street.

Larsson reported that the *Dimitrios* had set sail on time from Nörrkoping at five the previous evening, and should arrive in Tallinn at about midday.

At ten Lesser and Sõnn arrived after meeting Dr Kellassepp. The magistrate had decided there was no need to proceed with any case in regard to the deaths of Vladimir Krilenko and Igor Glasunov. These were clearly cases of self-defence. He was however not so satisfied with the facts in the case of Blind Rudi. The evidence was not conclusive that Artur Simm had acted in self-defence. However, he had to agree with the police officers that when the known character of Rudolf Pottsepp was compared with what was known about *Härra* Simm, it did appear that the balance of circumstance favoured Simm's account of events. "I'm not at all sure about that young man's honesty," was the magistrate's judgement, "but I don't see him as the type to set out to murder someone, particularly an experienced troublemaker like Pottsepp. So we'll have to put that one down to self-defence too. I just hope Simm's wife doesn't die in mysterious circumstances in the next few months."

Just before leaving, Sõnn had asked Dr Kellassepp to sign the warrant for the suspected distillery raid, presenting it as a routine matter. There was no problem.

Maslov and Hekk had gone down to the docks to keep an eye on things, and Hallmets later sent Ilves and Mürakas to assist them if more than one lorry set off from the warehouse. Two vanloads of uniformed officers were to be ready at Pikk Street for twelve o'clock. Hallmets didn't think any lorries from the warehouse would get to the Heinaküla estate before one o'clock, given the time it would take to unload the cargo from the *Dimitrios*. But it was best to be on the safe side. He checked that his own automatic was in working order and loaded.

Hallmets, Larsson, Lesser and Sõnn waited in the workroom. Marta brought up some open sandwiches with herring up from the canteen, but no-one was very hungry. There was a palpable build-up of anticipation as mid-day approached.

At twelve Larsson rang the harbour authorities who reported that *Dimitrios* was on its approach, and should be docked by half past. Hallmets sent Lesser down to the harbour to co-ordinate that end of the operation. At twenty to one, Maslov phoned to say that she was now tied up at the dock, and preparing to unload.

They had to move at just the right time. Hallmets had decided against assembling in some village near the estate. He knew how word of strangers hanging around could spread like wildfire in rural areas, even when there seemed to be no-one there. And he didn't want to give the distillery any advance warning. Not that it could be hidden very easily. The operation at Heinaküla was on a large scale. The still would be permanent, since it would have to be well-tuned to produce spirit of the quality of *Leikari* vodka. There would also be a bottling plant, and extensive storage. The operational areas would no doubt be disguised on the outside, probably as barns or storehouses. But there would be no way of disguising what was inside.

At half past one, Lesser phoned from the harbour. According to the Customs Office, *Dimitrios* was carrying a cargo of porcelain electrical insulators which were being shipped from Astiz AB in Nörrkoping to Krummfeldt & Co., Tallinn. By arrangement with Lesser, the customs officers had not asked too many questions. With a brief look at the nearest crate, like all the others, marked 'Astiz AB', and seeing rows of shiny dark red conical insulators packed in straw, they okayed the unloading.

By the time the unloading was finished, two unmarked lorries had appeared and parked outside the warehouse. Now the warehousemen manhandled the crates onto trollies and moved them into the warehouse. However, a man who'd come with the two lorries selected a number of crates which were left to one side by the warehousemen, and loaded into the lorries by the two drivers. Lesser suspected these crates were going directly to Heinaküla. Had the sorting out of the crates been intended to happen at Krummfeldt's plant, the whole shipment would surely have been collected by Krummfeldt's vehicles.

Hallmets agreed, and told Lesser to take all the men there and follow the two lorries.

"OK," he said to the others, "Time to go!"

63

Hallmets' orders were clear: the lorries were not to be intercepted until they had entered the estate. Lesser, Maslov and Hekk in one car and Ilves and Mürakas in another were following at a discreet distance. Meanwhile Hallmets, along with Larsson, Kadakas and Sõnn, and the uniformed officers, needed to get themselves to a point where they could wait unobtrusively.

The spot advised by Sõnn was a junction two kilometres from Heinaküla, through which the lorries would have to pass on their way to the estate. At the junction was an old inn with several run-down outbuildings. The two vans were concealed behind one of the outbuildings, the officers remaining inside. Lembit meanwhile parked the Volvo outside the inn and, in his chauffeur's uniform, made great show of opening the bonnet to let the engine cool as after a long journey; then he wiped the windscreen and windows, occasionally stopping to smoke a cigarette. Anyone passing would assume his wealthy passenger was in the inn. Sõnn reckoned himself in danger of recognition, and stayed in the car, sat on the floor by the rear seat. Hallmets, Larsson and Kadakas went in. Hallmets greeted the proprietor, said he and his friends were thirsty after a long drive and asked for bottles of *kvass*. It was mildly alcoholic, but not enough to dent their judgement. And plausible enough not to arouse the landlord's suspicions.

They sat by a window and watched the car through the layer of grime on the glass, while for the landlord's benefit making conversation about their journey over from Pärnu, the fashionable resort town on the Gulf of Riga. Larsson, it seemed, knew the road well and was able to talk at length about the various sights to be passed on the way. Kadakas responded enthusiastically and occasionally added some detail. Hallmets grunted agreement from time to time, yawned frequently, and was impressed by Larsson's encyclopaedic knowledge.

After fifteen minutes he saw Lembit throw aside his cigarette, stretch his arms and close the bonnet. The signal. "OK, that's it," he muttered to the others, and they drained their glasses and left, nodding farewell to the landlord.

As they reached the car, Lembit opened the door for them. "Yup," he said, "That's the lorries just gone past, and taken the Heinaküla Road." Hallmets and Larsson got in, whilst Sõnn and Kadakas went round to join the uniformed officers; their vans were to lead the raid. Hallmets felt that accompanying Sõnn would give Kadakas some useful experience. A minute later the two cars following the lorries arrived, the vans moved to the front, Hallmets' car took up the rear, and the convoy moved off up the Heinaküla Road. Hallmets was aware that they had to move fast. If the landlord at the inn was aware of the distillery, as, given his profession, he was likely to be, he'd guess that the purposeful convoy of vehicles was up to something. And since he had a telephone, as Hallmets had noticed, he'd be phoning the estate by now.

They passed through Heinaküla village and followed the road to the estate entrance. The gate was now closed, but the leading van was fitted with solid metal bars at the front, and smashed through it without stopping. The others followed. Four hundred metres took them a junction. To the left, a drive led to the front entrance to the manor house. They turned right and headed for a group of large outbuildings. They swung round the edge of the first they came to and found themselves in an deserted courtyard.

As Lembit swung into the courtyard behind the two CID cars, Hallmets could see the uniformed officers already pouring out of the vans, Sõnn directing them towards the largest of the wooden buildings facing the courtyard. As they approached it a man came out of a small door let into one of the large wooden double doors, spotted them and dashed back inside, slamming the door behind him. The police officers were well equipped however, one carrying a sledgehammer, another a large crowbar. They clustered round the little door. Maslov jumped out of one of the other cars and ran over to join them.

Hallmets and Larsson were now out of the car. While Sõnn's job was to secure the distillery, Lesser's was to locate the lorries. He called to Hallmets, "They can't have gone far, chief. There's a lot of dust around, we should spot the tyre tracks."

"Over here," shouted Ilves, from the opposite corner of the yard. Mürakas, Hekk and Lesser converged on him, Hallmets and Larsson following. The tracks in the earth were clear enough, and recent. They led round the back of the large barn to what looked like a coach-house, a rather dilapidated two-storey wooden construction with two large doors on the ground floor with a blank wall between, and windows above, presumeably once servants' quarters.

As they moved out of the shelter of the barn a shot rang out. They all dived for cover. Hallmets and Larsson were still by the barn, and dodged behind it. Ilves and Mürakas threw themselves on the ground behind a large trough and Lesser and Hekk nipped behind an empty wagon.

"Police!" shouted Lesser. "We have a warrant to search these premises. Put down your weapons and open up. Immediately!"

The response was a fusillade of shots from the windows on the upper storey.

Sheltered by the edge of the barn, Hallmets turned, out of habit from the war, to check their rear. A man stood in the courtyard, having just emerged from the broken door. He was pointing a pistol at them. Hallmets instinctively ducked, and a bullet ploughed into the woodwork where his head would have been. The man turned and ran towards the road. But Hallmets had recognised him: Kleber! Meanwhile Eva had produced a long-barrelled Mauser pistol, hardly the normal police issue, and levelled it at the running man.

"Do I take him out, boss?"

There was no choice. "Go for it."

She paused briefly, then fired. Kleber staggered as he ran, and fell over.

"Well done," said Hallmets, "Check him out. Arrest him if he's still alive...."

"He won't be," she said grimly.

"Check him anyway. Then go to the distillery and get some uniforms round here."

"Will do, chief!" and she was off.

Hallmets pulled out his Browning and joined the others in concentrating fire on the defenders in the stable block. Soon all the windows on the front of the block were smashed. There seemed to be six or maybe seven shooters. But both sides were well shielded, so it seemed a bit of a stalemate. Hallmets suspected this was just what the defenders wanted; it gave their fellows time to get the crates out of the lorries and into hiding. The deadlock needed to be broken.

Two minutes later it was. With a loud roar the van with the reinforced bars raced round the corner and smashed into the blank wall between the gates. The driver had guessed that the gates would be well bolted, but the wooden wall between would be weaker. He was right. The van's bonnet buried itself in the wall, splintering the wooden slats around it. The defenders' fire immediately turned on the van, but its roof and sides were armoured, and the shots had little effect. Lesser and his men increased their fire to cover the van's retreat. But it only reversed a few metres turned sharply, and came alongside the building, so that the passenger window was near the hole they'd made.

Hallmets smiled. He recognised this move from the war. He knew the passenger would now toss a stick bomb or hand grenade into the hole in the building. The van reversed suddenly and there was a loud explosion from inside the building. The van moved forward again and a few seconds later there was another explosion. This time some of the slats in the wall were blown out. Lesser ordered his men to concentrate their fire through the gaps in the hope of chasing out any of the men who had been unloading the lorries. The defenders returned fire, but only sporadically. Maybe they were trying to decide what to do next.

Their decision was hastened by a new bout of firing. Hallmets recognised rifle fire and peeped round the corner. Some of the men who'd secured the distillery had reached an upper floor at the rear of the barn, and were pouring rifle fire from a row of small windows down into the stable. The defenders would be unable to hold their position in the face of powerful fire coming down onto them. Now they would have to retreat, but where to?

The fire from the stable windows ceased, but there were no calls of surrender. Lesser waved the armoured van around the side of the stable, and he and his men followed in its wake. Hallmets went after them, pausing to call to the men in the barn to come after them.

As he came around the corner, Hallmets reached another, smaller, courtyard at the back of the stables. It was empty, apart from the armoured van parked by the rear door of the stable, to Halmets' left. Beyond it, in front of him, was the rear of the manor house. To his right was a low building with a thatched roof which he guessed was a smokehouse.

He saw Lesser and his men standing in the cover of the van's rear. "What's happened?" he asked.

"Saw two of them get into the manor house. One whole, one wounded. Shall we follow?"

"No, not yet. Check out the lorries first. We need all the evidence we can get before we go for the house."

Lesser waved his men into the stable through the rear door, and Hallmets followed. The scene reminded him of the war. The hand grenades had done what they were designed for: produce a localised but powerful blast that would destroy anything in the immediate vicinity, and cause injury further afield through flying debris. Two men lay dead. One had an arm and half his face missing, the other had been flung against the door of a lorry and lay like a broken doll by the mud-encrusted tyre. On the other side of the lorries they found two more men on the ground, at the foot of the staircase leading to the upper floor, both with bullet wounds, but still alive. Hekk was already by one, tying a makeshift bandage around a profusely bleeding head wound. "Two more dead up here," shouted Lesser from the top of the stairs.

"Well done," Hallmets called back. "Let's see to these wounded men first, then get some crates open." His concern for the injured men was not simply a gut reaction from wartime, to save whatever lives you can. He also knew that they needed living witnesses, who would confess to whatever had been going on before those at the top had time to summon their lawyers and prepare their alibis.

While the injured were being bandaged up, and that included Mürakas, who'd picked up a gash on the back of his hand, the men with the crowbar and sledgehammer arrived, along with Sergeant Larsson. She reported to Hallmets that the distillery had been secured, and five arrests made. They'd also found the bottling plant and a storeroom well-stocked with *Leikari* vodka, as well as a smaller amount of *Three Monks* Georgian brandy.

One of the wooden crates had already been removed from its lorry, and they all gathered as the crowbar man got to work. As the lid was lifted, all they could see was straw. Hallmets nodded to Lesser, who tentatively slipped his hands into the straw and after some rummaging produced a package just under a metre long wrapped in cloth. Lesser carefully peeled back the cloth. There was a few moments' silence as they all stared at the weapon, a little like a rifle with a much shortened vented steel barrel. They could smell the oil and see the sheen on the barrel.

"Sub-machine gun," said Lesser, "Looks brand-new. No magazine. They must be packed separately. Are they Swedish or German?"

Larsson leaned forward, "Let me have a good look." She took the gun carefully from Lesser's hands, examined the stock, felt the weight. "Finnish. Suomi KP/-31. Only came out in '31. State-of-the-art. Our army would die for these."

"Are they made there?" Hallmets asked her.

"The factory's in Jyväskylä, right in the middle of Finland. So they must have been taken by rail or truck to Turku, and loaded onto *Dimitrios* there. These weapons aren't cheap, chief."

"So the question is, who were they going to sell them on to?"

"If all these crates are full of them," said Lesser, "They could supply every gangster in the Baltic States, or equip a small army,."

"OK," said Hallmets, "We need to get this operation finished. From the fact those two ran to the manor house, and the amount of money that seems to be involved in this whole business, we have to suspect Heinrich von Langenstein of being party to it. But we need more people here, to examine the distillery, itemise this stuff, and search the whole estate."

"Inspector Sõnn's on that," said Larsson, "He phoned Pikk Street from the distillery. Their office is well-equipped. I suspect they've got records of every single shipment in the filing cabinet there."

Hallmets asked Ilves and Mürakas to guard the arms lorries until the reinforcements arrived. Then, pistol in hand, and followed by Lesser, Hekk and Larsson, he made for the rear door of the manor house.

64

The door was a very ordinary wooden one, once painted black, but now the paint was peeling. They entered a cramped and dim hallway with a stone floor; what light there was came through the grimy window over the outer door. A door to the left was closed, but one on the right was ajar, so Hallmets took that one, moving swiftly into a roomy kitchen. It was very warm, heated by a fire in the wide hearth at the far end. There was a smell of soup which reminded Hallmets of the beetroot soup his mother often made.

There was a big wooden table in the middle of the room, and he sensed rather than saw the two people hiding beneath it.

"Police. We are armed," he said firmly, "Come out, please, very slowly, hands first." Four hands appeared from behind the table. Then their owners, a middle aged woman and a girl of perhaps twelve. The woman regarded them impassively, the girl wide-eyed, wondering.

"Who are you?" asked Hallmets.

The older woman answered. "Veera. I'm the Baron's cook. This is Katja, my grand-daughter."

"Two men came in the back door a few minutes ago. One was wounded. Where did they go?"

She gestured towards a door half way along the inner wall of the kitchen. "The Baron and one of his Germans. They went through there. It's the service stair, goes directly to the dining room."

"Which one was wounded?" asked Lesser.

"His Lordship. But the German is armed. Be careful."

Hallmets opened the door and they made their way up the narrow staircase, dimly lit by tiny windows. He imagined how difficult it must be for the baron's servants bringing full dishes of soup or roast meat up here without tripping on the steep wooden steps. They tried to minimise the noise, but several of the stairs squeaked painfully. Hallmets reached the door at the top, turned the handle and peeped into the room. It was empty. Guns first, they moved in and circled the large dining table towards the closed double doors that formed the only other exit.

"Look, on the table," whispered Lesser, "A bloodstain." It was near the edge, staining the dark wood a darker purple, the imprint of a right hand. Someone had clearly leaned on the table as he passed, taking his hand off a bleeding wound in order to support himself.

Hallmets turned the handle of the double doors. Immediately a shot rang out in the next room and the bullet thumped into the stout wooden door. If it had been one of those hollow doors made of plywood they were putting into new houses, he'd have taken the bullet in his chest. But the old carpenters made doors to last.

He moved to the left side of the doors, signalled Larsson to his side and Lesser to the other, then gestured to Hekk to open the right hand door. Hekk dropped to his knees, turned the handle gently, and, keeping behind the door, swung it open. Instantly a barrage of fire erupted from the next room, shattering an elaborate ceramic lion sitting on the mantelpiece at the end of the room.

"Someone's got one of those sub-machine guns," muttered Lesser.

"Keep quiet!" hissed Larsson.

A second burst of fire sprayed bullets across the dining table, sending brass candlesticks flying, and ricocheting into the ceiling, tossing down fragments of plaster. At the end of the shooting came a small click. Instantly Larsson stepped into the door way, levelled her pistol and fired two shots in rapid succession. "OK," she said, and stepped into the room, swinging her pistol around to cover the corners.

As Hallmets followed, he saw a tall well-built young man with close-cropped blonde hair standing behind a leather-clad armchair. His right arm hung useless at his side, the fingers still clutching the sub-machine gun. He put his hand to his chest, where blood was beginning to seep into his shirt. "*Ich verstehe nicht,*" he gasped. He was beginning to understand that the members of the master race were still mortal. He shook his head in puzzlement and collapsed behind the chair.

"Hold your fire," called Hallmets, "Ilmar, check him out. I think I saw this fellow last time I was here, pretending to be a servant. Neat shooting, Eva, I'm glad you're on our side."

Hekk cautiously approached the armchair, weapon at the ready, then knelt down. "He's dead, chief." He searched his trouser pockets, then flourished a small card. "ID card. Hans Schriff. German citizen. Nazi party member. SS *Truppführer.*"

They approached the next set of doors. Once again, they prepared for shooting, but when Hekk opened the door there was no response. Larsson swung into the open doorway ready to fire, then, after panning her weapon round the room, stepped inside, the others following.

The room they entered was a smaller sitting room. Comfortable sofas flanked a fireplace on the inner wall. A writing table and chair sat under one of two windows looking to the front of the house. Under the other was a green-painted wooden chest.

On the sofa to the left of the fireplace lay Heinrich von Langenstein, clearly badly injured. Laura Vaher sat with one arm round him, the other pressed to his lower abdomen, trying to staunch blood flowing from a wound. She had pressed a scarf into the wound, and was holding it down. She simply said, "Heinie's dying. Please help him."

Hallmets told Lesser and Hekk to check the rest of the building and get an ambulance for the baron. He guessed that several would already be on their way after the battle at the stables. "Eva, can you wait here, with these two," he said, "I don't think they pose a threat."

Hallmets told von Langenstein the ambulance would be arriving soon, and they'd get him to hospital.

Heinrich waved Hallmets closer. "*Vielen Dank, Herr Hauptkomissar.* Please, you must believe me, Laura has nothing to do with all this."

Hallmets thought that highly improbable, but answered, "If you want me to believe that, *Herr* von Langenstein, I think you should tell me everything. If we know all the facts, it may be clear that she is not involved." It was clear to him what was happening. Heinrich was offering a deal: a confession in exchange for Laura's freedom. Hallmets assumed Laura was at least a competent actress, and would therefore probably be able to convince a jury she was just a simple woman, who was horrified when she found out what was going on. But Heinrich didn't want to take a chance on that.

Laura was holding the packed cloth firmly on the wound, there was only a little blood seeping out between her fingers. But how much internal damage had been done wasn't clear. The baron coughed and went on. "We were caught out when your people started firing down from the distillery. God knows where this bullet ended up. I'm not hopeful, Chief Inspector, I saw wounds like this in the war, they don't usually turn out well."

"You'll be surprised how much surgery has advanced since then, *Herr Baron.*" He could see the man was dying, now was not the time to begrudge him his title. "But you're right, this is not a good one. I think you need to talk to me now."

Hallmets sat himself at the bottom end of the sofa, by Heinrich's feet. Larsson sat on the other sofa. They put their guns away.

"We lost a lot in the land reform after the war, but our father was determined to stay here. 'This is our ancestors' soil. One day we'll reclaim it all,' he used to say. We worked hard to develop the farm, the horse-breeding."

"Yes, you mentioned that last time I talked with you."

"Of course. Anyway, Father died in '22. We had things running very efficiently, but it wasn't enough, not if we wanted to buy back some of the land that had been handed over to the peasants. That's when we came up with the idea for the distillery. We knew someone in another estate who'd built a legal distillery, but what with all the regulations and taxes, he wasn't making much out of it. It was Krummfeldt who suggested we do it illegally. He's a rather unpleasant little man, isn't he? He suggested he could help with the distribution, and no-one need even know where the stuff came from. We needed the money, so we took the risk. And indeed, it paid off. When we Germans do something, we do it well, eh?" He coughed and gasped, Hallmets could see the pain etched on his face. "Rather than just producing cheap hooch, we went for a quality product. We called it *Leikari* so people would think it came from Finland. You've tried it?"

"Yes, indeed, it really is very good."

Heinrich smiled. "So good that Krummfeldt suggested we send it abroad too. With prohibition in Finland we made lots of money. Then we started sending it to Sweden too. With the absurd price of legal alcohol there, people were flocking to buy illegal stuff that was just as good. And they even thought it came from Finland. We bought back two of the farms and added them to the estate, and invested money in good blood stock. Two top-class stallions. Beauties. You must come and see them sometime. We even managed to get hold of some excellent Georgian brandy."

"*Three Monks*?"

"You know of it? You grow in my estimation, *Herr Hauptkommissar*. It's well-known to connoisseurs. So hard to get after the Revolution. But it's so corrupt over there now, we only had to find the right officials to bribe. We almost thought of turning the distillery legal then, but there would have been too many awkward questions, and the money kept coming."

"Did Vaher go along with it?"

"Of course that was awkward, having a policeman in the family. However, we discovered he was very reasonable. His view was that the business of the police was catching real criminals – gangsters, pimps, murderers, thugs – and that making illegal booze was hardly a big deal. So we gave him a cut, and he was very happy with that. He was not a bad chap for an Estonian."

"He was all right," said Laura, with a sniff.

"Please, tell me about the guns. I can understand the vodka. But why were you bringing guns into the country? That's a whole new level of risk. And the punishment is very severe. Even as an accessory to that, Laura might face ten years in jail. Juries can sympathise with illegal alcohol – who doesn't want to buy his vodka cheap – but not with importing weapons."

Heinrich coughed and winced, caught hold of Hallmets' arm. "Albrecht was working in Germany with the Nazi party. I'm not sure exactly what he did. He and Krummfeldt were thick as thieves, and every time Albrecht came here, he'd go off with him. Finally they let me in on their plan. Krummfeldt is involved in a number of German Societies throughout the country – he puts money into them, too – and he thought that with the right leadership they could be brought together into something like the Nazi party. The plan was to use the money we made from the booze to import weapons. Then, when the time was ripe, we would mount a *coup d'etat*, restore power in Estonia to the Germans – the old families in the countryside and the businessmen in the cities – and declare an alliance with Germany."

"Why did you agree to it?"

"I hoped that if Estonia could then become a satellite of the Reich – a sort of Protectorate – with the rights of the Baltic Germans restored, we would get more of our land back. The settlement the Estonians forced on us was very unjust. Albrecht said his friend Alfred Rosenberg thought it was a great idea, and once Hitler was in power Germany would welcome it. He was posted to the embassy here to help prepare for the coup." He coughed again. More blood seeped through Laura's hand.

"Please," she pleaded, "Stop talking, Heinie, you need to rest. You can say all this later if you really want to."

He looked up at her. "No, Laura, it needs to be said before it's too late. I need to protect you."

Laura glared at the Chief Inspector. "Where's the ambulance? Why are they taking so long? A baron should be first in the queue."

"I stopped being a baron many years ago," gasped her brother. "Don't worry, they'll be here. Let me finish my story."

"Why didn't they just send you German weapons?" asked Hallmets.

"Come now, Chief Inspector, please allow us some intelligence. The point was that Germany itself should be entirely unconnected with the coup. The weapons were Finnish. The whole thing was to be an internal move by the German community here. There were even some

Estonians who would work with us."

"Did Vaher know about the plan?"

"That was a problem. We knew Vaher's opinions about law and order, and his admiration for what the Nazis were doing in Germany, so we hoped he'd support us, and bring some of his police colleagues along. But he said a *coup d'etat* in Estonia by us Germans was the last thing he wanted. And the idea that Germany was behind it appalled him. 'No patriotic Estonian will stand for Germans running the country again,' he said. He told us to drop the plan altogether, and and threatened to stop it if we didn't. I told Albrecht Nikolai was right, it wasn't going to work. Laura begged Albrecht to drop it too."

"Yes, that's true," Laura confirmed, wiping a tear away, "I did. I pleaded with him."

"Albrecht said he'd think about it. Next thing, Vaher was dead. We suspected Albrecht was behind it, although he denied it. He said some gangster must have killed him. He insisted that we go ahead with stockpiling weapons. He was confident there would soon be enough people to stage a coup. 'Even if we have to bring them in from Germany' he said."

"He always wanted his own way," added Laura, "Ever since he was a child. Our parents spoiled him, gave him whatever he wanted."

"So you don't know exactly who killed Vaher?" asked Hallmets."

The baron shook his head. "Albrecht denied he was there, but I didn't believe him. My little brother was always a bad liar. I suspect Hans Schriff, and maybe some of those so-called 'gardeners' we had. And that other policeman, the one Laura seemed to like ..."

"Lepp? Was he involved too?"

Laura shook her head. "No, not Indrek, Surely he wouldn't ..."

"Yes," her brother continued,"That was him. I never liked him, you know. No empathy for others, no sense of duty. He was very enthusiastic. For the coup, I mean. He longed to be one of the rulers. One of the new men, he called himself. But really, there was no breeding, no class. Like Hitler, eh?" Von Langenstein coughed. Blood dribbled down his chin.

"Thank you, *Herr Baron*, I think you should rest now."

"You must believe me that Laura was not involved. She is a woman after all, and this was men's work. She realised Albrecht was involved in the killing when she saw you had his pen."

Laura nodded tearfully. "Yes, it's true. He ..."

"But she knew her duty to the family, *Herr Hauptkommissar*. Her silence was only the proof of her breeding. There is no reason to punish her."

"Rest assured, we'll not be hard on her."

The baron fell back on the sofa exhausted.

"Eva," said Hallmets, then to Larsson, "Can you get the medics up here as fast as possible." He knew the baron had not long to live. He too had seen such wounds on the battlefield.

As Larsson got up and turned for the door, Hallmets saw Heinrich's expression freeze and Laura's mouth fall open.

"Hands in the air!" a sharp voice called.

Larsson and Hallmets obeyed. Hallmets turned around very slowly, to see who was there. He saw a man rising from the chest by the window, a thin man with dark hair oiled and combed back from his forehead, and a thin moustache beneath a thin and pointed nose. With a luger pistol in his hand.

"Albrecht!" gasped Laura.

The man climbed out of the chest. He was wearing an immaculate black suit and shiny black shoes. He seemed to Hallmets more like a gigolo than an aristocrat. "I got in there as soon as the fighting started. I'm not stupid. Well, Heinie, you've really spilled the beans there. Now I'm going to have to shoot these two cops before I go." He walked over to the doors leading to the centre of the house and turned the key in the lock. "That's better. We need a little privacy."

"So you and your thugs killed Vaher," said Hallmets clamly, "Because he loved his country more than your maniac scheme."

"He was pathetic," sneered Albrecht, "Countries, nationalities, they're all finished now. The new man is bigger than all that. He makes his own destiny, through the power of his will. He dominates, he seizes opportunities, he builds his own world, moulds the lives of others, makes them part of his universe. Who are the Estonians in the face of that? An insignificant race which we will supersede and transcend."

"Hiding in a clothes-chest doesn't sound very transcendent. The game's over now."

"You think I'm done here, Hallmets. Let me explain something. In one minute you and the woman will be dead. Then I'll go out the back door and slip away. I've got my diplomatic badge and my car's not far. I'll back in the embassy in half an hour." _

"Be a man and a von Langenstein, Albrecht," wheezed Heinrich. "Stand up and tell the truth. It's all over. Then you can flash your badge and scuttle back to your hideout."

"You don't understand, do you, my stupid big brother. History has left you behind. The future belongs to me. Too bad you won't see it.

I've been wanting to do this for thirty years." He shot Heinrich in the head. Blood and brain sprayed out the back of his skull onto Laura's lap. She looked at her bloody hands, then screamed. A long, terrible scream of rage and despair and loss. The sound of it filled the room, echoed from the walls, pressed at the windows, so that the drapes on either side seemed to shiver.

"Shut up, you stupid bitch!" yelled Albrecht, and fired a shot in her direction, as if to make his point. It caught her on the shoulder and spun her off the couch. She tumbled onto the floor in a heap. And stopped screaming.

But the noise had done its job. Footsteps could be heard in the next room. People had evidently come up the main staircase. Probably the medics with a stretcher for Heinrich. Someone tried the door, shook it.

"Shit," muttered Albrecht. He stared for a moment at Hallmets. "I'll get you two later, you have my word on that." And he ran to the door at the other end of the room, the one Hallmets had entered some fifteen minutes earlier, flung it open, dashed through and slammed it behind him.

Then a familiar voice. "Police, stop!" And a shot. And two more shots. And two more.

The door opened again.

"Who the hell was that?" said Kadakas. "I had to shoot him, he tried to kill me."

65

There was a lot of activity at the Heinaküla estate. Ambulances ferried the dead and injured away. Among the latter was Albrecht von Langenstein, wounded in his left thigh and right shoulder. Kadakas has shot him in the leg first, but von Langenstein had continued shooting, and the lieutenant had no alternative but to shoot him again. He himself suffered only a flesh wound in one arm.

All sorts of people now turned up at Heinaküla Manor. Police were searching the grounds and every building for further evidence. Officials from the internal revenue service came to examine the distillery and impound the stocks of vodka and brandy. A couple of army officers came to look at the weapons found in the crates. They were hoping the army would ultimately get them.

Among the first newcomers was Jaan Kallas. Hallmets had phoned Kallas as soon as he could, before anyone could tell him not to. He gave Kallas an interview, focusing on the discovery of the distillery and the smuggled weapons. He declined to comment on what had taken place within the manor house, or on the role of the von Langensteins, knowing that Kallas would draw his own conclusions. Tõnu the photographer was invited to take shots of the distillery equipment and the stores of illegal alcohol.

Captain Lind arrived to receive Hallmets' account of the matter and to congratulate him on tying up the Vaher case. As he said goodbye to Lind at the main door of the manor house, Hallmets noticed the captain's driver loading some crates into the car. "Spoils of war," said the captain, looking guilty, "The revenue people will only pour it away. Terrible waste of good vodka. I'll send you over a few bottles."

An hour later, he retold the story to Colonel Reinart.

"Very neatly done, I must say, Chief Inspector," said Reinart, smiling, "So it turns out the whole thing was about illicit alcohol production, and the resentment of a few members of the former ruling class. And Vaher was killed by hirelings of the ex-Baron, led by Schriff. All of whom died in the raid today."

"What about the German connection? Schriff was a member of the Nazi party."

"How many Germans do you think belong to the party? There are bound to be some bad eggs."

"We still have Albrecht von Langenstein. Hopefully he can be questioned."

"Oh, didn't I mention it? He passed away in the ambulance, on the way to hospital. One of my people was there with him. Wounded in three places, he didn't have much chance."

Hallmets said nothing. He knew how many times Albrecht had been wounded.

"It's just as well, really," the Colonel continued, "After all, he was a diplomat, and we'd never have been able to question him, let alone put him on trial. He'd have been back in the *Reich* in no time. We'll have to say that Albrecht knew nothing about the alcohol business. It was unfortunate that he arrived, purely to see his brother and sister, and quite by chance, in the middle of the raid and got caught in the crossfire. He must have taken a short cut from his car across a field, so that the police didn't spot him, or they would naturally have warned him off."

"What about the weapons? How are you going explain them away?"

"Obviously we can't reveal their plans for a seizure of power. That might put ideas into too many people's heads here. So we say the weapons were also part of the smuggling operation. They were to be sold on at a big profit to any government which would pay for them. They might even have been sold to our own army!"

"And Krummfeldt?"

"He claims he didn't realise his crates were being used by the smugglers. It would be very difficult to prove anything against him. His factory is important to our economy. But it's been suggested to him that he steps back from personally managing the plant, and takes himself to another country for a few years."

"So everything is nicely sewn up?"

"Your job is to solve the crime, Hallmets. Mine is to manage the political fallout, and make sure our country stays in one piece. Sometimes the narrative has to be massaged. We simply can't afford to fall out with Germany. That's the reality of where we are. Estonia is like a weasel in a bearpit – we just have to keep out of the way of the bears, and hope they don't take too much notice of us."

Hallmets sighed. "Yes, I understand. The only loose end that remains then is Lepp. The baron made it clear to me that he was involved in Vaher's death."

Reinart sighed. "Yes. Tucking him away in a backwater is not an option now. I sent someone round to his place but he'd already flown the coop. But we'll be keeping an eye out for him, and when we catch him, he'll get what's coming. By the way, the press haven't been here, have they?"

"I'm afraid so. Kallas turned up."

Reinart wasn't pleased. "Dammit! How the hell did he find out?"

"Didn't you notice as you came in. The place is swarming with people. Any one of them could have fancied a few crowns for the tip-off."

"Did you give him an interview?"

"Yes, I think it would have been worse not to, otherwise he'd just wander around and speak to anybody. I focused on the distillery. But soon they'll all be here."

The Colonel sighed. "Well, just give as little as you can. At least this has saved us from concocting the stuff about a Lithuanian gang. We'll have a press conference in a day or two."

There was plenty to do the rest of the afternoon. At six, Larsson popped her head in to say the team, were going for a post-case drink at a bar in Kuninga Street and they hoped he'd come along. He said he'd drop in at some point. His days of a night's drinking with colleagues were past, however, he thought it important that the boss put in an appearance. But didn't overstay his welcome.

Lembit dropped him back at the Imperial just before half past six. He needed a shower and a change of clothes. By seven he was feeling cleaner and more refreshed, and headed for Kuninga Street. Better to pop in there early than late.

The bar was in a basement, and he guessed it was one frequented by police personnel. Having hung up his coat, he soon spotted Lesser, Sõnn, Ilves, Mürakas, Maslov, Kadakas and Larsson sat round a table, eating blood sausage, pickled gherkins and fried potatoes. "Tonight's special," said Larsson as Hallmets sat down. "That'll do me too," he replied, and ordered a beer along with his food.

The atmosphere was relaxed rather than celebratory. Hallmets knew the feeling of relief when a case was finally tied up. You couldn't really cheer until the judge had passed sentence. But he guessed there would be few sentences after this one. Heinrich and Albrecht von Langenstein were dead, as was Kleber. The survivors of the battle at the stables would face the heaviest sentences. The distillery operatives had surrendered as soon as the police entered the barn; their sentences would be fairly light. He suspected laura Vaher would never come to trial. He wondered if she would move away, or stay on at the estate.

Hallmets' biggest regret was that they hadn't nailed Lepp, who appeared to have got away scot-free. He was no doubt out of the country by now. He wondered whether the colonel had given a helping hand there. But he might be tempted to return to Estonia one day. And then there would be a reckoning.

"So, you'll be off back to Tartu soon?" asked Sõnn.

"As soon as we get things tied up," said Hallmets, "But you and Lesser will get most of that done. Thanks for your help."

"Our pleasure," said Lesser, "But I suspect we'll see you again. What with Vaher gone and Lind soon to retire, they'll be wanting somebody to head up the CID here. My bet's on you, chief."

"I'll drink to that," said Sõnn.

"Well, let's just see what happens," muttered Hallmets.

Twenty minutes later he made his farewells and left them to it.

Back at the hotel, he phoned Kirsti to let her know how things stood, indicating that he'd be back in a day or two. "And looking forward to it," he added.

Day 9. Thursday 30th March

66

Hallmets was in no hurry to go in the next morning, and reached his office just after nine. Maslov and Larsson were both there, looking tired. He guessed the get-together had stretched well into the night. There was no sign of Kadakas.

He'd picked up a paper on the way in, and saw Kallas's scoop on the front page under the headline *'Baltic German Plot Foiled!'* with the sub-heading, *'Exclusive Report from Jaan Kallas.'* The story described how police, led by Chief Inspector Hallmets, had, after painstaking work piecing evidence together, swooped on the Heinaküla estate to uncover an illicit distillery. Kallas commented that it was ironic that this plant, built using the very latest distilling technology, was producing vodka of a better quality than most legal stuff. He referred readers to page five where the paper's drinks connoisseur would discuss the quality of *Leikari* vodka, and report on the demand from retail outlets that it be produced legally. Kallas then reported on the gun battle as police fought with *'armed conspirators'* to seize a consignment of weapons, *'of the very latest type,'* purchased with the profits of alcohol smuggling and brought into the country illegally. Hallmets wondered who else Kallas had talked to at the scene.

'What was the aim of the conspiracy?' asked Kallas, *'Nothing less than the overthrow of the state!'* He reported that a number of Germans had been killed or captured and this pointed clearly (to Kallas at least) to a conspiracy among the Baltic Germans to regain power in Estonia. Kallas hinted that the German government would probably have been sympathetic to the conspiracy, had it succeeded. He pointed out that one of Herr Hitler's top advisers was Alfred Rosenberg, born in Tallinn, the son of a wealthy Baltic German merchant. *'This man, who fled to Germany in 1919 when General von der Goltz and his mercenaries were defeated by our army of independence, is no doubt encouraging German landowners in the Baltic states to foment trouble and destabilise the governments, in the vain hope of seizing power again for themselves. But, just as the Reds were foiled in their attempted coup in 1924, so the former rulers have now been thwarted through the intelligent investigation and prompt action of our police. We salute Chief Inspector Hallmets as the saviour of our nation.'*

Hallmets permitted himself a smile. He turned to page five to see a detailed description of the captured distillery, along with a discussion by the paper's drinks expert of the smell, taste, texture, and afterfeel of *Leikari* vodka, pronouncing it one of the best vodkas he had encountered, and agreeing with suggestions that the distillery be brought into legal production. He also quoted an unnamed *'police expert on illegal alcohol'* who endorsed his opinion of the vodka, and also mentioned the important achievement of the smugglers in sourcing quantities of the hitherto unobtainable *Three Monks* brandy from Georgia. Hallmets read this bit out loud, watching Maslov as he blushed, chewed his pencil, and buried himself deeper in his form-filling. For the morning was taken up with all the paperwork that inevitably follows a major case, and the three of them plodded through it with dogged determination. Lesser and Sõnn were no doubt doing the same thing in their own offices.

He had lunch in the canteen with Maslov and Larsson. No-one spoke much. Hallmets sensed the anti-climax that can accompany the pen-pushing that follows the conclusion of a case.

"Guess Oleg and I will be off home soon," said Larsson, after they'd eaten. "Back to chasing pickpockets on the beach at Pärnu for me."

"And I'll be picking drunken Russians out of the gutter in Petseri again," added Maslov.

"Don't be too depressed," said Hallmets, "You've done well, both of you, and that will be recorded, I can assure you. It's not for me to say, but I don't think either of you will be too long back in Petseri or Pärnu. Good people should be well used. Our police have a high reputation, and it's especially important that after these events we demonstrate that we're using the best people in the best way. Eva, I also think we really need to work hard giving women a bigger role in the police force."

"You'll have to do a lot of persuading on that one," said Larsson, "There have been women police in Sweden since 1910, and in Germany even before that. I'm not the first here, but we're not even in double figures yet. There are still too many men here who think a woman should be cooking his meal and digging up his turnips, while he sits in his living room swigging vodka."

Hallmets had just got back to his office, when Marta announced Lieutenant Kadakas to see him. The lieutenant was back in a crisp army uniform.

"*Tere,* Ants. Come in. I wondered where you'd got to this morning. We've a lot of paperwork to do."

"Sorry, Sir, er, Chief. I had to do some thinking. And then talk to Colonel Reinart. And my superiors back at Army Headquarters."

Kadakas hesitated

"Ah, of course. We'll be sorry to lose you. You'd make a fine detective."

"But that's just what I want to do. I've been asking for a transfer. A permanent one. I don't want to go back to the army. Or wear a uniform. Here is where I want to be."

"And what's the result?"

"It's going to up to you, Sir. They'll send you a form to fill in. If you OK it, so will they."

"Ants, go home now. Take off the uniform. Then come back here. There's a mountain of paperwork for you."

At two thirty Hallmets was invited to Captain Lind's office. The Captain invited him to sit, then offered him a drink, to celebrate the successful conclusion of the case. On this occasion Hallmets accepted, and Lind produced a bottle of *Three Monks* brandy. They toasted the success. Hallmets turned down a second toast, though he admitted to the captain that he thought the brandy was good stuff.

"I'm glad you think so," muttered Lind, "I've sent a crate round to your hotel for you. It wouldn't have looked good handing it over in here. It's in a box marked 'Machine Parts'."

"Thanks," said Hallmets, "Is that what you called me down for?"

"No, no. Well, yes, partly. But no, there's more. I'll come straight to the point, Jüri. As you know, I'm retiring soon. I'm advising the Prefect that you should get the job."

"Thank you for thinking of me, Peeter. I'll have to think about it."

"What!" Lind frowned. "Jüri, what is there to think about? You're the obvious candidate. What possible objection could you have?"

"I have two. One is that it's not just about me. My family is settled in Tartu, and we like it there. My wife has a job, my daughter's at the University and my son's still at the Gymnasium. I'd have to consult them about any possible move."

"But surely ..."

"My other hesitation is that I'm not a politician. I can't accept the truth being twisted, or even thrown out of the window entirely, simply for political considerations. I'm not sure if Reinart and his pals in the Ministry would be happy with that."

"Well, Jüri, I don't know what the world's coming to when women and children get in the way of a man's career." Lind shook his head and poured himself another drink.

67

Exactly on four o'clock Hallmets was shown into Colonel Reinart's office in the Ministry. Reinart greeted him warmly, invited him to sit, ordered coffee for them both.

"Well, Chief Inspector, I want to thank you for your work here. I'm also authorised to pass on the appreciation of the Minister and the Prefect that the case has been tied up without undue delay. They will be holding a press conference tomorrow morning at ten. By then you'll be on your way back to Tartu. I'm sure the local people can tie up any loose ends. We feel that it will give the population a sense of closure to see you returning to your post, a sense that normality and the rule of law have returned."

"Thank you. I'll be happy to get back to my family, Colonel. Living in hotels – even one as comfortable as the Imperial – isn't really my cup of tea. I take it from your more relaxed demeanour that the political aspects of the case have been resolved?"

"Quite so. We were certainly relieved that the Germans didn't want to make a big issue of it. The Ambassador has accepted our explanation of Albrecht von Langenstein's unfortunate and entirely accidental death. He has also assured us that they would condemn any attempt by a small number of Baltic German malcontents to overthrow the Estonian Republic. By pointing the finger at the Baltic Germans rather than the German government, your friend *Härra* Kallas has also done us a favour."

"So everyone lives happily ever after?"

The Colonel smiled. "We went through that yesterday, Chief Inspector, there's no need for me to repeat anything. But we'll have to keep a close eye on the German community here from now on."

"What about Lepp? Are you going to reveal his part in all this?"

"No, I don't think that would help. But we'll be watching out for him, and if he steps back on Estonian soil we'll have him."

"A quiet shot in the back of the neck?"

"If there's compelling evidence, he'll go on trial."

Hallmets didn't believe that, but kept his counsel.

"There's one other thing I'd like to discuss with you," said the colonel. "We now have to replace Vaher, and soon Captain Lind will be retiring. Some of the newspapers have been calling for you to be appointed Head of CID here, in view of your success with this case, and Lind has recommended you very strongly to succeed him. But I'll be honest with you, that's not going to happen. You've not been happy with the fact that a number of decisions concerning the case have had to be made for political reasons. Would you agree with that?"

"Let's just say that I attach a lot of importance to transparency and honesty."

"Even when it brings more problems?"

"It doesn't create problems, it reveals problems that are already there. That need to be faced and dealt with. In a democracy, openness is always the best policy. Not always the easiest, but in the long run, the only way to protect democracy."

Reinart smiled thinly. "Those views aren't helpful when it comes to cases that have to be, er ..." For once Reinart seemed to be searching for a word.

"Spun?"

"Spun. Yes that's a neat, almost a poetic, way of putting it. We spin tales to keep people happy."

"What about truth?"

"Yes, there's always a bit of that in the tale somewhere too. It confirms the authenticity of the whole story. That's how politicians operate. I've spoken about this to the minister, of course. The sad fact is, that we need someone here who is more amenable to the political aspects of police work than you are. I'm sorry about that, but that's the way it is."

"Thank you for being so candid with me, Colonel." Hallmets began to rise from his seat.

"Sit down, please, Chief Inspector. I haven't finished yet. As I said when you arrived, we are very grateful for the speed and efficiency with which you solved the case, and indeed, contained all the complications surrounding it. And when I say we, I include also the State Elder, *Härra* Päts himself. We recognise that your skills, as a detective and as a team-leader, are valuable, and we want to be able to use them in the best way possible. Accordingly, I'm authorised to offer you a new role as co-ordinator of a Special Police Group, based here in Tallinn, to deal with difficult criminal cases throughout the country. What would you say to that?"

"How would this group be staffed?"

"That would be up to you. How many officers do you think would be necessary?"

"Hmm. I'd say we should start with half a dozen dedicated officers, women as well as men. If they're going to different areas, they'd have to be augmented by local officers who know the place. On the other hand, if there are times when they're not required, they could offer training to forces across the country."

"Ah, yes. I hadn't thought of that. And six officers is well within the budget we planned for the unit. Are there people you might want to suggest?"

"Yes, I'm sure there are. Keeping the number to six would be tricky though. There are …" Hallmets checked himself. "I'm sorry, I'm talking like I've already said yes. I can't give you an answer right now. I'd have to talk it over with my family. We're well settled in Tartu, and I'd have to be sure they're OK with moving here. We share every big decision."

"Democracy in action, eh?" The colonel smiled. "Of course, we can't demand a response immediately. Today's Thursday, so why not let me know sometime on Monday morning? Does that sound reasonable?"

"Yes, it does. Thank you, Colonel. That's quite a lot to think about. I'll call you on Monday."

"Tell you what. I'll even throw in the car, and Lembit as well, if you take the job."

Back in his office, he called the University Library in Tartu. The library was housed in the restored western end of the ruin of the great cathedral that once dominated the entire city from its position on the hill above it, and he could imagine someone making their way to the tiny basement room where Kirsti worked, cataloguing the library's English language collections.

"*Tere*, Jüri! Is something wrong? You don't usually have me dragged up from the crypt. Don't tell me you've to stay up there for another week after all."

"No, no. Quite the opposite. It's all done, and I'm coming home tomorrow."

"Fantastic. I'm off work at four, so if you're getting the one o'clock train from Tallinn, I can meet you at the station."

"Yes, that would be nice. There's something else, too. A job offer …"

Acknowledgements

Since our first visit to Estonia, we've grown to love the country, and I even made an effort to learn the language. So what better place to set a crime story. My wife Vivien is my First Reader and honest critic, and that makes a big difference. Thanks also to others who have read part or all of the book, especially Liz Pugh, to Maarika Teral for valuable comments from Estonia, and to Richard Foreman for deciding that this book was worth publishing.

Historical Note

I've tried to set the story in an accurate historical background. The only real historical figures who appear (very briefly) in the book are Ado Anderkop, Konstantin Päts, Viktor Rotenbork, and Jaan Tönisson. All other characters taking part in the action are fictitious. I have recreated 1930s Tallinn as accurately as possible, and apologise for any errors therein.

A Brief Overview of Estonian History

Although the Estonians have been settled at the eastern end of the Baltic Sea since at least the beginning of our era, Estonia only became an independent state in 1918. Up to the late twelfth century the tribes lived more-or-less undisturbed. But at the beginning of the thirteenth century foreign domination arrived, in the shape of the Knights of the Sword, a crusading order recruited mainly in Germany. Under the guise of bringing Christianity to pagans, the knights subjugated the tribes and seized their lands. The Germanic landowning class, known as Baltic Germans, remained in place for the next 700 years.

After a serious defeat in 1236, the Knights of the Sword were incorporated into the larger and more powerful Teutonic Order. The Estonian lands were divided into a patchwork of territories, owing allegiance to the Order, the Bishop of Ösel (on the island of Saaremaa) or the Bishop of Dorpat (Tartu), and this situation persisted up to the Reformation, when the area became Lutheran, and the Teutonic Order transformed itself into the Duchy of Prussia.

A major upheaval came in the late 1500s, when Ivan the Terrible, Tsar of Russia, attempted to incorporate the eastern Baltic shores into his empire. A bloody war followed, as other powers in the area invaded the Estonian lands to resist the Russian advance westwards. Ultimately the Swedes emerged supreme in the early 1600s, and their rule in Estonia was regarded as "the good old Swedish time." Although the Baltic Germans, now swearing allegiance to the King of Sweden, retained their lands, their powers were constrained by the Swedish authorities, and peasants gained rights they were not to regain until the 19th century.

By the early 18th century Swedish power was waning, and the Russia of Peter the Great on the move, and in the Great Northern War (1700-1720) Russian armies gained control of Estonia (as well as Latvia and Lithuania), and the Baltic states were incorporated into the Russian Empire. The Baltic German landowners once again retained their lands and now swore fealty to the Russian Tsar. They weren't unhappy about this, as the protection of peasants' rights given by the Swedes was swept away, and they could treat the indigenous people as their slaves once again.

The city of Tallinn had been founded by the Danes, during a short-lived involvement in Estonia's history in the twelfth century, hence the name (from *Taana Linn* = "Danish town"). They built a castle on the hilltop site of a native fort, and the town grew at the foot of the hill. A cathedral was built on the hill, hence its name *Toompea* (= "cathedral hill"), and here the governor's office was located, and the aristocracy built their townhouses.

With a good harbour, Tallinn became a major port, and during the Middle Ages was a member of the Hanseatic League. Most of the merchants who established themselves there were, like the landowners, of German extraction, and the German merchants ran the town council until well into the nineteenth century. Tallinn's trade was boosted by the incorporation of Estonia into the Russian Empire, as the port was ice-free in winter, yet not too far from the capital St. Petersburg, and much traffic now passed through its harbour.

During the nineteenth century an indigenous Estonian middle class emerged, and with it came a movement for cultural emancipation, focused on the use of the Estonian language, which had suvived as the language of the peasantry. This cultural movement was met with suspicion from both the Russian rulers and the German landowners. Nevertheless books were published in Estonian, dramas were performed, and a tradition of local choirs was founded, which fed into a national Song Festival held every four or five years.

Industry also grew, and the western links of German entrepreneurs enabled some large factories to develop, producing such materials as textiles and plywood for the huge Russian market. Tallinn grew as people moved from the land into the city in search of work. The port of Tallinn also continued to prosper as the winter gateway to Russia, goods being moved directly from ship to railway wagon for shipment eastward.

The First World War and its aftermath changed everything. Russian and German armies moved through the Baltic provinces. But Russia's archaic structure could not support modern warfare, and the result was mutiny and revolution in 1917. As Russia imploded into civil war, and the soldiers came home, the Baltic states saw an unexpected opportunity to free themselves. Estonia declared its independence on 24th February 1918, a few days before invading German armies arrived. But later that year Germany surrendered to its Western opponents. This marked the start of the two-year Independence War, as Estonian armies fought against the Red army on one front, trying to bring Estonia into the new Soviet Union, and a freelance German army seeking to make the Baltic states into a German duchy, supported by most of the Baltic German landowners. Finally the Estonians emerged victorious, beating off a number of Red army thrusts, and defeating the German mercenaries at Võnnu in Latvia, making possible both Latvian and Estonian independence.

The new state had much to do to build its social, economic and political infrastructure. The first task was land reform, and a radical measure confiscated most of the Baltic German-owned lands and redistributed them to Estonian farmers. Estonia was transformed from a nation of landless peasants to one of small farmers. Many of the Baltic Germans left for Germany. Those who remained were left enough land for a single farm, on which they were obliged to be resident. With the loss of the huge Russian market, industry too had to readjust itself to the comparatively tiny domestic market. But Estonians are a hard-working people, and new export markets were found, as Estonian agricultural produce, butter and bacon in particular, found ready customers in Britain and Germany. Estonians had to learn how to do politics too. The new constitution was thoroughly democratic, leading to constant coalitions, with the same politicians shuffling power between them.

With independence, a new police force was formed. Standards of recruitment were high and there was no shortage of applicants. Consequently, Estonia's police were held in high regard within the country. The police were formed into three divisions, the uniformed police, focused on minor crime and public order, the criminal police, focused on the solution of major crime, and the political police, focused on the identification and surveillance of individuals and groups judged to be a threat to the state. The police were under the control of the Ministry of the Interior.

Yet the country was not isolated from what was happening in the rest of Europe. The economic crash of 1929 was not good for Estonia, but gradually the country worked its way back towards prosperity. Politically there were threats from both ends of the spectrum. Estonians knew that over its Eastern border was a Soviet state eager to reclaim the provinces of the Old Russian Empire. A Soviet-sponsored coup had failed in 1924, and there was a constant sense of threat from Stalin's empire. But there was also the rise of totalitarian movements, which happened across the whole of Europe. But the accession of Hitler to power in Germany, with his claim to protect Germans everywhere, added a new source of worry. As the 1930s progressed, Estonians tried to enjoy the life of citizens of a modern European state. But the clouds were not going to go away.

Further Reading

The best history of Estonia available is still *Estonia and the Estonians* by Toivo U. Raun (Stanford, California, Hoover Institution Press, 2nd edition, 2001), which includes good coverage of the first independence period. For a wider view of the Baltic states, see *A Concise History of the Baltic States* by Andrejs Plakans (Cambridge, Cambridge University Press, 2011).

A Little Bit of Estonian

Estonian is similar to Finnish, and completely unlike the Romance or Germanic languages that have shaped English. When you see any Estonian words in the text – names of people, streets, towns, etc. – remember that every letter is pronounced. Even two vowels together are sounded separately. And unless you want to learn Estonian, don't worry about the accents.

Here are some useful words, which appear from time to time in the text. Any Estonian spoken by characters in the story is shown in italics. There isn't very much.

Tere! – Hello!

Härra – Mr.

Proua – Mrs., or, as in German, used to address any woman older than her mid-twenties.

Preili – Miss, or used to address any young woman.

Terviseks! – Cheers!

Ülemkomissar – Chief Inspector

Komissar – Inspector

Plats – Place, Square

Pealinna Uudised – Capital City News

Printed in Great Britain
by Amazon